GIANT SPECIAL EDITION!
TWICE THE ACTION AND ADVENTURE ON AMERICA'S UNTAMED FRONTIER—
IN ONE BIG VOLUME!

SHAFTED!

Flipping onto his back, Nate clawed at the pistol under his belt and hastily aimed at the bowman, who was notching another arrow. Before Nate could fire, the Ute disappeared as if swallowed up by the earth itself.

Free from danger for the moment, Nate headed up the side of the gully to retrieve his other flintlock and the rifle. Looking to the right, up the gully, Nate caught a hint of swift motion. One of the Indian mounts, he thought, until he glanced around and saw that it wasn't the horse that had moved, but someone behind the horse. Suddenly a Ute bowman stepped from concealment and took aim at Nate.

When the Ute released his arrow, it streaked straight at Nate's face....

The *Wilderness* series published by *Leisure Books:*

WILDERNESS
SEASON
OF THE WARRIOR
David Thompson

LEISURE BOOKS NEW YORK CITY

A LEISURE BOOK®

June 1993

Published by

Dorchester Publishing Co., Inc.
276 Fifth Avenue
New York, NY 10001

The name "Leisure Books" and the stylized "L" with design are
trademarks of Dorchester Publishing Co., Inc.

Printed in the United States of America.

Chapter One

Nate King was being followed. He couldn't say exactly how he knew this to be true since his ears had not detected any strange sounds and his eyes had not seen anything out of the ordinary, but he knew it as surely as he lived and breathed. So when he came to the crest of a steep ridge he abruptly reined in and wheeled his handsome black stallion. Quickly he scanned the forested slope below, the green valley beyond, and the surrounding pristine peaks. Nowhere was there evidence of another human being, which was not at all unusual considering he was high in the rugged vastness of the majestic Rockies, hundreds of miles from civilization.

But trappers weren't the only men roaming the mountains. There were also Indians. As an adopted Shoshone, Nate knew their habits better than most whites. So he heeded his finely honed instincts when they blared a strident mental warning that he was being stalked by unfriendly warriors, and since he was close to Ute country he had no trouble guessing the identity of the hostiles.

The Utes had been plaguing Nate for years, in part because they knew him to be friendly to the Shoshones, their bitter enemies, and in part because he lived in a rustic cabin on the edge of their acknowledged territory and had the temerity to hunt, fish, and above all trap in their vast domain. They rightfully resented the intrusion, and he resented their resentment. To his way of thinking, there was more than ample room enough in the mountains for all.

So periodically the Utes raided his cabin, and always he fought them off. They had come less frequently of late, which had led him to become complacent, and partially explained his presence now deep within their land and miles from his home, where his darling wife and young son eagerly awaited his return with the fresh meat he had promised to bring, meat that at the moment lay slumped over the back of his horse in the form of a small blacktail buck.

Nate had shot the buck not half an hour earlier, and he readily surmised that the blast of his Hawken had been heard by a wandering band of Utes who were now shadowing him, awaiting the perfect opportunity to separate him from his hair. He wasn't going to give them that chance if he could help it.

Turning the stallion, Nate headed due east down the slope into the shelter of dense firs. His mount's heavy hoofs made little noise on the carpet of pine needles, and like a wraith he wended among the trunks until he came out in a meadow where the grass grew three feet high. This he promptly crossed, pausing at the far end to check his back trail. The Utes were still hanging back.

Beyond the meadow grew more pines, and through these he rapidly made his way until a clearing afforded him a panoramic view of the valley below. The sight of a long line of cottonwoods brought a smile to his lips since cottonwoods often grew in close proximity to water.

Nate jabbed his heels into the black stallion's flanks and galloped to the valley floor. Repeated glances back failed to turn up the Utes, or anyone or anything else for that matter, and he was beginning to suspect his instincts had been faulty when a glimmer of sunlight off the ridge proved the contrary. Someone was up there with a gun or a lance.

Without hesitation, Nate made for the cottonwoods. He was taking a calculated gamble, but short of making a stand and battling until the Utes dropped him, this seemed a prudent course. Outrunning them in their own country would be virtually impossible, and he wasn't about to hide from them and have them go back to their village bragging about how they had run him off with his tail between his legs. He'd outsmart the devils.

Through the cottonwoods appeared a patch of blue-green. Seconds later the stallion stood on the bank of a swiftly flowing stream, into which Nate goaded it. Once in the middle, Nate turned northward, relying on the rush of water to eliminate any tracks the stallion made.

This was a trick Nate had used successfully before. The Utes would have to divide their forces, sending half south and half north, thereby reducing the odds he'd face if they caught him. He alertly observed the woodland on both sides as he rode, the Hawken resting across his thighs.

Two miles of safe travel saw Nate passing along the bottom of a winding canyon, its sheer, rocky walls rearing far above his head. He disliked the sensation of being hemmed in, and prayed the Utes wouldn't gain the heights above him where they could pick him off at their leisure.

Nate was beginning to breathe a little easier when the canyon drastically narrowed until there was scarcely a foot of space to the right and the left. Lacking room to turn around, he pressed on, hopeful an exit lay ahead. Another quarter of a mile saw his hope shattered by a flat wall of stone that barred his path. The stream plunged into a hole at the base of the wall to flow underground from that point on. The canyon was a dead end.

There was just enough space for Nate to bring the stallion around and retrace his steps. He moved with urgency, for now the whimsical hand of Fate had given the Utes time to gain ground on him and he would be lucky if he got out of the canyon before they appeared.

Halfway to the canyon mouth Nate spotted something he had missed on the way up, a game trail winding from the stream to the west rim. Since to keep following the stream invited an unwelcome encounter with the Utes, Nate urged the stallion out of the stream and took the game trail to the top. At times the going was flat and easy; at other times a severe incline had to be negotiated. By dismounting and leading the stallion by its reins now and then, Nate was able to reach the summit.

Here Nate stopped. A quarter of a mile south, heading slowly toward him, were four warriors. They had not seen him yet, but they'd notice his silhouette against the backdrop of blue sky any moment unless he got out of there, fast. Which he immediately did, entering dense forest.

By Nate's reckoning his cabin lay eight miles off to the northwest, so it was in this direction that he bent the stallion's steps. Dappled by alternating patches of sunlight and shade, he rode amidst a primeval scene of virgin splendor. Squirrels scampered among the branches. Birds twittered or flitted about. Chipmunks played among scattered boulders. And everywhere the air was permeated by the stimulating mixed scents of rich pine and musty earth, a scent unique to the mountains. Such soul-stirring magnificence never failed to stir his emotions.

Enraptured by the beauties of Nature, and believing he had lost the Utes or enjoyed a substantial lead, Nate rode relaxed, admiring the scenery. He heard a fly buzzing around the buck carcass. A butterfly flew among a cluster of flowers to his left. Somewhere a cricket chirped.

This was the life! Nate reflected happily. The life the Good Lord in His infinite wisdom must have intended for humankind. Living off the land as the Indians did, having one's daily needs provided by a guiding Providence, with no cause to fret about the disturbing petty concerns which were the common lot of those who dwelled back

in the States. He wouldn't trade his life for anything.

Nate glanced westward at the sun. In less than
two hours it would be dark. Either he found a
spot to camp or he rode straight through until he
reached his home, and since the latter was more
appealing, he planned out in his mind the route
he would follow.

One of the first rules of wilderness survival
Nate had learned from his mentor and best
friend, Shakespeare McNair, was to never take
anything for granted. Long since he had recognized the wisdom of the advice. But there were
times, such as now, when he took something for
granted without quite appreciating the fact.

In this instance, Nate had taken it for granted
that the four Utes were either still back in the
canyon or somewhere to his rear, tracking him.
It never occurred to him that they might have
seen him vanish over the rim, and shortly thereafter found the game trail to the top. From there
they had swung in a loop, galloping hard until
they were in front of him rather than dogging his
tracks.

So it was that Nate had no intimation of danger until, as he rode between two closely spaced
pines and turned his head to grin at a chatter-
ing squirrel, an arrow thudded into the tree on
his right. The shaft streaked by so close to his
face, the feathers brushed his cheek. Startled, he
looked around and saw the four Utes charging
from cover as they converged on him from three
sides.

Another lesson Nate had learned, during those
long winter nights when card playing was a

favorite diversion of whites and Shoshones alike, was that only a fool bucked a stacked deck. The instant he laid eyes on the screeching quartet, he yanked on the reins and headed back the way he had come, only at a full gallop.

A few arrows whizzed past his head or hit nearby trees. Then the stallion widened the gap and the deadly rain ceased. Arrows took a lot of work to make, and no warrior wanted to waste one. The Utes would hold their fire until they were sure.

Nate rode as if he and his stallion were one, skillfully avoiding obstacles such as logs and boulders and skirting thickets. He ducked under a low limb, was nicked on the face by a second, and had to lean flat along the stallion's neck to miss being knocked off by a third.

Under normal circumstances the black stallion would have easily outdistanced the war ponies of the Utes. But burdened by the extra weight of the buck, a weight which shifted with every sharp turn made, the stallion was hard pressed to maintain its top speed.

Aware of this, and knowing that an unforeseen mishap might at any moment dump him on the ground almost under the flying hoofs of the four horses behind him, Nate reluctantly did what was necessary in order for him to outdistance the warriors. He held the Hawken in the same hand as the reins, drew his big butcher knife, and twisting, slashed the rawhide rope holding the buck in place on the stallion.

The deer tumbled, bounced, and rolled.

Two of the warriors slowed and moved toward the carcass but the remaining pair maintained their pursuit.

Nate faced around, jammed his knife into the beaded sheath his wife Winona had made for him, and settled down to the serious business of riding like the wind. Unburdened, the stallion was a virtual blur, its mane and tail flying, its muscles rippling under its sleek hide.

Seconds dragged into minutes. Gradually the Utes fell farther and farther behind, and at length they gave up the chase, both bringing their mounts to a halt and venting their frustration with a few choice parting gestures.

Nate saw them, and to add insult to their irritation he smiled and waved. Then the intervening vegetation screened them from view. No sooner did it do so than he cut to the right so he could swing wide of the Indians and get back on his original course.

Inwardly Nate fumed at losing the buck. It had taken him hours of patient hunting to locate and kill one, and now he had to do it all over again. He would probably arrive at the cabin late, get a little sleep, and have to head out again at first light. Of all the luck.

The forest life had fallen silent during the chase, cowed by the war whoops of the Utes. Gradually the birds resumed their lively singing and the small animals resumed their everyday lives. A pair of jays followed Nate for a while, perhaps out of curiosity. Once a hawk took flight from a high tree and soared directly overhead, its shadow passing across his upturned face. It was so low he clearly heard the beating of its wings.

A vivid streak of red tinged the western horizon as the sun sank lower. From the northwest came a cool breeze that rustled the leaves of the aspens and set the tall grass in the high country holes, as the trappers referred to those small park-like valleys nestled among the stark peaks, to swaying as if in time to music.

In such an invigorating setting it was impossible for Nate to stay upset for very long. He had an urge to whistle as he rode, but wisely refrained; the Utes might be closer than he thought. Soon he came to more familiar territory and picked up the pace.

Nate knew of a spring situated five miles from his cabin, in a shallow gully, and since it was directly on the way he stopped there to give the stallion a brief breather. The horse had worked up a considerable sweat during the strenuous exertion of the chase, and once at the spring it greedily dipped its muzzle into the cold water to drink.

Letting the reins drop, Nate stretched his legs by walking around the edge of the spring. As he came to a spot directly across from the stallion, the breeze brought to his ears the low murmur of voices. Instantly he crouched and pressed the stock of the Hawken to his right shoulder. The voices were indistinct, but he could tell that the langauge being spoken was an Indian tongue, not English.

Warily Nate made his way to the top of the gully and risked a peek. Thirty yards away, to the south, were the same four Utes he'd narrowly escaped from earlier, and one of them had the buck draped over his war horse. "They're sure a persistent bunch," he said under his breath, noting their line of travel was taking them to the northwest—toward his cabin. He figured they had recognized him during the chase, and now they were trying to head him off before he reached home.

This new development demanded drastic action. Nate was unwilling to allow them to get close to his loved ones. For all he knew, they might be planning to lie in wait outside the cabin and ambush his family. He had to stop them, and stop them right that moment.

With the thought came action, and Nate had a bead on the foremost rider before the warrior's mount had taken two more steps. He hesitated, unwilling to slay anyone who didn't have a chance to defend himself, and lifting his head higher, shouted, "Hey!"

All four Utes whirled at the cry.

The booming retort of the Hawken rolled off across the mountains as a crimson hole blossomed squarely in the center of the lead Ute's forehead and he toppled soundlessly to the earth. His three companions galvanized into action, one urging his horse toward the gully, another grabbing an arrow from the quiver on his back, and the third diving from his mount into the brush.

Nate had no time to reload the rifle. Placing it on the ground, he grasped the pair of flintlocks wedged under his wide brown leather belt and drew them in a smooth, practiced motion. Both pistols leveled simultaneously; both were pointed at the onrushing brave, but only the right gun belched lead and smoke.

Struck in the chest, the reckless Ute was catapulted backwards and slammed onto his face.

Weakly, he tried to rise, gasped, and died.

Only two were left. Nate shifted to train his other flintlock on the warrior wielding the bow, but that individual was already taking shelter behind a convenient tree trunk, so Nate held his fire. Dropping down, he slid the spent pistol back under his belt.

The surviving Utes, Nate reasoned, would not dare try a frontal attack. They'd either flank him or else they'd wait for the cover of darkness and sneak in close. Grabbing the Hawken, he slid down the slope to the bottom and padded to the spring.

Since the top of the gully at that spot was about level with the stallion's shoulders, Nate feared for the animal's safety. The Utes might well put an arrow into its neck or head to prevent him from riding off. So, holding the stallion's head down, he guided the horse farther up the gully to its deepest point, where the Utes would be unable to shoot it unless they climbed an adjacent tree to get a clear shot.

That concern out of the way, Nate climbed back to the top. Lying flat, he raised his eyes high enough for him to see the forest. The dead Utes were right where they had fallen. Two of the four war horses had strayed off and the other two were idly grazing. There was no sign of the bowman and his companion.

Easing partway down, Nate stuck his pistol under his belt, opened his powder horn, and proceeded to pour the proper amount of black powder into his palm and from there into the Hawken. He did the same with the spent flintlock, laying the guns side by side so he could work faster. From his ammo pouch he took the lead balls and patches he needed. His fingers moving quickly, he extracted the ramrod from its housing under the rifle barrel and used it to finish loading both weapons.

Nate was replacing the ramrod when he heard the patter of footsteps, and glancing up he beheld one of the Utes charging toward him with an upraised war club. Nate clutched at the pistol at his feet, but already the warrior had gained the crest of the gully, and as Nate's fingers closed on the gun, the Ute uttered a piercing whoop and launched himself into the air.

The brutal impact bowled Nate completely over and sent him tumbling to the bottom of the gully. Disoriented and dazed, he struggled to his hands and knees just in time to see the warrior spring at him. Nate threw himself backwards, the war club just missing his head. His right hand brushed against his tomahawk, and in a heartbeat he had it out and up to deflect another swing of the war club.

The blow jarred Nate clear down to his shoulder. He rolled to the right, heard the club thud into the soil within inches of his head, and heaved upright to meet the next assault. The warrior wasted no time, leaping and aiming a vicious swipe at his forehead. Only Nate's finely honed reflexes enabled him to counter the swing.

Quickly Nate drove his tomahawk at the warrior's unprotected legs, but the man was cat-like and skipped out of reach. Separated by a mere two yards, they circled, each seeking an opening.

Nate tried not to think of the last Ute, the bowman, who might be aiming at his back at that very moment. The distraction could prove fatal.

He must take them one by one and hope the last Ute was still concealed in the trees.

The Ute with the club grinned, feinted, then lunged, trying to bash in Nate's head. Nate stepped to the side and retaliated by sinking his tomahawk in the warrior's thigh.

A screech born more of rage than pain tore from the Ute's lips and he staggered rearward, blood pouring down his leg. He glanced down, his features contorted into a mask of sheer hate, and then he closed, delivering a clout that would have caved in the skull of a grizzly.

But Nate's head was not there to receive it. He dived to the left, landed on his shoulder, and rolled again, but toward his adversary, not away. The bloody tomahawk glistened in the fading sunlight as it cleaved the air and bit deep into the Ute's leg, so deep Nate was unable to yank it loose before the unexpected transpired. The warrior sprawled on top of him, and a fraction of a second later Nate felt the man's fingers gouging into his throat.

The tomahawk was forgotten as Nate grabbed the Ute's wrists and tried to pry the man's hands apart so he could breathe again. Hate-filled eyes blazed into his. The warrior's warm breath fanned his face. Nate bucked, striving to pitch the Ute off, but the man clung tenaciously to his neck. Nate twisted from side to side but failed to dislodge his foe.

Nate had the feeling his throat was about to be pried apart like an overripe melon. In desperation he drove his right leg up and in, between the warrior's out-flung legs. His knee connected, and with a gurgling whine the Ute went momentarily slack.

Seizing the initiative, Nate arched his spine, hurling the man from him. Surging upright, he reached out and wrenched the tomahawk from the rising warrior's leg. In a flash he swept the tomahawk on high and brought the keen edge crashing down just as the Ute looked up. Like a log being splintered for firewood, the warrior's brow split down the middle and his brains and gore gushed out, dribbling over his wide eyes, across his nose, and into his gaping mouth. The only sound he uttered was a feeble groan. Then the Ute fell backwards.

Still clasping the tomahawk handle, Nate was nearly pulled off his feet. As it was, he stumbled forward and had to fling out his other arm to maintain his balance. Inadvertently, the movement saved his life, for as he stumbled he heard a whizzing overhead and something brushed his hair. Straightening, he saw an arrow embedded in the dirt a few feet from the slain Ute.

Without bothering to look around, Nate took a step and dived. As he came down another shaft smacked into the soil near his elbow. Flipping onto his back, he clawed at the pistol under his belt and hastily aimed at the bowman, who stood atop the gully and was notching another arrow to his buffalo-sinew bowstring. Before Nate could fire, the Ute disappeared as if swallowed up by the earth itself.

Free from danger for the moment, Nate headed up the side of the gully to retrieve his other flint-lock and the rifle. With both pistols again snug at his waist and the heavy Hawken in his hands, he snaked to the crest for a look-see.

The two horses were still there, one of them the animal bearing his buck, but the Ute was nowhere to be seen. In the quiet aftermath of the savage conflict, Nate realized his heart was pounding wildly in his chest and his pulse was racing madly. Taking deep breaths, he tried to calm his frayed nerves. Another close call like that would turn his hair gray!

Looking to the right, up the gully, Nate caught a hint of swift motion out of the corner of his eye. One of the Indian mounts, he thought, until he glanced around and saw that it wasn't the horse that had moved, but someone behind the horse. Suddenly a Ute bowman stepped from concealment and took aim at Nate.

When the Ute released his arrow, it streaked straight at Nate's face.

Chapter Two

An hour earlier a well-built man had ridden out of the mountains to the northwest, riding easily in the saddle, his shoulder-length hair, flowing beard, and long mustache all a striking white, the same color as his horse. Lake-blue eyes alertly studied the terrain below as he descended into a lush valley. In common with all his hardy breed, he wore buckskins. A brown beaver hat crowned his head, while crisscrossing his chest were a powder horn, an ammo pouch, and the ubiquitous possibles bag.

Shakespeare McNair was his name, and among the free and company trappers that name was legend, an honor Shakespeare had earned by living in the Rockies longer than any other white man alive. None knew the mountains better than he did, not even men like Jim Bridger or Joe Meek. Whenever a disagreement arose concerning anything having to do with the wilderness, Shakespeare was the man the trappers consulted for the straight truth.

Close to the valley floor, Shakespeare reined up and gazed in annoyance at a thick column of smoke spiraling skyward from a large camp located on the bank of a sluggish stream. It was the smoke that had drawn him here, a mile out of his way, and he was not in the least surprised at what he found.

"Damn greenhorns," Shakespeare muttered, and spat. "If they want to get themselves killed, it's no business of mine." He had lifted the reins to resume his journey when the tinkle of gay feminine laughter fluttered on the wind.

"A woman!" Shakespeare exclaimed, thunderstruck. "Tarnation!" He paused, then quoted from the man who was his namesake. "How brief the life of man runs his erring pilgrimage!" His knees nudged his horse. "Get along, there, you mangy bundle of bones and hide, and let's go take a gander at these pilgrims."

Down into the valley Shakespeare made his determined way until he stopped across the stream from the bustling camp. He counted ten in the party all told, nine men and a stunning young brunette. "Idiots," he addressed his horse. "Each year this world gets more filled up with idiots. One of these days they'll take over and there won't be a sane person left anywhere."

A shout from the camp indicated one of the men had finally noticed the newcomer, and there was a general commotion as men gathered up their arms and dashed to the water's edge. In the lead ran a dashing man of 25 or so attired in what was probably the latest sartorial splendor.

He held a polished English-made rifle that he threw to his shoulder and pointed at McNair.

"I wouldn't do that if I was you," Shakespeare called out, "unless you're not particularly fond of living." Across his thighs rested his trusty Hawken, which, by tilting slightly, he had trained on the man with the gun.

"I say!" the pilgrim declared, lowering his rifle. "You speak the Queen's English, so you can't be a bloody savage." He offered a friendly smile and beckoned. "Come on across, my dear fellow. Never let it be said any white man was refused hospitality by the son of the Duke of Graustark."

Against his better judgment, Shakespeare clucked his horse into the stream and forded to where the group waited. He scanned the faces of the rest of the party and didn't see a seasoned mountaineer in the bunch. "No wonder," he said.

"No wonder what?" the Englishman responded, inspecting McNair minutely.

"No wonder you dunderheads built your fire so big every Indian within ten miles knows you're here," Shakespeare elaborated.

"The fire?" the pilgrim repeated, glancing quizzically at the offending blaze. "I'm afraid I don't understand."

"Of course you don't," Shakespeare snapped. "Most shallow man! Thou worms-meat, in respect of a good piece of flesh indeed! Learn of the wise, and perpend."

Amazement etched the other's face. "I know that quote. It's from William Shakespeare's *As You Like It.*"

"There's some hope for you yet," Shakespeare said, swinging down. He reached out and patted the bulky roll tied behind his saddle. "I never go anywhere without old William S. He's been whispering in my ear since before you were born."

"Are you claiming to have the body of Shakespeare rolled up in that blanket?" the Englishman asked incredulously.

"Something better. A book of his complete works."

A grin creased the duke's son from ear to ear. "Oh, that's jolly good! What a wit! You'd have me believe a frontier ruffian totes the works of the greatest dramatist of all time all over these bloody mountains? How stupid do you think I am?"

"You really don't want to know," Shakespeare said harshly, and stepped up so close to the Englishman their noses were practically touching. "And since you asked, don't make a habit out of calling me a liar. It's not good for your health."

Clearly flustered, the young man backed up a stride and declared, "Now see here! I don't know who you think you're talking to, but I won't stand being abused by a commoner."

"That tears it," Shakespeare growled. With a flick of his wrists he extended his Hawken until the tip of the barrel touched the Englishman's chest. "One more insult and you're worm food."

For the span of five seconds no one moved. Then some of the other men turned their weapons on the mountain man, and a bewhiskered giant in an odd cap commented, "Go easy there, mate, or we'll have your guts for garters."

Although Shakespeare didn't quite understand the unusual expression, he got the general drift and responded with, "The choice is this pilgrim's. I rode in here to offer some advice, not to look for trouble."

None of the men answered him. None of them lowered their rifles or pistols. And it was at that moment, when the air itself seemed to crackle with the mounting tension, that a musical female voice stated, "For the love of God, William. Enough of this childishness! Invite the man to tea and let's find out what he's about."

Shakespeare gazed past the ring of men and firearms and spotted the brunette and another man, who was dressed in the same fancy manner as the duke's son, standing apart from the rest. She wore an expression of amused interest, he one of reserved dignity. Slowly Shakespeare let his rifle droop, and the others did likewise. "I'm obliged, ma'am," he said. "I hate to waste good lead on greenhorns."

"Pay no heed to my brother," she answered. "Poor William couldn't be civil if his life depended on it."

"It does in these parts," Shakespeare informed her, and without another glance at the fool he shouldered his way through the men to her side. "The handle is Shakespeare McNair, ma'am, and I'm right pleased to make your acquaintance."

"I'm Diana Templar," she revealed.

"Lady Graustark," interjected the man beside her in a tone that implied the name held some special significance.

"Who might you be, mister?" Shakespeare asked.

"Eric Nash, at your service, sir," Nash said, performing an exaggerated bow that made Diana

Templar giggle girlishly. He sported a shock of black hair and had eyes the hue of sparkling emeralds.

"And what might you be? A prince or something?"

Nash grinned and shook his head. "Sadly, sir, I'm a commoner like yourself, an artist by trade, a vagabond by nature, a lost soul by design." He encompassed the snow-crowned mountains with a sweep of his arm. "I've journeyed to your fair country to capture on canvas raw, elemental Nature and her illustrious denizens."

"And folks hereabouts claim I talk funny," Shakespeare marveled.

"Because you quote old William S., as you so quaintly call him?" Nash asked, and when the grizzled frontiersman nodded, he sighed. "Eloquence, my friend, is a dying art. Most people, out of a false pride that licks the dust they trod, secretly scoff at anyone who uses words of more than one syllable. My hat is off to you, sir, for having the courage to exercise your intellect."

Now it was Shakespeare's turn to grin. "I do believe I'm taking a liking to you, son. This old coon hasn't met too many real thinkers in his time, and I'm about convinced that two thirds of the human race have right puny noggins."

Both Nash and Lady Graustark laughed uproariously; then the latter looped her dainty arm through Shakespeare's and nodded at a red and white canopy that fluttered atop four straight poles. "Come into the shade and have some tea. I made it myself."

"In that case how can I refuse?" Shakespeare replied, cradling his Hawken in his other elbow.

His eyes alertly roved over the camp, missing nothing, not the three dozen horses that were as fine a bunch of animals as he'd ever seen, not the many huge piles of varied supplies, enough to outfit an army, nor the dozen large trunks that must contain personal effects. "You folks fixing to settle in these parts?" he casually inquired.

"Good heavens, no!" Lady Graustark bubbled merrily. "We came to America on holiday, and as a lark decided to take a tour of these grand mountains."

"Didn't anyone tell you these mountains can be a mite dangerous?" Shakespeare inquired as they arrived under the canopy where a small mahogany table and six matching chairs had been set up. He touched one and shook his head in disbelief.

"Oh, there were some army officers who tried to convince us we were making the biggest mistake of our lives."

"They were speaking with straight tongues, Lady Graustark," Shakespeare admonished.

"Call me Diana," she requested.

"You don't know what you're letting yourselves in for," Shakespeare went on. "These mountains are crawling with hostiles. If the Blackfeet, Piegans, Bloods, or Gros Ventres find out you're here, there ain't a one of you who will make it back to the States. And that's a fact."

"Surely they wouldn't attack a party our size."

"Ma'am, there are thousands of them and only ten of you. How do you expect to hold them off if they decide they want to add some scalps to their collections?"

"We have guns."

"And so do they. Not many, mind you. Fusees, they're called, cheap trade guns the Indians get in exchange for beaver pelts and such. Half the time they burst or misfire, so most of the warriors don't much care for them. They'd rather use their bows. And you should know, ma'am, that in the time it takes a white man to load and fire his rifle an Indian can get off twenty arrows. From a hundred yards out they could hit one of your pretty buttons without half trying."

"I had no idea," Diana said, her pale brow furrowed.

Shakespeare had opened his mouth to elaborate on the intricacies of Indian warfare when William Templar stormed onto the scene, moving between Shakespeare and the woman.

"That will be quite enough! I heard what you've been saying, and I resent you trying to scare my sister with your outlandish exaggerations."

No one there saw the mountain man's arm move. One moment he was standing quietly in front of the irate nobleman. The next moment William Templar lay on the ground, dazed, blood trickling from the corner of his mouth.

"I warned you once," Shakespeare said.

The duke's son sat up slowly, rubbing his chin. A finger touched the blood and he looked at the red drop, aghast. Primal fury transformed his finely chiseled features into an ugly mask. He put his hands down to shove to his feet, exploding with, "You insufferable cretin! I'll—" But he got no further. His body had risen mere inches when the razor tip of a large butcher knife pressed lightly against his throat, freezing him in place.

"You don't learn very fast, do you?" Shakespeare said Softly. "This isn't England, you uppity son of a bitch. You're in the wilderness now. The nearest civilization is five hundred miles east of here. In these mountains men make their own laws. You can't go around insulting folks without paying the price." He moved his hand, lightly running the blade over Graustark's trembling throat without breaking the skin, and quoted, "How long will a man lie in the earth ere he rot?"

Eric Nash took a step toward them. "For love of God, forbear him," he declared.

Shakespeare glanced up in mild surprise. "So you also know old William S." Lips pursed, he straightened. "All right. For the lady's sake I won't spoil her tea party. But if this pup doesn't mind his manners, I won't be responsible for the outcome." The knife went into its sheath and he took a beat, careful to lean the Hawken against his leg so it would be handy.

Diana Templar, Lady Graustark, gazed in bewilderment at the buckskin-clad apparition who had twice in as many minutes threatened the life of her brother. By all rights she should be outraged and indignantly insist McNair leave, but she could not bring herself to utter the words. She liked this brash, untamed hooligan, with his bronzed, weathered visage, greasy hair, and smelly buckskins, and she flattered herself that she saw through his gruff exterior into a heart of solid gold.

Her brother, William, didn't share her sentiments. As Nash assisted him to his feet, William averted his face from McNair so the mountain man wouldn't detect the smoldering resentment he harbored. Twice now the ignorant savage had upbraided William in front of others, and the humiliation was almost more than William could bear. Had they been in England, William would have had the scoundrel locked in leg irons and tossed into jail.

Eric Nash was having difficulty maintaining a straight face. Secretly he had reveled in William's comeuppance, which in his estimation had been long overdue. The marquis was notorious for his arrogant airs, and had it not been for sweet Diana, Eric would have had nothing to do with her overbearing brother. Now, taking a seat, he surreptitiously admired her profile while she puttered about pouring tea into four china cups. She took the first cup to their guest, and as his gaze followed her his eyes caught McNair's and the mountain man smiled and winked.

"I give you my word my brother shall behave himself from now on," Diana said as she moved to a chair close to McNair's. "He always has had difficulty adjusting to the customs of the locals. Africa, India, China, South America, wherever we go, he invariably gets on someone's wick."

"You've been to all those places?" Shakespeare asked, and took a sip. The tea had a mild minty flavor with an underlying taste of honey.

"Those and many, many more," Diana said. "For three years now we've been traveling the globe, visiting out-of-the-way spots no one else has ever been to. We've dined with yak herders, Masai lion killers, Hindu holy men, and Amazonian primitives. We've ridden camels and elephants. I daresay by the time we're through there won't be a corner of this planet we haven't explored."

"Why?"

Diana paused with the cup halfway to her mouth. "I beg your pardon?"

"Why the blazes is an elegant lady like yourself traipsing all over creation? Do you have ants in your drawers? You should latch onto some handsome rascal and do yourself proud by rearing a passel of young'uns."

William Templar stiffened, his lips compressed. Eric Nash started to laugh, then caught himself and coughed, his eyes twinkling.

Only Diana displayed no hint of the emotions she was feeling, except in the slight edge to her voice when she answered, "I see. You believe a woman's lot in life is to be a dutiful, obedient wife?"

"Not at all," Shakespeare said. "I admire any woman who can hold her own in a world where men hold all the high cards, and I've always been right partial to those with an independent streak. But there comes a time when everyone, women and men, have to put their noses to the grindstone and do what the Good Lord put us here to do."

"Which is?"

"To have a home and rear a family, of course."

"Hear, hear!" Eric cried lightheartedly. "I have long maintained the same, sweet prince. But the woman for whom I feel a perfect and boundless attachment refuses to commit herself." He punctuated his comments with a meaningful look at the Lady Graustark.

"Women can be contrary critters sometimes," Shakespeare philosophized. "And once you marry them, it gets worse. When you want to stay home and rest, they want to go out and visit kin. When you want to go off fishing, they want you to fix up something around the cabin. It never fails."

"Is this experience speaking?" Diana asked.

"Yes, ma'am. I'm married to the most beautiful woman ever born."

"Is she white?" William threw in.

"No, she's a Flathead. Her name is Blue Water Woman."

William Templar had a sarcastic remark on the tip of his tongue, intending to demonstrate his social superiority by putting the upstart frontiersman in his place. But there was something in the glance McNair shot in his direction that gave William the impression of a volcano about to explode. He looked at the mountain man's knife and changed his mind about saying anything.

"Where is your wife now?" Diana asked.

"Back at our cabin. We spend about half the year there and the other half with her people." Shakespeare polished off the tea in a single gulp. "Right now I'm on my way to visit a friend and escort him and his woman to our place for a visit." He studied her a moment. "Where might you be headed?"

Diana shifted to stare longingly at the majestic peaks to the west. "Deeper into these glorious mountains. William thought we might head north until we strike the Canadian border, then go east to the Great Lakes. From there it should be relatively simple to find our way to Chicago. Then it's on to New York and passage on a ship to London."

"You sure have it all worked out."

"Is something wrong with our plan?"

"Only this." Shakespeare placed the cup and saucer on the table. "If you go north, you'll soon be in the heart of Blackfoot country."

"The ones you mentioned earlier?"

"Yes, ma'am. And they hate whites. Have ever since they tangled with Meriwether Lewis's party and one of them was killed while trying to steal a gun. More trappers have lost their hair to the Blackfeet than to all the other tribes combined. You go up there and every man in your party will be slaughtered and you'll end up as the wife of a Blackfoot warrior."

"Oh, dear."

William could no longer hold his tongue. "I'm not calling you a liar, McNair," he began, "but surely it's not as bad as you make it out to be. We have two rifles for every man and plenty of horses. I should think we can hold our own against the entire Blackfoot nation. From what I hear, Indians are inveterate cowards."

"Who told you such a bald-faced lie?" Shakespeare responded testily. "A drunk in a tavern?" He gestured at the horses, the supplies, and the trunks. "I'll admit you've brought along enough provisions to last you a lifetime, but that's exactly what will do you in. An Indian's eyes would bug out of his head on seeing so many goods just waiting to be stolen. Your horses alone are reason enough for them to kill you, not to mention all the guns."

William pointed at the bewhiskered giant in the odd cap, who was engaged in rubbing down a horse. "Do you see that gentleman? His name is Jarvis, and he was a sergeant in the Dragoon

Guards. If trouble comes he'll know how to deal with it. He's an expert in all forms of combat, and I dare say he's killed more men than you can count on your fingers and toes."

"William!" Diana declared angrily.

"Let him have his fun," Shakespeare said, and fixed a smirk on the irritated nobleman. "Thou art armed, Gloucester. Let thy trumpet sound!"

"Do you doubt Jarvis's ability?" William snapped.

"No doubt he was a dandy soldier," Shakespeare replied, "but if he's never fought Indians, then he has no idea what to expect from them. Besides, he's just one man."

"Do you have any advice to offer us about our travels?" Diana asked.

"Sis, please!" William said.

"Quiet. I want to hear Mr. McNair out."

Shakespeare was about to sit back down when he detected a hint of movement on a hill to the south. Without being too obvious, he surveyed the hill from bottom to top as he spoke, "I'd change my plans if I was you, Diana. Instead of going all the way to Canada, go north until you hit the Yellowstone River and follow it northeast to the junction with the Missouri. From there, head south and eventually you'll wind up at Independence. You'll get to see a sizeable chunk of the country and the tribes you run into will be mostly friendly."

"Mostly?"

William made a pyramid of his fingers and tapped them against his pointed chin. "If we do as this man wants, we'll see very little of the mountains. And I thought you were keenest on that idea."

"I was," Diana said, "but not at the cost of our lives. If Mr. McNair believes the danger is too great, I think we should accept his judgment and modify our plans."

"Really!" William snorted.

The mountain man turned, his countenance inscrutable. "Are any of these other men as good as your Jarvis?"

"They're all highly competent or I wouldn't have retained their services," William bragged. "Some have been with me for years, and without your help we managed to survive native uprisings, drought, near-starvation, and wild beasts."

"Then I reckon it's only fitting that they might die with you."

"What?"

"How bloodily the sun begins to peer above yon busky hill!" Shakespeare quoted. "The day looks pale at his distemperature."

"You're raving, old fellow," William scoffed.

"No, I'm trying to tell you that your camp is about to be attacked by a hostile war party."

Chapter Three

There was a twinkling of an instant for Nate King to act before the glittering shaft struck him. Had he been accustomed to sitting at a desk or working behind a counter day after day, his atrophied muscles would have been unequal to the occasion and he would have died on the spot. But Nate had left his accounting job in New York City years ago for the uncertainties of the violent frontier, and his unending fight for survival in a primitive land where unfriendly Indians and fierce predators might lurk behind every bend in the trail had honed his reflexes to a lightning-like degree. So it was that he threw himself to one side as the arrow streaked at his face and avoided being transfixed, but the shaft passed so close to him the feathers tickled the underside of his nose.

Quickly Nate whipped up the Hawken, yet he

was not quite quick enough, for the Ute bounded into the undergrowth and disappeared. Sinking down, Nate exhaled and calmed his ragged nerves. That one had been too close! He glanced at the black stallion, then moved down the gully away from it. The Ute would expect him to stay close to the horse, so by doing the opposite he might be able to catch the warrior off guard.

Twenty yards brought him to a spot where the left bank had been partially eroded away, leaving a gap a yard wide and about the same height. Here was his salvation. Dropping to his hands and knees, he crawled into the opening and advanced until he was in danger of exposing himself to the Ute. Cautiously, he eased his head out just far enough for him to scan the wall of vegetation. Wherever the Ute was, he was well hidden.

Nate paid particular attention to the trees nearest where the stallion stood. If the Ute intended to steal or shoot the horse, that was where the warrior would show himself. Cocking the Hawken, he settled down to wait he knew not how long.

After a while the insects came to life again, with the buzzing cicadas and a chorus of crickets vying for the honor of which could be the loudest.

The Ute might as well have been a ghost for all the sign there was of his presence. Nate wondered if the warrior would sneak around to the other side of the gully to come at him from the rear, and from then on he glanced repeatedly over his shoulder to forestall such an attempt.

The blazing sun vanished, painting the western

horizon a vivid red. Twilight afforded scant illumination and lent the landscape an eerie aspect.

Nate fought his own impatience. Eager to reach home, he wanted to end the stalemate as soon as possible, but he knew better than to commit a reckless act that would only get him slain.

At last Nate's patience paid off. He saw a dark shadow detach itself from the trunk of a tree, glide noiselessly to another tree, and begin climbing. The Ute was going high in the hope of getting a clear shot.

Nate rested the rifle barrel on the top edge of the gap and took purposeful aim on the shadow. It was hard to distinguish the warrior's head so Nate went for a body shot, his sights fixed on where he believed the man's chest to be. Slowly he let his breath out so the rhythm of his breathing wouldn't cause the barrel to waver, then he touched his forefinger to the cool metal trigger and applied gentle pressure.

Simultaneously with the blast of the Hawken the shadow threw up its arms, screeched, and plummeted, hitting the ground with a dull thud.

There was no time to lose. Drawing a flintlock, Nate vaulted over the gap and sped to where the body lay, ready to finish the warrior off if it should be necessary. But it wasn't. The ball had penetrated the right side of the Ute's chest, torn completely through both lungs, and exploded out the other side. Already a spreading red pool stained the grass.

Nate tucked the pistol under his belt and mopped his perspiring brow. He had been incredibly lucky and he knew it. The next time he might not be, and as sure as the sun rose there would be a next time, because the Utes were not about to let him live where he did in peace. He toyed with the notion of leaving, then shook his head. Too much time and energy had been invested in the building of his cabin and the developing of his land for him to tuck his tail between his legs and slink off somewhere else. He'd stay, come what may.

The better part of an hour was spent gathering weapons and rounding up three of the four war horses. The fourth was long gone, no doubt making a beeline back to the Ute village where its arrival would create quite a stir. The Utes would have no way of knowing the fate of the four warriors, although a few shrewd individuals might guess the truth.

By the time Nate had the three horses in tow and had resumed his trek toward his cabin, the moon had risen, bathing the virgin terrain in a pale, diffuse light, and enabling him to see plainly enough to avoid downed trees and thickets. The crisp, rarified air carried sounds exceptionally well, especially at night, so to his ears came the rumbling grunts of roaming bears, the guttural snarls of prowling panthers, and now and again the howling of wolves or the yipping of coyotes. Mixed in intermittently were the screech of night birds. Occasionally the air was rent by the terrified squeal of an animal in the grip of one of the predators, a sound which never failed to set his nerves on edge.

There was only a mile to go when Nate became aware of a crackling in the brush to his left. It stopped, then went on again for several seconds. Once more silence reigned, only to be broken by the sharp snap of a twig. Something big was paralleling his course, perhaps stalking him. He rested the rifle stock on his right thigh and probed the darkness, ready for the worst. It might be a panther after the horses, or perhaps a grizzly that had caught the scent of the buck. Whichever, he wasn't relinquishing the meat he had fought so hard to keep.

The creature skulking in the shadows grew braver and came nearer. Shortly, Nate could see a vague outline, but it was impossible to determine its size or shape. Then he heard the pad of heavy feet and knew the identity of the beast: a grizzly. The big cats seldom made so much noise, and no other animal, not even a bull buffalo, had such a ponderous tread.

Soon Nate also heard the bear's raspy breathing, and knew it wasn't more than ten feet away. Had it been daylight he might have risked a shot. In the dark, though, he couldn't be sure of hitting a vital spot, and if he only wounded the animal his life would be forfeit. Wounded grizzlies were fury incarnate, unstoppable in their wrath, capable of shredding a man to ribbons with their iron claws.

So Nate rode on, hoping against hope the bear would decide to go elsewhere. Presently he spied a square patch of light ahead and knew it was the cabin window. At his wife's insistence he had recently added an expensive glass pane window to admit more daylight and keep out dust, although he had protested that doing so made their home more vulnerable to an attack. She had pointed out that, with three of them able to shoot, defending their home should be no problem.

As usual when they had a dispute, she had won.

Now Nate slowed, listening to the ponderous thud of the bear's paws. He didn't want the brute to get any closer to his home. Should his wife or son, for any reason, be out and about, it might go after them. What should he do? A moment's deliberation prompted him to draw a flintlock and point it at the ground.

The bear had also slowed and seemed to be creeping closer.

"That settles it," Nate said aloud, and banged off the pistol. His stallion fidgeted at the retort, as did the war horses, so for several vital seconds he was distracted, trying to regain control. When next he glanced to his right the grizzly was gone and from a hundred feet away arose the sound of a bush being trampled under its immense bulk.

"Good riddance," Nate declared, grinning.

Suddenly light flared outside the cabin, capturing two people in its rosy illumination. One was a lovely woman with raven hair who held a torch, the other a young boy armed with a long Kentucky rifle.

"Pa?" the boy called. "Is that you?"

Jabbing his heels into the stallion, Nate trotted to the sturdy pole enclosure he had made for his stock and swung down. His wife reached him first, her free hand tenderly touching his cheek, her eyes reading his features as he might read a book.

"You had trouble," Winona said, bobbing her chin at the extra horses.

"The Utes again," Nate disclosed, and let the subject drop. So accustomed had he become to his harrowing life in the Rockies that the encounter with the four warriors qualified as mundanely routine and not worthy of a protracted discussion. He faced his pride and joy. "What if it hadn't been me, Zach?"

"Pa?"

"Haven't I taught you better than to come running out in the middle of the night when you hear a shot? What if it had been hostiles trying to lure you into the open?"

Zachary blinked, pursed his lips, and shuffled his feet self-consciously. How well he recollected the many times his father had told him the Utes would try any devious trick to draw them into an ambush. Since in his father's absence he was the man of the house, as Nate had repeatedly stressed, he should not have been so rash. The only excuse he could think of was the one he mumbled. "Ma did it too."

"Which doesn't make it right," Nate said, and whereas his own father would have given him a tarring he would never forget for the blunder, he merely walked over to his son and affectionately draped an arm over Zach's slender shoulders. "No harm was done, this time. Just be sure it doesn't happen again."

"You can count on me, Pa."

Winona held the torch while father and son stripped the animals and put them in the horse pen. Two trips were required before all the weapons and the buck were transferred indoors, and at last Nate was able to fully relax. He sat in the rocking chair he had built with his own hands in front of the stone fireplace he had constructed years ago and let the warmth permeate every

pore, soothing his aches and melting his cares
away.

"I missed you," Nate said softly when Winona
brought him a steaming cup of coffee.

"And I you," she answered in English.

Nate admired her beauty in the firelight: the
healthy glow of her skin, the lively glint in her
brown eyes, her full lips and luxuriant tresses.
He counted himself the luckiest man alive to have
earned her love, and touched a palm to the front
of her beaded buckskin dress. "How many more
moons, do you figure?"

"Five at the most," Winona answered. She
smiled at his frown of disappointment, then
commented, "The baby will come when it is
ready to come and not before. No matter how
much you fret, our daughter can not be rushed."

"What makes you so all-fired sure it will be
a girl?"

"I know."

"How?" Nate persisted, mystified by her unfath-
omable certainty. Common sense assured him
that predicting the sex of a baby was impossible,
and he would have told her as much if not for the
many inexplicable instances in the past where she
had exhibited an uncanny intuition.

"I just know," Winona said enigmatically, and
went to the wide counter on which the buck had
been placed. From a hook on the wall she removed
a big butcher knife.

"That can wait until tomorrow," Nate suggested.

"Tomorrow we are leaving for Shakespeare's.
Or don't you remember?"

Nate straightened and glanced at the frayed

calendar hanging on the west wall. He'd swapped for it at a Rendezvous, only because it helped Zach get a better understanding of the white man's conception of time and he wanted the boy to know all there was to know about white ways in case they ever ventured to the States again. They'd only gone once before, on a trip to St. Louis, and Zach had just been a sprout. So rarely did he consult the calendar himself that he'd plumb forgotten it was there. "I do now," he said. "Shakespeare was supposed to show up today and help us pack."

Winona laughed as she rolled the deer over and began to slit open the buck's hind legs. "Blue Water Woman wanted him to help us since she was afraid you would have me do all the work."

"She knows better than that," Nate responded, pretending to be slightly indignant. "The real reason he's coming is because they think we can't tie a knot without them showing us how its done. Sometimes they act as if they're our parents and we're their young'uns."

"What harm does that do, since both my parents and your parents are dead?"

"None, I guess. I realize they'll never have children of their own. But I'm a mite old to be treated the same way I treat Zach." Nate stretched his legs toward the crackling flames. "It upsets me to think that Shakespeare doesn't have that much confidence in me after all we've been through."

"He has more than you think."

In silence Nate sipped his coffee and mentally reviewed his long association with the reclusive mountain man. Had Shakespeare not taken a liking to him and taken him under his wing, Nate wouldn't have lasted out a single winter. McNair had taught him virtually everything important he knew about the Rockies, the wildlife, and the various tribes. And in his heart Nate knew he cared deeply for the cantankerous cuss, more deeply than he had ever cared for his own father, perhaps because Shakespeare had always let him make his own decisions and learn things the hard way rather than browbeating him to do what Shakespeare thought best, which was how his father had treated him. It was one of the most important lessons he had ever learned, and God willing, he'd be able to raise Zach without making the same mistakes his father had made rearing him.

Suddenly a book was thrust in front of Nate's face, shattering his reflection. "Will you read a bit, Pa, before I turn in?"

Nate nodded and set the book in his lap. He stared at the cover and said softly, *"The Last of the Mohicans."* It was old, the pages somewhat faded, the edges dog-eared, as well they should be since James Fenimore Cooper was his favorite author and he'd read the book several times through since purchasing it on his initial trip west from New York City. He flipped the pages until he came to a thin piece of leather.

Zach had sat down with his back to the fireplace and gazed up eagerly. This was one of his favorite times of the day, a family tradition stemming from his childhood. "Just pick up where you left off."

Nodding, Nate read: *"I know that the pale-faces are a proud and hungry race. I know that they claim not only to have the earth, but that the meanest of*

*their color is better than the sachems of the redman.
The dogs and crows of their tribes,"* continued the
earnest old chieftain, *without heeding the wounded
spirit of his listener, whose head was nearly crushed
to the earth in shame, as he proceeded,* "would bark
and caw before they would take a woman to their
wigwams whose blood was not of the color of snow.
But let them not boast before the face of the Manitou
too loud. They entered the land at the rising, and
may yet go off at the setting sun."

Nate paused. For some odd reason he could
not get Shakespeare out of his mind. Before continuing, he said to no one in particular, "I hope
the old buzzard is all right."

Fifteen miles to the northeast, in a narrow valley
nestled among a ring of regal peaks, the object of
Nate King's anxiety approached the spot where
Diana Templar, her brother William, and the artist
Eric Nash stood behind a pair of stacked trunks.
"I'm leaving now," he announced.

All three turned, Diana and Eric jolted into
registering different degrees of shock, William
displaying outright outrage.

"Leaving?" Lord Graustark exploded. "You're
running out on us at a critical time like this? You
balmy Yank! First you tell us there's a horde of
red savages about to swoop down on us, then
you have us work feverishly to erect a perimeter
barricade, and now you up and leave!" He started
to raise the rifle he held, as if about to swing the
stock, but checked the motion. "Go ahead, then!
Show your true color. But I sure as hell would
like to know where these bloody savages of yours
have gotten to!"

Shakespeare took the tirade calmly. Sighing, he addressed Diana and Eric, refusing to dignify William's presence with so much as a condescending look. "The Indians are still out there. They haven't attacked yet because the sun set shortly after they found us, and many tribes don't like to fight at night. They'll come at us at dawn. If we're not ready, there won't be one of us left alive by noon except maybe you, ma'am." He gave the top trunk a whack. "That's why I advised you to pile all your goods in a big circle."

"And a fine idea it was, mate," declared a deep voice as out of the dark strode the giant ex-soldier, Jarvis. "We used the same type of fortification when fighting the Bantus in Africa. Kept them at bay, it did, them buggers with their wicked long spears that could tear through a man like a knife through butter."

William made an impatient gesture. "Are you here for a reason or simply to interrupt our conversation?"

The giant stiffened as if snapping to attention. "Begging your pardon, your lordship, but you requested to be kept informed of anything having a bearing on our defense of the camp."

"Yes. So?"

"So I've set up sleeping schedules for the men so they'll get at least a fair bit of rest before morning. Each one—"

"Are you daft?" William said, cutting him off. "How can you let them sleep at a time like this? Keep them armed and at their posts until I tell you otherwise."

"As you wish, sir," Jarvis said, the words clipped and precise. Digging in a heel, he turned.

"Hold on there, old coon," Shakespeare said to stop him. Then he gave the duke's son a glance that would have shriveled a plant. "Jarvis here has the right idea. If your men are worn out they won't be much good when it matters the most. Let them get some sleep. Until dawn you'll be safe."

Whatever William would have answered was made irrelevant by a statement from Diana. "Mr. McNair has a valid point. Jarvis, do as you want with sleeping arrangements. Just be certain every man is awake well before daylight."

"Never fear, Lady Templar. I won't let you down," the giant asserted, and left.

William waited until Jarvis was out of earshot, then snapped, "Let's get to the point! McNair still hasn't explained this business about his running out on us."

"Why *are* you leaving?" Diana asked in a hurt tone.

"I'm no flash in the pan, if that's what is bothering you," Shakespeare replied. "I'll be back after I find out how many Indians are out there and what tribe they belong to."

"You're going out there all by yourself?"

"Someone has to, ma'am. We need to know what we're up against."

"It's too dangerous. I won't have it."

Shakespeare smiled, and to William's chagrin reached out and patted her arm. "Afraid you don't have any say-so. I'm a grown man and can do as I please. Just spread the word to your men so none of them mistake me for an Indian and shoot me by mistake."

"William, see to it," Diana said.

"But—"

"*Now*, William."

In a huff, her brother stalked off, his fists clenched so tight around his flintlock that his knuckles were white. Shortly thereafter they could hear him bellowing orders.

"The marquis loves telling others what to do but he doesn't like being on the receiving end," Eric remarked sarcastically.

"What the dickens is a marquis?" Shakespeare inquired.

"The son of a duke holds the rank of marquis but is called a lord," Eric explained. "While a duke's daughter, like Diana here, has the title of lady."

"I don't know much about this nobility business," Shakespeare mentioned. "So sometimes I have a hard time following the trail old William S. takes when he throws in all those princes and earls and such."

"You just have to know the various titles and their relationship to one another," Eric said. "The peerage, for instance, includes dukes, marquis, earls, viscounts, and barons."

"What's the peerage?"

"It's another name for the nobility. It means they're all peers, or equals."

The mountain man digested the revelation for several seconds. "What does that make those who don't have titles? Less than equal?"

"In the eyes of some nobles, yes," Eric confessed.

Shakespeare stared in the direction William had gone. "I think I'm beginning to understand a bit more of what all the fuss was about back in '76. In this country we won't stand still for anyone lording it over us like they're God's gift to all Creation, and those who don't wake up to the fact often as not find themselves pushing up flowers." Squaring his shoulders, he stepped close to the trunks and placed his hand on the top one. "Remember, no fires," was all he said; then, with a lithe rippling of his sinews, he vaulted over and within moments had been swallowed by the night.

"He's a strange one, isn't he?" Eric remarked.

"One in a million," Diana said pensively.

"You like him, I gather?"

"Immensely. You?"

"Very much. He's the most colorful character we've met in all our travels." Eric leaned on the trunks and peered toward the nearest inky slope. "Let's hope we see him again."

Chapter Four

A brisk, cool breeze from the northwest fanned Shakespeare's beard and his shoulder-length hair as he ran over the flat ground toward the hill where he had first spied the Indians. There had been more than a dozen, but they had sought cover so quickly he'd been unable to make a precise count. By concealing themselves as they had they'd revealed they were enemies, since friendly Indians invariably approached white camps without reservation, staying out in the open to demonstrate their peaceful intentions.

Twenty yards from the barricade Shakespeare halted and went to ground, flattening and straining his keen ears to catch the faintest sounds. To his rear some of the horses inside the perimeter were fidgeting and nickering lightly, no doubt sensing that something was wrong from the nervousness of the whites. Many animals, horses and dogs included, could smell the scent of fear, and although Templar's men were putting on a brave show, Shakespeare suspected they were inwardly terrified at the thought of doing battle with a superior force of Indians.

The mountain man didn't blame them. Whether the war party was Piegan, Blood, Blackfoot, or Gros Ventre was of no real consequence since the fate of the whites would be the same if they were overwhelmed. Those not killed in the attack would be tortured to test their bravery; then they'd be horribly mutilated, made to endure a grisly death, and finally scalped, a prospect terrifying enough to inspire fear in any man.

Shakespeare thought of Diana Templar and Eric Nash and wanted to kick himself for being so soft in the heart. This fight was none of his affair, but he'd gone and taken a shine to those two. If not for them, he would have ridden off hours ago and left the rest to face the Indians alone. Although, now that he considered it, he sort of liked the old soldier, Jarvis, too.

Up on the hill an owl suddenly hooted, and was promptly answered by another from a spot not fifty feet away.

Grinning impishly, Shakespeare snaked to his left, working in a loop toward the warrior concealed in the high grass. Every movement now was slow and controlled. He must make no sound whatsoever since there was no telling how many of the warriors were watching the camp and where they might be hiding.

Decades of wilderness living had imbued Shakespeare with the stealth of a panther. His passage through the grass was eerily silent. Often he paused to look and listen. Soon he was near the spot where the warrior should be, but he saw no one. Rigid as a log, the Hawken clenched firmly in his left hand, he let only his eyes rove back and forth. Just when he began to wonder if he was mistaken, a black shape rose six feet away and hastened toward the hill.

So skillfully did Shakespeare blend into the shadowy background that the brave passed within two yards of the frontiersman and never noticed him. In the moonlight Shakespeare could plainly see the other's face, but it was the hair he was most interested in. No two tribes wore their hair exactly alike, so if a man knew the different styles he could identify warriors accordingly.

This man had the lower portion of his long hair in a braid, with the front clipped in bangs that fell to just above his eyes, and at the back of his head there was a fan-shaped roach of animal hair. The style was quite popular with Piegan men.

Shakespeare smelled the bear fat the warrior had used to slick the hair as the man went by. He followed the brave's progress with just his eyes until the Piegan was out of sight, then rose in a crouched and trailed him. Now he knew their identity. He also needed to know how many the English greenhorns were up against.

From the valley floor the way led up and over the thickly forested slope of the hill. Beyond, at its base, flickered the tiny fire the Piegans had built where the whites could not see it.

On the crest Shakespeare stopped in the shelter of a boulder. None of the warriors were sleeping and it was doubtful any would. They were too excited, and would spend the night planning

their strategy, sharpening their knives, toma-
hawks, and arrows, and checking their charms.
Like many tribes, the Piegans were superstitious.
They believed that certain objects could impart
strong medicine to the owner, and regarded some
charms as having protective powers in battle. A
lucky talisman might be something so simple as a
seed or a stone or a bear or eagle claw, but whatever it was a warrior would not think to go into a
fight without it. Usually he wrapped his charm in
a soft piece of skin, then tied it around his body
or neck. Sometimes such charms were offered for
trade, and Shakespeare knew of several instances
where a particularly powerful charm had cost the
purchaser a half-dozen fine horses.

By the low light of the fire Shakespeare counted
11 warriors. He calculated another six or seven
might be keeping an eye on the whites' camp,
which brought the total close to 20. Steep odds,
but not formidable.

Having accomplished all he could, Shakespeare
had turned to depart when faintly from the other
side of the hill came the crunch of a dry twig.
Another warrior was returning to the fire, and
not wishing to be spotted, Shakespeare scooted
around the boulder and ducked low.

Seconds later low voices confirmed that not one
but two braves were coming back. Their excitement was obvious from their rapid speech. They
were eager to count coup and take scalps, to go
back to their people crowned with glory.

The mountain man, flush with the boulder,
observed their descent. As he squatted there,
pondering how best to handle the defense of the
camp, an idea occurred to him that lit up his eyes

with mischievous delight. The one thing Indians feared more than anything was bad medicine. Often they'd abandon an enterprise if the omens weren't just right. So what would happen, he asked himself, if he arranged a little bad medicine for the Piegan war party? Or at least threw a scare into them?

The idea was tantalizing. Shakespeare sank to his hands and knees and cautiously worked his way lower. The Piegans were talking animatedly, confident they were safe from the besieged whites, never imagining one of their enemies would have the audacity to pay them a visit.

A thicket grew within ten feet of the fire. Into this Shakespeare crawled, and here he had to be extremely careful not to snag his buckskins or the Hawken. The bushes were so tightly spaced that at times he was compelled to twist sideways to slide through the gap. At length, though, he succeeded in worming close to where the Piegans were huddled in a circle around their crackling blaze.

Keeping his face screened by intervening branches, Shakespeare lay and listened for the better part of an hour. During that time four Piegans returned from the valley and four more were sent to take their place. The warriors joked and laughed, thoroughly at ease, a drastic contrast to the prevailing attitude among the marquis's party.

During Shakespeare's wide-ranging travels he'd learned a half-dozen Indian tongues and picked up a smattering of many more. But since his contact with the Piegans had been limited, invariably involving the business end of a Piegan lance, he knew few of their words, certainly not enough to make hide or hair of their conversation.

Presently Shakespeare decided the time was right. What he had in mind was risky—some might say insane—but it would so spook the Piegans they might take it as a bad sign and call off the attack. Slowly he eased backwards, retracing his route until he lay just within the outer margin of the thicket. Girding his legs under him, he sucked air deep into his lungs, held his breath a moment, then threw his head back and did his best imitation of a grizzly's roar.

For the span of five seconds the night was totally still. Abruptly, the Piegans leaped to their feet with much yelling and gesturing.

Shakespeare knew he had to get out of there before they thought to surround the thicket. Grabbing a bush on either side, he shook them vigorously while venting another animalistic roar. In the dancing glow of the fire the effect must have been little less than spectacularly frightening, because the very next instant three of the youngest Piegans were in full flight.

To cap his performance, Shakespeare suddenly roared a third time and burst out of the thicket with his arms flailing, the play of firelight lending him a spectral aspect. Two more Piegans were frantically retreating while the rest were rooted to where they stood as if mesmerized.

Whirling, Shakespeare sprinted into the comforting shadows and angled up the steep hill. If he didn't cover a lot of ground quickly he'd never set his eyes on Blue Water Woman again. He was almost to the boulder when shouts of rage erupted, and looking back he saw the war party in frenzied pursuit. They had figured out he was flesh and blood. Some might even have recognized him as being with the marquis's bunch. Now his life depended on his being faster and cleverer than they were.

The mountain man skirted the boulder, dug in his moccasins to gain extra purchase, and jogged to the crest. Once more he glanced behind him to see if the Piegans were gaining, and the next instant he collided with something barring his path and was nearly knocked off his feet. Recovering his balance, he faced forward, and was flabbergasted to behold an equally stunned warrior holding a war club.

The Piegan gathered his wits swiftly. Sweeping the club up, he sprang.

Shakespeare dared not become embroiled in a prolonged fight. Since he already had the Hawken at waist height, it was the work of a moment to cock the hammer, level the barrel, and squeeze off a shot. Caught in mid-leap inches from the muzzle, the Piegan was catapulted backwards by the blast.

Without stopping to gauge whether the shot had proven fatal, Shakespeare ran like the wind down the far side, wincing now and again as branches tore into him. There was quite a commotion at the camp, but it was dwarfed by the uproar made by the enraged Piegans as they reached the top of the hill and discovered their fallen fellow.

Shakespeare hit the flat valley floor on the run and made for the makeshift barricade. The Piegans behind him weren't his only problem now. There were others lurking in the tall grass and they might try to intercept him. On top of that, he had little confidence the men in the marquis's employ wouldn't shoot if they saw a vague figure running toward them despite being cautioned not to.

In his younger days Shakespeare had won foot race after foot race in friendly competitions with Flathead, Nez Percé, and Shoshone runners, and the experience served him in good stead in the present as he raced for his life, enabling him to pace himself so he didn't tire prematurely. He breathed deeply, his arms swinging easily at his side, his legs pumping steadily. The grass swirled around his ankles, and the wind blew through his hair.

Scores of yards separated him from the barricade when a scarecrow-like form streamed out of nowhere with a lance held aloft.

Shakespeare swerved as the warrior's arm flashed down. He glimpsed the lance, then felt a jarring blow to his left shoulder as the tip nicked him, tearing his shirt and his flesh. Unfazed, he closed his right hand on one of the pistols at his waist. The Piegan was elevating a knife when a ball cored his brain.

On Shakespeare sped, thrusting the flintlock under his belt. Behind him stormed the main body of Piegans. To his right and left arose strident cries as those warriors who had been keeping watch on the camp realized what was happening and joined in the chase. An arrow sailed from out of the dark sky and thudded into the soil a hand's width from his foot.

Adding to the clamor were shouts from behind the barricade. Someone—it sounded like the soldier, Jarvis—was telling the rest not to shoot unless he gave the order to do so.

Then Shakespeare was close enough to see Lady Templar, the marquis, and Eric Nash behind the trunks. The artist spied him and waved him on. Diana cupped a hand to her mouth and urged him to hurry. Looking back, he saw why. A skinny Piegan with the stamina of an antelope was hot on his heels, eight feet away and reducing the distance swiftly. The warrior gripped a knife he would never get to use, as Shakespeare's other pistol proved quickly.

Rather than stop to climb over the trunks and thereby give the Piegans a chance to pick him off, Shakespeare, pistol in one hand and rifle in the other, increased his speed, coiled, and leaped, clearing the top with half a foot to spare. Diana, William, and Eric barely got out of the way in time. He hit on his right shoulder, rolled, and swept erect, his features as composed as if he had just taken a stroll in a city park.

Jarvis suddenly gave the command to fire, and the men on the west side of the barricade opened up on the onrushing Piegans. A single volley was all that was needed to disperse them as, like ghosts, they vanished in the grass.

In the silence that subsequently enveloped the camp a Piegan could be heard groaning in pain.

"Dear Lord!" William Templar breathed, his face the pallor of a sheet, his forehead damp with perspiration. The tip of his tongue touched his lower lip and was withdrawn.

"What on earth did you do out there?" Eric asked McNair. "It sounded as if you started an Indian uprising single-handed."

"I reduced the odds a mite," Shakespeare said, and replaced the second pistol under his belt to free his hand so he could examine his wound. The lance had gouged half an inch into his shoulder and drawn blood, but already the flow had reduced to a trickle.

"My word!" Diana exclaimed, moving toward him. "You've been hurt."

"It's just a scratch, ma'am," Shakespeare said.

"You let me be the judge of that. I've had practice bandaging wounded." Diana glanced at her brother. "Be a dear and bring the bag with the ointments."

"I don't know where it is," William protested sullenly.

"It's with the personal things we kept out of the trunks," Diana reminded him, adding curtly, "Now be off with you! This man is in pain."

Exhibiting as much enthusiasm as if he were being sent to the guillotine, Lord Templar sulked off, his spiteful gaze lingering long and hard on the man he blamed for his sister's ill manners. William was not one to forgive slights. Forgiveness, in his estimation, was for weaklings, a failing caused by inordinate compassion for those who deserved none. But he was a patient man. Sooner or later an opportunity would arise for him to have his vengeance on the mountain man, and he could hardly wait.

Watching the marquis leave, Eric Nash remarked absently, "You're a brave man, Mr. McNair. It's a pity that in the greater scheme of things our lives are paltry by comparison."

"Some lives, maybe," Shakespeare said, and neither of them had to ask if he had someone special in mind. Diana had peeled back the edge of the torn buckskin and was gently determining the extent of the wound.

Eric leaned his back on the trunks and folded his arms. "All of us, I'm afraid, live and strive and die in vain. Our petty triumphs, our many defeats, what do they matter? Do they advance the progress of humanity through the gloomy and torturous byways of history one little centimeter? I should say they do not. All is for naught, sir, for naught. Even your wondrous deed we've witnessed this night."

"I didn't know you're such a gloomy cuss," Shakespeare said.

"He has his moods," Diana interjected. "The temperament of an artist and all that. But sometimes—" and she stared at Nash "—his moods are bloody inconvenient."

"Now, now, Diana," Eric chided. "Remember you're a lady."

"And you remember that your self-appointed purpose in life is to keep me happy, not depress me. You should be grateful to Mr. MaNair for his valiant efforts in our behalf, not lecturing him on your morbid outlook on life." She glanced out over the barricade. "In any event, of much more interest to me is whether the savages have desisted for the night or whether we should fear an attack before dawn now that they are so stirred up."

"Don't fret in that regard," Shakespeare said. "They lost three men, so they'll be busy committing the spirits of their dead to the spirit land. That will keep most of them occupied until morning."

"Heathens believe in an afterlife?" Eric exclaimed, and laughed. "Now I truly have heard everything."

"Why do you find that so peculiar?" Shakespeare asked. "Sure, Indians believe in a spirit world, and most of them believe in God, only they call Him the Great Mystery or the Great Medicine or the Great Spirit or some other name depending on the tribe."

"We were told all Indians are crude and barbaric, brutal primitives who have no religion," Eric said.

"Some of them feel the same away about whites," Shakespeare commented. He had been scouring the valley and felt positive the Piegans were indeed gone. The moaning had ceased, and the only sound now was the sighing of the wind through the grass. "Take the Utes," he detailed. "To their way of thinking the afterlife is divided up into three levels. The highest is just for them. The middle level is for buffalo and other game. The lowest level is for the few whites who reach the other side."

"How marvelous," Eric said. "Tell us more."

"Why are you so curious?" Shakespeare responded. "Do you really give a damn about their beliefs, or are you just like most other whites? Folks in the States generally despise Indians. Think they're a nuisance and should be killed in the name of progress. The government hasn't helped matters much by making it official policy to relocate all Indians still living in the States west of the Mississippi." He frowned. "Why, even a senator came out and said that if every Indian was to disappear tomorrow it would be no great loss to the world."

"You sound rather bitter," Eric said.

"Bitter, nothing! I'm mad as hell. If the government ever tries to drive off the tribes in these parts, I'll be the first in line to help the Indians."

Diana had been listening in growing puzzlement. "I do not understand you at all, Mr. McNair. By your own admission you slew three Indians several minutes ago, yet now you defend them and their way of life? Isn't that being inconsistent?"

"Not at all. Some tribes, such as the Shoshones and the Flatheads, have never harmed a hair on a white man's head. They're decent, honorable folks, and when you make a friend of one you have a loyal friend for life. They sure as blazes deserve to be treated better than the Cherokees."

"But what about the Indians you just fought?" Diana brought up. "Do they deserve fair treatment?"

"The Piegans? Of course they do. Part of this land was their territory before the white man ever stepped off the *Mayflower*. They hate whites with good reason. They've seen the beaver trapped off, and the buffalo killed in greater numbers than ever before. They know that white men think they have a God-given right to do as they please with the land and everything in it, and they see us as destroyers of their way of life."

"What rubbish! They're blowing the white presence out of all proportion," Eric declared.

"Are they? Already there are hundreds of trappers roaming these mountains, and quite a few settlers like myself who have dug in roots and aim to stay. And more and more are coming every year."

"So what would you do if formulating Indian policy was up to you?" Diana asked.

"I'd keep the whites east of the Mississippi and the Indians west of it."

"And where would that leave you?"

"On this side of the river," Shakespeare said with a grin. "I'm an adopted Flathead."

Eric and Diana laughed merrily, and it was to this scene that William returned bearing a satchel. "Here are our medicines," he stated, dropping the bag at his sister's feet. Sniffing loudly, he wheeled and walked off.

"If you don't mind my saying so, ma'am," Shakespeare told Diana, "your brother should give some thought to joining the human race." Then, almost as an afterthought, he quoted William S.: "Having his ear full of his airy fame, grows dainty of his worth, and in his tent lies mocking our designs."

"I say," Eric chuckled. "You know Shakespeare almost as well as I know Byron."

"Who?"

"George Gordon Lord Byron. The greatest poet of all time. The master weaver of words in rhyme."

"Never heard of him," Shakespeare said. He felt a tug on his sleeve and looking down, found the satchel open and Diana on her knees waiting for him to sit so she could minister to his wound without having to stretch. "You're making a fuss over nothing," he grumbled as he eased to the ground.

Diana's deft fingers soon had the gash cleaned and bandaged. The pale moonlight, bathing her smooth skin, presented the illusion her face had been sculpted from marble. Eric Nash's eyes never left it for a moment.

When she was done, Shakespeare stood, Hawken in hand. "Thank you for your trouble, Lady Templar. Now I'd best cheek on my horse. It gets lonesome without me." Then he melted into the dark.

"What an odd, fascinating character," Eric said. "Did you notice how he lost his mountain twang and stopped using all that slang after he became worked up over the Indian issue?"

"Yes. I'd like to know what he did before he came to these mountains to live. I'd wager he was a lawyer or a politician perhaps."

"McNair a political bloodsucker? I think not."

From out of the night came a gravelly voice. "You two had better quit chawing like a pair of chipmunks and get some sleep. Come first light those Piegans are going to pay us a visit and it won't be no social call."

Chapter Five

Dawn had yet to tinge the eastern horizon when Nate King opened his eyes. Snuggled beside him lay Winona, her rich black hair wreathing her face, her bosom rising and falling as she breathed. For the longest while he simply stared at her, reveling in her beauty. Then he pecked her on the tip of her nose, eased off the bed, and stood.

Across the room snored Zach, his limbs askew, his mouth gaping wide.

Nate grinned, went to the table where his clothes, pistols, and rifle had been placed before he retired, and donned his britches. Then he jammed a flintlock under his belt. In bare feet he padded to the door, silently worked the wooden latch, and stepped out into the brisk morning air. Immediately goose flesh covered him and he inadvertently shivered.

Down at the lake the ducks, geese, and brants

floated in idyllic tranquillity. Once the sun rose they would rouse to life and create a racket with their quacking and honking.

Nate softly closed the door, stretched, and yawned. Walking around the corner, he entered the trees and went a short distance before relieving himself. He strolled back, went past the door, and to the far end of the long, low cabin where the horse pen stood. The animals were huddled together in one corner. His stallion, spying him, came over to be greeted, and he accommodated by stroking its neck and rubbing around its ears.

This was one of Nate's favorite times, the quiet hour before the advent of the blazing sun heralded another day. Even the air seemed to be stilled with expectation. He gazed at the regal mountains to the south, among them the lofty peak that had earned the name Long's Peak in honor of the explorations conducted in the region by Major Stephen Long back in 1820. Long, like most Easterners, had no conception of the grandeur of the territory he had surveyed, even going so far as to brand the plains as the "Great American Desert," and informing his superiors that the well-nigh limitless prairies were inhospitable to man and beast and of no worth to people depending on agriculture for a living. Thanks to Long, maps now labeled the land between the Mississippi and the Rockies as a desert.

Nate had to shake his head and grin every time he thought of it. How was it, he mused, that two people could look at the exact same thing and each see something entirely different? When he'd first crossed the plains, instead of comparing them to a desert, he'd been astounded by the teeming varieties of life with which the prairie abounded. Hadn't Long realized the plains were home to millions upon millions of buffalo, antelope, deer, and other animals? And why hadn't Long been impressed by the fact that some Indian tribes successfully tilled the arid soil? Rather than being a desert, the plains were a verdant garden waiting to be claimed by enterprising souls hardy enough to endure the many hardships of frontier life.

But as much as Nate appreciated the prairie, his appreciation paled in comparison to his passionate devotion to the mountains. For as long as he lived he would never forget his first sight of the towering ramparts with their glistening crowns of snow. He could still recall the shiver of awe that rippled through his soul. And now, as he admired the sweeping vista of monumental crags, sublime rocky palisades, and ivory summits touching the very clouds, he felt the same familiar thrill.

Nate knew he would spend the remainder of his life right where he was. He would live and die in the mountains, and when he was gone he wanted the Shoshones to accord him a proper burial right there in the land he loved. If he never saw the States again he would not suffer in the least. Back there he had been so dependent on everyone and everything: on his parents for their guidance, on his employer for his livelihood, on merchants for his clothing, food, and other essentials. He'd been forced to rely on society for his very life, much like a bird in a cage was dependent on its owner for its sustenance, and he hadn't realized the fact until he'd learned the meaning

of true freedom by coming to the mountains and
making do on his own.

What a difference genuine freedom made in a
man's life! Nate reflected. He owed no one, was
beholden to no one. All the decisions that affec-
ted his life were made by him and him alone.
He had total responsibility for his existence, and
instead of quaking with fear at being thrown on
his own resources, he was daily exhilarated by
wrestling with the realities of life. Struggling and
hardship brought out the best in people, made
them better than they had been. Total depend-
ence on others, on the other hand, brought out
the very worst in human nature and made people slaves to their baser instincts. Or so he firmly believed after giving the matter considerable
thought.

Nate patted the stallion and strolled back
toward the cabin door. Somewhere far across
the valley an elk bugled, which was unusual at
that time of year since normally a person only
heard a bull elk in the fall, during rutting season.
He saw several sparrows frolicking in a nearby
tree, and smiled.

Back in New York City he would have been
breathing air filled with soot from burning coal
and wood. He would have had to contend with
garbage in the gutter, refuse in the alleys, and
the reek of human waste. Crossing a street was
a hazardous undertaking due to the volume of
carriage traffic. And the only "wildlife" to speak
of were hoards of stray dogs and cats that only
added to the general stench.

And now look! The air was sparkling fresh. The
only scents were those of pine and musty earth,

and occasionally a hint of mint from the patch Winona had planted by the cabin. There was no one trying to run him down, and nary a dog or cat in sight. Just the wolf.

Nate stopped and watched as the cub, sporting a bright patch of white on its chest, trotted out of the brush and up to his legs. "Good morning, Blaze," he addressed Zach's pet. "You were out all night again and Zach was worried." Squatting, he scratched under the wolf's tapered chin, and was licked on the face in return. "Just what I need to start the day. A bath of wolf slobber."

"We could go for a swim so you can wash the slobber off."

Nate glanced around. Winona, bundled in a heavy buffalo robe, was framed in the doorway, her disheveled hair adding to her incomparable beauty. "Forget the swim. Let's go off in the woods and fool around."

Her smile was devastating. "We fooled around plenty last night, as I recall. And me as big as a basket!"

"Don't blame me," Nate said, rising. "I was lying there minding my own business until these hands started roaming all over me. What was I supposed to do? Bite my tongue and whimper a lot?"

Winona, laughing, walked into his arms and they embraced, their lips locked. Eventually she pushed him back and said in mock anger, "Keep doing this every day and we will wind up with fifteen children!"

"What's wrong with that? When they get old enough they can do all the work around here while you and I take it easy."

She clasped his hand and headed for the lake,

the robe slipping down to reveal her shapely shoulders. "You tossed and turned a lot last night. Is something bothering you?"

"No," Nate said. But after going a few more yards, he confessed, "Well, maybe. I have this nagging feeling that Shakespeare might be in trouble, although I know darn well there isn't a problem he can't handle. He hasn't gotten all that white hair by being careless."

"Perhaps he will arrive today and put your fears at rest."

"I hope so." Nate stared northward. "I sure as blazes hope so."

Shakespeare McNair had not slept a wink. He hadn't tried to. As he'd told Diana and the rest, he doubted very much the Piegans would attack before dawn, but since he couldn't be one hundred percent certain of that, and since he *was* certain that when the Piegans closed in they would be able to sneak right up to the perimeter without the greenhorns being the wiser, he deemed it prudent to stay awake and alert.

First light was not far off. Already a faint rosy streak rimmed the eastern skyline. Shakespeare halted beside a pile of provisions and gazed at the hill screening the Piegan camp from view. He thought he might detect some evidence of their coming, but all was peaceful. Close at hand a guard dozed. Across the camp two men were whispering and casting bitter glances at the slumbering marquis.

From the snatches of conversation Shakespeare had overheard during the long night, he gathered that most of the men despised William Templar.

They stayed in the marquis's service out of devotion to his sterling sister, not to him. Some of them, apparently, had worked for the family for many years under the duke himself. One was their butler and back in England, another was William's valet, and another some other sort of manservant. They were good men, and they'd been through severe trials during their many travels with the Templars, but they were hardly competent enough to fend off seasoned warriors despite William's boasts to the contrary.

Shakespeare hadn't said anything to any of them, but he was sorely perplexed by their willingness to be a servant to any man or woman. Servitude smacked of slavery, and Shakespeare never had been partial to that institution. Back in the States a sharp division had arisen between States in favor of the practice and those against it. Some, like Pennsylvania and New York, had banned the slave trade. The years ahead promised to be rife with discord over the issue.

"Morning, mate."

So unexpected was the greeting that Shakespeare nearly jumped. He hadn't heard anyone approach, which was quite extraordinary given his acute senses. Spinning, he looked into the twinkling eyes of the giant. "Make that a habit and you're liable to get your head blowed clean off."

Jarvis chortled and rested the stock of his rifle on the ground. "Sorry, gov. A soldier's training is hard to break." He leaned on his gun and surveyed the scenery. "Right pretty country you've got here, Mr. McNair. I haven't seen the like since Tibet."

"I hear tell they've got a few sizeable mountains there," Shakespeare allowed.

"A few," Jarvis said, grinning. "One, they claim, is the highest in the world. The natives call it Chomolungma." Raising a huge finger, he scratched his right whisker. "I got to climb it partway. Took a shot at a snow leopard and missed. Pity too. It would have looked fine mounted over my fireplace."

"You like traveling around the world with the Templars, do you?"

"Yes, sir, I truly do. Started when I was in the Dragoon Guards, and I've never regretted my urge to roam," Jarvis said wistfully. "I've seen the Himalayas and the Alps. I've watched the sun rise over the Ganges and set on the Tiber. I've eaten yak and hippopotamus, which isn't hard to swallow if you hold your nose." He glanced at the mountain man. "You must be able to understand."

"Better than you think," Shakespeare said. "Do you ever get the itch to settle down?"

"Not yet, but a body never knows. Maybe one day I'll meet a bit of goods who will get her claws into me and never let go. Until then, I want to enjoy what life has to offer."

"Let's hope the Piegans don't end your traveling days," Shakespeare remarked, scanning the valley. The eastern sky was now aglow, the stars fading.

"Are they really the devils you make them out to be?"

"When their dander is up there's no stopping them this side of the grave."

Jarvis stared at the tent containing Diana

Templar. "I would hate to see anything happen to her. She's such a sweet little thing. There isn't a nasty bone in her body." Shifting, he scowled at William. "Which is more than can be said of her brother."

"And Mr. Nash?" Shakespeare inquired.

"He's a mystery, mate. A nit could tell he's sweet on Lady Templar, but I don't think she's quite as sweet on him. She is is his patron, though, which gives him an excuse to stay close to her."

"His patron?"

"You do know he's a painter? Well, most painters and poets and sculptors and the like are so busy creating their art, as they call it, that they'd forget to eat if they didn't have a patron to pay their bills and keep food on the table."

"She gives him the money to live on?"

"Enough for him to make ends meet. Thousands and thousands of pounds each year. But don't mistake her purpose. Most of the money she spends to buy his paintings, and although I'm not much on culture, I will admit his works are inspiring. Very true to life. One day he might even be famous."

"Interesting," was Shakespeare's comment.

To the west a jay shrieked, the first bird to hail the new day.

At the sound the giant stiffened and raised his rifle. "Was that the real thing, Mr. McNair?"

"Call me Shakespeare. Yes, it was."

Jarvis nodded. "I've heard that these Indians use bird and animal cries to signal back and forth."

"That they do. And it takes years before a man can tell the difference." Shakespeare heard a loud yawn. Turning, he saw the marquis sitting up in his blankets, which had been positioned directly in front of Diana's tent. Beside William, Eric stirred.

"I'd best see to the men before his lordship gets up," Jarvis said. "If they're not all at their posts he'll have a bloody fit." He hurried away.

The timing was perfect. Shakespeare had been about to make that very suggestion since a golden halo framed the horizon, portending the imminent rising of the sun. He moved along the west side of the barricade, scouring the tall grass and the nearest slopes. Either he was slipping in his old age or the Piegans were in no great rush to attack.

Soon Jarvis had every man up and ready to meet the onslaught. The marquis insisted on having a silver basin set up in front of a mirror so he could wash and shave. Eric Nash tarried around the tent until Diana emerged, looking absolutely resplendent in a stunning blue dress adorned with frilly lace at the throat and at the ends of both sleeves.

Fully ten minutes after the sun rose, as Shakespeare stood pondering the situation, the three came toward him.

"So where are the heathens?" William demanded while still yards off. Gesturing angrily at the mountains, he declared, "Obviously, you got us all worked up for no reason! Because of you I had terrible nightmares all night long."

"How did *you* sleep?" Shakespeare asked Lady Templar.

"Well enough under the circumstances," Diana

answered. "I woke up several times and looked out, and each time I saw you walking the perimeter. You must be quite fatigued."

"I'll get by."

"Really, sis," William said. "If I didn't know better I'd swear you care more about his welfare than mine." He jabbed a the finger at the trunks, supplies, and brush comprising the barricade. "Since this whole affair has been a false alarm, I say we pack up and head north to Canada as we originally planned. These savages are really timid at heart, and this delay has been unnecessary."

"Don't you ever get tired of being wrong?" Shakespeare asked.

"Your impertinence, sir, is resented."

"Tell that to them," Shakespeare said, and pointed at the crown of the hill where over a dozen warriors were silhouetted against the sky, the tips of their lances glittering in the growing light of the rising sun. The Piegans had materialized moments ago. Strangely, they were making no move to come any closer.

"My word!" the marquis exclaimed. "They certainly are wicked-looking blighters!" He faced McNair. "I owe you an apology, sir. My outburst was uncalled for. Please forgive me."

A grunt constituted Shakespeare's assent. He was too preoccupied by the Piegans to pay much attention to Templar, although in the back of his mind he did wonder why William was being so charitable with his apologies all of a sudden.

"Is it normal for them to stand and stare like they're doing?" Eric Nash asked.

"No," Shakespeare said. "Frankly, I don't know what to make of it."

"Perhaps they have decided to leave us alone," Diana suggested.

"Hardly. They're bloodthirsty as sin where whites are concerned. If they're not attacking, they have a damn good reason."

"What could it be?" Diana wondered.

"I'll be dogged if I know. But it's a cinch we're not going anywhere until they show their cards. Keep everyone inside the barricade and have them eat at their posts. When the attack does come, we might not have much warning."

"We could charge them," William proposed. "I can take half the men and drive the savages off without working up much of a sweat."

Shakespeare shook his head. "You go charging through that high grass and none of your men will reach the hill alive. There are more warriors hidden out there just waiting for us to pull a stupid stunt so they can pick us off one by one."

"So it's a stalemate, then," William said. "So be it. In the meantime, I'm famished. I'll have our man cook an extra portion for you, McNair."

The mountain man paid no heed. He focused on adjacent hills and mountains, seeking anything that might explain the behavior of the Piegans. "A gloomy peace this morning with it brings," he quoted distractedly. "All we can do is wait them out."

An uneventful hour went by. Breakfast for the men was distributed by Jarvis, while the marquis, his sister, and Nash sat at a table near the tent and partook of a fare seldom seen in the Rockies: kidney pie left over from the night before, biscuits, sweets, and tea.

Shakespeare was invited to sit at the table with

them, but politely declined. He stayed at the barricade, munching on the cold kidney pie, the taste of which he found he liked even though it couldn't hold a candle to roast venison or panther meat. The Piegans, the whole time, stayed in plain sight on the hill. Some were seated with their backs to trees or boulders, others standing. Now and again one or another would glance off toward the northwest, and it was this that caused a sinking feeling in Shakespeare's gut. He had a hunch why the war party was lounging about and he prayed he was wrong.

By mid-morning the men were much more relaxed, convinced their show of strength had given the Piegans second thoughts. This attitude was fostered by the marquis, who made the rounds and boasted that "the overrated heathens are scared to death of us." Some took to shouting challenges at the Indians, daring the Piegans to prove their mettle.

Toward noon, as Shakespeare leaned on a trunk in the company of Diana, Eric, and Jarvis, the Piegans all stood, vented hearty whoops, and shook their weapons overhead. Shakespeare quickly spotted the cause of their jubilation marching in single file into the west end of the valley.

"More of them!" Eric exclaimed.

"Yep," Shakespeare said grimly. "This is what they've been waiting for. The ones who have kept us pinned down here were part of a much larger war party, and last night they sent a runner to bring the rest here."

No one said anything else as the new arrivals spread out across the valley floor and were joined by those from the hill. Soon their purpose became apparent; they were forming a ring around the whites.

"I count thirty-five of them," Eric said.

"And there are more in the grass yet," Shakespeare mentioned. Catching Jarvis's eye, he advised, "Have your men check their pieces. Instruct them not to fire until the braves are so close they can't miss. And if any of the Piegans get inside the barricade, have them use their knives instead of their guns. A wild shot could hit one of us."

"Sound advice, mate," the giant replied as he left.

A pall of deathly silence hung over the valley. Two thirds of the enveloping ring had been completed when Lady Templar excused herself to go to her tent, and no sooner was she gone than Eric Nash touched the mountain man's shoulder.

"Should I save a ball for Diana?" he whispered.

"We won't let them get her."

"But you can't guarantee they won't. And there are horrid tales of what they do to white women." Eric bit his lower lip and looked askance at the rifle in his hands. "I should tell you, McNair, I'm not much of a fighter. My experience with firearms is severely limited, and I doubt I hit what I aim at one time out of ten."

"Don't worry. You'll do better today."

"How can you be so sure?"

"Because you'll be fighting for your life. It's one thing to set up a target and try to hit the mark when you don't much care if you do or not, and it's another to take aim at a man you know is going to bury a tomahawk in your brain if you

don't bring him down. Necessity makes medio-
cre marksmen better than they ever figured they
could be."

"I regret our association has been so fleeting,
Shakespeare. I find your frontier insights quite
appealing."

"We'll palaver again after we teach these Piegans
a lesson in humility."

"Your optimism, sir, is outrageous."

Further conversation was forgotten as the circle of Piegans voiced a collective series of war
whoops while waving their weapons, and then to
a man they swarmed toward the barricade.

Chapter Six

Shakespeare McNair had been in more fights with Indians than most men alive, and he had the scars to prove it. He'd been stabbed with a knife, struck by a tomahawk, pierced by a lance, and transfixed by arrows. He'd been jumped from ambush numerous times, caught in raids on villages in which he happened to be staying, and gone on raids himself with friendly warriors. Few whites knew as much about the varied aspects of Indian warfare.

So when Shakespeare saw the Piegans brazenly surrounding the camp he knew the war party was confident of victory and would never retreat once the attack began. Indians much preferred to have the element of surprise in their favor in any conflict. They'd rather strike from concealment, sneaking up on their enemies and pouncing when their foes were distracted. That the Piegans disdained doing so indicated they held the whites in utter contempt.

As the warriors raced forward through the waving grass, Shakespeare was the first to fire. Given his proven marksmanship he didn't have to fear wasting the lead, and true to form, his initial shot dropped a Piegan 40 yards out.

Swiftly Shakespeare reloaded, his fingers a blur. Arrows rained down from all directions, some imbedding themselves in the ground, others thwacking into the trunks and provisions. He was pleased to note Jarvis was holding the other men in check, preventing them from firing until the Piegans were closer just as he had instructed.

The screeching warriors were 20 yards out when Shakespeare squeezed off his second shot. As before, a Piegan pitched to the earth, and a second later guns opened up all around the perimeter. More Piegans dropped. So did a couple of the defenders, one with a shaft clear through his neck.

Eric Nash joined the battle. As he'd predicted, he missed.

And then the Piegans were at the barricade and leaping over it with the smooth, flowing motions of blacktail deer leaping logs or scrambling to the top where they could find a purchase. By now most of the frantic defenders had expended the shots in their two rifles, so they met the confident braves with knives or pistols or their rifles wielded as clubs.

Shakespeare employed the last method as a pair of Piegans vaulted over the trunks in front

of him. The first he clipped with a vicious swing,
catapulting the warrior backwards, but the second
alighted on his side of the barrier and whirled to
impale him with a lance. Twisting, Shakespeare
avoided the blow and heard the lance thud into
the bottom trunk. The stock of his rifle curled
in a tight arc, catching the Piegan full on the
face and crushing the man's nose in a spray of
blood. Gurgling, the warrior backed away, trying
to buy time to recover, time Shakespeare was not
going to give him. A single bound brought the
mountain man to his adversary, and he drove
the stock into the Piegan's throat. There was
a loud crunch, then the brave fell, wheezing
pitiably.

The interior of the barricade was now a swirling melee of men engaged in desperate life-or-
death struggles. War whoops, curses, screams,
and inarticulate cries rent the air. Shakespeare
saw one of the defenders down and dead and
being scalped. He spotted Jarvis, hemmed in by
three Piegans but holding his own. A glance back
showed Eric Nash rigid as a pole, terrified by the
carnage.

Then Shakespeare thought of Lady Templar.
He looked at the tent, and the short hairs at the
nape of his neck prickled. A swarthy warrior was
almost to the flap, tomahawk in hand. "Diana!"
Shakespeare shouted, and raced to her rescue
knowing he couldn't possibly get there in time
but resolved to try anyway. A chill seized him
as he watched the Piegan grab hold of the flap
and throw it open. The warrior grinned, took a
step. That was as far as he got, for out of the tent
poked the barrel of a rifle, and its booming retort

sent the Piegan crashing to the grass.

Diana stepped outside, her features like granite, just as Shakespeare reached her. "Get back inside!" he yelled. "I'll protect you."

"The Templars fight their own fights!" she responded.

Arguing under such circumstances would be ridiculous. Shakespeare had his hands full anyhow, as around the tent rushed a stocky Piegan whose knife leaped at the frontiersman's throat. Shakespeare got his rifle up to block the blade in the nick of time, but the impact of the heavy warrior drove him backwards, making him lose his balance, and they both went down. Hands clawed at his eyes, striving to gouge them out. The knife narrowly missed his temple.

Coiling his stomach muscles, Shakespeare heaved upward and dislodged his antagonist. The Piegan rolled as he was flipped and jumped up in the blink of an eye, his knife at the ready. Before the brave could pounce, a rifle stock slammed into his temple from behind, staggering him. Never one to let an opportunity go by, Shakespeare whipped out one of his pistols and shot the brave dead.

Diana Templar hefted her rifle, staring at the crimson stain on the stock. "I couldn't let him kill you," she said softly.

"I'm obliged," was all Shakespeare had time to say, because the tide of battle had turned in drastic favor of the Piegans and several were racing toward the tent, each eager to be the first to count coup on the grizzled mountain man or to take the fair female captive. Elsewhere, four of the marquis's party were dead, two more severely wounded. Jarvis had slain four braves but was still hard-pressed.

Releasing the Hawken and the spent pistol, Shakespeare drew his other flintlock and his tomahawk, which he'd rather use in close combat than his knife; the handle was longer, giving him a greater reach, and the heavy head could be used to smash as well as slash.

The foremost Piegan was grinning as his arm streaked back to throw his lance.

Shakespeare put a ball squarely in the center of the man's teeth. The gun now useless, he let it join the other weapons at his feet and moved between Diana and the onrushing warriors. The outcome was virtually a foregone conclusion, but he wasn't one to die meekly. Lips curled in a mocking smile, he crouched to meet them head on.

All around was sheer bedlam. The ground was spattered with blood and gore. Terror-stricken by the uproar, the horses had panicked and were stampeding around inside the circle, adding to the confusion.

The two Piegans were ten feet from Shakespeare when his gaze flicked past them for an instant and he beheld the most wonderful sight in all the world.

Attired in a beaver hat and a mackinaw coat, a tall rider astride a magnificent black stallion sailed over the barricade and came down in the midst of the pandemonium. While still in mid-air he voiced a bloodcurdling war whoop that seemed to cut through the other cries and drew the attention of every man, red and white alike. In his right hand he clutched a cocked Hawken, in his left a cocked Kentucky rifle. As the stallion landed, the rider pointed the Kentucky at a Piegan and from a range of 12 inches shot the man in the forehead. The next instant the stallion rammed into the warriors trying to bring Jarvis down, scattering them like so much chaff in the wind.

Out beyond the barricade other riders, hollering at the top of their lungs, were rapidly approaching.

The two Piegans almost on Shakespeare halted in confusion. This new development was not to their liking. They logically concluded that more whites had arrived to reinforce those they fought. And when they saw the tall rider dispatch a second of their number with the Hawken and ride a third down under driving hoofs, they whirled and dashed to the barrier.

Other warriors were doing the same, scattering every which way. Some were wounded and had to be helped by companions. Had the majority of the remaining defenders not been so shocked by the unexpected turn of events, they could have slain many more warriors before the Piegans scaled the barricade, but most simply stood and gaped as the Indians fled. With a notable exception. Jarvis, armed with a large war club he had stripped from a fallen foe, was wreaking havoc right and left, going after every Piegan in sight. He'd been driven to the brink of a berserker rage by seeing his fellows die and nearly being killed himself, and his wrath was fearsome to behold. Three additional Piegans died at his hands before the remnants of the war party made good their escape.

Once over the barrier, the Indians fled to the north, south, and east, but not to the west. From that direction were galloping two whooping riders who knew how to shoot on the fly, and proved it by picking off a pair of Piegans who had the brash temerity to charge them.

In the aftermath of the battle, Shakespeare felt a familiar sensation in his limbs, an agitated quivering brought on by the blood still pumping furiously through his veins. Suddenly tired to his core, he surveyed the dead and dying littering the ground, then glanced up as the tall rider came over to him.

"I can't leave you alone for a minute without you getting yourself into heaps of trouble," Nate King quipped.

"As I recollect, it's usually the other way around," Shakespeare responded with a mock air of offended dignity. He brushed the back of a hand across his perspiring brow and nodded at the nearest body of a Piegan. "You sure showed at the right time. Another few moments and . . ." He let the statement trail off.

"I couldn't very well let you be killed," Nate responded jokingly, although he was profoundly upset at how close his mentor had come to being slain. He'd seen the Piegans closing in on McNair as he bore down on the barrier, and for several anxious seconds he'd feared that he'd be too late to do any good. "I'd have to put up with my son bawling like a baby for a week."

Diana Templar, now that the fighting was over and she had a chance to think about what she had just been through, began trembling ever so slightly. She fully realized that Shakespeare was right.

If not for the arrival of the handsome stranger, she would have ended her days in a Piegan lodge or suffered an even more horrible fate. With an effort she cleared her throat and commented, "I don't know who you are, kind sir, but I am forever in your debt. I'm Diana Templar."

"Nate King, at your service," Nate responded, and indicted the two other riders who were now at the barricade. "And yonder is my wife, Winona, and our son, Zachary."

"Your *wife*?" Diana said in amazement as she watched a lovely Indian woman mounted on a sorrel vault the barricade at a low point, followed immediately by a boy of nine or so riding a mare. Then her attention shifted to another point along the barrier and she stiffened and gasped. "William!"

Lord Templar was rising from the ground, a hand clasped to a nasty gash on his temple from which blood dripped in great drops. He looked toward the tent, took a faltering stride, and fell to his knees.

Instantly Diana sprinted to his aid. She was halfway there when she saw Eric Nash off to her right, his hands over his abdomen, shuffling awkwardly as if gravely wounded. He spotted her and reached out a hand in mute appeal. Diana slowed, torn between going to her brother or to Nash. Then, ruefully, the tie of family being stronger than the tie that linked her to the artist, she made a decision that unknown to her was to have shattering consequences later on. She ran to her brother.

Eric Nash halted. No one there saw the intense hurt his eyes reflected, nor did anyone notice the hardening of his pale features. He'd expected Lady Templar to run to him, which she would have done if she loved him as much as he believed he loved her. A sharp pang flared in his chest and he doubled over, wishing he could die on the spot.

"Where did those no-account bastards get you?"

The deep voice brought Eric up with a start, and he found their bearded savior standing beside him, regarding him solicitously. "What?" he blurted out.

"Where are you hurt, mister?" Nate asked, seeking sign of blood.

"I'm not," Eric said, blushing. "I'm just sick, is all."

"Sick?"

"I've never witnessed such terrible savagery before. The glee those devils took in their killing! Why, it was like seeing the gates of Hades swing open and out spill red demons bent on human destruction. I saw one of them cut off the hair of poor Jensen. His hair! Why would they commit such a meaningless, horrible act?"

"The hair is a trophy of sorts."

"How bloody revolting!"

"It's called scalping, a practice that a lot of tribes indulge in. You see, Indians value bravery above all else, and one way for a warrior to show off his bravery is by having a collection of scalps hanging in his lodge or tied to his coup stick." Nate paused. "Quite a few mountaineers take hair too."

"White men take part in such grisly barbarism?"

"Mainly those who have taken up Indian ways. They have to earn respect just like anyone else."

"I've gone mad," Eric muttered. "Either that, or I've been transported by arcane sorcery to an ethereal realm where madness rules and all human virtue is dead."

"Are you sure you weren't hit on the head?" Nate asked.

"No," Eric said, sobering. He straightened and lowered his arms. "I assure you I'm fine. But I thank you for your concern."

"Then I'd best lend a hand elsewhere," Nate said, moving off. He glanced back once, saw the man staring blankly at the sky, and wondered if the Englishman might be a bit touched in the head. Then he recalled the very first time he had witnessed the killing of another human being, and how intensely upsetting the experience had been. It seemed like a lifetime ago, yet hadn't been more than eight or nine years. In the interval he'd slain dozens of enemies without batting an eye, not because he liked killing but because he'd had to kill to stay alive. The deaths didn't bother him, though, as they once had, and he sometimes questioned whether he was becoming calloused or whether he had maturely learned to accept an inevitable aspect of wilderness life and merely did whatever it took to survive. Shrugging, he put the matter from his mind and concentrated on helping get the camp in order.

For the next hour everyone was busy. The dead Piegans were dragged to the barricade and thrown over. Those only wounded were dispatched by Jarvis, who appeared to derive inordinate satisfaction from doing so. The four slain members of the marquis's party were buried at the base of a knoll, while the wounded were placed on blankets near the tent and tended by Lady Templar and Winona.

Diana said little the whole time. After she'd bandaged her brother, whose gash turned out to be minor, she'd gone to Eric Nash to ask if he was all right, and he had responded to all her queries with curt, cold answers. She saw no rhyme or reason for his attitude, and she had been deeply stung when he'd turned his back on her and declared that he should be aiding the other men and not wasting his time talking to her.

On the heels of that thunderbolt had come another when the Indian woman had walked up to Diana and asked in faultless English to help out with the wounded. Now, as they finished wrapping the arm of the last man, Diana rose and regarded the woman intently. "Winona, isn't it? I'm afraid I've been terribly remiss in my manners." She introduced herself.

Winona offered a tentative smile. She'd been aware of the many stares the white woman had tossed her way while they worked, and she did not know what to make of them since her experience with women of Nate's race was limited. At a recent Rendezvous she had met two wives of missionaries, women who had impressed her with their gentle, friendly natures. But in a subsequent visit to St. Louis she had run up against a white woman who had tried to kill her, and during her stay in that frightening maze of stone and wood lodges the point had been driven painfully home that in the eyes of many she was an inferior, a "lowly savage" as one woman had tactlessly described her within her hearing. It had been extremely unsettling to learn that most white women despised her simply because she was not white. So now Winona made bold to inquire, "How do you know my name?"

"Your husband told me," Diana said, racking her brain for more to say. This was the first Indian woman she had ever met, and she wanted to learn all she could about the fascinating creature and her way of life. "He is quite a man, I gather."

"There is no one like Grizzly Killer," Winona said proudly.

"Who?" Diana replied, thinking the reference was to someone else, perhaps a member of Winona's tribe.

"Grizzly Killer is Nate's Indian name. It was given to him by a mighty Cheyenne warrior when Nate first came west, on the day he killed his first grizzly."

"We saw some on our journey here, great brutes capable of shredding a man with a single swipe of their long claws. Or so we've been told. And we were advised to stay away from them at all costs."

"Sound advice," Winona said. "Only the bravest of warriors dare face a silver-tip and live to tell of it. My husband has killed more than any man alive, white or Indian."

"How is it he's been able to kill so many?" Diana wanted to know.

"He is Nate," Winona said simply.

"Oh. I see. Of course." Diana turned away so the woman wouldn't see the laughter in her eyes. Such puppyish devotion to a man was utterly absurd, and must be the result, she reasoned, of Winona being overawed by her white husband. She'd seen the same thing in Africa, Asia, and South America. Native women everywhere couldn't help but look up to their white betters. Composing herself, she turned and remarked, "I hope that one day I find a man as worthy of my love as Nate is of yours."

"You are very kind," Winona said, pleased at the Englishwoman's unaffected frankness. On an impulse, she added, "Perhaps you would like to visit our cabin and stay with us a while? It is so seldom that we get visitors, and I would enjoy female company."

How sweet! Diana thought. Out loud she said, "Thank you for the gracious offer, but our plans are in such disarray that I don't know what we will do next." She gazed at the wounded. "We've lost so many men, I'm afraid we may need to head back to St. Louis just as soon as these gentlemen are up and about again." A sigh whispered from her lips. "And I was so hoping to see more of this mysterious land and its many marvels."

"I understand," Winona said. "If there is anything I can do for you, please ask."

Here was a golden opportunity, and Diana quickly answered, "Just promise me you'll stay with us until we know what we're doing next. I would so like to chat with you over tea and hear of your life and your people." She paused. "Which tribe do you belong to, by the way?"

"I am Shoshone."

"Will you stay?"

"If you want," Winona said, and leaned forward to confide, "I can use the rest. We rode hard to find Shakespeare, and when I am pregnant I tire more easily than I usually do."

Diana blinked, unsure whether she had heard correctly. "You're pregnant?" she whispered in astonishment, remembering how Winona had fought the Piegans and then leaped the barricade on horseback. Here was something the friends in her social circle would never believe!

"Yes."

"My word!"

Diana brought a chair out of the tent and insisted on having Winona sit down. Then, excusing herself, she went in search of Jarvis, and found him in the company of Nate King and Shakespeare McNair. They were rounding up the last of the horses. "I'm glad you're all together," she informed them. "I'd like to invite you to my tent for supper and a meeting this evening."

"All three of us, Lady Templar?" Jarvis asked doubtfully. Rarely in all the time of his service to the Templars had he been asked to dine with them. To tea, yes. But the intimacies of meals were reserved for their social peers or special guests. Or for the locals in the exotic parts of the world they visited, whom the Templars plied for information so they would have more to relate when they returned to London.

"Yes. We have much to discuss. I would like to hear all of your opinions as to the best way to proceed. In light of our losses today, I don't want to make the wrong decision."

"We'll be there," Shakespeare promised, and grinned as she headed for the tent. "Now there's a woman with gumption, Nate. You should have seen the way she stood up to the Piegans."

"Winona and her seem to be hitting it off," Nate mentioned. "I reckon we'll stick around for a spell and see what we can do to help her out."

"It's decent of you to see her right," Jarvis said in gratitude. "This is one time I'm out of my element, mates. I thought I knew all there was to know about fighting, but I've never seen anything like these bloody heathens. There's no halfway with them, is there? They keep coming at a man until they drop him or he drops them."

"I wish you wouldn't do that," Nate said.

"Sir?"

"Refer to Indians as bloody heathens. They're no better or worse than our kind." Nate's right hand, perhaps unconsciously, rested on a pistol. "And I'd like to remind you that my *wife* is an Indian."

"I meant no offense, Mr. King," Jarvis said. "Don't get your dander up. To me, people are people no matter what color their skin happens to be."

"Do the Templars share your view?"

"William doesn't, but then he's a bit of a cad. As for Lady Diana—" and Jarvis, out of loyalty, hedged "—she's more open-minded than he is."

"That's right good to hear," Nate said. "Maybe Winona has found herself a new friend."

Chapter Seven

Lady Diana Templar put on a magnificent front at supper, smiling and chatting animatedly despite the nightmare the day had been. Four of their party had perished; three more were wounded, although not seriously. Only Jarvis and Eric Nash, of all the men in the marquis's employ, had escaped unscathed—Jarvis by virtue of his skill acquired while a soldier for the Crown, Eric because the Piegans had been rightfully more concerned with the defenders who were resisting them than with one quaking white-eyes.

Since Diana had no time to prepare steak pie, as she had been wont to do from deer slain by the party, she made do with scones, sandwiches layered thick with the last of the tasty jam she had brought all the way from England, and tarts. She apologized profusely for such meager fare, and was glad none of her close friends could see the culinary depths to which she had fallen.

Present around the table were the two frontiersmen, Winona and Zach, the Templars, Eric,
and Jarvis.

"I'm happy you were all so kind to join us,"
Diana said to her guests after the sandwiches
were consumed. "Because of the critical situation in which the attack has placed us, I must
rely on sound suggestions from you. What should
we do? Clearly, staying in the mountains is
impractical, as is the idea to go to Canada.
We are now so few that we could never hope
to fend off another attack. We must head for
civilization, and the sooner, the better. But
should we retrace our steps or take another
route?"

Nate put down the tart he had been eating.
"From what I've been told, you came almost
due west after leaving Independence until you
struck the mountains. Then you came north. Is
that right?"

"Correct," Diana said.

"Then you don't want to go back the same way,
not if you value your hides," Nate declared. "How
you got by the Sioux and the Pawnees the first
time without being spotted is beyond me, but you
might not be so lucky again."

"What would you propose?"

Shakespeare spoke before Nate could. "Remember what I told you before about going to the
Yellowstone River and following it until you hit
the Missouri? There would be your safest bet.
You'd have plenty of grass and water for your
horses and you wouldn't have to worry about
getting lost."

"What about the Piegans and others of their ilk?"

"The Blackfeet and Piegans have territory north of the Yellowstone and they seldom cross it except on raids. That's what those we tangled with today were doing here. It's doubtful there's another Piegan war party this far south at the same time, so all you'd have to keep your eyes peeled for would be Blackfeet." Shakespeare stroked his beard. "And maybe a few Bloods. And Gros Ventres."

"You're not very encouraging, Mr. McNair."

"I don't aim to be. You'll be in danger no matter which way you pick, but I figure you'll be in less danger along the Yellowstone and the Missouri than you would be if you cut directly across the prairie." Shakespeare swallowed some tea. "And once you reach Mandan country you'll be as safe as a baby in a cradleboard."

"Mandan country? I don't believe I've heard of it."

"Mandans are Indians, ma'am, but they're as friendly a bunch as you'll find anywhere. Like the Shoshones and the Flatheads, they've never taken a white scalp. They like being our friends. They're honest in all their dealings, and they'll give you the last morsel of food in their lodge if you're hungry."

William, who had morosely listened to the conversation, finally chimed in with, "You make the devils sound like saints."

"They're as close to it as Indians come," Shakespeare said, refusing to be nettled. "And once you reach their villages, you'll have a straight shot down the Missouri River to Independence with little to fear except maybe the Rees, who have been doing all they can to make life miserable for whites ever since Colonel Henry Leavenworth moved heaven and earth to show them how puny the white man can be when he puts his mind to it."

"What did he do?" William asked.

"Back in '23 the Rees kicked up their heels a mite. They were upset with some trappers who had lent a hand to the Sioux. This was before the Sioux took to being unfriendly themselves." Shakespeare leaned back in his chair. "Anyway, the Rees drove off some trappers who were going up the Missouri, killing about a dozen. Colonel Henry Leavenworth put together about six companies to punish the Rees and headed for their villages, taking along a couple of cannons and swivel guns for good measure. Along the way he was joined by seven hundred Sioux and a lot of trappers. By time he reached the Ree villages he had over a thousand men under him."

"What happened?" Jarvis prompted when the mountain man stopped.

"Leavenworth proved he was a flash in the pan. He surrounded the Rees and tried to parley with them, which made the Sioux so disgusted they all left. By the time the colonel got around to attacking, the Rees had slipped away in the middle of the night. Ever since the Rees think all whites are no account."

"So they'll attack us if they see us?" Diana asked.

"Probably. But all you have to do is take a page out of their book and sneak by their villages after dark. Once you do, you're home free."

"Tell me, Mr. McNair," William said. "How long will it take us to reach Independence from here?"

"Weeks and weeks. Maybe months, even if you push hard and have more luck than most."

"And you expect that the six of us can travel a thousand miles or so through hostile territory—except for the bleeding Mandan country—and reach Independence safely? That's going it a bit much, isn't it?"

"A body can do anything he puts his mind to. Like I always say, where there's a will there's a way."

"How delightful," William snorted.

Diana rose and began moving around the table, her hands clasped behind her back. "I don't want to be too hasty. We've already proven we don't know what we're doing once, and I'd hate to repeat our mistake." She stopped next to McNair. "What we need is a guide, someone who knows this country and can see us all the way to Independence. Someone like you."

The front legs of Shakespeare's chair hit the ground with a thud. "Hold on there, ma'am. I'm flattered you'd ask me, but I really can't spare the time."

"For me," Diana said, resting a hand on his shoulder. "Please."

"My wife would have a fit. We're supposed to join her people at Bear Lake in three weeks."

"I'll pay you."

"No-sir-ee. I don't see how I could."

"A thousand American dollars for your services."

"A thousand!" Shakespeare declared. "It would take me half a year of steady trapping to earn that much."

"What do you think, Mr. King?" Diana expectedly asked. "Is a thousand dollars a fair amount?"

Nate had been listening to the exchange with amusement. He knew his mentor had taken a liking to the Englishwoman, and he was eager to see whether Shakespeare would succumb to her charms and as a result get into hot water with Blue Water Woman. He failed to see his connection with the proposition, and so answered, "It's up to Shakespeare what he thinks is fair, Lady Templar."

"What about you?" she persevered.

"Me?"

"Would you take a thousand dollars to be our guide if it was offered to you?"

"I might," Nate said, "but since I'd never leave Winona and Zach for that long a spell, there isn't much use in talking about it."

"What if you could bring your wife and son along?"

Suddenly Nate perceived an underlying motive to her probing and he glanced at Winona, whose expression told him she had already discerned the truth and was seriously mulling over a decision. But then, she always was one step ahead of him. He had never been loath to acknowledge that she was mentally sharper than he could ever hope to be, as demonstrated by her excellent grasp of English while his grasp of the Shoshone tongue was merely adequate. He took pride in her brilliance, and counted himself fortunate to have her as his wife.

"The reason I am asking is because I would like to invite all of you to come along," Diana was elaborating. "You, your wife and son, and Mr. McNair if he so desires. And I'm quite serious about the amount. A thousand dollars each is a paltry sum to pay for safe passage back to the States."

"We would have to think it over," Nate said.

Diana glanced at McNair. "And you? Is there anything I can say that would change your mind?"

"Oh, you could give me a week to ride home and spring the question on Blue Water Woman," Shakespeare responded without any real thought of being taken seriously.

"Go right ahead."

Nate and Shakespeare exchanged glances; then the older mountain man stood. "You'd be willing to sit here that long when there's no guarantee I'll agree?"

"We will need at least a week for our wounded to recover sufficiently to make the journey, and since there are fewer of us now I must decide what to take along and what to leave. The delay will be well worth it if you agree to help. At any rate, you have my heartfelt thanks for going to so much trouble on our behalf."

"So please you, save the thanks this prince expects," Shakespeare quoted. "The luster in your eye, heaven in your cheek, pleads your fair usage."

Diana laughed merrily and touched McNair's cheek. "I do believe you have a dash of rogue in you."

"Doesn't every man?"

The rest of the conversation concerned small talk about England, and Diana went on at length about how great a man her father was, and how he thoroughly approved of his offspring receiving an education in the practical affairs of the world through their many travels. William contributed little to the discussion, Eric Nash even less.

Nate was the first to excuse himself and his family so they could turn in, and Shakespeare promptly did likewise. As they strolled toward where Winona and Nate had chosen to sleep, his friend put a hand on Nate's arm.

"I've been meaning to ask you something," Shakespeare said. "Don't take this wrong, but what the hell brought you here today? I thought you were waiting for me at your cabin."

"We were, until I told Winona I had this bad feeling about you. She told me that she'd learned long ago never to buck her intuition, so we figured we'd ride toward your cabin and maybe meet you on the way since we know the trail you usually take to reach our place." Nate chuckled. "And there we were, riding along, when we heard all this shooting and hollering and came for a look-see. The rest you know."

"Maybe some day this old coon can return the favor."

Under a cottonwood tree Winona spread their blankets. She tucked Zach in while Shakespeare took Nate aside.

"I'll be leaving before sunup. I asked for a week but it won't take near that long, so expect me back in three days, if you're still here."

Nate gazed at his wife. "Something tells me we will be."

"Keep your eyes peeled. I doubt the Piegans will bother these greenhorns again after the licking we gave them, but you never know. They might want revenge."

"Rest easy. I'll watch over these people until you come back."

"Thanks." Shakespeare showed his teeth, then said, "For ever and for ever farewell, Brutus! If we do meet again, we'll smile indeed. If not, 'tis true this parting was well made."

"Shoot sharps the word," Nate said, and stood there until McNair was lost in the shadows. They'd previously agreed to sleep at opposite ends of the camp to reduce the chance of the Piegans sneaking in among the marquis's party undetected. Turning, he strolled to his blanket and sat down beside his wife. "What do you think about Lady Templar's proposition?"

"I would like to go."

"Have you forgotten you're heavy with child?"

Winona's laugh tinkled on the breeze. "How could a woman ever forget such a thing? Every time she moves, every time she breathes, she is reminded of the new life stirring within her."

"Then we have to tell Diana no."

"I did not say that, husband," Winona said. "Our daughter will not enter this world for five moons yet, so there is more than enough time for us to travel to Independence and return."

"What if something goes wrong? What if there's an unforeseen delay? We could be stuck out on the prairie when you give birth."

"Which would be good. The prairie is flat, so we do not need to worry about her rolling downhill if she doesn't slide out onto the buffalo robe as she should."

Nate shook his head in exasperation. "Sometimes your sense of humor is downright peculiar."

"Our baby will be fine whether I give birth in our cabin or out on the plains," Winona said, her hand caressing his wrist. "And I would very much like to go."

"Me too, Pa," Zach said from under his blanket.

"Get to sleep," Nate groused. His reservations notwithstanding, he was also inclined to accept the proposition, but his motive was the money and he didn't care to have his greed put his family at risk. A thousand dollars made a tidy sum, a nest egg they could set aside for the future, for the day when the beaver were played out as they must eventually be due to the heavy toll taken on their number each year by free and company trappers.

As if Winona could read his thoughts, she startled him by casually commenting, "Diana has made us a very generous offer. We would be fools to pass up an opportunity to earn a thousand dollars."

"Since when do you care about money?"

"I am thinking of you," Winona answered. "You value it much more than I ever could."

"As you like to say, we'll get by no matter what happens, money or no money. If this was New York it would be a different story, but in the mountains we can live off the land and never go hungry or without clothes. Everything we need is right here for the taking." Nate put his hands down and braced his palms on the ground. "This is the way life is meant to be. Once, it's true, I believed earning money was the main purpose to our lives. Now I know better, and I thank God I learned what truly matters before I was gray and wrinkled."

"If, as you claim, you no longer care about such things, then agree to go for my sake. Diana Templar truly likes me. She does not think I am less of a person than she is because we are different." Winona gazed at the tent, which was highlighted by a small fire dancing in front of it. "I have long wanted to know about white women and why they do the things they do. Perhaps, through Diana, I will learn to better understand them."

Nate had long known of his wife's continuing fascination with women of his own kind, and of her keen desire to learn why many white women despised her when she had done them no wrong. He recollected how bitterly disturbed she had been after their visit to St. Louis, and how he had been unable to answer her many questions to her satisfaction. Being a man, he found womanly nature to be one of life's great mysteries, a mystery so profound no man since the dawn of time had been able to pierce its veil, to overcome the insurmountable obstacle posed by the inherent differences between the two sexes.

"There is another reason I ask this," Winona was saying. "For many sleeps now have I been cooped up in the cabin, and I would like to get out in the fresh air for a while, to travel and see sights I have never seen." She gestured at the inky outline of the mountains, barely visible under the shimmering stars. "To you this land is much different from the land in which you were raised, and so you never tire of exploring it. But I was born here, and the mountains are not new to me." She sighed. "The plains are. My people only go there to hunt buffalo for a short while, and then we go right back to the mountains. I would like to see more of the prairie, husband. I would like to feel the same thrill you do every day."

The passionate appeal touched Nate deeply. "That's two good reasons you've given me," he said. "And I don't see how I can object." Smiling, he shifted to kiss her cheek. "You can tell Lady Templar that we'll guide them to Independence, but make it clear to her that if the trip turns out to be more than you bargained for, if you fall sick or have any problems with the baby, then we're turning around right then and there and heading for your village so old Raven Woman can tend you. She knows more about nursing pregnant women than anyone."

"I will tell Diana now," Winona declared excitedly, and rising, hurried off to the tent.

"You made Ma real happy, Pa," remarked a youthful voice from under the blankets.

"And you remember to do the same with your wife when you tie the knot," Nate replied. "A man has an obligation to do what he can to please his wife so long as it doesn't break his spirit."

The blanket lifted and out popped Zach's head crowned by a thatch of tousled dark hair. "What do you mean by that spirit part?"

"A marriage should be like a partnership, son. The man and the woman share the work fairly even, and when big decisions have to be made they sit down and talk it over together." Nate heard a soft crunch to his rear and twisted to peer into the dark shadows along the barricade. "Some marriages don't work that way, though. Either the man or the woman wants to have the power, wants to have everything done just the way they want. They don't know how to give and take. So they do all in their power to make life miserable for the other one in order to have their way."

"I still don't understand about a woman breaking a man's spirit."

"There are things a woman can do that twist a man all up inside and slowly wear him down," Nate explained. "Things like nagging or always carping or always criticizing whatever the man does. Things like making him out to be a fool around others, or always siding with her family against him." He stopped to listen and heard a faint footstep. Without being obvious, his hand drifted to the Hawken at his side. "Or worse," he then went on as if nothing out of the ordinary was occurring, "the woman can stay so attached to her folks that she never cuts the apron strings. She always wants to stick close to them, and runs to them for advice instead of to her husband. The husband winds up being third in her affections instead of first like he should be, and he spends his days miserable."

Nate had kept on talking while he pinpointed the sounds. Seconds later he spied a vague figure moving along the brush wall, and he was raising

the Hawken when he recognized the gigantic outline of Jarvis.

The giant ambled toward them, a rifle slanted
across his exceptionally wide shoulders, a brace
of pistols under his belt. "Evening mate. And you
too, lad."

"You might be happy to hear that we've decided to guide your party back to the States," Nate
mentioned.

"All right by me!" Jarvis said. "I'm not a wee
bit ashamed to admit we need your help. I tried
to have his nibs hire someone before we left St.
Louis, but he wouldn't hear of it. Said he'd survived bloody Africa and South America and had
nothing to fear in America." He sighed loudly.
"A nod is as good as a wink to a blind horse, I
suppose."

Zach sat up and stated, "You sure do use funny
words sometimes, Mr. Jarvis. Don't they speak
proper English where you come from?"

"Call me Ben, boy," the giant replied. "And no,
since a child I've been mangling the Queen's own.
I suppose I'm six pennies' worth of half-pence in
the langauge department."

"There you go again," Zach said.

Laughing, Jarvis stepped closer and squatted.
"If I may be so bold, Mr. King, I can use your
help tonight."

"What do you need?" Nate asked.

"With his lordship and the others laid up, there's
only the painter and me to guard the camp at
night. Much as I admire Mr. Nash's talent, he's
as thick as a plank where fighting is concerned.
So I was wondering if you would be willing to
take it in turns with Mr. McNair and me? Mr.

McNair has already agreed to take a shift. If you lend a hand, we can each take four hours, which will see us until dawn."

"You can count on me. Just wake me when my time comes."

"Thank you. You're well and truly a gentleman, sir, even if you do run around all covered with animal hides." Rising, he smiled down at Zach. "Be seeing you, then."

"Do you think I'll ever grow that big, Pa?" the boy asked wistfully as the giant faded into the night.

"I wouldn't get my hopes up," Nate responded. He glanced at the tent, saw Winona and Lady Templar talking, and lay down on his back, a hand under his head. It was good that Winona was taking a shine to the Englishwoman. Perhaps, after this, she wouldn't think most white women were heartless and cruel. And truth to tell, he was rather excited at the idea of venturing into new country and beholding new sights. He also was enthused by the likelihood of meeting the Mandans, about whom he had heard so much from other trappers. Mandan hospitality, everyone claimed, was excellent.

As for the element of danger, there was *always* the possibility of finding one's life threatened anywhere in the wilderness. At any given minute of any given day a ferocious beast or a bloodthirsty enemy might appear. It was an unavoidable part of life, like having to hunt game and seek out water in order to stay alive, something to be taken in stride as it cropped up. All he could do was hope that his loved ones survived.

Rolling onto his side, Nate reached out and touched his son. "Good night, Stalking Coyote." His voice lowered. "I love you."

"Are you all right, Pa?"

"Fine. Why?"

"You sound as if you're coming down with a cold."

Chapter Eight

The next three days were quiet ones.

Nate made repeated sweeps of the countryside, but saw no evidence the Piegans were still in the vicinity. He also took it on himself to supply all the meat the marquis's party would need, and as a result he was absent from the camp much of the time.

Winona and Lady Templar became inseparable. Winona was delighted by the countless questions her newfound friend asked about the Indian way of life in general and the Shoshones in particular, questions Winona believed demonstrated Diana's sincere interest in her and her people. For her part, she learned a great deal about English polite society, and couldn't get enough of hearing about balls and parties and sundry gala functions.

William Templar was on his feet the day after the battle, his surly disposition still intact. He shunned Nate and Winona as much as possible, preferring the company of his countrymen, who in turn were taken aback by this sudden familiarity on his part, although they never let on to him.

In addition to Jarvis and the now perpetually moody Nash, there was the valet, Harrison, and a stocky, taciturn man named Fletcher, all that remained of the original nine. Harrison had taken an arrow in the fleshy part of the shoulder, and had to go about for a while with his arm in a sling. Fletcher had been cut in the thigh by a knife, a deep cut that required stitching.

Lady Templar had despaired of being able to seal the wicked wound, leading Fletcher to fear infection might set in and make amputation necessary. At that point Winona had stepped up to him, a parfleche under her arm. From the bag she withdrew a thin sewing needle made from buffalo bone and the Indian equivalent of thread, a lengthy coil of buffalo sinew. In short order she had endeared herself to Flether by stitching him up as expertly as if a physician had done the task. From that moment on, he would abide no slurs against her, as the marquis learned when he made a few snide references in Fletcher's presence.

Zachary spent much of his time in the company of Jarvis, who regaled him with gory tales of brutal combat in foreign jungles and on the burning sands of alien deserts, filling the boy's mind with images of swarthy Arabs, ebony natives, and Asian pirates.

It was the third day after Shakespeare's departure that Lady Templar found herself temporarily alone late in the afternoon. Winona was spending time with Zach, so Diana took her rifle and strolled down toward the stream. Earlier she had observed Eric Nash, easel, paints, and brushes in hand, going in that direction. She found him on the bank, engrossed in capturing the primal beauty of a stark peak on canvas.

"Mind a bit of company?"

Eric glanced around. The corners of his mouth twitched downward; then he nodded curtly and resumed painting. His strokes, usually so delicate and graceful, were hard and forceful, almost as if he was attacking the canvas.

"Care to talk about it?"

"About what?"

"Please, Eric. Don't insult my intelligence. You've been behaving strangely toward me for days and I would like to know why."

"Would you now?"

Stung by his tone, Diana stepped to where he could see her and she could see his face. "Yes, I most definitely would. I thought we were friends, yet you've been treating me as if I was an ogre. You hardly pass a comment my way anymore."

"My apologies," Eric said crisply, raising his brush from the canvas and fixing her with a frigid stare. "You can be assured that we have been, are now, and will always be *friends*."

The last word was spat out as if it was an insult, and Diana blinked in confusion. "I must be dense," she stated. "For I haven't the foggiest why you are so mad at me. Tell me what is bothering you."

"You're too naive by half."

"I beg your pardon?"

His shoulders slumping, Nash set his brush and palette down carefully. "Have you ever been in love, Diana?" he asked as he straightened.

"Of course."

"With whom, might I ask?"

"I love my parents for their gentle, giving natures. I love William despite himself because he's my brother." Diana paused. "And I love you."

"As a friend."

"Yes. What difference does that make? Why do you keep harping on our friendship?"

A haunted look came over Nash. "Because I had deluded myself that your affection for me was based on more than platonic friendship. Flighty dreamer that I am, I cherished the idea of one day being your husband."

"Eric," Diana said softly.

"Hear me out! I want to clear the air so we can spend the rest of our association together being civil to one another."

Diana tried to alleviate his somber demeanor by injecting some humor. "Is that what you call our relationship?" she laughed. "An association?"

"A rose by any other name," Eric said, then went on in a rush. "What else would you call it? You are my patron, nothing more, despite the years we have spent together and the intensely personal feelings I have revealed to you time and again. Always you have put me off with the excuse that you didn't quite feel for me as I feel for you."

"If you'd just give me more time . . ."

"Maybe you'll come around?" Eric said. "Bother! Quit deceiving yourself. The other day you conclusively proved the depth of your affection when you ran to William's aid and not to me."

"Please—"

Eric broke in. "Take it as done, Diana," he snapped with an angry motion, "and let the matter be. Rest assured that once we reach England, I will no longer impose myself on you. And you can do us both a great favor by finding someone else to patronize." Then, oddly, he grinned.

"I take your point, but I think you're being highly unfair to me and blowing what I did out of all proportion. There was blood all over poor William's face, and for all I knew he might be dying. Was I to just leave him lying there in the dirt unattended?"

"Spare me your feeble excuses."

"Feeble!" Diana responded irately, her pale cheeks changing to a bright crimson. She burned with a yearning to tell him off, to show that every statement he'd made had been wrong, but the words choked off in her throat. Her rifle clenched tight in her left fist, she stormed off toward the camp, smashing through low bushes in her path instead of skirting them. At one point her dress snagged on a branch and she jerked it loose with an oath. Twenty yards from the stream she halted, her breath coming in ragged gasps as tears filled her eyes. She bowed her head, bit her lower lip, and trembled. "Oh, Eric," she whispered. "Sweet, sweet Eric."

The tears gushed, and Diana was glad trees screened her from those within the barricade. Silently she cried for many minutes, until the shriek of a jay jarred her back to reality. Sniffling, she moved on, using her sleeve to dry her face.

At the barrier Diana halted and gazed sadly over her shoulder. A glimpse of Eric could be seen through the trees. "You're right, of course," she said quietly. "And I'm sorry. So very, very sorry."

On the fourth day Shakespeare returned.

Nate was a mile northwest of the valley hunting deer when he saw the white horse and its rider emerge from pine trees directly ahead. Putting his heels to the stallion, he was soon close enough to see the broad smile that creased his best friend's mouth. "I gather Blue Water Woman gave her blessing," he said as he reined up.

"That she did, young Hamlet," the mountain man answered heartily. "So I'm off to the Mandan country, and the devil take any hostiles that stand in my way."

"Blue Water Woman didn't want to come along?"

"No. I asked her to. When she refused, I offered to take her to the nearest Flathead village so she can spend time with kin until I get back. But she declined."

"Did she give a reason?"

"She wants to be alone."

"What on earth will she do all by herself?"

"Think a lot, mostly. And probably do a heap of wandering," Shakespeare said, then quoted, "Over hill, over dale, through bush, through brier, over park, over pale, through flood, through fire."

"I should think she'd prefer our company to her own."

"How green you are and fresh in this old world!" Shakespeare exclaimed. "Everyone likes to have time to themselves every so often so they can piece together the puzzle of their life and maybe make sense of the whole mad scheme."

"Not me. I'd rather be with Winona than by myself any day."

"Of course you would," Shakespeare said, and reverted to his inevitable habit: "Your mind is all as youthful as your blood."

"I love her, is all."

McNair chuckled and goaded the mare forward, musing aloud, "I do much wonder that one man, seeing how much another man is a fool when he dedicates his behaviours to love, will, after he hath laughed at such shallow follies in others, become the argument of his own scorn by falling in love."

"If I didn't know you better I'd take that as an insult."

"Perish the thought, dear Romeo. I was merely stating a fact of life."

"A minute ago you called me Hamlet. Make up your mind which one I'm supposed to be."

"Truly, you're both of them and many more besides," Shakespeare said. "You'll have no cause to complain unless I take to calling you Juliet."

Nate smiled. "I swear that every day you get stranger and stranger. If I don't watch myself, some of whatever afflicts you might rub off on me."

"It would do you a world of good. Like most folks, your mind is confined by mental bars of your own devising. But there is a glimmer of hope for you. Once a month or so you actually come up with an original notion."

"I'll try to do it more often in the future."

They crossed a valley and climbed a gradual slope to the shoulder of a mountain. From their lofty height they saw the camp far below.

"Say, young pup, you haven't told me whether Winona and you have decided to go along," Shakespeare said.

"We have," Nate disclosed, and went on to tell about the events of the past several days, concluding with, "Lady Templar and Eric Nash are acting like they hardly know each other. When they do talk, they're so damn polite I can hardly hold in the laughter."

"They must have had a falling out," Shakespeare deduced. "I saw it coming. He thinks with his heart and she thinks with her head, which is a poor combination."

"How can a man think with his heart?" Nate inquired.

"Men do it all the time, but they won't own up to the fact because they're afraid everyone will say they're less manly than they should be. Women pretend they do it all the time, when the truth is they think with their heads more than we do, but they're afraid to own up to it because they don't want men to know how level-headed they really are."

Mirth exploded from Nate. "Where *do* you get these harebrained notions of yours?"

"Live another fifty years," Shakespeare said testily, "then see if my notions are half as crazy as you think they are now. Experience has a way of sweating the fat off a brain."

Nate assumed the lead as they wound down to where the stream bubbled and gurgled its way eastward. "I haven't seen hide nor hair of the Piegans," he mentioned.

"And you won't. I crossed their trail on my way back here. They're on their way north, heading for home."

"See any other sign?"

"Just critters."

"Let's hope the whole journey is that way."

Lady Templar had spied them coming from a ways off, and was eagerly waiting at the barrier. When she learned the good news, she broke into a grin and began issuing instructions to her brother, who in turn relayed them to the men. The upshot was that at first light the next morning the marquis's party began their homeward trek. In order to travel light and thus make better time, a dozen heavy trunks were left behind, as well as the table and chairs, the canopy, and a host of other items Nate and Shakespeare had decided were nonessential.

Only William Templar complained. As they were heading out, he drew up alongside Nate and remarked, "I still fail to see why we can't pack all of our belongings with us. Possessions cost money, my good man. Were they yours, I'd wager you wouldn't be so free-handed in dispensing with them."

"In the first place," Nate replied, "I wouldn't be caught dead with such worthless trifles as your gold-embossed chamber pot, especially not out here in the middle of the damn mountains where a body can heed Nature's call behind the nearest tree or bush." He nodded at the string of horses.

"And in the second place, now a third of your stock isn't carrying any weight at all, so we can switch loads when others tire and cover more ground each day. And if we have to trade, we can use the extra horses."

"Trade with whom?"

"Indians. Sometimes they'll let you go through their territory if you give them a few trinkets to show them your good will."

"Blimey! Are you daft? My horses are hardly trinkets. Each one cost me hundreds of pounds."

"Look at it this way. Would you rather part with a few horses or with your life?"

"See here, King! I've half a mind to bill you and your simpleton friend for my losses on this expedition, and by God, if we don't reach Independence safely, I will. My solicitors will wring the money out of you if they have to."

Nate's Hawken was resting across his thighs. Casually, he placed both hands on top of it and leaned toward the marquis. "I've never met a man so intent on giving up the ghost in all my born days, and if you keep spouting off the way you do, you're liable to get your wish."

Snorting in contempt, William prodded his horse into a trot and left Nate stewing.

The rest of the day passed without incident. Once they reached the prairie, they hugged the edge of the foothills where they could seek cover fast if an enemy war party appeared. Twice they stopped to rest. That night they camped at the mouth of a canyon into which they could retreat if set upon.

The second day was a repeat of the first, with everyone worn out by evening and ready for a decent night's sleep. The same with the third day, and the fourth. Usually they rode strung out in single file, although sometimes two or more of them would bunch up to talk. Either Nate or Shakespeare always held the lead, and one or the other was constantly roving far afield to make certain no unwelcome surprise awaited them over the horizon.

They saw countless shaggy buffalo grazing leisurely, and almost as many timid antelope that bounded off at incredible speeds at their approach. Wolves and coyotes were also in abundance, trailing the herds, the wolves waiting to pick off sick and aged stragglers and the coyotes waiting to pick over whatever the wolves left. Smaller animals were likewise plentiful, such as prairie dogs, ferrets, and foxes.

On numerous occasions they spotted the monarchs of the wild, the massive, feared grizzlies, but the size of their party deterred the normally aggressive bears from disputing their passage. One night, though, their horses began whinnying in a panic, and the next morning, when a count could be made, one of the animals was missing. Huge paw prints and a bloody smear led them into the nearby brush, where they discovered the head and neck of the hapless horse, covered thick with flies. The grizzly had torn them from the body, then dragged the rest off.

Nate and Shakespeare were all for pursuing the bear and dispatching it, but William, after studying the tracks for some time, decided to keep the party intact and press on. As he put it, "What's the loss of one horse when we have so many? Besides, this bear might circle around and attack us while you're gone, and the next time it might grab one of the women."

On a crystal-clear night, with a myriad of stars decorating the firmament and a cool breeze waving the high grass, they camped east of a small mountain range. Shakespeare entertained them by telling the history of the region.

"These here mountains," he began, "are called the Hammer Mountains by the Arapahos and the Medicine Bow Mountains by the Shoshones. Both tribes, and the Sioux and Cheyenne besides, come here every so often for the wood they use in making their bows. The Shoshones are partial to ash and cedar, while the Arapahos like mountain birch. And I think the Sioux favor mountain mahogany."

"The bloody beggars can't even agree on which wood makes the best bow!" William commented contemptuously.

"Do you wear the same clothes as everyone else?" Shakespeare retorted. "No. Every man has his favorites, whether it's clothes or weapons. The Indians are just like us in that regard."

"I say, Mr. McNair," Harrison said. "Is there any chance of our running into the Arapahos or Sioux or any of the others you mentioned."

"There's always a chance."

That night William insisted on posting two men on each shift, but changed his mind when Nate pointed out that since he was the only one interested in doubling the guard, he should pull the extra duty himself.

The next day, at mid-morning, Nate caught up with Shakespeare, who was a hundred yards in advance of the column. "You seem to have a knack for reading human nature," Nate said.

"Years of experience, son. A man can learn a lot if he keeps his eyes and ears open."

"What do you make of the marquis?"

"Troubled about him, are you?"

"The man has what most folks would consider is everything that life has to offer. He's as rich as Midas, or will be once his father dies and leaves him his share of the inheritance. He has all the prestige a man could want being part of the nobility and all. And he's a handsome cuss, a man practically any white woman would gladly marry."

"So?"

"So the man is yellow through and through. He's one of the biggest cowards it's been my displeasure to ever meet."

"Every gem, they say, has at least one imperfection," Shakespeare said, and smirked. "Course, in his case there's a heap more than one."

"We all have our flaws," Nate said. "I figure one of our purposes in life is to try to try and correct them before we die. Be perfect, the Good Book says."

"Tarnation!" Shakespeare exulted. "You did it again."

"Did what?"

"Had another original notion. I've got to get me something to write with so I can make a record of them for your grandchildren."

"We're straying off the trail."

"Which was?"

"William Templar. Lord Graustark. The marquis."

"Can you be more specific?"

"Why does a man like him, who has so much to live for and so much to lose, and who deep down is scared of his own shadow, travel all over the world and put himself in situations where he's in great peril? Why does he go out of his way to court danger?"

"Some men like to face the things they're most afeared of to prove to themselves they're not afraid," Shakespeare said, and cocked his head to observe the younger man's profile. "But I have to say I don't see eye to eye with you on this. The marquis isn't the total coward you make him out to be. Look at how well he fought against the Piegans, and he didn't whine or moan about his wound afterward."

"But the bear!" Nate countered. "And last night when he wanted to have extra men stand watch?"

"You could be mistaking caution for coward-ice. Our friend William is the kind of man who never takes risks he doesn't have to, but once danger comes he holds his own without complaint."

"I don't know," Nate said uncertainly.

"Would you do anything to put Winona's life in jeopardy? No. Templar feels the same about his sister. I'd imagine she's one of the few people he really and truly loves—besides himself, naturally."

"Then you like him?"

"I never made any such claim. I'd be lying if I did." Shakespeare gazed to the north, then squinted, his brow furrowing. "But I learned long ago not to go around judging folks by their faults. Hell, if we all did that, none of us would have anything to do with anyone else. So I take people as I find them, and if they rankle me, then I make it a point to have as little to do with them as possible."

"Yet you hired on to guide Templar to Missouri."

"I hired on to get his sister there. William could be scalped tomorrow and I'd dance a jig." Shakespeare frowned and drew rein. "And he just might be."

"What are you raving about now?"

"See for yourself," Shakespeare said, pointing.

Nate did, and his skin crawled. Less than two miles distant, atop a sheer butte, rose a smoke signal.

Chapter Nine

Indians rarely used smoke signals in the mountains for the simple reason that intervening peaks, crags, cliffs, and hills invariably hid their billowing puffs from those they wanted to see the message. On the flat plains, though, where visibility stretched for miles, smoke signals were an ideal method of communicating over long distances. In this case the sender had just begun, as evidenced by the two lone puffs rising slowly on the air currents.

"What is he saying?" Nate asked urgently.

"Hold your britches on, Mercutio, until he finishes the message," Shakespeare replied.

More puffs blossomed, forming a vertical string, rising until they mingled with the passing clouds.

"Well?" Nate prompted.

"It's short and sweet," Shakespeare said. "White men. Many horses. Come quick."

"Any idea which tribe?"

"From the smoke?"

Nate scanned the level expanse on all sides. "Damn. There's no cover except for that butte. Maybe we should make a run for it. There must be boulders or clefts we can use for shelter."

"We'd never make it."

"Why not?"

Shakespeare extended a finger to the west where a small dust cloud was rapidly growing in size. "They'll be on us before we do."

Galvanized into action, Nate whirled the black stallion and raced to the others. Winona and Zach were in the company of Lady Templar, and all three had been so engrossed in their conversation they had failed to see the smoke signals. They looked up in alarm as Nate reined up so sharply the hoofs of his stallion sent clods of dirt flying.

"My word!" Diana exclaimed. "What has you so worked up?"

"Indians!" Nate explained, raising his voice so the marquis, Jarvis, and Eric could hear. "We have no time to lose. Bunch the horses together and stand by your guns."

With that Nate was off, racing along the line until he reached Fletcher and Harrison, who were both bringing up the rear in order to keep an eye on their many horses and prevent any of the animals from straying off. Quickly he told them of the impending danger. "Fan out on either side of the horses," he ordered, "and keep them packed tight. Be ready to cut and run though, if we're attacked."

Both men nodded. Both had the look of men who sincerely wished they were somewhere else.

In a flash Nate was galloping back toward the front of the column. Out on the plain the dust cloud had swelled tremendously, and a number of riders had materialized at its swirling base. Nate tried to count them, but the dust and distance thwarted him.

Shakespeare, meanwhile, had joined the women and Zach, and was moving around the horses to a point where he would be directly between the Indians and their own party. The men took up positions at regular intervals in front of their small herd.

"Recognize them yet?" Nate asked as he stopped alongside his mentor.

"Not yet," Shakespeare responded. "But at least we know they're not Blackfeet."

Nate nodded. The Blackfeet, like their allies the Piegans, routinely conducted raids beyond their own territory afoot. They did so more out of adherence to tribal tradition than due to any advantage being on foot gave them. One day soon, Nate knew, they would have to change their ways in order to withstand the Sioux and the Cheyenne, who had adapted to the horse so readily and now were regularly winning victories over the conservative Blackfeet.

Twisting, Nate saw that everyone had a rifle at the ready. Zach's face was set in lines of solemn determination that filled Nate with pride. William Templar, to Nate's surprise and annoyance since it proved Shakespeare to be right yet again, displayed no fear at all.

"We can breathe a mite easier," Shakespeare suddenly announced, cradling his rifle in his elbow.

"How so?"

"They're Crows."

This was welcome news to Nate. While not always as friendly to whites as the Shoshones were, the Crows had never killed a white man so far as Nate knew. They did sometimes resort to thievery, on several occasions having stolen horses from free trappers.

At one time the Crows had been one of the most powerful tribes west of the Mississippi, and their nation had numbered about eight thousand souls. But constant warfare, and later a smallpox epidemic, had so ravaged them that now only two thousand of their number were left, and of those approximately twelve hundred were women. Consequently, most warriors had more than one wife. Chiefs often had three or four.

Soon the band was close enough for Nate to make a head count, which came to 22 braves. This bothered him a bit, since often when a large Crow band encountered a smaller group of whites, the Crows would insolently insist on receiving gifts as tokens of the good will of the interlopers in their country.

"Let me do the chawing," Shakespeare suggested.

"Gladly."

"Whatever happens, don't let any of them get past us and in among the horses. One shout will scatter the whole bunch and we'll never see half of them again."

Then the rumble of hoofs heralded the arrival of the Crow party. Neither the warriors nor their horses were painted for war, which told Nate this was a hunting party probably out after buffalo. He wished he spoke the Crow tongue, as Shakespeare did, so he could understand what was going to be said.

Only when the Crows had all halted and were appraising them did Shakespeare break the ice by addressing them in sign language. "Greetings. I am Wolverine Killer," he said, using the sign equivalent of the name bestowed on him many years ago by the Flatheads.

Nate was puzzled. Why was McNair using sign when he spoke Crow fairly fluently? Insight made him grin. His friend was doing so for *his* benefit so he could follow the drift of the talk and be prepared for trouble should the Crows turn out to be belligerent.

"I have heard of you," a lean Crow answered. "They say you are a friend of our people. I know that many winters ago you stayed in a village of our tribe for ten or twelve moons." He paused. "I am Four Horns."

"I know of you," Shakespeare signed, repaying the compliment. "They say you are a man of honor, a man who has never given his white brothers cause to take offense."

Nate saw some of the Crows muttering among themselves, younger warriors who sat behind the front row of more seasoned men. If a conflict arose, it would be these young ones, who were eager to prove their manhood by demonstrating their courage, who would start it.

"What are Wolverine Killer and his friends doing in the land of the Crows?" Four Horns asked.

"We pass through on our way to Mandan country," Shakespeare revealed.

"You have not come to trade with us?" Four Horns inquired, and several of the younger warriors displayed indignation.

"We are in a hurry," Shakespeare explained. "Not many sleeps ago the Piegans tried to take our hair. We drove them off, but we lost some of our men in doing so. Now these people must return to the white man's land and tell the loved ones of those who died what has happened."

Four Horns glanced at the women, then at the other white men. "The Piegans are our enemies also. They raid us often, killing young and old alike. Anyone who slays them is our friend." He motioned northward. "You may go in peace."

Nate relaxed, and had started to lift his reins to leave when one of the younger warriors shouldered through the front line and stopped beside Four Horns.

"I am Plenty Hole, and I say you cannot leave until you show us you are our friends. Words can hide lies, but horses are proof of the truth."

"Are you saying I do not speak with a straight tongue?" Shakespeare signed angrily.

Plenty Hole stared at the rifle poised in the mountain man's lap, and smiled deviously. "You have lived in the mountains since the time of our grandfathers, Wolverine Killer, and all of us know of you. We know you would never talk with a forked tongue. We also know you have shown your friendship to our people many times." He nodded at the clustered horses. "Is it wrong to show your friendship to us by giving us some of your horses? You have so many. You will not miss a few."

This was the moment of truth. Nate had his

right hand resting on his Hawken, and he tensed, set to whip it up and fire.

"I never thought I would see the day when the Crows would try to take advantage of my friendship with them," Shakespeare signed indignantly. "If you were hungry, I would share my food with you. If you were hurt, I would help mend you. But I will not give up horses that are not mine to warriors who already have fine horses of their own."

"They are not yours?" Plenty Hole signed quizzically.

"They belong to this man," Shakespeare said, indicating William Templar.

"Ask him to give some to us."

"Ask him yourself."

Plenty Hole swung toward William Templar. His hands and arms worked feverishly. Then he stopped, awaiting a reply.

Realizing he was the focus of attention but completely ignorant of the proceedings, William turned to Nate and demanded, "Why the devil is this bloody beggar looking at me the way he is?"

"He wants you to give him some of your horses to show him you're his friend."

"The cheeky blighter! I don't even know him," William snapped. "Tell him he can't have any of my horses, and if he doesn't trot along like a good little savage I'll have his head on toast."

Plenty Hole was impatient. "What does he say?" he asked.

"He says he has already proven his friendship by killing many Piegans who would have killed many Crows had they lived," Shakespeare replied. "He says he is offended that you would insist on taking horses from one who has recently lost friends who died killing your enemies." He paused, his features flinty. "And he says that if you try to take the horses or molest us in any way, we will cover the ground with the guts and blood of many foolish Crows."

Nate half expected Plenty Hole and some of the other young warriors to fly into a rage. His thumb curled around the hammer, and his finger touched the trigger.

The next moment Shakespeare turned his white horse and resumed their journey without condescending to give the Crows a parting word or look. He sat at ease in the saddle, showing by his posture that he was unafraid.

Following the grizzled frontiersman's lead, Nate wheeled the black stallion and motioned to the others to head out. Unlike McNair, he watched the Crows out of the corner of his eye and saw a bitter argument erupt between Four Horns and Plenty Hole. Soon all the Crows were taking sides, and they were still arguing when Nate glanced back after covering over five hundred yards.

"I'll remember that Plenty Hole," Shakespeare remarked.

They were halfway to the butte when faint whoops came to Nate's ears. Fearing the worst, he stopped, but the Crows were riding to the south, not attacking. He watched until the dust they raised was lost in the distance; then, breaking into a relieved smile, he clapped McNair on the back. "My hat is off to you, sir," he said, doffing his. "Well done! You called their bluff."

Shakespeare shrugged. "They were after meat,

not out to lift hair. I figured they wouldn't risk theirs for a few horses." He gave his mustache a pull. "Still, we'd best stay extra alert tonight. I wouldn't put it past Plenty Hole and some of his young friends to sneak back and try to take some horses."

Lady Templar came over to them. Burning with curiosity, she wanted to know everything that had been said, so as they rode along Nate recounted the exchange as best his memory permitted. When he got to the part where Shakespeare had told Plenty Hole the horses belonged to her brother, she faced McNair.

"Those horses are half mine. You know that. Why didn't you say as much?"

"There would have been hell to pay. They would have wanted to know exactly which ones were yours, and then they might have ridden right up and grabbed them for themselves."

"But they wouldn't have touched William's?"

"Not once they knew about yours."

"I must be terribly dense, Mr. McNair. Why would they be so brazen as to take mine but not his?"

"Because you're a woman."

"It matters that much to them?"

"Makes a world of difference," Shakespeare replied. "In Indian society the women get the hind end of the deal. It's the men who are lords and masters of their lodges, and their word is law. If a woman doesn't do as she's told, she might be beaten. If the man doesn't want her anymore, he can throw her away. In some tribes, like the Apaches, women are not even allowed to have their own names. In almost all of them, the women have no voice in public matters. They do as the men want or else."

"How . . ." Lady Templar began indignantly. Then she paused, seeking the right word, but all she could think of was, "How *primitive!*"

"By your standards, yes, ma'am," Shakespeare said. "But the Indians have been living this way for as long as any of them can remember, and the women don't complain."

"They wouldn't dare after being bullied into submission."

"It's not like that at all. The men usually treat their wives with love and kindness. They're good husbands and providers, and most Indian women are proud to be the wives of the warriors they marry. And while the women don't have much say at the councils, in their own lodges it's a different story. Many a wife is the boss of her family and her husband doesn't realize the fact."

"I still say it's reprehensible."

Shakespeare sighed. "You'd have to live as an Indian for a spell before you could understand their views on things. Believe me. The women are rarely abused. And they take a lot of pride in the work they do in keeping up the lodge and making clothes and cooking. In some tribes they have special societies for the women in which they advance depending on how well they do their crafts and such."

"Slavery, Mr. McNair. The Indian way is nothing more or less than utter slavery. To think of all those poor women overworked and overburdened by common drudgery. I am incensed."

"I'm sure you are. But for the last time, conditions aren't as bad as you think. Yes, the women work hard, but so do the men. And at least the women have help from the other wives in their lodge."

Lady Templar's nose scrunched up. "Other wives? Then it's true what I heard? Indians practice polygamy?"

"They practice what?"

"The men have more than one wife."

"In some tribes, they do. Many of the men die young, so there's never enough of them to go around. If a woman wants a husband she has to share him with another woman. Or maybe two. Or three."

Diana made a sniffing sound and frowned, as if she had smelled a foul odor. "But what does all of this have to do with them taking my horses?"

"In some tribes women can't own horses. In others they can own a few, but it's the warriors who have the most. The men need good horses for raids and hunting buffalo, which is why they steal all they can get their hands on."

"You're deliberately evading the issue. Why? So I won't think even less of Indian society?"

The mountain man looked at her. "They would have tried to take your horses because to their way of thinking it wouldn't be fitting for a weak woman to own so many fine animals."

Nate had listened to the dispute with suppressed amusement. At one time he'd shared many of Lady Templar's sentiments, but subsequent experience had taught him how decently Indian women in general were treated, and he'd learned to accept their way of life. Few of the warriors he personally knew routinely beat their wives, and those that did were often rebuked by the older men.

He studied the butte as they passed it. Whoever had sent the smoke signal was undoubtedly long gone, back with the band. He saw a ribbon of a trail that wound from the base to the escarpment, which explained how the warrior had ascended. Then the Englishwoman posed a question that perked up his ears.

"Have you ever had more than one wife at one time, Mr. McNair?"

There was a prolonged silence before Shakespeare answered. "Yes, Diana, I have. Back when I lived with the Crows."

"How many, may I ask?"

"Five."

"You lived with five women at *once?*"

"I was young then."

"Meaning you didn't know right from wrong?"

"No, meaning I could keep up with all five and not be worn to a frazzle. Now it would be different. I have a heap of trouble just keeping up with one."

"Well, I never!" Lady Templar declared, and moved off to ride with her brother. Her cheeks were scarlet, her chin jutting high. Decorum dictated that she be outraged by McNair's conduct, but inwardly she was delighted more than she was shocked. Here was a juicy tidbit she couldn't wait to tell her friends!

Nate let several minutes go by before he said, "You never mentioned having five wives to me. For that matter, you never mentioned living with the Crows. And here I thought that I'm the closest friend you have."

"You are, but being someone's friend doesn't entitle you to know every little fact about their whole life. Being a friend means you accept them for what they are, not what they've been."

There was an edge of hurt to McNair's tone, leaving Nate to conclude he had offended him. "I'd never think less of you for keeping your past private." He laughed. "And I sure wouldn't think less of you for having five wives. Some day you'll have to tell me how you made do."

Shakespeare cracked a smile, glanced at Nate, and guffawed rowdily. "It wasn't easy!" he declared. "You don't know what marriage is really like until you're being nagged by five women at the same time."

Evening found them on the south bank of a sluggish stream, camped in a tract of cottonwoods. While Harrison made the fire, Shakespeare went off into the brush after meat for the cooking pot and the rest of the men watered the horses. Nate tied rope between a half-dozen trees so that once the animals had slaked their thirst they could be tethered for the night.

Not long after, the crack of a rifle carried from downstream, and in due order Shakespeare strolled back bearing a young black-tailed doe over his shoulders. He volunteered to do the butchering, Winona did the cooking, and under a starry celestial spectacle they all sat down to a meal of roast venison.

Nate devoured his chunks in great bites, chewing greedily as he savored the delicious taste. He saw William and Diana unpack their fine china and silverware before they sat down to eat, and he wondered why it was that some people became so habit-bound they lugged their habits around with them like so much old baggage they were unwilling to give up for anything newer. By doing the same thing day in and day out, they dug themselves into a rut, and sometimes got down so deep they couldn't dig themselves out if they tried.

He thanked God that he'd had the horse sense to change as his environment changed. To go from the streets of New York City to the wide-open spaces of the frontier had been a drastic step to take, yet he had learned to adjust, had learned to mold himself to the new conditions that arose and to wrest a living from the land. He took pride in that fact. Many came west and never survived. They succumbed to the elements, to the beasts, to the Indians, or to some weakness in themselves. Defying the odds, he had prevailed.

Most of their party were done eating when Zach spoke up. "Uncle Shakespeare, will you quote for us some tonight? I'd sure like to hear more of old William S."

"I don't know," McNair hedged. "I expect everyone else has had their fill by now."

"Indulge the boy, McNair," William said. "I love hearing the Bard mangled by your recitations."

"Do you now?" Shakespeare replied. To Zach he said, "This above all: to thine own self be true. And it must follow, as the night the day, thou canst not then be false to any man."

"That's one of your favorites," the boy said. "I've heard it many times before. Why didn't you do something new?"

"I figured maybe the marquis hadn't ever heard it," Shakespeare said, and rose oblivious to the glare he received from William Templar. "Now if you'll excuse me, I want to spread out my blanket and turn in. My old bones ain't as spry as they used to be."

Everyone turned in early, except for the two men chosen to stand the first watch. It had been decided that two were needed in case the Crows should put in an appearance, and the early stint fell to Jarvis and Harrison.

Nate had agreed to handle the second watch, with Fletcher, so he was soon snug under his robe and serenely contemplating the heavens. The drone of Winona and Diana talking lulled him to sleep. How long he slept, he couldn't say. But there was no mistaking the sounds that woke him up—an ear-splitting war whoop followed by the blast of a rifle.

Chapter Ten

Eight years of living in the wilderness had honed Nate's reflexes until they were razor sharp. As a result, no sooner did the war whoop rent the night than he was up and in a crouch, the Hawken in his hands. Swiveling, he spied a commotion among the horses and trotted toward them. On the heels of the shot, more bloodcurdling whoops confirmed that more than one warrior was out there.

The majority of the horses were neighing in fright and trying to pull free of the tether ropes. Several had either succeeded or been aided by human hands, because they were moving deeper into the trees.

The fire had long since gone out. In the gloom Nate had difficulty discerning movement, and so it was that at first he didn't see the stealthy figure gliding toward his black stallion. When the stallion whinnied, he recognized its cry and spun, the Hawken fully cocked.

A dull glint of starlight on a drawn blade betokened the purpose of the figure. In a heartbeat Nate had the Hawken to his shoulder and a bead on the center of the black shape. Then he fired.

At the booming retort two things happened simultaneously. The figure dropped in its tracks, and out of the darkness hurtled a fiery whirlwind with an upraised tomahawk. Nate sensed rather than saw his attacker, and by sheer luck got the rifle up in time to counter the initial brutal blow. Turning, he countered a second, and a third, the tomahawk handle thudding against the rifle barrel with such force the barrel smacked into his forehead.

Growling, his assailant backed up a stride, shifted, and came at him from a different angle.

Nate aimed a vicious swipe at the warrior's head and missed. His left shoulder flared with explosive agony as the brave connected, and suddenly the Hawken was ripped from his grasp. Once more the tomahawk cleaved the air, streaking for his face. and Nate threw himself to the side, his hand closing on his own tomahawk in midair. Hitting on his elbows and knees, he instantly rolled and heard the warrior's weapon bite into the earth.

And then Nate was flat on his back with his attacker looming above him and the man's tomahawk sweeping up for another strike. But Nate had other ideas. Bending forward, he sank his own tomahawk into the warrior's leg, and was gratified by the squawk it elicited. The brave, without thinking, doubled over, his face inches from Nate's, and in that moment Nate identified Plenty Hole. Shoulders rippling, Nate swept his tomahawk straight up and buried it in the Crow's throat.

Warm drops spattered on Nate's face. He skipped to the left, knowing full well a wounded man was still capable of landing a fatal blow, and threw back his arm to strike once more. It proved unnecessary.

Plenty Hole had gone to his knees, his hands pressed over the gushing spout where his throat had been. Sputtering, spraying crimson like a geyser, he swayed, wailed, and pitched forward, the wail dying as he did so that the cry and his life ended the second he struck the ground.

Breathing heavily, Nate backed away a few feet, then thought to glance around and see how his companions were faring. To the south rose shouts and the popping of guns. Most of the horses were where they should be, but five or six were missing.

Nate wiped his tomahawk on Plenty Hole's leggings, shoved it under his belt, and reclaimed the Hawken. He began to sprint in the direction of the shots, and had covered ten yards when a high-pitched moan drew him up short. It came from tall weeds to his right. Sinking low, he crept forward until he spotted the form of a man lying sprawled on his stomach. Even in the dark he could tell the man was white, and by the clothes he could tell it was one of the Englishmen.

Swiftly Nate reached the man's side and knelt. Slowly, he rolled the stricken Britisher over. It was Harrison, the valet. A large hole in Harrison's chest had been left by a lance that had penetrated deep into his body.

"Who?" Harrison croaked weakly, his eyelids

quivering.

"Nate King," Nate said, taking the man's hand in his. "Lie still. Don't strain yourself."

"How bad?" Harrison asked.

Nate made no reply.

"That bed, eh? I feared as such." Harrison abruptly coughed violently, shaking from head to toe, and an odd sucking noise came from the hole in his chest. At length he subsided and lay quietly. "I never saw the blooming heathen, sir. So help me."

"I believe you," Nate answered softly.

"Where's Lady Templar? Or Jarvis? I'd like to say good-bye to them."

"I don't know. Sorry."

"Typical. That's been my life since the day I was born." Harrison closed his eyes and groaned again, louder. He tried to lift his other hand, got it an inch off the grass, and gave up the effort with a gasp.

"I wish there was something I could do for you," Nate said guiltily, and meant it. This man, he reflected, had no business being in the wilderness. Harrison was accustomed to all the cultured refinements civilization had to offer, and was like a fish out of water when not in a city; he should never have left foggy London.

"There is," Harrison whispered, his lips flecked with spittle. "Please tell Lady Diana . . ." He stopped, inhaled noisily. "Please tell her . . ."

Nate waited for the Englishman to finish the request, but no more words were uttered. After several seconds he felt for a pulse and found none. "And now there are five," he said to himself as he closed the dead man's eyes.

Standing, Nate walked southward. He soon heard voices and saw several people coming toward him. The moving mountain in the lead had to be Jarvis, and beside the giant was Shakespeare. Behind them came the women and a small form that could only be Zach.

"Who's there?" Jarvis suddenly bellowed, leveling his rifle in Nate's direction. But Shakespeare was faster and swatted the barrel aside.

"Whoa there, old coon! You wouldn't want to be putting a ball into a mountainee man, would you?"

"King?" Jarvis blurted out. "Sorry, mate. I mistook you for an Indian in the dark. You look just like one except for that beard of yours."

Nate advanced as William Templar and Eric Nash caught up with the others. "What's the count?" he asked.

"The mangy bastards got seven of the horses," Shakespeare answered. "We chased them as far as we could, but they were mounted and we weren't. I think I winged one."

"Serves the savages bloody well right," William said. "They're errant thieves, no more, no less. I'm sorry we didn't kill some of them to teach them a lesson."

"We did," Nate said, jerking his thumb over his shoulder. "I killed two. One was Plenty Hole."

"Couldn't have happened to a more deserving bastard," Shakespeare said with a grin. "If you haven't scalped him yet, do go. We'll use his hair to wipe the dirt and mud off our moccasins at night."

"There's more, and it's bad. They killed one of ours."

In the confusion of being rudely awakened in the middle of the night and the heated excitement of the chase, none of then had realized one of their party was missing. Now, everyone looked at everyone else as they sought to determine which one of their group Nate meant.

William Templar was the first to blurt out, "Harrison! Where the deuce is Harrison?"

Wordlessly, Nate beckoned and turned, taking them to where the hapless valet lay still and pale. "His last words were of Lady Templar," he reported.

"The poor dear," Diana said.

William Templar surprised all present by sinking to his knees and taking the dead man's limp hand in his. His voice was choked when he declared, "Harrison was a damn good man. Been with the family for almost twenty years." He broke off and gazed blankly into the distance. "I hardly ever had to reprimand him for a shoddy performance of his duties."

"There's an epitaph for you," Shakespeare muttered to Nate.

One by one or in pairs they moved off, leaving the marquis alone. William was glad they left, glad they wouldn't observe the acute torment that now contorted his fine features. He would never confess as much, but he blamed himself for the deaths that had occurred. Indirectly at least, he was responsible since it had been his inspiration to take a jolly jaunt to the colonies and get a taste of genuine American frontier life. Diana, as she always did because she loved to travel, had readily been caught up in the whimsical enterprise. Nash came because she did. But the others had been men specifically chosen by William for their competence and their steadfast qualities. Some of them had been on previous trips, and he knew them well. And while generally he disdained to fraternize with commoners, on occasion he'd mingled with them and found them to be honorable and true in their simple way.

Rising, William cleared his throat and walked to where McNair was starting a fire. He saw his sister in earnest conversation with King's wife, and barely restrained an urge to curse. Of late Diana had been spending an inordinate amount of time in the company of the Shoshone woman, so much that she had been unable to spend time with him. At the outset he had chalked up Diana's interest to her usual fascination with native cultures, but now he was not so certain. He was beginning to suspect a bona fide friendship was developing between the two, which was patently absurd, Winona being a lowly heathen and all.

A few yards away, Nate noticed the odd look the marquis bestowed on his wife and Diana and wondered why. Most likely, Nate thought, the duke's son was upset that his sister was associating so freely with an Indian woman. In his opinion, it was unfortunate Harrison had died instead of William Templar.

A loud crackling signaled the fire had caught, and Shakespeare sat back on his haunches and held his palms out to the rising flames. The circle of depressed faces ringing him prompted him to remark, "I know we're all upset by what has happened, but it's not the end of the world. We can still make it to the Mandan country in one piece if we all pull together. There are more than enough horses left to pack the supplies along, and with game being plentiful we won't go hungry."

"How can you talk about such trifles with Harrison lying over there and not yet cold?" William asked irritably.

"I'm sorry he was killed, Templar," Shakespeare responded. "No man should have to die because of another man's greed. But out here we learn one thing about death real quick,. Life always goes on. No matter who dies or how many, everything carries on just like before. The sun and moon rise and set. The birds sing. Buffalo roll in their wallows. The world is unchanged."

"Mr. McNair!" Diana said. "I'm shocked at your callous attitude."

"I don't mean to offend you. I'm just trying to make the point that we have to pick up the pieces and get on with our lives. Tomorrow is another day, and if we're not real careful one or more of us could end the day just like Harrison did."

"Are you thinking the Crows will come back?" Jarvis asked.

"I doubt it. The young ones paid a steep price for stealing only seven horses, and they won't bother us again. They're more concerned right now with having to go back to their village and tell everyone what happened."

"Why should that bother them?" Diana inquired.

"Indians hate to lose men on a raid. They see it as bad medicine. Losing two is an outright calamity, and the young warriors who took part will have to prove themselves in battle or by earning some other honors before the shame of this night will be erased."

"I hope they all die," William growled.

"As for us," Shakespeare said, "we should turn in. It's safe to leave just one man on watch, but we should also keep the fire going on the off chance I'm wrong and some of them sneak back to find Plenty Hole and the other one Nate killed." He stood. "If they see the fire they'll figure we're all awake and leave us alone."

"What about the bodies?" Fletcher asked, breaking his typical silence.

"Nate and I will drag then off into the brush."

The marquis took a step forward. "Like hell you will. Harrison deserves a proper Christian burial and I aim to give it to him."

"What will you dig with?" Shakespeare said, and stamped his foot several times. "This ground is as hard as a boulder and we don't have spades."

"I'll use my fingers if need be," William said. "One way or the other Harrison is going to be buried so the animals don't get at him."

"I'll lend a hand, sir," Jarvis offered.

"Count me in," Fletcher said.

"You'll be up half the night and won't be able to stay awake in the saddle tomorrow," Shakespeare pointed out, trying to convince them of the folly of burying their companion.

"So be it," William stated. "King and you can keep watch. Harrison was one of us, so I don't expect you to sacrifice on his behalf."

The Englishmen moved off, and Lady Templar gave McNair a disapproving glance. "You continue to shock me. I flattered myself that I knew you, but clearly I was imagining qualities in you

that you do not possess. Haven't you a shred of
basic human decency?"

"I'm just being practical," Shakespeare said.

"Hang your practicality!" Diana said, and spinning, she walked away in a huff. She was piqued
not only at the old mountain man but also at
herself for taking a liking to him when she
should have known her affection would be
betrayed. Americans were a hopeless lot, she
fused, barbarians at heart, and it was well and
good Britain had lost the so-called Revolutionary
War. Good riddance to bad rubbish!

In her pique, Diana had her head down and
her fists clenched, and had no idea where she
was going or what was in front of her until she
abruptly collided with someone. Fearing it might
be a savage, she jumped back as she looked up,
then smiled in grateful relief. "Eric! I didn't see
you."

"Your brother has us looking for a suitable spot
to bury Harrison. I'm afraid I wasn't paying much
attention either." He started to leave.

"It's good to hear your voice again," Diana said
quickly. "You've hardly spoken three words to me
in days."

"You know why."

"Yes, I do. But does that mean we can't be
friends? That we can't chat now and then?"

"I suppose not," Eric answered.

Eager to keep him talking, Diana alluded to
what was uppermost on her mind. "What do you
think of McNair's attitude? Have you ever witnessed anything so crass in your life?"

"He has his reasons."

"You're defending him?"

"Haven't King and Shakespeare demonstrated time and again that they know this country inside out? They know Indians, they know the wildlife. I should think we would be grateful for any advice they offer instead of criticizing them all the time."

"But Harrison—!"

"Is dead and gone. It will make no difference at all to his whether his body wastes away in a grave or is consumed by scavengers."

"Would *you* like to be left to rot on the prairie?"

"If that's my fate, so be it. The world will suffer no great loss."

"How can you talk so? My word. You sound like McNair."

"Do I?" Eric responded, and chuckled. "I knew I was changing, but that much? Thank you for the compliment."

"I don't understand you anymore," Diana confessed. "What happened to the carefree artist who so charmed me with his wit and vigor?"

"His wit died when he realized what a fool he was making of himself. His vigor has flown on the same wind that swept away his zest for life." Eric gazed sadly into the darkness. "As for being carefree, I stopped being so juvenile the day I discovered I was a coward."

Diana blinked and tried to read his expression, but the deep shadows frustrated the attempt. Even though she had admitted to herself and to him that she didn't love him enough to contemplate marriage, she still cared about his welfare as a proper friend should. They had been close for far too long for her to summarily dispense with her feelings.

"When those Piegans attacked us," Eric went on in a low tone, "I was so paralyzed with fear and horror I couldn't move. And do you know that until that very moment I had always regarded myself as a rather courageous chap?"

"You're mistaken," Diana said. She took a step and rested a reassuring hand on his arm. "You're no coward, Eric Nash."

He pulled away, then looked down at the spot she had touched. "You have no conception, my dear, because you have never felt the sheer terror I did at the sight of the Piegans ruthlessly butchering our fellows. You grabbed your gun and fought like the tigress you are, while I cringed in a corner, too frightened to even pray for deliverance."

"I think you're being unduly hard on yourself. You had never seen an Indian attack before."

"Neither had you," Eric said, and was gone, hastening into the night, a roving specter among the trees.

Baffled and upset, Diana tried to think of words of comfort she could say to him later, something that would alleviate his despair and dispel his somber mood. Turning, she headed for the fire to warm herself, then suddenly became aware of someone standing nearby. "Who?" she declared.

"It's me," Nate King announced, stepping into the open. "I didn't mean to eavesdrop. Shakespeare sent me after more wood."

"You heard?"

"Some of what he said, yes."

"What can I do, Mr. King? I hate to see him this way."

"There's nothing you can do. Some problems a man has to work out for himself."

"Ever the rugged individualist," Diana said testily.

"Ma'am?"

"You mountain men are so damned self-sufficient, it's galling. You rely on no one or nothing, and you believe you are honor-bound to handle every difficulty you encounter by yourself. Imposing on others is taboo. You'd rather suffer in silence than ask for help."

"I think you're stretching the point a mite."

"You haven't even heard my point yet, which is that not all people are like Mr. McNair and you. Civilized people, people with breeding, reach out helping hands to those in need."

"Like Shakespeare and I have done in offering to see you safely to Independence?"

In a day crammed with more conflicts than Diana Templar normally experienced in a month, having her own argument thrown in her face was the last straw. She rudely shoved past King and stomped to the fire. Ignoring everyone else, she sat down, rested her chin in her hands, and wished to high heaven she had never left England.

Out in the cottonwoods, Nate stared at her stiff back for a bit, then made his way further into the trees, picking up branches as he went along. Soon he spotted the artist up ahead. Increasing his stride, he drew within a few yards and asked, "Found a spot yet?"

Eric stopped. "No. It's hopeless. There are no soft areas where the digging would be easy."

"You might try closer to the stream. Flash floods are pretty common hereabouts, and all that extra water makes the soil near streams and rivers a bit softer than the ground elsewhere."

"Thank you. I never would have thought of that." Eric smiled, and started to retrace his steps.

"Hold on. I wanted to ask you a favor."

"How may I be of service?"

"We're getting close to the southern part of Blackfoot country," Nate said. "Shakespeare and I have decided that one of us should keep on scouting around as we travel so we're not taken by surprise by a war party. One man alone, though, is easy for Indians to pick off from ambush. We figure on having two men scout around together. That way, if one goes down, the other can escape it and warn the rest."

"Yes?" Eric said, missing the inference.

"I'd like you to ride out with me when it's my turn."

"Me!" Eric exclaimed. "Why me?"

"Why not?"

"Well . . . I'm a . . . that is . . ." Eric stammered, and finally got out, "You'd be wiser to pick Jarvis or Fletcher."

"I want you. Will you do it?"

"This is most unexpected," Eric mumbled, running a hand through his hair. "I suppose, though, if you insist, I'd have to agree."

"Fine. Make sure your rifle is loaded and you have plenty of ammunition and black powder."

"I will. I won't let you down," Eric said. "Now if you'll excuse me, I have to tell William about the soil near the stream." Mustering a smile, he swiftly strode off, and there was more bounce in his stride than there had been for days.

Nate King watched Nash's departure with pursed lips, and when the Englishman was beyond hearing range, grumbled, "I just hope to hell I know what I'm doing."

Chapter Eleven

The days that followed the Crow horse-stealing incident were ones Eric Nash would never forget. As he rode with Nate King hour after hour over the flat expanse of prairie, he found himself liking the young trapper more and more. They talked constantly. Eric besieged Nate with countless questions about the pristine land, its many creatures, and, of course, Indians. He learned more about wilderness survival and basic woodlore in just the first two days than he had learned during the 24 years of his entire life.

Eric became adept at recognizing various animals at a distance by their outlines and the way they moved. He learned how to distinguish a wolf track from a coyote print, that of a bull buffalo from a cow. He grew skillful at reading the weather, telling by the shape and speed of the clouds and the scent of the air whether rain would fall later in the day.

His horizons were expanded in other regards as well. Periodically, while they rested far from the main body, Nate gave Eric lessons in shooting, and before long Eric could consistently hit a target the size of his hand at 50 paces. He also acquired proficiency in using the tomahawk and the butcher knife, and could throw both with reasonable accuracy.

Without Eric consciously being aware of it, his confidence grew by leaps and bounds. But one thing he was aware of, a discussion he would always cherish, took place on their very first scout together, when they had gone barely a mile from the others. They had been riding quietly side by side. Suddenly his horse nickered and fidgeted, its ears pricked, its nostrils flaring.

"What the bloody hell!" Eric snapped.

"There's your reason," Nate said, pointing at a huge shape a quarter of a mile off, moving away from them. "Your horse got wind of it."

"What in the world is that monster? An elephant?"

Nate laughed. "No, my friend. That there is a grizzly bear. White bears, some call them. Others call them silver-tips. Whatever the name, they're terror on four legs, and if one ever comes after you, don't be ashamed if you're scared hell West and cook."

"If I what?"

"Run for your life."

Eric rode on, thinking of his fear during the Piegan battle. "Have you ever been afraid of anything, Mr. King?"

"Lord, yes. Why, the first time I tangled with a grizzly, I about stained my pants. I didn't know the true meaning of fear until that day in the Republican Fork of the Kansas River when a big old bear caught me napping." Nate shook his head. "I was as green as grass back then."

"Did you run?"

"I was too scared to run."

"What did you do, then?"

"I accidentally killed it."

Eric glanced around to see if the frontiersman was in earnest, and was amazed to confirm such was the case. "How, pray tell, does one *accidentally* slay a brute that size?"

"Luck. Pure dumb luck. I had a knife with me and I stabbed it in the eye by chance. Next thing, the bear up and keeled over."

"There must have been more to it than that."

"Not really," Nate said. "And that wasn't the only time I've been scared half to death. My first fight with Indians was against a bunch of Kiowas. The whole while my heart was in my throat."

"Still, you *did* fight them."

"There was no other choice. Either I fought or I died, and I wasn't partial to giving up the ghost just then." Nate sighed. "Fear is like a cold chill. It burrows deep inside you and turns you to ice, and the only way I know to overcome it is to not think of how afraid you are but to get on with doing what has to be done."

"Perhaps you're right," Eric said. "But how does a person shut fear from their mind so they can get on with the matter at hand?"

"You don't try to shut it out. Just let it lie there while you do what you have to."

GET
4 FREE BOOKS!

You can have the best Westerns delivered to your door for less than what you'd pay in a bookstore or online. Sign up for one of our book clubs today, and we'll send you **4 FREE* BOOKS**, worth $23.96, just for trying it out...**with no obligation to buy, ever!**

Authors include classic writers such as
LOUIS L'AMOUR, MAX BRAND, ZANE GREY
and more; PLUS new authors such as
COTTON SMITH, TIM CHAMPLIN, JOHNNY D. BOGGS
and others.

As a book club member you also receive the following special benefits:
- **30% OFF** all orders through our website & telecenter!
- **Exclusive access** to special discounts!
- **Convenient** home delivery **and 10 days to return any books you don't want to keep.**

There is no minimum number of books to buy,
and you may cancel membership at any time.
See back to sign up!

*Please include $2.00 for shipping and handling.

YES!

Sign me up for the Leisure Western Book Club and send my FOUR FREE BOOKS! If I choose to stay in the club, I will pay only $14.00* each month, a savings of $9.96!

NAME: _____

ADDRESS: _____

_____

TELEPHONE: _____

E-MAIL: _____

☐ I WANT TO PAY BY CREDIT CARD.

☐ VISA   ☐ MasterCard   ☐ DISCOVER

ACCOUNT #: _____

EXPIRATION DATE: _____

SIGNATURE: _____

Send this card along with $2.00 shipping & handling to:

**Leisure Western Book Club
20 Academy Street
Norwalk, CT 06850-4032**

Or fax (must include credit card information!) to: 610.995.9274.
You can also sign up online at www.dorchesterpub.com.

*Plus $2.00 for shipping. Offer open to residents of the U.S. and Canada only.
Canadian residents please call 1.800.481.9191 for pricing information.
If under 18, a parent or guardian must sign. Terms, prices and conditions subject to change. Subscription subject
to acceptance. Dorchester Publishing reserves the right to reject any order or cancel any subscription.

JOIN NOW!

Eric uttered a low, disbelieving laugh. "You make it sound so easy."

"Most things in this life are until we try to figure them out and make a mess of the figuring."

"You missed your calling, my friend. You should have been a philosopher."

Nate King snorted. "Not on your life. Those fancy thinkers don't know a plew from a plow. I'm content just the way I am."

Which, now that Eric gave it some thought several days later, was a remarkable statement in itself. He doubted there had been a single day of his existence where he had known perfect contentment, even the months spent in Lady Templar's company. There had always been dissatisfaction with one element in his life or another. If it wasn't his failure to paint the masterpieces he thought should flow from his brush, it was unhappiness at being repeatedly put off by Diana.

Yet, as the days followed one after the other, Eric was surprised to note a degree of contentment in his own prowess he had never known before. He eagerly looked forward to his rides with Nate, and sucked up knowledge just as eagerly.

The limitless sea of waving grass fascinated Eric. Several times he tried to capture the essence of the beautiful scenery on his canvas, and fell short of his expectations. How was it possible, he reflected, to recreate the sense of flowing motion, of life and vitality, the prairie radiated?

There came a day when dark clouds to the west betokened an afternoon thunderstorm. Nate and Eric were two miles ahead of the others, as always scouring the land for hostile Indians. In front of them appeared one of the low hillocks that intermittently dotted the plains, and Nate was in the lead as they rode to the top.

Suddenly the black stallion whinnied shrilly and swung to one side. Nate, caught off guard, was nearly unhorsed, and had to grab the reins with both hands. His Hawken fell to the ground. Engrossed in regaining control of his mount, he didn't see the sight that sent a shiver of consternation down Eric's back: an enormous grizzly coming at them over the hill.

Few animals are as formidable at close range as the grizzly. Possessed of a massive build, with a length often reaching seven feet and a weight in excess of a thousand pounds, a grizzly is a veritable engine of destruction when aroused. Equipped with gigantic teeth and claws nearly four inches long, it is more than a match for any creature in its domain.

As Eric saw the bear sweep over the crest, he nearly fainted from fright. He would have turned and fled—the thought was uppermost on his mind—had he not realized there was no hope for Nate. The trapper couldn't possibly get his horse turned in time to avoid the bear's rush. So without thinking, Eric jammed his heels into his animal, rode in close to the grizzly, and fired into its head.

Eric didn't see the mighty paw that flashed out and hit his horse in the shoulder. He heard the thud, and a loud crack, and then his horse was falling to the left and he was falling with it. At the last possible moment he thought to throw himself clear so he wasn't pinned underneath.

Impetus carried Eric into a roll. Any second he dreaded the sensation of sharp pain as the grizzly tore into him, but he shoved to his feet without being set upon. Then he saw why.

The enraged bear was in hot pursuit of Nate. Displaying surprising swiftness for a creature having such a huge bulk, the grizzly was close on the heels of the fleeing black stallion. Nate had a flintlock out and cocked and trained on the brute, but inexplicably, he didn't fire.

Eric was waiting for the stallion to go down, the grizzly was so close. But the horse put on a burst of speed that took it far in advance of its pursuer, and the bear, lacking the stamina to run long distances, soon slowed and gave up the chase entirely.

A dismaying thought struck Eric: What if the grizzly turned around and came after him? He took a half step, intending to flee, then changed his mind when he recalled being told by Nate that a horse was faster than a grizzly but a grizzly was much faster than a man. He wouldn't get 20 yards before the bear overtook him.

Eric's next idea was to reload, but he was still too slow at it and might not get the powder and ball down his rifle in time. Then he remembered that Nate had dropped the Hawken, and spinning, he ran to the rifle and scooped it up. As he straightened he saw Nate riding up to him.

"Are you hurt?"

"No, I'm fine, thank you," Eric said, and glanced back at his mount. Torn wide open from its shoulder to its elbow, it was thrashing in a spreading pool of blood and neighing pitiably. "Which is more than I can say for my horse."

"William will throw a fit."

"Hang William! Where's the bear?" Eric asked, looking out across the prairie. He was stunned not to see it, and couldn't comprehend how so large a creature could simply disappear. Then the black stallion took a few more steps and far out beyond it he spotted the bear moving rapidly to the east. Not only that, he saw two smaller versions of the beast trailing along behind it. "What are those?" he asked in bewilderment.

"Haven't you ever laid eyes on cubs before?"

"The grizzly was a female?" Eric said, his sensitive artist's soul recoiling at the idea of shooting a mother bear even if she had been on the verge of ripping Nate apart.

"Sure was. Sometimes the cubs stay with the mother for a year or longer. I saw them as I was trying to lead her away from you so I held off putting lead into her. Figured if I could outrun her there wouldn't be any need kill her." Nate reached down for his Hawken and added, "I hate to kill anything unless I don't have any choice."

"You deliberately led her off? You let her get that close to you knowing what she'd do if she got close enough?"

"I saw you were afoot," Nate said simply.

Eric stared after the fleeing bears. "I shot her, though. Now the mother will die and the cubs won't be able to take care of themselves."

"Those cubs are old enough to get by on their own," Nate responded. "And don't worry about the mother. I had a good look at her face and your shot only creased her thick skull. She probably didn't even notice."

"You really think she'll be all right?"

Nate cocked his head and scrutinized the artist's anxious upturned countenance. "I guarantee it," he said after a bit. "Now why don't you strip your saddle off your horse, do what has to be done, and we'll head back to get you a new animal."

"What else has to be done?" Eric inquired innocently.

"You have to put the horse out of its misery."

Every drop of blood seemed to drain from Eric's face. He opened his mouth, closed it again, and his throat bobbed. "I have to shoot it?"

"Would you rather the poor animal lies there for hours in the hot sun, suffering the whole time?"

"But couldn't you do the chore for me?"

"No. Some things a man has to do himself." Nate was inspecting his rifle, insuring there were no cracks or chips. His next comment was spoken so casually that Eric never suspected the motivation behind it. "I don't rightly see why you're so upset. A few minutes ago you charged a grizzly. And now you don't have the gumption to do an act of mercy?"

The reminder shook Eric. He *had* charged a raging bear, hadn't he? Ridden right up to it and put lead into its skull, as his trapper friend would say, which was hardly the act of a coward. Perhaps, just perhaps, he wasn't the hopeless person he'd imagined. "Very well," he declared, and walked over to the still-struggling horse. The scarlet pool of blood framed its sweaty head and neck, while from its slack mouth came feeble whinnies.

Eric slowly reloaded his rifle, his fingers shaking a little as he poured in the black powder. He nearly forgot to use a patch, but he did remember to push the ball down the bore with a rapid, steady stroke instead of tapping it down. He also remembered not to place his hands over the end of the ramrod when he seated the ball. As King had explained, sometimes there were embers in the barrel from an earlier shot, which might cause the gun to go off prematurely. At last he was ready.

"Try for the forehead," Nate suggested. "A shot to the brain is quick and painless."

Dully, Eric nodded, his mind awhirl with the harsh reality of the grim task he was about to perform. He'd never, ever killed a living creature before, and he didn't know if he could now. The grizzly had been different, what with King's life endangered. This was cold, calculated, premeditated. Or was it? What was so heartless about ending the life of an animal in agony? King had been right. It would be more humane to spare the horse further torment.

"Eric?" Nate said.

"I'm ready," Eric declared, and touched the stock to his shoulder. As he pointed the barrel, the horse looked up at him with its great, moist, dark eyes, causing him to hesitate. Did it know? he wondered. What was it thinking? He heard a sharp click and realized he had cocked the hammer. His mouth was dry, his palms damp, when his forefinger pressed lightly on the trigger.

At the blast the horse threw its head high, neighed once, and collapsed, its tongue protruding as death claimed it.

Eric inhaled the acrid smoke, coughed, and stepped back. He glanced up at the young trapper, then said, "To you something like this must be easy, but my whole being has been dedicated to preserving all life on canvas for future generations to enjoy. I worship the pervading spirit that animates all things, and I strive to reflect that spirit in my art. The thought of killing anything has always been like sacrilege to me. Do you see what I'm saying? Do you realize what I've done here?"

"You shot a horse."

"You don't see," Eric said sadly.

"Let me ask you something," Nate said. "If a Piegan was to come rushing at you right this second with a lance in his hand ready to throw, what would you do?"

There was no pause on Erie's part. "I'd shoot the blighter."

Nate nodded and moved his stallion closer. "You'll do to ride the high country with." He stared at the dead horse. "Except for one little mistake."

"What?"

"You forgot to strip off your saddle first. Now you've got more blood on it than before."

"Why didn't you remind me?"

"I didn't want you to have too much time to think about what you were doing," Nate answered, and grinned broadly like he might if his son had just done something that made him especially proud.

"You know," Eric said, as the truth commenced to dawn, "I'm beginning to think you duped me."

"I did."

And they both laughed.

If one member of the marquis's party was enjoying himself immensely and expanding his personal horizons in the bargain, another was profoundly distraught at the outcome of their trip to America, and becoming increasingly embittered toward everyone and everything connected with the country she was growing to despise.

Diana Templar kept more and more to herself the farther north they traveled. Until the loss of Harrison she had withstood the emotional ravages of their setbacks with her customary poise and self-control. But his death, even though she had rarely associated with him on a personal basis, upset her tremendously.

For the first time Diana realized that *she* might die before they reached civilization and safety. During the Piegan attack she had been so busy she had barely given a moment's thought to harm befalling her. Afterward, involved with her plans for the trek and diverted by Winona's attachment to her, she had not had occasion to dwell on the subject.

Now, though, traveling mile after mile over boring terrain that annoyed her with its unending sameness, Diana had little else to do when not chatting with Winona other than to think, and of late her thoughts were straying more and more to her possible death.

As she gazed out over the monotonous ocean of rippling grass, Diana could conceive of no worse fate than perishing in this godforsaken land populated by teeming savages and fierce animals, where her bleached bones would lie undisturbed forever. No one in England would know of her fate. They would all wonder, all speculate endlessly over the mystery. Her father would undoubtedly send a party to try and find William and her, and his heart would be crushed when the search party failed.

Perhaps, Diana reasoned, her days of flitting around the globe like a vagrant hummingbird in search of stimulating sights and sounds should come to an end. Perhaps she should give serious consideration to settling down, to doing as that old ruffian McNair had suggested and finding herself a husband.

That thought brought Eric's image into her mind, and Diana found herself debating the merits of what it would be like as his wife. He was witty, charming, and gallant, if a tad timid, and as devoted to her as a man could be. Or he had been until she spurned him. Had she made a mistake?

Diana suddenly heard a horse riding up close to hers, and the next second Winona appeared at her side.

"Are you feeling ill?" Winona asked.

"Not at all. Why?"

"I have watched you today and you seem very upset. Is there anything I can do for you?"

"No, thank you," Diana said, grinning at the childish devotion the simple Shoshone was constantly showing her. "I'm fine. Really."

To the north a distant rider appeared, and Shakespeare immediately bellowed for everyone to halt. Shortly thereafter they could see that there were two men astride the animal, and presently they recognized Nate and Eric on the black stallion. Everyone except Fletcher, who was at the rear of the column minding the horses, clustered forward to learn what had happened.

Diana was struck by the happy glow infusing Eric's face as the pair galloped up. He had the look of a boy on a great adventure, of someone deliriously thrilled at being alive. She listened as King told McNair about an encounter with a she-bear, as King called it, and heard about the fate of Eric's mount.

Eric was walking past her on his way back to the horses to pick a new animal to ride. Diana bestowed her friendliest smile on him and said, "That must have been a very frightening experience for you, yet you're remarkably chipper."

Stopping, Eric regarded her coolly. "I did what I had to," he said proudly.

Diana didn't quite understand his attitude. He could easily have been killed, and that bothered her. So she said, "Perhaps you should inform Mr. King that he can scout alone or with Jarvis from here on out. There's no earthly reason why you should risk *your* life."

"Are you implying I can't take care of myself?"

"No. Don't be silly. I just don't see why you, a man who dabbles with paints and brushes for his livelihood, should be required to bear arms and fight off animals and savages like the other men do," Diana stated, and instantly knew she had said something terribly wrong.

Eric Nash might have been chiseled from marble, so drawn were his handsome features. His next words were uttered in a gravelly tone Diana had never heard before. "I'll thank you, Lady Templar, to keep your opinions regarding my limitations to yourself. For your information, I shall continue to assist Nate in whatever he wants me to do, and I shall do so gladly. Unlike *some*, he doesn't judge a person's ability by what they *dabble* in." Back erect, Eric abruptly stalked off.

"Oh, dear," Diana said. "What have I done?"

"No man likes to be told he is not a warrior at heart," Winona commented.

"Eric? A warrior?" Diana laughed at the ridiculous concept. "He's never harmed a living soul. He's a painter, my dear. An artist. A devotee of harmony and tranquility. Eric knows nothing of the martial spirit."

"There are men in my tribe who are artists," Winona mentioned. "They paint the history of our tribe on buffalo hides, and they paint as they are asked on our lodges so that everyone can tell whose lodge is whose by the paintings on it. Their paintings are very true to life." She paused. "These men are also brave warriors, and when an enemy attacks they fight just like the men who are not artists."

"What are you saying? That Eric wants to be a warrior like them?" Diana shook her head. "I'm afraid you don't know him like I do. He prefers a life of ease and luxury to one of fighting and bloodshed."

"I am not saying he likes to fight. I am saying he can if he has to."

Diana glanced over he shoulder and saw Eric selecting a new mount. She knew she was right, yet she was troubled. Eric had been changing lately, not behaving as he typically did. What if he should go so far as to recklessly expose himself to danger and be slain, now of all times, when she was finally beginning to respond to his previous romantic interest in her?

Surveying the prairie, Diana frowned. It was this awful land that was changing him for the worse, she reflected. This horribly primitive country that brought out the primitive in all its inhabitants. "I hate this land and everything about it," she said bitterly to herself. "I can't wait until we're safe and sound back in England."

Winona, if she heard, made no response.

Chapter Twelve

At long last they reached the Yellowstone River and followed along its shore to the northeast, making for the junction of the Yellowstone and the Missouri. Nate and Shakespeare practiced more diligence than ever for now they were at the southern boundary of the land the Blackfeet called home. They were in daily risk of running into a Blackfoot war party or a band of warriors out hunting, and unlike the divided reception the Crows had given them, they could count on the Blackfeet showing nothing but hostility.

Fortune favored them at first. Always present were herds of buffalo or antelope or deer, which enabled them to easily live off the land. And they came on no evidence of Blackfoot activity, not until they were within 20 miles of the junction, by Shakespeare's reckoning.

That morning had dawned bright, clear, and promising. Nate and Eric headed out ahead of the rest to do their daily scouting duties. Recently the Englishman's confidence had grown to such an extent that he often separated from Nate and rode a half mile to the east of their main group to further reduce the possibility of their being taken unawares.

So it was that Nate was riding alone within a hundred yards of the river when his keen eyes spotted curling tendrils of gray smoke rising from a point not quite a hundred yards in front of him and close to the water. Instantly he turned the stallion to the left, hunched low, and rode into the sparse trees growing along that particular stretch.

His Hawken cocked, Nate dismounted, tied the stallion to a tree limb, and then trotted toward the thin wisps. Avoiding snags and twigs, he worked close enough to see the charred, smoldering embers of a fire. The ground around it was empty. No voices wafted on the morning air. Nor did he see any horses. He suspected that whoever had made camp there was gone, but he still advanced warily to confirm it.

Tracks told the story. Four Indians, Blackfeet by the cut of their moccasins, had rested overnight and moved out at dawn. They were now riding to the northeast, in the exact same direction as the marquis's party, in a leisurely fashion.

Nate squatted and scratched his chin. The Blackfeet, he mused, must be four or five miles ahead and were no threat so long as they maintained that distance. Since there were only four, he guessed they were after game and not on a raid, but he couldn't be positive of that. Often raiding parties were quite small.

Hurrying to the stallion, Nate swung up and trotted back to warn Shakespeare and the others. They would be all right so long as they slowed up a bit. In his haste, though, he completely forgot about Eric Nash.

Half a mile to the east, the Englishman was thrilling to the glorious experience of being on his own. He surveyed all around him as if he was the master of his domain, although in truth he knew he was being a bit cocky and had to watch himself lest he blunder onto a grizzly or some other peril.

Eric held his long rifle tilted upward in one hand, the stock braced on his thigh. Under his black belt rested a loaded pistol, at his side a large knife. He wished he had a tomahawk, but neither Nate nor Shakespeare had one they could spare.

Also high on Eric's new list of wants was a complete set of buckskins, including the high moccasins Nate was partial to. He'd made mention of his desire to Nate. And how pleased he had been when his trapper friend had offered to start keeping the hides of the deer they killed so that Winona and he could work on curing the skins and making the buckskins! Regrettably, they could only work as time permitted, during the evening after they halted for the day, so it would be a week or more before the buckskins were ready. Eric could hardly wait.

As Eric rode, he now and again absently caressed the smooth, cool rifle barrel as a lover might caress the silken limb of a loved one. He'd mildly shocked himself by becoming quite attached to the rifle, which was quite normal according to Nate. Many trappers went so far as to give their long guns names, and they would no more part with their favorite rifle than they would with their life.

On several occasions Nate had let Eric shoot a deer or a rabbit for the supper pot. But as yet, Eric had not tested his mettle alone, and he was keen on shooting something to take back for their meal, to show everyone, especially Diana Templar, that he could contribute his fair share.

It was still early in the day, but Eric didn't consider that when he spotted a pair of black-tailed does grazing in the open a quarter of a mile ahead of him. Putting his horse to a gallop, he raced toward them. Predictably, they whirled and fled, and while not as fleet as antelope, they were remarkably fast, so much so that they distanced themselves from the horse with every minute the chase lasted. At length they slanted toward the river, and were soon lost in the brush along its border.

Eric did not give up easily. He angled to the strip of vegetation and rode along it, peering into the tangled growth for the does. Nate, he felt certain, would be proud of him if he bagged one, and he was determined to do so if it took him all day.

As time went by Eric knew they had eluded him, but he stubbornly rode on anyway. He just might flush something else, and shortly he did, although not at all what he expected.

There came a slight curve in the river where a stand of trees hid whatever lay beyond. Eric plunged into the trees rather than go around them, in the hope of spooking more deer, although by then he would have gladly settled for a rabbit. He saw the flowing water, and beside it a narrow, clear strip of bare earth, and thinking that he should water his mount he rode out of the trees and hopped down.

As Eric guided his horse to the water's edge, he happened to glance down at his feet. His brow rippled in trepidation when he beheld moccasin tracks there in the soft earth, tracks so fresh even he could tell they had been made a short while ago.

Nate had to be warned. With that in mind, Eric gripped the saddle, and had started to lift his leg to a stirrup when a guttural laugh froze the blood in his veins, and glancing to his left he discovered four Indians watching him with amused detachment. Behind them stood four war horses. "Good God!" he exclaimed, and began to level his rifle.

Quickly the four were on the Englishman, one of them tearing the gun from his grasp while the other three threw him to the ground and stripped him of his pistol and his knife. Then, ignoring him, they yipped and waved his weapons in the air.

Eric was in a daze, his fledgling confidence shattered. The mountain men had warned him this was Blackfoot country, and although he couldn't identify the four warriors by the style of their buckskins or their hair, he assumed they were indeed the feared Blackfeet and that he was

in dire straits. He tried to rise, but one of the braves
pressed a foot on his chest, pinning him down.

Gradually Eric took possession of his senses.
For some reason his captors did not seem to rate
him as much of a threat. Not one of them bothered to cover him as they jabbered excitedly and
pointed repeatedly toward him, evidently decid-
ing his fate.

Would they kill him then and there, or take
him with them to their village to torture him at
their pleasure? That was the question uppermost
in Eric's mind. He'd learned enough of Indian
ways to know the gory end in store for him, one
way or the other, and he was quite amazed to
find he was totally unwilling to meekly accept
whatever they had in store. He wanted to *live*,
and by God he would!

Eric lashed out with his arm, batting the brave's
leg aside, and shoved to his feet, or tried to. He had
only gotten halfway up when a warrior slammed
into him and they both toppled backwards, the
warrior's arms pinning his arms to his sides. The
cold embrace of the water was a shock. He'd forgotten all about the river being to his rear.

Water gushed into Eric's open mouth as he
went under. He sputtered and thrashed, striving
to break free before he drowned, but the Blackfoot
was determined on holding him under. His chest
began to ache abominably. In his thrashing his
knee accidentally swept up into the brave's groin,
and suddenly he was released.

Eric shot to the surface and gasped for fresh air.
Spluttering, he backed away, and saw two other
warriors entering the river after him. One held
a tomahawk, the other a knife. He turned and

dove, swimming underwater for as many yards as he could before his protesting lungs demanded air again. Then, rising, he twisted and saw the Blackfeet looking all around them in confusion. One spied him and gave a shout.

Again Eric dived, swimming awkwardly, his movements retarded by his clothing and his shoes. He entertained the hope of outdistancing the Blackfeet and seeking shelter in the trees. Pumping his arms and legs, he rose once more.

Two of the Blackfeet were on horseback and racing up the river bank to catch him.

Eric hadn't counted on this. He surged to the shore, reached firm ground, and had started to run when his left foot slipped on a flat rock. Down he sprawled. Before he could push upright, the pounding of hoofs was on him. Something snatched at his back; then he was plucked up as if he only weighed a gram and slung over the back of one of the horses.

Everything had happened so fast, Eric was thoroughly addled. He attempted to sit up, but was knocked back down. Dimly, he realized another warrior was riding right beside the horse over which he had been draped. He listened to the pair talking, and shortly all four were together again next to his own horse.

The next thing Eric knew, he was roughly yanked to the ground, hurting his elbows and shins when he hit. One of the Blackfeet gestured at him, and at his horse. The command was self-explanatory.

Eric grunted as he stood and shuffled to his horse. He had to concentrate to get his arms and legs working properly before he could climb up.

As he straightened, all hell broke loose.

From the trees burst a tall figure on a black stallion who gave voice to a strident whoop. It was Nate King, Hawken in hand. He rode straight into the clustered Blackfeet, the stallion bowling over the two who were standing and then ramming into one of the war horses, sending that animal crashing backwards into the river. The last warrior was raising a lance when the stock of the Hawken clipped him on the jaw, tumbling him from his horse.

"Ride, Eric, ride!" Nate shouted, and gave Eric's mount a smack on the hind end.

Like a bolt, Eric shot through the trees.

On the Englishman's heels came Nate. Holding the Hawken and the reins in his right hand, he drew a pistol with his left and looked back, prepared to cut down the first Blackfoot who gave chase. The one he had clipped and one of those the stallion had knocked over were still down, unconscious, while the warrior in the river was struggling to get his horse under control and the last brave was staring sullenly after them.

For a mile Nate let the animals race along the river. Then he pulled abreast of Eric and gestured for him to stop. The artist was pale, but grinning. "You had a close shave there," Nate said. "If I hadn't come on you when I did, you'd be on your way to the nearest Blackfoot village."

"How did you find me?" Eric asked breathlessly.

"I rode back to warn Shakespeare there were Blackfeet around. Then I went to warn you. Found your tracks and saw where you chased the deer. So I figured I'd better check on you.'" Nate replaced the pistol. "Had to ride like the wind to get to you in time."

"I'm in your debt. Again."

"Just don't go making a habit out of getting caught. I won't always be able to pull your fat out of the fire." Nate studied their back trail. Convinced the Blackfeet weren't in pursuit, and puzzled by their absence, he continued to the southeast. "How did they capture you anyhow?"

Eric detailed the incident in detail, ending with, "I don't understand why they were laughing at me, and why they didn't appear to think of me as much of a danger to them."

"The Blackfeet hold all whites in contempt," Nate said. "As for their laughter . . ." He raked Eric from head to toe and rolled his eyes.

"My clothes?"

"Those fancy outfits of yours are enough to give a man a fit."

"In Europe they're the height of fashion," Eric said lamely, "but I'm glad I'll soon be wearing buckskins. Then no Indian will laugh at me."

Nate glanced at him. "Be thankful you weren't wearing buckskins when those Blackfeet set eyes on you, or they might have mistook you for a trapper and killed you on the spot. The way you're dressed, they probably couldn't figure out just what you were, so they came right up to you to see."

Eric touched his silk shirt, then his jacket. "I owe my life to my tailor," he said, and laughed.

Within five minutes they were reunited with their friends. While Eric related his misadventure to Jarvis, Winona, and Zach, Nate huddled with his mentor.

"I'll go back up the river and find what became of those varmints. It's strange they didn't chase us."

"Damned strange," Shakespeare agreed. "Keep your eyes peeled. Where there's four there might be more."

"I should have wiped them out right there, but I was afraid one of them would bring Nash down before I finished."

"Good thinking. We want to get to Independence with at least one of these English left alive."

After giving a wave to his wife and son, Nate rode hard for the next quarter of an hour in an easterly direction, swinging well wide of the curve in the Yellowstone where the Blackfeet had jumped the Englishman. Then, turning to the river again, he came on the trees from the opposite direction, his every sense alert.

The Blackfeet had gone.

Nate rode to the strip of earth, got down, and read the tale the prints revealed. After he had ridden off with Nash, the warriors had mounted up and headed straight across to the far bank. One of them had been helped up by another brave, so at least one was seriously hurt.

Putting a hand over his eyes, Nate scoured the opposite shore for as far as he could see and the prairie beyond. Other than a few antelope, nothing moved. He stepped into the stirrups and backtracked the Blackfeet, soon learning that they had been several hundred yards northeast of the curve when they saw Nash chasing the deer and turned around to sneak up on him.

Nate knew he should be glad they were gone, yet he was still bothered by the way they had up and ridden off like that. Blackfeet were as persistent as they were warlike, and no one ever had or ever would accuse them of being cowards. So why the devil had they left? He pondered hard, and the only logical conclusion he could reach was that they were satisfied with the guns they had taken. To a Blackfoot the stealing of a gun counted almost as much as the slaying of any enemy. In fact, so important did the Blackfeet regard the taking of a rifle or pistol, their word for an honor earned in war, *namachkani*, meant, literally, a gun had been taken.

Just to be safe, Nate rode along the river for a considerable spell, checking to see if the four braves might have recrossed farther up. He was relieved to find no evidence of such trickery.

The afternoon was waning when Nate turned the stallion around. Vivid red, orange, and yellow streaks had transformed the western horizon into a rainbow blaze of colors. Engrossed in admiring the unique display, he had no idea anyone was approaching until the faint drumming of hooves made him face forward to discover Eric Nash, a new rifle in hand, riding to intercept him.

"Is something wrong?" Nate asked when the Englishman was close enough.

"I needed an excuse to get away so I came along to see what was keeping you," Eric said. A shadow clouded his glowing visage. "Quite frankly, old friend, I can't tolerate being around Diana for very long. She hovers over me now like my mum, and keeps insisting I stay with her and the others." He encompassed the landscape in a sweeping look. "I've tried to explain why I like going off by myself now, but I might as well be speaking to a cat."

"She's just concerned for your welfare," Nate said in her defense.

"For the welfare of a *friend*," Eric said, adeptly turning his horse so he was now beside Nate.

"Everyone needs friends."

"Point taken. But there is more to it that I'm not at liberty to divulge. Suffice it to say I've learned my lesson, and I'll never fall in love again."

"Never say never, especially about love. Shakespeare likes to say a man never knows when Cupid will poke him with one of those puny arrows. Usually when he least expects it."

"The man is a fount of frontier witticisms," Eric replied. "But I meant what I said. I've the whole of my life in front of me, and I'm in no hurry to have my heart wounded again."

Not one to pry into the personal affairs of others, Nate made no further pertinent remarks. A mile further he idly mentioned, "Tomorrow we'll reach the junction."

"How far to Mandan country from there?"

"I'm not rightly sure. I've never been in this territory before, but Shakespeare has. Ask him."

"You care for that old fellow a lot, don't you?"

"Like he was my own father," Nate answered, and rode several yards before he realized the significance of what he had said. How many days ago was it he had been criticizing McNair for his fatherly attitude? In the future he would know better.

"I don't blame you," Eric said. "He's got no flies on him."

"Is that an insult? I'll have you know he takes a bath every six months whether he thinks he needs one or not."

"Goodness, no. I wouldn't insult either of you. You've given me a new lease on my life." Eric chuckled. "I alluded to the fact that he's nobody's fool."

"They don't come much smarter," Nate agreed.

"And that woman of yours! Where did you ever find such a gem? She's a smashing woman for—" Eric said, about to praise Winona, when an iron clamp closed on his arm. The look in the trapper's eyes was enough to cause his breath to catch in his throat.

"Over here, Eric," Nate said softly, "men don't go around talking about the wives of other men if they care to stay healthy."

"I say. But I—"

"This isn't England. If you were in camp with a bunch of trappers and you took it into your head to compliment another man's wife, he'd be well within his rights to separate your head from your shoulders." Nate released his hold. "But I'm your friend so I won't get my dander up."

"Over such a trifle?"

"You should know by now that Americans are a mite touchy about matters that are none of anyone else's business. We cherish our privacy above all else, and we'll beat the tar out of anyone who gets too nosy for their own good."

"That's part of your independent natures."

"That too. We've got an independent streak in us a mile wide and a yard thick, as your King George found out the hard way when he tried to grind us under his heel."

"I will say this," Eric remarked. "You Americans are a most peculiar breed. You make your way as you see fit and don't give a tinker's damn what anyone else thinks of you." Pausing, he suddenly stared at Nate, then asked softly, "Did you mean what you just said?"

"About Americans?"

"About my being your friend?"

"I sure did. You've earned the right to hang your hat in my cabin any time you're passing by."

"Why, thank you, Nate," Eric said, sincerely touched, his throat involuntarily tightening. He turned away so the trapper wouldn't see the effect on him. How could he explain why the commendation of this forthright backwoodsman meant more to him at that moment in time than all the flattery he had ever received about his art from all the nobility in England and in Europe? King, McNair, and their ilk were men stripped of all pretense, of all those artificial qualities bred into those trapped in the gilded cage of culture. If he had earned King's friendship, then he was indeed a dramatically changed man from the fop who had set sail from England months ago.

A camp was being set up when they arrived. Jarvis and Fletcher were watering the horses. Winona and Zach were gathering wood. The Templars were standing by the river, admiring the setting sun. And Shakespeare was prowling around like a nervous panther until he caught sight of them.

"Anything?" he inquired of Nate as they were climbing down.

"They're long gone."

"I still don't like the smell of this. We'll keep two men on guard again all night long. You and Eric can take the first watch, Jarvis and me the second, and Fletcher and the marquis the third."

"Zach has been wanting to help out more."

"Tell him it's his job to protect the women if we're attacked again. With Winona in the family way, we have to take extra good care of her."

Eric glanced at Nate. "You're wife is pregnant?"

"Yep."

The Englishman was speechless. He thought of all the hardships they had endured so far, and how Winona had borne them without uttering a single complaint. In all his life he had never known such exceptional people as these, so strong, so self-reliant. What he wouldn't give to be one of them! A germ of an idea sprouted in his brain, an idea so breathtaking, so startling, that he had to go sit down to mull it over.

Later, as Diana Templar strolled past him, she wondered why he looked at her and laughed.

Chapter Thirteen

Nate King awakened with a distinct, uneasy feeling that something was wrong. He lay still for half a minute, listening, sorting the sounds to determine if there were any out of the ordinary. A few crickets were chirping. Close by someone was snoring. He heard someone else toss in their sleep. Since the sky was still dark and the first resplendent rays of sunshine would not appear for perhaps half an hour, the birds had not yet commenced with their morning ritual of singing with boisterous abandon.

Slowly Nate rolled over and surveyed the camp through slitted lids, feigning sleep in case hostile eyes were watching. Winona and Zach were slumbering peacefully to his left, Shakespeare off to his right. Not far from Winona slept Diana Templar. Across the charred remains of the fire lay the giant, Jarvis, and Eric Nash. Only Fletcher and the marquis were missing, and they were both on watch.

Nate shifted position again and gazed toward the horses. Or rather, toward where the string of tethered animals should be, because as he faced in that direction he was shocked to see every last horse was gone. Flabbergasted, he looked right and left, unwilling to accept the testimony of his own eyes. Then he sat bolt upright, grabbed the Hawken, and cautiously rose.

Jarvis snorted and mumbled something in his sleep.

Staying low, Nate moved to the cottonwoods 15 yards away. The first thing he saw was the long, buff-colored rawhide rope that had been stretched between two of the trees now lying on the ground like a stricken snake. It had been cut at both ends. Turning, he walked the length of the rope, trying to make sense of the few tracks plain enough to see in the dim light. That was when he spied the feet.

A pair of black boots was jutting out from behind a nearby thicket.

Dreading what he would find, Nate edged to the thicket. In the dark the large black stain on Fletcher's chest resembled ink more than it did blood, and the wide slit in Fletcher's throat resembled another mouth more than it did the fatal cut made by a razor-sharp knife.

Pivoting, Nate sought sign of the marquis. He didn't raise a cry as yet, because he didn't know if the Blackfeet were still close at hand; doing so might initiate an attack. Bent at the waist, he crept in a circle around the area where the horses had been tied, and in a patch of high grass he nearly tripped over the body.

William Templar, son of the Duke of Graustark, was on his face in the grass, a pair of arrows sticking from the center of his back.

Nate crouched and gently lifted the marquis a few inches for a better look. There was a big welt on Templar's forehead, possibly put there by a war club. He touched a finger to William's neck and was surprised to discover a pulse.

Suddenly, to Nate's rear, there was a footstep. He whirled, bringing the Hawken to bear, his thumb freezing on the hammer when he saw who it was. "Trying to get yourself killed?" he whispered.

Shakespeare nodded at the marquis. "Did they kill him?"

"He's still alive but in a bad way."

"Pity," Shakespeare whispered, and there was no telling if he meant it was a pity the marquis was still alive or a pity the marquis was in a bad way. "Have you had a look-see all around to make sure they're gone?"

"Not yet."

"Then let's get cracking."

It didn't take long thanks to the rapid fading of the night. The horses had been led one at time through the trees to the open prairie, far enough from the camp so the noise wouldn't be heard when they were herded in a bunch to the northwest.

"They're clever devils, I'll say that for them," Shakespeare remarked, on one knee with a hand running lightly over prints he had found. "They must have brought the horses out one at a time so they could keep the critters quiet. Probably took the better part of an hour."

"The four I tangled with, you reckon?" Nate asked.

"Hard to tell, but that would be my guess. By now they're miles off and having a fine laugh at our expense."

"I wonder why they didn't try to kill us in our sleep."

"They didn't want to risk spoiling a good thing. It isn't every day the Blackfeet can steal pretty near thirty prime horses without shedding a little of their blood in the attempt. Why, when they get back to their village they'll be hailed as the best damn horse thieves in the whole Blackfoot nation," Shakespeare said, not without a touch of envy.

"Or there might be another reason," Nate said gravely.

"Such as there are more of the bastards within a day's ride or so, and our four friends plan to get the horses to safety, then come back with reinforcements to finish the job?"

"Could be."

"I had the same notion." Shakespeare stood and frowned. "This is a hell of a note. We'll be picked off like rabbits."

"Not if I can help it," Nate vowed.

Together, they carried William Templar back to camp. Jarvis was just waking up, and at his bellowed oath of surprise their whole party was awake and on their feet. Questions were answered, orders issued, and the next hour was a whirlwind of activity.

Shakespeare, by virtue of prior experience, was best qualified to extract the two arrows from between William's shoulder blades. Diana and Winona assisted. Working carefully, he inserted the tip of his butcher knife, which he had heated until it was red hot in the rekindled fire, into William's flesh, and pried gingerly at the shafts and the arrowheads. The heads were his main worry since they were designed to come loose in the victim's body once the sinews used to fasten the barbed points to the shafts were loosened by warm blood.

Few greenhorns or Easterners realized it, but over half of all arrow wounds where a vital organ was spared, as was the case with William, resulted in death from infection or the poison Indians sometimes liberally applied to the arrowheads. The Blackfeet, Shakespeare knew, were partial to dipping their arrows into dead animals or coating the points with rattlesnake venom, but he had no way of telling if these had been.

It was with exquisite care that the seasoned mountain man dug and prodded and tugged until at long last he succeeded in removing the first shaft intact. Winona mopped Shakespeare's brow as he applied the knife to the second arrow. A pale Diana Templar wiped the blood that trickled out of the wound off her brother's fair skin.

Meanwhile, Jarvis was busy burying Fletcher. Since the others were all busy with pressing needs that had to be accomplished before the Blackfeet returned, he alone stood over the shallow grave, bowed his huge head, and said softly, "So long, mate. You were a right upstanding lad who kept to himself and never used bad language. You were always decent to the birds, and kind to children. I never knew you to get your knickers in a twist, not once." He paused to cough. "I'm not one of God's own, so I don't know quite what else to say except I hope you reach those Pearly Gates."

During the burial, Nate, Zach, and Eric Nash were occupied with hastily preparing a cache for the supplies they would be unable to take with them now that they were deprived of their horses. A case of extra rifles, spare ammunition, and black powder and various other provisions had to be hidden so the Blackfeet couldn't get their hands on so much plunder. Since they lacked proper digging utensils, they had to make do with broken branches and flat stones, scooping and rooting and excavating as best they were able until they had a roughly oval pit into which they placed everything. The dirt was heaped back on top, then leaves and bits of broken limbs were gathered from under the trees and strewn on top of the dirt.

When they were finished, Nate stepped back and critically inspected their handiwork. To a casual observer the cache was not readily noticeable. An alert Blackfoot might notice some irregularities and poke around the spot, but that couldn't be helped. He went to the fire, arriving just as Shakespeare, with a cry of joy, removed the second shaft.

"Did you get both heads out?" Nate asked.

"Sure did. I'll cauterize him while you rig up a litter."

"Cauterize?" Diana Templar said, watching King and the other two walk off. "How do you propose to do that, may I ask?"

"Watch and learn, little lady," Shakespeare answered. With a quick snap of his wrists, he broke the arrow off below the point and tossed the head aside. Then, turning, his hand curled around the owl feather fletching, he held the broken end out and let the fire lap at the wood. Soon the tip of the shaft was in flames. Then, with a quick motion, he swung around to the marquis, braced one hand beside the two wounds, and inserted the flaming tip into one of the holes.

"Oh, my God!" Diana exclaimed, covering her nose and her mouth with her hand when the pungent odor of burning flesh assailed her. She saw her brother twist and groan, but he didn't revive.

Working methodically, Shakespeare repeated the procedure with the other wound, searing the openings shut and stopping the bleeding. With a sigh he threw the arrow from him and slowly stood. "There you go, ma'am. If his brain isn't addled by the blow he received, and if there wasn't poison on those arrowheads, and if the wounds don't get infected, he should recover."

"Dear William," Diana said, tenderly resting her hand on his hot cheek. "I fear he has the beginning of a fever."

"Check him now and then," Shakespeare advised. "If it gets worse, then he's infected and we'll have to take special steps to pull him through."

"I can't thank you enough."

"Don't thank me yet. We're not out of the woods yet," Shakespeare said. He hurried to where Nate and the others were constructing a crude litter. "Need a hand?"

"Join in," Nate said as he delivered a stroke of his tomahawk to a slender sapling. In short order he had a half dozen, and these, in combination with a pair of long, straight, stout limbs that Shakespeare collected and a sufficient quantity of rawhide cord brought by Zach, enabled him to have the litter put together before the sun cleared the eastern horizon.

Blankets and a robe were piled on the litter, then William Templar was placed on top of them and another robe was thrown over him to keep him warm. Jarvis and Eric Nash offered to carry the marquis during the early going.

Nate had everyone pack along as many parfleches as they could comfortably carry. Cords were looped to the bags so they could sling the parfleches over their shoulders and thus leave their hands free to meet whatever emergency might arise. Everyone had a rifle. Everyone had two pistols, even the women and Zach. Everyone brought along a powder horn and an ammo pouch.

In single file they marched to the northeast, staying close to the Yellowstone River where there was plenty of cover. Nate walked at the forefront, Shakespeare brought up the rear. They maintained a brisk pace, aware they might not have much time to put as much distance as they could between their camp and themselves. If the Blackfeet did come back in force, they had to be far away.

The sun climbed steadily higher. The river widened, leading Shakespeare to announce, "We're near the junction!" Midday found them at the point where the Yellowstone merged with the bigger Missouri, and here the combined river widened even more as it flowed eastward across the plains.

Nate called a halt. Hard biscuits were passed out. Munching on his, he knelt by the litter and held his palm to William Templar's damp brow; the skin was hot enough to melt butter. "His fever is much worse," he declared.

"What do we do?" Diana asked anxiously. "He needs rest. I don't think we should move him until the fever goes down."

"We can't stop yet," Nate responded, and glanced at Winona. "We'll have to keep our eyes peeled for any roots or plants that will help."

"And acorns," Winona reminded him.

"What good can they do?" Diana asked.

Nate answered her. "You take a couple of handfuls and boil them for a few hours. The water helps fight infection." He scanned the nearest vegetation. "But I haven't seen any oak trees hereabouts."

"Please don't let him die. He means everything to me."

"We'll do what we can," Nate promised. Rising, he walked back to where Shakespeare stood, studying the country they had traversed, and said in a low voice so none of the others would overhear, "What about Fort Union?"

Established in 1828 as a trading post by the American Fur Company, Fort Union was situated on the north bank of the Missouri about three miles above the convergence with the Yellowstone. Manned by trappers and visited regularly by friendly Indians, it was the only refuge within hundreds of miles.

"I thought about that," Shakespeare responded. "But those ornery Blackfeet would expect for us to head there and they might be waiting somewhere along the way. They might not even have gone back to our camp."

"True," Nate said. "Maybe one of us should go for help then. We'd stand the best chance of eluding them."

"And leave just three men to watch over the women, your boy, and the royal pain in the hind end?"

"You go. I'll stay."

"If you sure that's what you want. But keep in mind it'll take me the better part of the day to get there, what with having to watch out for the Blackfeet every step of the way and then having to swim the damn river. And I'm not much of a swimmer. The earliest I could possibly make it back would be sometime tomorrow, probably late tomorrow at that."

Nate hesitated. If Shakespeare was right about the Blackfeet guessing their intent, then chances were slim his friend would reach the fort. Besides that, with Shakespeare gone the burden of responsibility for taking care of the others fell on his shoulders alone, and he could hardly lead them and keep an eye on their back trail at the same time.

"If you want my opinion," Shakespeare said, sensing Nate's indecision, "we should just keep on going. Pretty soon we'll be close to Mandan country, and the Blackfeet will think twice before following us that far. The Mandans and them have been feuding for years."

"But the marquis—"

"Which is more important, his life or the lives of the rest of us? Because I feel it in my gut that

if we head for Fort Union, the Blackfeet will sure
as blazes cut us off."

The decision had to be made quickly. Nodding,
Nate returned to the head of the line and gestured
for them to head out. He hugged the shoreline,
his eyes lingering often on the north shore on
the off chance that other Blackfeet might appear,
spot his small party, and ride along the opposite
side until they were far ahead, then cross and
wait in ambush. No Indians appeared, although
several animals showed themselves on his side:
white-tailed deer, rabbits, a weasel, and a beaver
out in the water.

At the rear of the little group Shakespeare constantly stopped to scour the land behind them.
Sooner or later the Blackfeet would appear; he
knew it as surely as he did the sun would set
that evening and rise the next day. If his hunch
was correct and they were lying in wait near the
fort, eventually it would occur to those buzzards
that they had blundered and their quarry wasn't
coming. They'd head for the camp, pick up the
trail, and practically kill their horses catching up.
He had to spot the warriors early enough to give
his companions time to conceal themselves. If he
was negligent, the Blackfeet might be on them
before they could get off a shot.

Toward the middle of the afternoon Nate called
another halt to check on William Templar. The
marquis was worse off, his fever consuming him
like a wildfire. Diana held her brother's head in
her lap while Winona let some cold water trickle
down his parched throat. All William did was
mumble and toss his head every so often as if
in the throes of delirium.

As Nate stood silently observing, Shakespeare came up to him.

"You know, son, I've been using my noggin, and it's occurred to me that we're going about this all wrong."

"How do you figure?"

Shakespeare smiled and wagged his rifle at the Missouri River, which had broadened until it was close to a mile wide. "We'd make better time and leave no tracks at all if we took to the water."

"Sure. We'll sprout feathers and pretend we're ducks."

"Mercutio it was and Mercutio it still is."

"What?"

"I have two words for you," Shakespeare said, smiling craftily. "Bull boats."

Nate reacted as if someone had smacked him with the flat of a tomahawk. He recoiled, glanced at the river, then at McNair, and a matching smile creased his mouth. "We'd only need two if we crammed everyone in real tight."

"That's right. And have you noticed the willow trees we've been passing for the better part of an hour?"

Elation and hope pumped through Nate's veins. They just might make it! Except for one little hitch. "We haven't seen any buffalo in a long time."

"Then it behooves us to keep our eyes peeled."

"Behooves?"

"Sometimes, young sir, your ignorance is appalling. Get thee to a nunnery."

"A what?" Nate responded, thinking that his friend couldn't possibly have said what Nate thought he just said.

"Give a yell if you see any," Shakespeare replied,

and cackling like a madman he strolled to the end of the line once again.

They made slower progress once their journey was resumed. Everyone was fatigued. Jarvis held up well despite having borne the litter for so many hours, but Eric Nash faltered and kept stumbling, so Nate took his place until the blazing sun perched on the western rim of the earth.

In a secluded clearing they camped, positioning the litter near the river so water could be conveniently brought to William at regular intervals. The fire was kept low. Nate took the first watch, Shakespeare the second, Jarvis the third, and Eric Nash the watch prior to daylight.

Before dawn painted the heavens they were all up and on their way, the giant and the artist again bearing the litter. The previous evening Winona had dug up a root and concocted a tea that was forced into William although he balked at its bitter taste. His fever abated but did not break entirely. Diana hovered near the litter, attentive to her sibling's every sound.

Their steps were not as brisk this day, yet they made good time. The last of their biscuits were consumed as they hiked. Periodically game appeared on the prairie to their right, either deer or antelope or wolves, but always at a respectful distance, and there were never any buffalo.

Halfway through the morning, as Nate looked up after having his attention diverted by a squirrel that had scurried across his path, he spied a pair of big coyotes 70 yards off. They were just sitting there, watching him. Instantly he halted and held up his arm so the others would do the same. Twisting, he used sign language to inform

Shakespeare what he saw, and in seconds the white-haired mountain man was at his side.

"They're not wolves, but they'll do."

"Which one do you want?"

"The one on the left. But we should get closer."

Nate and Shakespeare advanced slowly so as not to scare the coyotes off before they were so close they couldn't miss, both holding their rifles tucked to their shoulders and cocked. Nate hoped he hadn't accidentally underestimated the amount of black powder the last time he'd loaded his rifle, as insufficient powder resulted in a rainbow sort of trajectory at distances over 50 yards and made accurate aiming virtually impossible.

The coyotes were not about to let two humans get much nearer. When the men were still 40 yards off, they rose and padded southward, walking slowing, the male in front of the female, their gaze riveted to the humans.

"We ain't got no choice," Shakespeare declared, taking deliberate aim.

Nate imitated his friend, sighting on the larger animal, at an invisible spot just behind its front shoulder. Tensing his left arm, he held the barrel steady, said, "Now!" and stroked the trigger.

Twin retorts cracked across the plain. The male coyote leaped straight up in the air, lips curled back over his pointed teeth, and yowled, falling silent by the time he fell to the ground. In contrast, the female keeled over right where she was, twitched a few times, and was still.

Nate sprinted toward them, drawing a flintlock. Another shot, however, was not needed; both coyotes were as dead as dead could be. He hefted one to his shoulder, McNair took the other, and they returned to their party.

"Are *those* what we are supposed to eat this evening?" Diana asked, her nose puckered. "I'd much rather have venison."

"These aren't for eating," Nate said, throwing his burden down and drawing his butcher knife. He looked at his wife and son. "Lend us a hand, would you?"

Between the four of them they soon had both coyotes completely skinned. Since they could not afford the time necessary to properly cure the hides, they simply cracked both skulls, removed the brains, and then rubbed the brains over the inner surface of each hide so the pelts would retain some of their natural suppleness once they dried.

Diana Templar had to turn away halfway through the skinning and gasp for air to keep from being ill.

The first one done, Nate held his trophy aloft and chuckled. "Now all we need are some buffalo."

Little did he know he would get his wish much sooner than he anticipated.

Chapter Fourteen

It was almost two o'clock by the position of the sun when Nate, who was a dozen yards in the lead, looked northward across the sluggishly flowing Missouri as the faintest of rumbling sounds carried to his keen ears. Puzzled, he scrutinized the other shore, which at that point was much closer than it had been previously because the river had temporarily narrowed. He saw birds start up in fright from the trees and take wing.

Mystified, Nate took several steps toward the water. The rumbling was growing louder, almost but not quite like the noise of far distant thunder. He felt he should know what caused it, but the answer eluded him until from the back of the line came a fiery yell.

"Get moving or we're all done for! Run like your lives depend on it!"

At the same moment Nate noticed the state

of the earth underfoot and saw the countless hoofprints, some old, some made recently. "Buffalo!" he exclaimed, stunned. "This is a buffalo crossing!"

Quickly Nate ran to the litter and took over from Eric Nash. Jarvis broke into a shuffling run. Nate kept pace, Winona and Zach staying by his side.

Shakespeare assumed the lead. Diana and Eric shadowed him. Everyone had their eyes on the north side of the Missouri, and it wasn't long before a great roiling line of enormous dark shapes materialized, giving the impression the horizon itself was in motion, rolling toward them like a living wave.

Actually, there was a living wave, but it was composed of muscle and bone and thick, hairy hides. Thousands upon thousands of buffalo were on the move, a massive herd of the largest animals in North America, the bulls standing six feet at the shoulders and weighing close to two thousand pounds, the cows only slightly smaller with a shoulder height of five feet and a total weight of one thousand pounds. Their powerful legs flying, they surged toward the river, toward the crossing they had used for generations.

On the other side of the Missouri, Nate's heart raced faster than his feet. He tried to judge how far the line of buffalo extended and whether he and the others could get beyond that spot before the herd reached them, but the distance prevented him from making a fair assessment.

William Templar, jostled by the swaying and bouncing of the litter, was muttering, tossing, and turning. Once he unaccountably laughed.

The rumbling became a mighty thundering as thousands of hoofs drummed the earth. Never slowing, neither looking to right nor left, the leading row of behemoths drew ever nearer the opposite shore.

By the herd's speed, Nate suspected they had been stampeded, although by what he had no idea. Truth was, he didn't much care. All that mattered was getting to safety before the buffalo swept down upon them. There would be no stopping the single-minded brutes. Shouting would not do it, guns could not do it. Their sole hope was to get past the crossing.

Every minute was an eternity. Nate ran and ran and didn't seemed to be making any headway. The end of the line of buffalo still hadn't appeared. He realized they might not make it, and gulped.

Much too soon, the leading rows of buffalo came to the brink of the north shore and plunged into the water. A writhing, grunting, bellowing mass, they swam for the south side, buoyant monsters, their heads, humps, and tails remaining above the surface.

"We'll never make it!" Shakespeare yelled, confirming Nate's conviction.

Then, as Nate's lungs labored and he breathed in ragged spurts, he spied their possible salvation ahead, a small area where high winds or some other upheaval had felled dozens of closely packed trees, resulting in a terrific logjam right at the water's edge. The thickly intermingled fallen trees formed an imposing barrier 30 feet wide and ten feet high. "There!" he cried. "Take cover there!"

Shakespeare had been marking the advance of the approaching herd. He faced front, took in the situation at a glance, and hustled Diana and Eric behind the logjam.

Nate and the others joined them moments later, moving to the very middle of the logs where the shelter was best. There, the marquis was deposited next to the lowest log.

"You can't intend to stay here!" Diana protested. "We'll be smashed to pieces!"

"Get down!" Shakespeare said, shoving her low and crouching beside her.

They huddled together, Winona sheltering Zach with her own body and Nate sheltering her. Jarvis had adopted a protective stance over the marquis. Eric glanced at Lady Templar but made no move toward her.

Through cracks between the logs they could see the front ranks of buffalo bearing down on them. Dark eyes wide, heads upthrust, the powerful beasts churned the water into white foam. The din they created was tremendous.

"Brace yourselves!" Shakespeare warned. "And whatever you do, stay close to these logs!"

No one needed the advice; they were not about to move an inch. Hugging the logjam, they waited in tense expectation, listening to the splashing and snorting of the adults and the bawling of the young calves. It sounded as if the river itself was rising up against them, and just when they thought the clamor could get no louder, it did.

The herd reached the south shore. Without slowing the buffalo rose from the water and hurtled toward the prairie, shoulder to hairy shoulder, their iron hoofs pummeling the ground in a continuous booming roar. The air itself vibrated as if pulsing with life, while the ground shook as if in the grip of an earthquake.

Nate pressed tight to Winona's back, his arms around both her and Zach. Out of the corner of his eye he saw Diana Templar's mouth wide in a scream of sheer terror, but he couldn't hear her for the riotous, near-deafening crescendo of incredible sound created by the tumultuous buffaloes as they swept past on either side of the logjam. He felt himself shaking. He felt Winona and Zach shaking. He glimpsed the logs trembling in a fit of ague. A pungent odor tingled his nostrils.

Thick clouds of dust swirled into the air, forming a choking cloak that obscured everything. Nate coughed violently, then held his face close to Winona's hair so he wouldn't inhale as many of the fine particles. The logs in front of them swayed and jerked forward, threatening to crush them. He imagined what would happen if the buffalo smashed into the barrier instead of going around, and steeled himself to do what he could to spare his loved ones from harm.

To the right there was an immense crash attended by a barely audible wavering shriek.

Nate dared not investigate. He clasped his family close and prayed as he had never prayed before for deliverance from their ordeal. Something struck the back of his left leg, and for a few harrowing seconds he thought that the buffalo were on them. But he wasn't struck again. Rigid as a rail, he waited and waited for the herd to pass.

There were repeated loud smashing noises. There were crunching noises. Snapping noises.

It sounded like the whole world was being pulverized to bits and pieces, being demolished by an irresistible force as elemental as a tornado or an earthquake. For minutes that seemed like hours the bedlam went on and on and on.

Then, of a sudden, the uproar diminished, the smashing and crunching and snapping stopped, and the sound of the hammering hoofs began to fade to the south.

"The bull boats!" Shakespeare shouted through the hovering cloud of dust. "Now, Hamlet, now!"

Nate knew this might be their only opportunity. If they let it pass, the Blackfeet might be on them before they came on more buffalo. He gripped his Hawken firmly, said into Winona's ear "Stay here!" whirled and raced after the herd. It was impossible to see for more than a half dozen yards, but the further he ran, the more the dust thinned, so by the time he reached the edge of the flattened grass he could see for 50 yards or so.

Forty yards away was the trailing edge of the herd consisting mainly of cows and calves and old bulls whose age was taking its inexorable toll on their speed and stamina.

To the left a rifle boomed, and out on the plain a shaggy bull pitched headfirst to the ground and rolled over twice before coming to rest.

Nate whipped the Hawken to his shoulder, cocked the hammer, and took careful aim on another fleeing bull. He would much rather have shot it from the side so he could better judge where its vital organs were located, but he had no choice. Mentally compensating for the angle, he took a deep breath, held it, and squeezed off the shot.

In a whirl of limbs and tail the bull tumbled, sliding a dozen feet until it came to a lurching stop. It tried to rise, got its head off the ground, then sank down and went limp.

Lowering the Hawken, Nate promptly began reloading. As he uncapped his powder horn he glanced around and saw Shakespeare already taking a bead. Momentarily his mentor's rifle spat lead and smoke, and a third buffalo went down. "I thought we only needed two hides," he called.

"I got to thinking," Shakespeare responded. "The marquis will need to lay down, and that Jarvis will about take up a whole boat all by his lonesome."

"Too bad about those coyotes," Nate mentioned.

At that instant, from the logjam, came Winona's upraised, tense voice. "Nate! Quickly! We need you!"

In a flash Nate spun and was off, not even bothering to finish reloading in his haste to reach his wife. He imagined the worst—a straggling bull had spied them crouched behind the felled trees and was about to attack. Seconds later, he saw the reason for her cry.

One of the big logs near the top of the tangle had been dislodged. It would have fallen directly onto William Templar had not Jarvis apparently seen it dropping and shielded the unconscious marquis with his own body. The log had caught Jarvis in the chest, knocking him over, and now the giant was flat on his back with the log on his chest and his legs on top of the marquis.

Winona, Zach, Eric, and Diana were vainly striving to move the heavy weight off Jarvis, who lay stunned, unable to assist.

Shakespeare was only steps behind Nate. Setting their rifles aside, they each took an end of the log, letting the others apply themselves to the middle.

"When I give the word," Nate said, bending over and hooking his hands under the rough bark. He bunched his shoulder muscles, steeled his legs, and swept the others with a glance to see if they were ready. "All right. Lift."

The strain was such that Nate's face turned a beet red and his veins bulged in his neck. Slowly, though, the log rose. Once they had it off the giant they had to beware lest the log slip and crash down onto the giant's unprotected face. Shifting slowly, some of them grunting from the exertion, they levered the log clear of Jarvis, and at a nod from Nate released their collective hold.

A loud thud heralded their success.

Winona was immediately at the giant's side, examining him to gauge the severity of the blow he had received. Her deft fingers probed his chest and his arms, and at length she looked up at Nate. "None of his bones are broken but he will be very sore for many sleeps."

"If it had been anyone else," Eric commented, "they'd be dead. Their ribs would have been caved in."

"I'll get some water and revive him," Diana offered.

"Go with her, Zach," Nate directed.

"The river is only twenty feet from where we stand," Diana said in the act of turning. "I'll be fine."

"Go with her anyway, Zach," Nate repeated. "And keep alert for Blackfeet."

"Like a hawk, Pa," the boy pledged. Dutifully, he trailed after Lady Templar, his long rifle clasped at his waist, his eyes darting every which way.

Winona had risen and stepped over to Nate. "How many buffalo did you shoot?"

"Three. We'll be real busy the next few hours."

She glanced down at the rolled hides lying near the litter and echoed his own sentiments by remarking, "It is unfortunate we did not run into the buffalo before we shot them."

"They won't go to waste," Nate said. "Zach's never hunted buffalo that way. I'll take him out the first chance I get."

Eric Nash had overheard. The Englishman stared at the coyote pelts, then at the frontiersman and his wife. "I don't understand. What did you plan to do with those skins?"

"Buffalo can be right temperamental," Nate said. "Sometimes they'll let you get close to them; other times they'll run off as soon as they see you or get a whiff of your scent. But they never pay any mind to coyotes, so Shakespeare and I were going to throw on a hide and crawl right up to the first buffaloes we saw."

"How ingenious."

"It's an old Indian trick," Shakespeare threw in. "Sometimes they use coyotes pelts, sometimes wolf pelts. Years back I knew a young warrior who thought he'd try something different and wrapped himself in a panther skin." He laughed lightly and shook his head.

"What happened?" Eric prompted.

"The buffalo turned on him and tried to gore him to death. He was damned lucky he got away with his own hide intact."

The next moment their conversation was interrupted by Zach, who raced around the end of the barrier and announced, "Smoke, Pa. To the northwest."

Nate lost no time in hurrying to the river. Sure enough, a thin grayish-white spiral indicated there was a campfire about two miles from the Missouri. But who had made it? As he watched, two more columns of smoke appeared. Soon a third was added, all within the same general area. Now he knew what had spooked the buffalo herd.

"Could they be white men?" Diana asked hopefully.

"No," Nate said. "They're Blackfeet. A whole village of them. The warriors went after the buffalo a while ago, which is why the critters stampeded. Now the women and children are setting up to butcher the carcasses. They'll be camped there for days."

"They're too bloody close to us for my liking," Eric said "What if some of them come to the river for water?"

"They probably will." Nate faced his son. "Zach, while we're making the bull boats it'll be up to you to keep watch. Stay under cover. If you see any Blackfeet, make tracks to tell us."

"I won't let you down," the boy declared, squaring his slender shoulders.

In quick order they brought Jarvis around, insured he was unharmed, and carried the litter out onto the prairie where Nate, Shakespeare, and Winona drew their butcher knives to tackle the first dead buffalo. Working as a team, they expertly skinned the great beast from head to tail, leaving the latter on the hide.

Eric Nash was a fascinated observer of everything they did. He noted every cut, how they slit down the back of the hind legs and then made a straight slash from the tail to the chin down the middle of the belly. He saw how they cut the front legs, and then how the hide was peeled from the body like an orange skin from an orange. Drawing his own knife, he moved forward and said, "Can I help out with the next one?"

Nate, his hands and forearms covered with blood and gore, glanced up. A slow smile curled his mouth. "Be our guest. Just try not to stick one of us by mistake."

Skinning the second buffalo took longer because Eric slowed them down, but neither Nate, Winona, or Shakespeare objected. Nate was secretly pleased at the enthusiasm the Englishman showed, and corrected him where necessary.

When, in due course, the job was done, Eric stepped back with a childish grin and held his arms up to inspect the fresh blood and bits of tendon and flesh sticking to his forearms and upturned sleeves. Breaking into laughter, he waved his arms toward Diana and said. "Do you see? I'm virtually a mountain man!"

Diana turned her nose up and sniffed, "I see. And I think you're a sorry sight."

Eric kept on laughing. "I say, if I don't get those buckskins soon, I'll reek to high heaven."

"I will have them done in four or five sleeps," Winona promised.

Nate was already on his way to the last bull. He

hadn't known that his wife had lugged the half-made clothes along when they fled from their camp, but it was just like her, he mused, to bear the extra weight if it meant helping someone else out.

The third buffalo was skinned swiftly. All three hides were stretched out, and while Winona scraped them clean both Nate and Shakespeare sought out willow trees along the Missouri and stripped off enough branches for the frames. Since they were all keenly appreciative that time was critical, they worked much faster than they ordinarily would have, and by evening had finished the bull boats to their satisfaction.

Eric, Jarvis, and even Diana Templar lent a hand. It was the giant who dragged two of the completed boats to the river's edge. Eric took the third.

"Anything?" Nate asked his son as he tossed an armload of parfleches and the coyote skins into one of the boats.

"Not a sign of a soul, Pa," Zach answered. "I saw a few deer come for a drink, and once a grizzly."

"Are we going to launch these craft now?" Diana inquired somewhat nervously. She gazed at the setting sun, which had painted the western sky with a riotous blaze of colors, then at the bull boats, and lastly at the swirling current. Everyone present could read her thoughts. She didn't trust the boats a whit.

"I reckon not," Shakespeare answered. "If the ones who are after us haven't come by now, they won't until tomorrow sometime. Indians don't much like to travel at night."

Right there on the bank they made camp, dividing up the chores as they normally did with one exception. Nate returned to the buffalo carcasses to slice off enough thick steaks to satisfy their hunger. But he wasn't the only one interested in eating. Five gray wolves had been drawn to the remains by the scent, and were now tearing into the buffalo Nate had slain.

On spying him, three of the wolves slunk away from the kill. Their fellows were not so meekly disposed, and stood next to the grisly bulk with their teeth bared and feral growls rumbling from their throats.

Nate didn't bother contesting their right to feast on the carcass, not when there were two other buffalo to choose from. He had reloaded the rifle and had the pistols at his belt, so he was ready should the pack prove quarrelsome, which he doubted would happen. By and large wolves avoided conflict with humans. The only times he'd seen this violated had been when the wolves were nearly starved or driven to madness.

The pack watched Nate hack off a half-dozen large pieces. One wolf snarled at him as he departed, and when he was almost to the river they all resumed feeding in a frenzy.

A fire was crackling in the shelter of several cottonwoods. William Templar's litter had been aligned close to it and a robe draped over him up to his chin. Diana knelt beside her brother looking worried.

"How is his fever?" Nate asked after giving the meat to Winona.

Diana forced a smile. "A bit better. The medicine your wife gave him has done wonders. What was the name of those roots she used again?"

Nate told her the Shoshone name, adding, "There is no word for the plant in English. Doctors back in the States have never heard of it." He leaned his rifle against a tree and sat down with his back to the trunk. "There are a lot of cures the Indians use that white people know nothing about, which isn't surprising since the Indians have been living off the land for ages. They know all about the plants found here. They know which roots, stems, and leaves can be used to treat all manner of diseases, and I've seen them cure ailments that would have proven fatal east of the Mississippi."

"The way you talk about white people sometimes," Diana said, "gives one the impression you don't consider yourself one of us any longer. Do you? Or have you gone totally Indian?"

The question surprised Nate since he'd not been aware of any attitude toward whites on his part and had never given the matter much attention. "I'm an adopted Shoshone and I'm right proud of the fact," he responded.

"Does that mean you're white or an Indian?"

"Some of both, I suppose," Nate said.

"And you truly *like* being the way you are?"

"I've never been happier."

Lady Templar shifted to stare at Eric Nash, who stood ten yards off with Zach watching the antics of ducks out on the broad river. "Someone else is acting happier than I can ever remember, and I don't like it."

"Why the blazes not?"

"Don't hold it against me for saying this, Nate, but he's an artist, not a ruddy frontiersman like you and Mr. McNair. If he's not careful he'll get in deep trouble. Some people are not meant to be anything other than what they always have been."

"You're making a mountain out of a molehill," Nate told her. "What harm can it do?"

"Time will tell."

Chapter Fifteen

Nate was on watch when the war party came. He'd volunteered for the final stint of the night, between roughly three A.M. and dawn, since that was when the Blackfeet had struck before and he guessed they might do the same again.

Stars still dominated the heavens, although to the east a pale glow signified they would soon be gone, when Nate, walking along the shore with his Hawken slanted across his shoulder, detected the shriek of a startled bird to the west. Ordinarily such cries would not arouse much interest since birds were forever being stalked by predators, but this time Nate looked and saw a flock of grosbeaks take wing. He identified them by their distinctive, shrill calls of *p-teer, p-teer, p-teer*.

Nate figured the birds were a hundred yards distant, possibly more. Crouching, he scanned the shoreline, and was soon rewarded for his diligence by spying the black outlines of several figures moving slowly eastward. They would be on the camp in less than two minutes.

Turning, Nate dashed to Shakespeare and nudged his friend once, all it took for the mountain man's eyes to snap open. "Company calling," Nate whispered. "We have to get everyone into the boats."

Quickly they went from sleeper to sleeper, rousing each quietly. The last to be awakened was Diana Templar. Nate sank to one knee, lightly touched her shoulder, and shook gently, as he had done with Winona and Zach. Both of them had simply woken up without saying a word; they knew better than to make any noise. But not so Diana. The instant his fingers contacted her body, she let out a screech and sat bolt upright, eyes wide in fright.

"What?" she blurted out, yelling. "What is it?"

"Hush!" Nate said, clamping a hand over her mouth before she could compound her mistake. Putting his lips to her ear, he whispered urgently, "Blackfeet. Get in the same bull boat as Winona. Hurry."

Swiftly, the parfleches were loaded. Jarvis and Nate carried the litter to the water's edge. There, Jarvis lifted the marquis into a boat in which Shakespere waited, then stepped in beside them. They were cramped for room, but Nate, Shakespeare, and Winona had decided before retiring that they should each be in separate boats since the greenhorns had no experience handling the crafts and they did.

The previous evening Nate had given instructions in how to properly handle the shallow boats. Long, wide branches had been chopped from trees and trimmed down to make serviceable poles for steering and paddling. Pieces of wood had been tied to the tails. At a question from Eric Nash, Nate had explained that the tails of the buffalo were left on the hides for that very purpose as they stopped the crafts from spinning.

Now Nate handed a pole to Jarvis and gave the bobbing boat a shove. He moved to the next one, which contained Winona, Diana, and Zach, and did the same. Only when they were safely away did he step to the last boat, place his Hawken inside, and press both palms to the buffalo hide to push.

"Behind you!" Eric Nash shouted.

A glance revealed a dozen or more silent, ghostly shapes flitting toward them, coming along the shore and from the trees. When they realized they had been spotted, the Blackfeet uttered a savage chorus of whoops and screeches and bounded ahead, each anxious to be the first one to count coup.

Nate's shoulders rippled as he applied his might to the boat and sent it sliding out into the current. He held tight to the top edge and let himself be hauled into the water. Then, by hooking a leg over the rim, he slid in beside the Englishman. None too soon.

The four fleetest warriors had reached the spot from which the craft had been launched. One let fly with an arrow, the shaft narrowly missing Eric's head. Two others plunged into the river and swam after the boat, which was not yet traveling fast enough to outdistance them.

But Nate wasn't worried. The swimmers had eight or nine yards to cover. Drawing both pistols, he extended his arms, and was about to send the Blackfeet into eternity when an abrupt shift in the current caused the bull boat to swing around toward shore. The very next second the craft righted itself and floated on downriver, but by then the damage had been done. The unexpected movement had pitched Nate to one side, on top of Nash, and before Nate could scramble to his knees one of the warriors reached the side of the boat.

Nate saw the brave rise up, dripping wet, a war club in the man's grasp. Snaking a hand out, he leveled the pistol at the warrior's forehead, then fired.

The ball ripped into the Blackfoot's cranium and sent him flying backwards into the river with a loud accompanying splash.

Meanwhile, the other warrior had caught hold of the craft and was working his way around to the far side so he could get at the two white men from the rear.

Unaware of this, Nate pushed onto his right knee and saw the majority of the Blackfeet moving along the shore, paralleling the course of the boat, which was now 30 feet from the water's edge and gaining distance rapidly. He heard an arrow buzz overhead and ducked low, his eyes at the rim, seeking some sign of the other warrior who had dived into the Missouri. His perplexity was intense when he saw no one.

Eric Nash had struggled to a sitting posture and grabbed one of the poles. Leaning to his left, he paddled as he'd been taught, in short, clean strokes.

"Where is the other one?" Nate wondered aloud.

"Maybe he knew he couldn't reach us in time and swam back to land," Eric opined.

"No Blackfoot ever gave up so easily," Nate disagreed, glancing at the artist. Behind Nash the Blackfoot surged into view, a tomahawk held high in the air. So instantaneous was Nate's reaction that a ball cored the warrior's brain before Nate quite realized he had fired his other flintlock.

From the bank came howls of rage.

Grabbing the second pole, Nate threw his weight into paddling and steered the boat further out. Ahead were the dark silhouettes of the other two boats. The current increased, adding to their speed, soon carrying them beyond the reach of arrows or lances.

A golden halo crowned the eastern sky, a halo that expanded to become a belt of yellow, which in turn expanded into the glory of a new day as the sun peeked out over the world, imbuing the surface of the Missouri with a fiery hue that lent the river the appearance of molten lava.

Nate looked back twice. The first time, the Blackfeet were in persistent if futile pursuit. The second, the war party had halted and was screaming insults. Even if they went back for horses, they had no hope of getting anywhere near the boats without being picked off, and they knew it.

"We did it!" Eric cried.

"But we're not out of danger yet," Nate informed him. "We're not quite in Mandan country. For the next twenty miles we always have to be on our guard for more Blackfeet."

"If I never see another one again my life will be complete," Eric muttered.

Traveling on the flat, smooth surface was like floating on a sea of glass. They held the boat a quarter of a mile from land, and stayed well behind the others so that they would have time to avert a collision should one of the leaders hit a snag.

For the first time in days Nate could relax, and he felt the tension drain from him like water from a sieve. During a tranquil spell, while Eric guided the boat alone, he leaned back and reloaded his pistols.

Nash glanced at the trapper repeatedly. He had made up his mind to bring up a subject dear and near to his heart, yet he had refrained for fear of seeming an idiot. Now, taking a breath, he declared, "This is nothing to do with you, but there is a question I need to ask."

"Go on."

"What would you say if I told you that I want to stay in this country when the Templars leave?"

"Your life is your own."

"But do you think I can make a go of it? There's no joy for me in England anymore, not after having experienced the thrill of living like you do."

Nate adjusted his ammo pouch and powder horn, stalling so he might consider how best to respond. Uppermost in his thoughts were the comments made by Diana Templar. "What will you do to live?" he asked with a grin. "Take up trapping beaver?"

"Hardly. I don't know the first thing about the trade. Somehow I'd like to continue as an artist, although how I can do that while living in the wilderness is beyond me at the moment."

"Some other painters have gone around making portraits of the Indians and buffalo and such," Nate said.

"I recall hearing about some of them. Even saw a little of their work," Eric said, his expression reflective. "One is a man named Catlin, I believe, from Philadelphia, who has done more than any-one else. They say he brings the Indians to life as no one can."

"I heard tell he nearly got himself scalped."

"How?"

"He paid the Sioux a visit. They're none too friendly to most whites, but they let him stay with them a while and paint portraits. One day he painted a prominent warrior. Some other Sioux were watching, and one of them poked fun at the portrait. Naturally, the warrior didn't like it much, and the next thing Catlin knew there were warriors going at one another tooth and nail. The warrior he had painted was killed and Catlin barely got out of the village alive."

"Yet he kept on painting," Eric said softly. "And there is another man, a Swiss by the name of Karl Bodmer. He visited the frontier with a German prince named Maximilian and brought back paintings that captivated Europe."

"I didn't know about him," Nate said.

Eric didn't respond. Absorbed in serious delib-erations, he paddled mechanically, hardly aware his arms were moving. If, he asked himself, Catlin and Bodmer could make a record of Indians and wilderness life in general, why couldn't he do the same? Only he would do a more thorough job. They had only worked here and there as they traveled about; so much more remained to be done, and he was just the man to do it.

Nate could see the Englishman was deep in thought and he didn't know what to make of it. He hoped Diana wasn't right, and that Nash wouldn't make a grave mistake he'd long regret. To give up one's whole life and start over in another country was a big step for anyone to take. For Nash, who was accustomed to mingling with nobility and the very rich, the change would be drastic.

Picking up his pole, Nate bent his arms to rowing. He smiled at Zach when the boy looked back at him and waved. Later Winona did the same. In the lead boat Shakespeare and Jarvis were making rapid headway despite the craft being burdened by the giant's great weight and the unconscious marquis.

As always, Nate kept a lookout on the two shores, his main concern being that they would meet a band of Blackfeet with canoes or bull boats of their own, a slim prospect since the Blackfeet were not known to travel often on the waterways. Gradually the sun climbed and reached its midday zenith. A few dark clouds materialized on the western horizon, to the north of the Missouri, and sailed eastward.

Nate hoped they would find one of the Mandan villages soon. There were several, exactly how many he didn't know, strung out on a long stretch of river. Each village, Shakespeare had informed him, was headed by two leaders, one a war chief, the second a man who oversaw everyday peacetime affairs, while over the whole nation presided a single grand chief.

Unique to the Mandans was their love of farming. They were the only tribe Nate knew of who routinely cultivated the soil. The women did, anyway. The men, as in most tribes, were more involved with warfare, buffalo hunting, and religious ceremonies.

Nate wondered if the Mandan women were as beautiful as everyone claimed. Trappers and traders who had visited them were all unanimous in their insistence that Mandan women possessed physical charms few could rival. Crow, Flathead, and Shoshone women were also noted for their lovely features, but the Mandans were supposedly the most fair of all.

As the hours went by, Nate became drowsy. He'd enjoyed little sleep during the night, and what with the constant stress he had been under since the Blackfoot trouble began, his overwrought body craved a long, restful sleep. By shaking his head vigorously and occasionally pinching himself, he managed to stay awake.

The majestic Missouri River flowed peacefully onward, serenaded by the chirping of birds along its banks, attended by the frequent splashing of leaping fish, and visited by countless animals that came to the shore to quench their thirsts.

Nate made a mental note to use river travel more often in the future. The dangers were few and far between, and they could make better time than they otherwise would if they traveled overland on horseback.

Back in the early days of trapping, the trappers had always used the rivers and streams to get around. Not until later, when the Rees had denied them access to the northern reaches of the

Missouri, did the trappers take to using horses most of the time. And by then they were familiar enough with the land and its inhabitants to get by without being killed.

There was a story making the rounds that a steamboat was regularly plying the waters of the Missouri, serving the river outposts of the American Fur Company. Nate hoped he would see such a wonderful sight. He'd heard tales about the big boats, but had yet to behold one himself.

Infrequently Nate would gaze northward, and on each instance he noticed a few more dark clouds scuttling eastward. A storm was brewing, he deduced, but if it stayed well north of the river their journey would be uninterrupted.

Toward the middle of the afternoon Shakespeare gave a shout and pointed to the south. Silhouetted against the backdrop of blue sky were several warriors on horseback who were watching the bull boats.

"Mandans, you think?" Eric asked.

"Could be," Nate said. "Or they might be Sioux."

Shortly thereafter the small group turned their war horses and sped southward, tending to confirm his guess since the Sioux homeland lay in that direction.

Another hour elapsed. Nate was paddling idly, his thoughts drifting with the current, when he spotted a few huge animals on the north shore. On drawing almost abreast of them he saw they were buffalo, strays from a larger herd. There were five, one of which was quite big and must be a bull, the rest all smaller and probably cows.

As Nate stared at them, he saw another huge

shape appear out of a thicket near where the buffaloes were drinking. His interest promptly perked up, for the newcomer was a grizzly. Ignoring the buffalo, the bear ambled toward the water, and it was in the middle of an open space when the bull charged.

Now here was a scene of no common occurrence, yet not utterly unusual in that such incidents were typical in a violent land overrun by savage beasts. Everyone slacked off from paddling to view the confrontation, and all three boats were guided closer to the north shore so they wouldn't miss this rare spectacle.

The bull had the edge in size, but not by much. The bear had a slight edge in agility, since when aroused a grizzly displayed a nimble prowess belying its great bulk. And the bear also had the edge in having ten razor claws to the bull's two wicked horns, although the latter dwarfed the former and had a spread of three feet compared to a length of four or five inches for the claws.

Bellowing and snorting, the buffalo rammed into the grizzly, rolling the bear completely over. In the blink of an eye it was up, though, and turning to meet the bull's next rush. This time the bear dodged, but not before tearing the buffalo open with a swipe of its front paw.

Again the bull charged, head lowered, horns outthrust. It speared them low at the moment of contact, trying to disembowel the grizzly, but aimed too low and merely knocked the bear for a loop. This time when the grizzly rose it became the aggressor, going after the bull with its claws flying.

The two titans met in the center of the clearing

and battled head to head, the buffalo swiping and gouging with its horns, the grizzly using its paws to devastating effect. Like boxers, they circled, sparred, and connected. Blood flowed over both their coats. The bull drove a horn into the bear's side and tore upwards, tearing a vicious hole in the grizzly. Moments later the bear retaliated by ripping open part of the buffalo's skull.

Both animals tired quickly. It wasn't death that decided the outcome, but fatigue. As if by mutual consent, the combatants suddenly parted and went their separate ways, the grizzly limping into the brush while the bloody but unbowed bull rejoined his little harem.

"My word!" Eric exclaimed excitedly when the fight was over. "One day I will have to record that fight on canvas. I only hope my memory serves me in good stead."

"Some sights are never forgotten," Nate said. "I still remember the first time I saw the Rockies as if it took place yesterday."

"It's curious how our minds work," Eric replied, stroking lazily. "How we so readily recall pleasant things that make us feel good, but how we tend to forget the bad unless reluctantly reminded of them."

"Why dwell on that which makes us unhappy? I don't figure we were put on God's green earth to go through our whole lives miserable."

"Point taken," Eric said, and stared northward. "My goodness! Look at all that lightning."

A vast, writhing black mass engulfed most of the northern sky. Lightning crackled incessantly, dancing in wild arcs of yellow light, piercing the clouds like celestial spears. Faintly on the wind came the muted clap of thunder.

"Do you think that mess will come our way?" Eric inquired.

"Not unless the wind changes. It's blowing from west to east, so we should be safe."

"I hope so. I'd hate to be caught out on this river in a raging thunderstorm."

They continued eastward, Nate often checking the position of the tempest. To his relief the prevailing wind held fairly steady, although the storm did drift to within a mile of the Missouri, at which time the breeze picked up tremendously and turbulently shook the branches of the trees lining the north shore.

So intent was Nate on the bad weather that he didn't realize Eric and he were falling a bit behind the others until the Englishman made a joking remark.

"We had better paddle faster or we'll be making camp by ourselves tonight."

Nate looked and saw that Winona's boat was 60 yards in front of theirs, while Shakespeare's craft was another 50 or 60 yards ahead of Winona's. For some reason that bothered him. None of them were in any danger at the moment, and they were all as safe as they could be from hostile Indians, so he was puzzled as to why he felt so uneasy.

Shrugging, Nate applied his muscles to the pole. Eric, on seeing this, did likewise. Bull boats were not built for speed, however. Their craft narrowed the gap at an irritatingly slow pace.

Eric gave a little laugh.

"What strikes you as funny?" Nate inquired without taking his gaze off his wife and son.

"I was just thinking of how my cultured friends

in England and Europe would react if they could see me now, floating along this wild river in the heart of this untamed land in a primitive boat."

"What would they say?"

"They'd think I've gone mad. You see, in the comfort of their parlors and their drawing rooms they like to talk about the many adventures they would like to have in foreign lands among strange peoples, but they would never actually get out of their chairs and go book passage on the first ship to wherever it is they would like to visit."

"Why not?"

"Because it is one thing to intellectually dissect the nature of hardship and danger while safely secure in one's own home or club, and quite another to go out and experience hardship and danger firsthand. To do so would entail sacrifice, and they are unwilling to even temporarily give up their luxuries and comforts." Eric paused. "That was one of the things that attracted me to Diana and her brother. Unlike most of their peers, they have always been willing to take risks, to explore where others only talked about exploring, to actually do what others dream about doing." He paused again. "I thought that by associating with them and joining them in their far-flung travels I would be able to paint scenes and people no man had ever painted before."

"Hasn't it worked out that way?" Nate asked, more to be polite than out of any intent interest in their conversation. He was still watching Winona and Zach, still doing his best to catch up with them. Yet he had not gained much; they were still 40 yards ahead.

Suddenly Nate spied a narrow break in the north

shoreline approximately parallel with the position of Winona and Zach's boat. No sooner did he set eyes on it than to his ears came an odd noise, a grumbling hiss of incredible magnitude, as if a million snakes were all hissing at once. With the sound dawned comprehension, and as stark fear lanced through him he cupped a hand to his mouth and screamed at the top of his lungs, "Winona! Zach! Paddle for your lives!"

Chapter Sixteen

A minute earlier Winona had been moving down
the river without giving much thought to what
she was doing or her immediate surroundings.
Instead, she was preoccupied with a burning
question: Why was it that white women were
so moody? She had noticed this inexplicable
trait during her stay in St. Louis, and now
Diana Templar was demonstrating the same
behavior. The Englishwoman seldom talked as
freely to her as had been the case when first they
met. Indeed, Diana was becoming less talkative
the further they traveled despite Winona's many
efforts to engage her new friend in conversation.
She had told Lady Templar all there was to know
about the Shoshones, and was eager to learn
more about English society, but Diana was,
now strangely reticent on that and every other
subject.

Absorbed in her musings, Winona scarcely gave much thought to the storm to the north. Nor did she make special note of the break in the shoreline. Only when she heard her husband's sharp yell of warning did she glance up, hear the ominous hissing, and perceive the peril she was in.

"Ma?" Zach was asking. "What is Pa all upset about?"

"The stream!" Winona answered as she stabbed her pole into the water.

"What stream?" Zach responded, glancing in all directions in confusion.

"There!" Winona said. She took a hand from the pole long enough to point at the gap in the shore, then paddled with redoubled vigor. Years ago she had lost a favorite cousin who had been out hunting and thoughtlessly wandered into a gully just as a thunderstorm swooped down on the mountain above him. He had died horribly, drowning after the torrent had carried him along with it for a great distance, battering him against boulders and trees. When they found his body, nearly every bone in it had been broken.

Diana Templar, seated at the back of the boat, stared at the small tributary of the wide Missouri and was puzzled. Until a few moments ago she had been brooding over the tragic turns of events that had befallen their expedition and pondering her future should she make it back alive to civilization. On hearing Nate King's shout she had twisted to see him waving frantically. She didn't comprehend the cause for his alarm, and Winona's sudden concern aggravated her bewilderment. "What is all the fuss about?" she wanted to know.

"Flash flood," Winona said.

"A what?"

Winona nodded at the dark bank of clouds to the north. "The heavy rain has made the stream rise swiftly, so fast there will be a flash flood."

"But we're over a hundred yards from the mouth of that stream. Surely we're safe."

As if in answer, the hissing rose to a crescendo and a foaming wall of water over 25 feet high appeared up the tributary. Like a living juggernaut it rolled down to the junction with the river and surged outward, pushing a smaller wall of water ahead of it, making directly across the Missouri—directly toward the middle bull boat. In the midst of the foam and water swirled boulders and logs large enough to crush the craft completely.

Nate King was shouting himself horse, urging his wife and son to hurry. He wished now that they had never gone closer to the north shore to witness the battle between the grizzly and the buffalo. His own boat was far enough back so that the gigantic swell would miss it. Similarly, Shakespeare was so far ahead that his boat would also be spared. Only Winona, Zach, and Diana were in danger, and there was no hope of them escaping.

Winona saw this. She knew the wave would catch them broadside. Whirling, she grabbed Lady Templar's wrist. "Can you swim?"

"Yes. But why—?" Diana began, and stifled an urge to scream as Winona hauled on her arm and sent her sailing over the right side of the bull boat. She had no chance to protest, to resist. The cold water enveloped her from head to toe, shocking her senses, and fortunately she remembered to close her mouth as she struck. Then, furious at the way she had been unceremoniously treated, she shot to the surface just as Winona and Zach dived overboard.

In seconds Winona's head was above the surface and she shouted, "Swim for the south shore!" Suiting her actions to her words, she knifed southward using short but powerful strokes.

Zach shot after her.

But Diana Templar, wrestling with her anger, hesitated. She felt Winona's action was reckless, bordering on insane. Until she turned her head and saw the enormous wall of water and debris bearing down on the frail bull boat with all the destructive force of a rampaging cyclone. Then the gravity of her situation hit her, and with a gasp of terror she swam for her life.

Diana was a dozen feet to the rear of the Kings, who swam skillfully. Her clothes hampered her, her shoes made her legs leaden. She tried to catch the Kings, but couldn't. Never one to quit at anything, she gritted her teeth and put all her strength into pumping her arms and legs.

The hissing was much louder, eclipsing all other noises. Diana refused to look back and see how close the wall of water was, since to do so would delay her for precious seconds she might need to get away. Then an explosive crashing and rending sound caused her to forget herself and glance over her shoulder.

The bull boat had been torn apart.

Diana saw that the huge wave was only half the size it had been when it gushed out of the stream, but it was still devastating enough to smash her to pieces. Spitting out water, she swam for all she was worth. Winona and Zach had even more of a lead, and she despaired of ever overtaking them. Suddenly Winona looked around, spotted her, and came swimming back toward her.

Why? Diana wondered. The next heartbeat all other considerations were forgotten as the hissing seemed to fill the entire universe and an invisible hand seized her legs and lifted her into the air. Despite herself, Diana screamed. As she did a watery fist wrapped her in its wet embrace, smothering her at the same time it flung her deep into the river. Vaguely she was aware of tumbling end over end. She hit something with her shoulder and winced. Seconds passed, and she hit something else, only with her head this time. The world went black.

Winona King had seen the Englishwoman caught by the cresting wave, and rather than flee for her own safety she swam to rescue her friend. She gave no thought to her own welfare, or to the new life taking form within her. She simply saw someone in need, and she responded to that need the only way she knew.

"Ma!" Zach screeched.

The wall of water slammed into Winona and hurled her along with it. She spotted Lady Templar sweeping past and clutched at Diana's leg but missed. Twisting and churning, she tried to keep an eye on the Englishwoman while avoiding the logs and boulders all around her. But it was hopeless. The wave upended her, flipped her, bore her helpless in its grasp.

Winona had prudently held her breath just as she was enveloped. She could do so for a minute or two with no discomfort. Presently, however, her lungs commenced to ache and burn. She longed for a breath of fresh air, yet the force of the current showed no signs of abating.

Abruptly, a hand seized her wrist. Winona, startled, managed to twist her head and found her son clinging to her. Fighting the current, she was able to curl an arm around him protectively, and together they were propelled through the river like lead balls blasted from a gun.

Everything was happening so fast, Winona had no time to think. She glimpsed objects in the water near her, debris from the flood, but saw no sign of Diana Templar. Her lungs ached terribly. She feared she would soon have to open her mouth whether she wanted to or not. Then, just when her consciousness was swimming and the pain had become nearly overwhelming, the irresistible pull slackened and she was cast upward, breaking the surface with her son at her elbow.

Winona sucked the cool air in ragged gasps as she floated weakly on her back in a sea of froth. She felt utterly exhausted, drained of all energy. Beside her Zach was sputtering and coughing, and she compelled her body to move, to turn toward him. "Are you hurt?" she rasped.

"Not really, Ma," the boy answered gamely. "I almost passed out, is all."

Winona hugged him, then scanned the river. She was astonished to discover they were within three hundred yards of the south shore. Shattered trees, limbs, and twigs floated all around her. Among them bobbed a limp figure in a dress.

"Diana!" Winona exclaimed, and pulled Zach along as she moved forward. "We must help her."

Lady Templar was face down, her arms outstretched, her dress clinging in soaked folds to her body. She showed no trace of life when Winona gripped her around the waist, nor did she after Winona had rolled her over.

Looping her forearm under Diana's chin, Winona swam for the south shore. Where she found the strength, she had no idea. Zach helped as best he could, and between the two of them they brought the Englishwoman onto dry land and gently placed her on her back.

Winona didn't know what to do next. She felt for a pulse, and thought she detected a weak beat in the woman's wrist. But Lady Templar did not appear to be breathing.

Acting on the assumption that Diana had swallowed too much water, Winona flipped her onto her stomach. Then Winona began pressing down hard in a pumping motion, trying to force the excess water out of Diana's mouth. There was no response, no change in Diana's condition, and Winona feared she had reached her friend too late.

For half a minute Winona pumped. For a minute. Suddenly Lady Templar twitched and voiced a gurgling groan as river water spurted from her parted lips. Overjoyed, Winona kept pumping until the Englishwoman stopped spitting up. Diana was panting like a horse that had galloped for miles when Winona eased her over and said, "You are safe now. The flood did not claim you."

Diana's eyes were fluttering uncontrollably. Uttering a gasp, she opened them all the way and locked them on the happy face above hers. "You saved me?" she croaked.

"My ma sure did," Zach declared. "If not for her, you'd be dead right now."

"Son," Winona chided softly.

"Well, it's true."

The import of the boy's words slowly sank in, and Diana Templar shuddered. She vividly recalled the flash flood and the horrendous wave that had swamped her. She remembered the cold, clammy sensation of being submerged, and the nasty blow to the head she had received. But most memorable of all was the image of Winona swimming toward her as the wave crashed down. "Thank you," she whispered.

"You would have done the same for me," Winona said, giving the Englishwoman's shoulder a tender squeeze.

Diana Templar did not reply. Her insides felt all twisted up, and she wanted to curl into a ball and cry. Not because of the horror of the nightmare she had just experienced, but the horror she felt over the way she had treated the Shoshone woman. She had regarded Winona as an inferior, a barbaric, ignorant savage deserving of her pity and at times her scarcely concealed contempt. She had pretended to befriend Winona to learn about Indian ways, not out of genuine interest in Winona as a person. She had, simply put, used King's wife for her own ends.

And now look at what had happened! Diana closed her eyes and moaned. The woman she had despised had risked all to save her. The primitive she had judged as inferior had proven herself endowed with qualities Diana had long flattered herself that she too possessed. But the plain truth was that she probably would *not* have gone to Winona's aid as Winona had come to hers. The plain truth was that this simple Indian woman, in her own way, was more noble than most members of Diana's select social circle.

Winona heard the moan and misunderstood. Thinking that her friend was in agony, she sought some trace of a wound, and when she found none, she feared that Diana had suffered an internal injury. "I will make medicine for you," she offered, starting to rise.

Diana clutched at Winona's wrist and held tight. "No," she said. "I'm fine. Believe me."

"We should not take chances. I would not want any harm to come to you," Winona said. Again she began to stand, but to her amazement Lady Templar suddenly vented a wail of despair, lunged upward, and embraced her. Winona held herself still, listening to the Englishwoman's racking sobs. Uncertain of what had brought on the outpouring of grief, she waited for the sobbing to subside.

"I am so sorry," Diana said after a while, sniffling as she sat up and moved back.

Once again Winona misunderstood. "It is not a sign of weakness to cry after such an experience. It is joy at being alive."

"I can never repay you adequately for what you've done."

Winona smiled. "What is to repay between friends?"

At that instant a voice hailed them from out on the river. Nate and Eric were paddling furiously toward shore, while 20 yards behind them came the other bull boat.

Nate's heart had nearly stopped when he saw his wife and son go under, and his joy at finding them alive and well was boundless. The moment his boat touched the ground he was out and at their side, giving them both long, passionate hugs. Moisture filled his eyes. Tears trickled down his cheeks. "I thought I'd lost you," he said hoarsely.

"Ma saved us," Zach said. "Saved both of us."

Eric Nash, just joining them, overheard as he squatted next to Diana Templar. "You were fortunate that Winona was so handy," he said.

"No one knows it more than I do," Diana replied, brushing at the wet hair plastered to her face.

"I'll get a fire going so we can dry your clothes," Eric offered. "Otherwise you might catch your death."

"Wait," Diana said softly before he could walk off into the trees.

"What is it?"

"I want to apologize for the way I've treated you in the past. It's no wonder you felt jilted. But I was the one to blame. I didn't deserve your love."

"Now is hardly the proper time," Eric said, casting a meaningful glance at the Kings. "Be a bit more discreet and we'll discuss this later."

"Now is as good a time as any." Diana touched his hand. "This is important. I want you to know I've reconsidered. I would very much like to be your wife."

"My wife!" Eric burst out, forgetting himself. He could not have been more shocked had she risen and kissed him full on the mouth. "But I haven't proposed to you."

"Isn't that what you planned to do eventually?"

"Once, yes," Eric admitted. He saw Nate looking at him and felt unaccountably embarrassed. Bending closer to Diana, he whispered, "This *really* isn't the right time to air our dirty linen, love. Wait until we can be alone with no prying ears about."

"I don't care if they do hear. They're our friends."

"I care," Eric declared. "There are some things a man just doesn't talk about in front of others."

Diana grinned. "I do believe that you're beginning to sound more and more like Shakespeare and Nate every day."

"Thank you."

There was a loud splash as the last bull boat arrived. Jarvis hopped out, and by dint of his prodigious might pulled the craft clean out of the water while Shakespeare and the marquis were still inside. The mountain man was kneeling next to William Templar, who was awake, though pale and slick with perspiration, and seated with his back propped against a side.

"Diana?"

"Billy!" Diana cried in sheer joy. Unmindful of her weakened condition, she pushed to her feet, rushed past Nash, and stepped to the boat. "You've come around!"

The marquis nodded, righting his head with an effort. "Lend me a hand up, would you, old man?" he asked McNair.

Shakespeare and Jarvis both hoisted Templar out and set him down on soft grass yards from the river. Diana flew into William's arms, and the frontiersman and the giant moved off so the brother and sister could have their reunion in private.

No one needed to announce they would make camp at that particular spot; everyone just set about doing what was necessary, and soon a fire was blazing and enough wood had been gathered to last the night. Half an hour later a rifle shot shattered the stillness, and as the blood-red sun alighted on the western horizon, Shakespeare strolled back with an antelope over his shoulders.

By then Diana Templar was wonderfully warm once again thanks to Winona, who had escorted Diana into the brush and wrapped her in a pair of heavy blankets, then hung her dress and undergarments on the end of long sticks over the fire until the clothes were dry.

Nowhere on the sprawling plains was there a happier group that night as they sat around the flickering flames and talked about the events of the day. Even William Templar shed his customary cheerless disposition and joined in the banter and joking spawned by the heartfelt relief everyone there felt.

With a singular exception. Eric Nash stayed aloof from the rest. Balanced on a log ten feet away, he listened with half an ear and commented only when addressed.

After the supper, Diana rose, clasped her slim hands behind her back, and sauntered over to him. "Mind if I join you, kind sir?" she asked gaily.

"Feel free," Eric replied, sliding down to make room for her. She sat, but so close their elbows were touching, causing him to slide further.

"I won't bite," Diana said.

"Your levity is ill-timed."

"What in the world is wrong with you? Why are you so out of sorts?"

"It isn't every day a woman up and tells me she wants to marry me."

Leaning back, Diana tossed her head, swirling her shiny hair. "I should think you'd be happy I've finally come to my senses. It's taken me long enough." Her eyes caressed his. "For which I'm profoundly sorry. Until recently I never, ever gave thought to you as other than a dear friend. But so much has happened in the past few weeks, so much that was fresh and disturbing, that I've acquired a whole new perspective on life."

Eric let her talk.

"Take today, for instance. This morning I was depressed, lamenting my fate and despising this land and everything in it. Then the flash flood caught us—" Diana broke off, gazed at the serene waterway, and shuddered "—and when I came around I began to see what a bloody fool I've been."

"Diana . . ."

"Let me finish, please. I want you to fully understand so you will know I'm in dead earnest. This is no frivolous decision. To come back from the dead, as it were, is an intensely unsettling experience. It makes you love life more, if you see my meaning." Diana paused. "It made me realize how stupid I've behaved, and how I've had the man of my dreams in front of my nose for years and never seen him for the treasure he is."

"I'm no treasure."

"You're too modest by half. You're articulate, intelligent, and a devoted suitor. How you found the patience to bear with me is a mystery. Today I realized the injustice I've done you and I want to make amends."

"There is no need."

"There damn well is! You opened your heart to me and I threw it back in your face. Can you ever forgive me?"

"I already have."

"Sweet Eric," Diana said, extending her arm to stroke his cheek. "The one constant in my forever changing life. I wish I had seen the truth sooner."

"Indeed."

"You don't believe me?"

"I was referring to my being the sole constant in your life. It's patently untrue. Your parents and your brother are your anchors, and I daresay there's no room for a husband anywhere on your little ship except possibly on the gangplank."

Diana stiffened in indignation. "What an outlandish comparison! And what is wrong about having a very natural attachment to one's own family? Does that mean I can't love you? Can't live with you wherever we wish?"

"Perhaps not. In any event, it's all irrelevant."

"Then why quibble over it? I've told you how much I've changed, and I've acquitted myself well if I do say so myself." Diana moved nearer to him. "Forget about my family. Think only of me. Look me in the face and share your innermost feelings, the feelings you've keep penned up for so long. I want to hear them, dearest. I want to love you as you deserve to be loved."

For the longest while Eric Nash sat there gazing inscrutably into her beseeching eyes, his shoulders slumped in resignation. Then standing, he put a hand on her shoulder, squeezed affectionately, and said softly to insure none could hear, "There's just one little problem."

"What is it? Together we can surmount anything. Share it with me and I'll do whatever it takes to eliminate it."

Sadness etched Eric's countenance as he responded. "I don't want you anymore." And turning, he walked into the night.

Chapter Seventeen

Then came the day they arrived at the Mandan village of Mato-tope.

It was early morning, the air cool and crisp and filled with the songs of birds perched in the willow, ash, elm, and cottonwood trees lining both shores. Abundant deer were spotted on the banks. Rich grass of a greener shade than was common on the plains grew all along the river.

The initial intimation Nate King had that they were nearing their destination came when they rounded a bend and before them unfolded tilled tracts devoted to beans, corn, squash, and sunflowers. These were the first large farmlands Nate had seen since leaving the States years before. He admired the orderly rows that reflected the pride the Mandan women took in cultivating the soil.

There was another bend not far ahead, and when Nate's bull boat passed it he beheld a sight that made his mouth go slack in astonishment. For nothing he had heard could quite prepare him for the reality of seeing a Mandan village with his own eyes.

As with all Mandan villages, this one was located atop a prominent rise bordering the Missouri, a vantage point that gave the Mandans a sweeping view of the surrounding countryside and rendered a surprise attack by their enemies virtually impossible. A sturdy palisade formed the perimeter, while visible inside it were many odd domed roofs. Jutting high into the sky from the center of the village were a half-dozen tall poles from which dangled fluttering objects Nate could not quite identify.

The Mandans knew they were coming. A commotion was taking place in the village, and shortly from the front of the palisade spilled warriors on horseback and afoot who were trailed by a great many women and children. They descended to a level area at the base of the rise and awaited the two boats.

Nate unconsciously fingered one of his flintlocks, then reminded himself that the Mandans were famous for their friendliness to all whites. He glanced at Winona, who was staring in awe at the village, then at Zach, who wore a grin of youthful delight. Behind them in the cramped craft was Eric Nash, whose expression was one of rapture; Nash was drinking in every sight much as a man dying of thirst would quench his parched throat at the first oasis he found.

Since their boat was in the lead, they landed first. Nate held the craft steady while the others climbed out, then with Nash's assistance pulled it completely out of the water. Turning, he cradled the Hawken in his left elbow and advanced toward the waiting phalanx of painted warriors, Winona striding proudly at his side.

A tall warrior stepped forward to meet them. It was obvious that here was a man of considerable stature in the tribe, not only from the way he carried himself, but from the many locks of hair that adorned his quilled buckskin shirt and leggings and the many feathers in his flowing bonnet that reached down to the ground. The right side of his shirt and his right legging had been painted a deep red, while covering the shirt were many symbols attesting to his prowess in battle, among them the painted semblance of a hand which indicated he had killed an enemy in hand-to-hand combat. In his right hand was a lance liberally decorated with scalps and eagle feathers.

Nate halted and made the Indian sign for friend, which was done by holding his right hand in front of his neck with his palm outward and his index and second fingers pointing straight up, then raising his hand until the tips of his fingers were as high as his head.

A wry smile creased the stately warrior's bronzed face. "I am glad," he signed in response after leaning his lance against his broad chest, "or we would have to kill you."

Nate couldn't help but laugh. He introduced himself, using his Shoshone name.

"Grizzly Killer is a fine name, as is any name that tells of a man who can kill the mighty white bears. I am Four Bears, chief over all my people," the warrior disclosed with a twinkle in his eyes, and then he tapped his chest and spoke his name in the Mandan tongue. "Mato-tope."

In order Nate introduced his wife, his son, and Eric Nash, speaking the latter's name in English since there was no sign language equivalent. The second bull boat touched land as he was doing so, and the rest of their party came over and was promptly presented to the chief.

"What are you doing in Mandan country?" Four Bears asked when the preliminaries were out of the way.

"We are helping these people reach the white man's land," Nate answered, pointing to the four Britishers. "Along the way we have been attacked by Blackfeet and caught in a flood. This man—" and Nate jerked his thumb at the marquis "—is still weak from wounds he received and needs much rest." He paused to stare up at the palisade. "We have heard much of the hospitality of the Mandans, and we are hoping you will agree to let us stay with you for a while, until we are fit enough to finish our journey."

"Four Bears has never turned a white man in need away from his lodge," the chief signed. "My people have always welcomed whites to our villages. You may stay with us for as long as you like."

"We thank you," Nate signed sincerely.

Turning, Four Bears beckoned. Other warriors came forward to be introduced, among them the war chief and the peacetime or civil chief of the village, both of whom were clearly held in lesser esteem than Mato-tope, and then some more important warriors. When they were done, the chief's immediate family advanced, and he took particular delight in introducing his wives and many children. Among them was a young daughter of exceptionally singular beauty, a smiling maiden of noble bearing whose black hair was streaked silver-gray in parts, a peculiar characteristic of most Mandans.

When it was Eric Nash's turn to greet her, he shuffled forward like one who was sleepwalking and gaped dumbly at her ravishing face. Only when Nate nudged him did Nash blurt out a hello in English, and then think to make the Indian sign for friend as Nate had taught him to do during their long trip down the Missouri.

Morning Dew, for that was the maiden's name, glanced coyly away and smiled, at which some of her sisters giggled merrily. Later, as they climbed to the village, Morning Dew repeatedly cast shy looks at Nash, who in turn beamed from ear to ear.

Nate noticed the exchange and grinned to himself. If he knew anything about women—and he had learned as little as any man knew during the course of his marriage—Eric Nash was in for an interesting stay among the Mandans. His deduction was borne out when Four Bears got around to assigning the members of their party to various lodges. Nate, Winona, and Zach were invited to stay with the chief's family. Shakespeare and Jarvis were assigned to the lodge of a relative. The Templars were invited to yet another dwelling. Finally it was Nash's turn, and Four Bears was about to have him go with the marquis and Diana when Morning Dew stepped forward and whispered into her father's ear. Four Bears glanced at her, then requested that Nash also take up residence in his own lodge rather than in one of the others.

And such lodges they were! Nate had never beheld the like. They were conical in shape, earthen mounds of great size with large holes on the crowns of the domes for ventilation. Scores of lodges were clustered around a central plaza, in the middle of which reared the poles Nate had glimpsed from the river. At close range he was able to establish that the fluttering objects were scalps.

One of the most remarkable aspects about the lodges was the Mandan practice of using the roofs for everything from dozing in the sun to playing games on them, as the children often did. As Nate was led toward Mato-tope's lodge, he saw dozens of men and women observing his party from above. On top of several dwellings rested bull boats the women employed when traveling along the river to work on their crops. A number of buffalo skulls were also in evidence.

Four Bears occupied a lodge near the central plaza. He stood aside and motioned for Nate to enter through the rectangular doorway braced by stout beams.

Once inside Nate noted other beams used to support the structure. To his right was a long rail to which were tied a number of sleek war horses, mares, and colts. Dogs scampered about. Baskets, shields, and parfleches hung from the beams, while lances and paddles leaned against them. At the base of one post was another buffalo skull.

Illumination was afforded by the sunlight streaming in through the large hole in the roof. Directly under the hole buffalo robes had been spread, and near these four women were busy preparing food and drink for their guests. Bashful children hung back, watching from the outer shadows.

Nate was accorded the seat of honor on Mato-tope's left. Zach was alloted the seat on the chief's right, with Eric Nash beside him. Winona, according to Indians custom, squatted to Nate's left and slightly behind him.

Once everyone was comfortable, Four Bears broke out his favorite pipe and it was passed around from man to man. In addition to the grand chief, there were four other warriors present at this welcoming ceremony, one the war chief of the village, another the peace chief.

In keeping with tradition, Four Bears made a short speech, using sign. "Once again we have a chance to show our love for our white brothers by helping these friends who are now among us. Many times have the whites shown their affection for us by giving us many gifts. But the most precious gift they have brought us is the gift of peace. When the two known as Lewis and Clark came among us many winters ago, in the time when Black Cat was grand chief of all the Mandans, they insisted we make peace with our old enemies the Pawnees, and since that day our people have been able to hunt without fear of being attacked by them, and our woman can take off their moccasins at night. This is good."

Nate recollected hearing about the winter the Lewis and Clark expedition spent in the vicinity of the Mandans and the aid that had been rendered.

"Thanks to the whites," the venerable chief was saying, "we have made peace with all our enemies except the Sioux, who continue to plague us with their raids. My people are in dread of them, which is why we seldom go out to hunt buffalo anymore except in large groups. Perhaps, in the future, the whites will help us make peace with them as well so that all may live in peace and harmony."

The frank appeal touched Nate, and he responded as eloquently as he was able: "Were it in my power to bring about peace between the Sioux and the Mandans, know that I would do so. But I do not know the Sioux. From the stories I have been told, they do not like whites, and kill and scalp us when they can. So I say that if the Sioux should attack our friends the Mandans while we are staying in your village, we will help the Mandans fight them off. Your happiness is our happiness, and your sorrows are our sorrows."

Four Bears appeared quite moved, and impulsively gripped Nate's shoulders as a token of their mutual devotion. Then he gave commands and the women brought food and drink.

While they ate, Four Bears talked of his people, revealing there were about nine thousand Mandans living in six villages. In close proximity lived a smaller tribe, the Hidatsa, who spoke a different tongue but were otherwise so much like the Mandans in their dress and conventions that it was impossible to tell the two tribes apart.

Through extensive trade with the whites, the Mandans had become one of the richest tribes west of the Mississippi. They owned many blankets, axes, and knives obtained from traders, and they could also boast of owning more guns than any other Indians. They were a prosperous, thriving people, whose dispositions were always sunny and whose manners were above reproach. There was none of the petty thievery so common among some of the plains tribes, nor were they given to lying and trickery.

Nate found the tales about them to be completely true. He was much impressed by the bearing of the warriors and the beauty of the women, and he silently gave thanks that he had encountered the Shoshones first and not the Mandans, or he might well have ended up with a Mandan wife instead of Winona.

During the meal, Morning Dew made it a point to personally serve Eric Nash whatever he desired. She hovered over him like a hawk, ready to refill his bowl the moment it was empty. When he thanked her, as he did every time she waited on him, she bestowed a smile that would have melted butter.

"My people have almost used up our supply of meat," Four Bears revealed after the food was consumed. "When the sun sets this day the Bull Society will perform the Buffalo Calling Dance so that many buffalo will come and fall under our lances, arrows, and guns. You are invited to attend."

"We would be honored," Nate signed, and inquired, "Am I to understand the Mandans have a number of special societies just as the Shoshones and others do?"

"Yes. For the men there is the Bull Society, the Okipa Society, and others. There are also some for the women." Four Bears nodded at his daughter. "Morning Dew is in the White Buffalo Cow Women society. They will hold their own dance this night so that the herds will graze near our village."

"My wife would like to attend," Nate signed, knowing she would and speaking on her behalf according to Indian protocol.

"The White Buffalo Cow Women would be glad to have her."

After the welcoming ceremonies, Nate and his family were given a tour of the village by Mato-tope. The orderliness and cleanliness were above reproach. Every Mandan they encountered offered a friendly smile, while frolicking flocks of small children trailed in their wake, whispering and giggling.

As they neared the north palisade, Nate peered between the poles and saw dozens upon dozens of open scaffolds dotting the prairie. "Your dead?" he asked their host.

"Come and see," Four Bears signed. He led them from the village and over to the scaffolds, which were just high enough so that the bodies were out of the reach of roving beasts. Here and there among the platforms were circles consisting of human skulls, and in the center of each circle were two buffalo skulls and two long lances tipped with feathers.

Nate halted near one such circle and watched an elderly woman approach. She stepped over the ring of skulls, knelt in the middle in front of one, and placed a bowl of squash on the ground beside it. "What is she doing?" he asked.

Four Bears pointed at the scaffolds. "When the flesh has wasted away, the skulls are taken and put into circles. Relatives and friends come here to honor those who have died and to bring them food they will eat in the spirit world."

This was a new Indian custom to Nate. He wondered how those who had departed were supposed to eat real food, but made no comment in this regard as many Indians were quite touchy about their burial practices and often regarded any skepticism as an insult.

On their way into the village Nate spotted a man doing a dance atop one of the lodges. The warrior was chanting and waving a stick laden heavy with feathers. He glanced at the chief and arched his eyebrows quizzically.

"The rainmaker," Four Bears explained. "We have not had rain for many sleeps and our cornfields are becoming dry."

They walked on, and as they rounded a lodge encountered a Mandan dressed in a most spectacular manner, with a robe of white wolfskins hanging from his shoulders, medicine pipes in his hands, and fox tails tied to the heels of his moccasins. His body had been daubed with clay and he was painted red on his forearms and forehead.

"This is Old Bear, the greatest of our medicine men," Four Bears said, presenting the aged healer. The two Mandans conversed briefly, then the chief added, "He has heard about your friend who was wounded and he is going to cure him for you."

Nate expressed his gratitude in sign language. While he might be dubious about certain burial practices, long ago he had learned not to discount the ability of medicine men and women to effect incredible cures. He'd personally witnessed such events, healings no white doctor was capable of doing, sometimes with the use of unknown herbs and other plants and sometimes involving spiritual techniques only the healers themselves knew.

Old Bear was about to walk off when his gaze fell on Winona. He stared at her stomach, then addressed Nate. "Your wife will give birth in three moons. The baby will be a girl, and she will be healthy." Smiling, he hastened away.

Winona pressed a hand to her abdomen and grinned, pleased the renowned medicine man had confirmed her feelings. She was also glad to learn the birth would not take place for three more months, since that would give them time to return to their cabin high in the Rockies.

Nate was bemused by the medicine man's predictions. By now Winona was showing her condition so that anyone could see she was pregnant, but the business about the baby being a girl and the time until the birth was baffling.

As they neared the chief's lodge, they found Shakespeare and Jarvis waiting for them.

"Stalking Wolf told us about the warrior who was killed two sleeps ago," the mountain man said to Four Bears. "And we would like to ride along with the men who are going out to scout around. Stalking Wolf has offered to let us use two of his horses, if you have no objections."

"Tell my brother I have none," the grand chief responded.

"What is this all about?" Nate inquired of McNair.

"Two warriors were out hunting the other day and they were set on by a band of Sioux," Shakespeare detailed. "One was shot with an arrow. It happened not far from here, too close to the village for the Mandans' liking. So they want to make sure the Sioux have left the area before they have their big buffalo ceremony tonight. The last thing they want is for the Sioux to spring a surprise attack while they're all busy dancing and singing."

"I'd like to come along if it's all right with you," Nate signed to Four Bears.

"Good. You can use my best horse, a gelding as fast as the wind."

"What about you?" Nate said to Nash. "Care to join us? There might be some excitement."

The Englishman glanced at the chief's lodge, where Morning Dew stood framed in the entrance, and shook his head. "Thanks, but I'll stick around here."

"I wonder why," Nate muttered, and followed Four Bears into the lodge, where he was given a magnificent white gelding with a flowing black mane and tail. The animal shied until Nate stroked its neck, rubbed under its chin, and spoke soothingly in its ear.

As the warriors who were going gathered in front of Mato-tope's lodge, it became apparent there were 15 comprising the scouting party. Zach asked to go too, but Nate refused out of worry over the danger to his son should they run into any Sioux. Stalking Wolf, a tall, lean warrior dressed much like Four Bears, assumed the lead as they rode from the village. They bore to the east, crossed the Missouri at a shallow point, and headed into the prairie.

Nate rode beside his mentor, Jarvis behind them.

"So what do you think of the Mandans?" Shakespeare inquired after they had covered the better part of a mile.

"I like them as much as I do the Shoshones, and I've only been among them for a few hours."

"There are no people finer anywhere," Shakespeare agreed. "What gets me, though, is how damn happy they are all the time. I've never met a tribe so contented with their lot in life, making the most of all life has to offer."

"How long should we impose on their hospitality?"

"Until the marquis mends or they throw us out," Shakespeare joked. "Whichever happens first."

The giant prodded his mount forward to join them. "I couldn't help but overhear," he commented. "I like this bunch my own self. They're not bad for heathens." He chuckled, then declared, "Of course, I don't like them half as much as Mr. Nash apparently does."

"Why do you say that?"

"When you were in the high chief's house, Nash confided to me that he's thinking of staying on with them once we've gone."

"What? Did he give a reason?" Shakespeare asked.

"No, sir. But it doesn't take a genius to figure out why. He's taken a fancy to the high chief's daughter. Morning Dew is her name, if I remember correctly."

"Do tell," Shakespeare said thoughtfully. "Life is just plumb full of little surprises. I only hope he knows what he's getting himself into."

"How so, sir?"

"If he starts fooling around with her, he'd better be serious about his intentions or there will be hell to pay. Not even the Mandans will abide having their women treated with disrespect. If he should get them mad at him, there's no telling what they might do with the rest of us."

"I say. Maybe we should have a word with Nash and warn him."

"Not me. I hardly know the man. You should do it, Jarvis. You're his countryman."

"True, sir. But it would be a bit awkward."

"I'll do it," Nate offered. "Nash and I are friends. He'll listen to me."

"Don't be too sure," Shakespeare said. "When love flies in the ear of most men, their brains fly out the other."

"Old William S. again?"

"No. Me."

"Hold on," Jarvis suddenly exclaimed, gazing straight ahead. "What the devil is that savage going on about?"

Nate looked, and saw Stalking Wolf gesturing sharply at a small group of riders several miles to the south. "He's using sign language," he translated for the ex-soldier's benefit, "to inform us that those riders are Sioux."

Chapter Eighteen

The next moment the Mandans were off, racing in hot pursuit of the fleeing Sioux. Nate, Shakespeare, and Jarvis joined in the chase, but the Englishman, having difficulty controlling his spirited horse, soon fell to the rear.

Nate's own horse was everything Four Bears had claimed, and he shortly was in the lead alongside Stalking Wolf. Accustomed as he was to riding bareback, he had no problem handling the animal. The Mandans did use saddles, but usually only for ceremonial occasions. On long rides or when off to make war, they preferred to do without them.

Rather quickly it became apparent that the Sioux would not be easy to overtake. Their own mounts fairly flew over the ground, and the Sioux rode them as if each man and his steed were one creature.

Much had been bandied around the campfires of the trappers concerning the horsemanship of the Sioux, rumored to be second only to that of the Comanches, who were the generally acknowledged masters at both horse breeding and riding. Now Nate had the chance to see the truth of the assertions, and he was convinced every word he had heard was true. He'd seen Comanches once, the time he paid a visit to Santa Fe, so he could make a firsthand comparison.

But the Mandans were a persistent lot. For miles the chase continued through the high grass, spooking antelope and small game right and left. The warriors lashed their animals relentlessly with their quirts, but the Sioux maintained their lead throughout. Eventually the Mandan horses became winded and the reluctant warriors had to stop.

Nate was glad when they did. He would gladly have tangled with the Sioux, but he feared riding Mato-tope's horse into the ground to catch them. If he should ruin the animal, courtesy demanded that he give the chief a horse of equal or better breeding.

As they were sitting there watching the Sioux vanish in the distance, Stalking Wolf signed, "There were five of them, just as Broken Claw claimed. I do not think they are part of a bigger war party or we would have seen more."

"Most of them looked young to me," Shakespeare signed. "My guess would be they are out to prove their manhood by coming here and hanging around your village. They hope to go back to their tribe and boast of the many coup they have counted."

"If we catch them they will never count coup again."

"Will you advise your brother to go on with the ceremony tonight?" Nate inquired.

"The Mandans do not fear children. We will have our buffalo dance."

Preparations were in full swing when the scouting party rode into the village. The men belonging to the Bull Society had stripped down to their breechclouts, painted their bodies as was customary, and donned buffalo masks made from the skins of the great beasts. Complete with horns, the masks were amazingly lifelike. Many carried painted shields, some bows, some rifles, and others lances.

Not to be outdone, the members of the White Buffalo Cow Women had attired themselves in their finest dresses, thrown their prettiest blankets around their shoulders, and put on white conical headdresses crowned with feathers. They were congregating at the west end of the plaza, where they would perform their dance.

Everyone in the village gathered for the celebration, many standing around the outer margin of the plaza while almost as many more took to the roofs. The children were in their element, squealing with glee as they dashed to and fro and got underfoot now and then.

Four Bears had received the report of the Sioux band in somber silence. At his brother's behest he had agreed the dances should indeed be held, but he had also given orders that commencing the very next day there would be warriors out on the prairie at all times searching for the young Sioux.

Nate and his party were allotted positions on the north side of the plaza where they had an unobstructed view of the unfolding ceremony. From where he stood Nate could see Winona and Diana Templar to the west, observing the women.

"Have you ever known anything so exciting in your whole life?" Eric Nash asked as they stood watching the last-minute arrangements of the Bull Society.

"Enjoying this, are you?"

"There are no words to describe these marvelous people. I feel as if I've stumbled on another Eden, and all around us are a new race of Adams and Eves."

"You're exaggerating a mite, wouldn't you say?"

"Not at all," Eric replied, sighing contentedly. He encompassed the plaza with a sweep of his arm. "Look at them, Nate. *Really* look at them. Not one of them has a devious bone anywhere in his or her body. Their pristine souls have never known the wickedness and vice that corrupts our own social fabric. They are living as all humankind was meant to live, free and in perfect accordance with Nature."

The artist's fiery passion made Nate study him intently. "Indians are no different than any other people," he finally responded. "There are good ones and there are bad ones in every tribe. The Mandans are no exception."

"On the contrary. I have never known people as noble as these. Not in Asia, nor in South America. And certainly not in Europe." Eric twisted and pointed at the lodges. "If by no other standard, measure them by how clean everything is here. Why, there are cities in Europe where you can hardly walk down a street without becoming dirtied by the filth underfoot. Some gutters run deep with garbage and urine. Believe me, I've seen it." He lowered his head and shuddered. "The worst was the recent smallpox epidemic. Did you hear about it?"

"Can't say as I did."

"Thousands died. I was on the Continent at the time, and I had to pass through the stricken cities on my return to England. The dead were lying in the open, their foul bodies reeking, their skin covered with blisters filled with pus. The authorities say that all the filth contributes to the spread of such diseases, and I can see why." Eric smiled at the assembled Mandans. "Gaze around you, my friend. The cleanliness of this village is a reflection of the inner cleanliness of its inhabitants. Whether you agree or not, here is paradise. I respect them more than you can ever know."

"I'm beginning to see that," Nate said. He had never heard Indians described in such glowing terms before, and he was troubled by Nash's lack of perspective. The man was so fond of the Mandans that he was blind to reality. Yes, they were friendly. Yes, they had many admirable traits. But they would torture and scalp a captive, just like any other tribe, and they were not above exterminating their enemies if given the chance. In short, when the occasion called for it they could be as bloodthirsty as the Apaches or the Blackfeet.

"I may never leave here." Eric said softly.

"So I heard. Have you given the matter a lot of thought?"

"What's to think about?" Eric retorted. "I've found heaven on earth, and I'd be a bloody fool to give it up."

"What about England?"

"What about it? My family and friends will get by without me." Eric placed his hands on his hips and nodded. "And they might even accept what I've done once they understand the lofty purpose motivating me."

Nate glanced at the White Buffalo Cow Women and spied Morning Dew among them. "What is your lofty purpose?"

"To do what no man—no white man—has ever done before. I intend to use my talent to paint and sketch every single aspect of Mandan life, to show them in all their glory for all the world to see."

"But what about those two other painters, Catlin and Bodmer?" Nate asked. "I thought you told me they've already paid the Mandans a visit and done some paintings of the tribe?"

"That's just it! They stayed with the Mandans a short season and painted whatever impressed them the most," Eric said, gazing appreciatively over the tableau before him. "I, on the other hand, intend to capture each little part and particle of Mandan existence, to record their way of life as no man has ever done before. I'll make a complete record that will so captivate your fellow countrymen back in the States and my own in England that the name of the tribe will be on everyone's lips. And once they are so well known, no one, not even your government, will dare try to force them off their lands as you told me has already been done with the Cherokees and other tribes."

This argument gave Nate pause. He remembered the conversation well, one of many during their long trek across the plains, but at the time he had merely been venting his spleen over a government policy he considered tyrannical and unsound. He hadn't been trying to convert Nash to an ardent supporter of the Indian cause.

And Nash had a point. If he did make an artistic record of the Mandans and have the paintings displayed in the States and elsewhere, it might cause public opinion to sway in favor of the tribe should there ever develop a conflict with the government over the tribe's right to live along the Missouri.

So Nate let the matter drop for the time being while he gave it more thought. In his heart he still felt Nash might be about to make a mistake that would only bring sadness in the years ahead, but he could not bring himself to say as much when he had no solid reason for saying so. And Nash was, after all, a grown man. If the Englishman wanted to give up a life of luxury to live with the Mandans, that was Nash's business, not Nate's. Moments later the Bull Society started their ceremony, and Nate temporarily shut the problem from his mind to concentrate on the warriors.

Eric Nash was also riveted to the dance, his blood pulsing in rhythm to the beat of the drums as he drank in the sights and sounds. He watched, fascinated, as the warriors began dancing in a large circle, often bending at the waist and uncoiling again, spinning and whipping from side to side as they flowed gracefully in imitation of the mighty beasts they were working their magic on. As they danced they yipped and howled and whooped in fierce abandon.

Many of the spectators also joined in, some swaying in time to the drums, others shuffling their feet, others whooping. A few fired their guns into the air.

While this was going on, the White Buffalo Cow Women were performing their own dance, a more sedate one to be sure, moving in a circle, as did the men, but chanting and singing rather than voicing savage cries.

Soon the whole tribe was swept up in the frenzy of buffalo fever. The dancing went on and on and showed no sign of letting up. Eric Nash didn't mind. He reveled in the rite, clapping and stamping his feet and occasionally uttering shrieks worthy of a true Mandan. More and more, however, his glance strayed from the dance of the Bull Society to that of the White Buffalo Cow Women. He spotted Morning Dew and locked his eyes on her, feasting on her loveliness. When, at length, she glanced at him and smiled, he felt warm inside.

Night came on. Stars sparkled on high. Yet still the dancers went around and around. Fatigue began to take its toll, and some of the younger members of the Bull Society faltered.

Then Nash witnessed a curious display. He saw one of the male dancers stumble and nearly drop from weariness, and when that happened, another dancer armed with a bow stepped in close and shot the stumbler with a blunt arrow. Spectators then laid hold of the exhausted man, dragged him from the circle, and drew their knives. With the panting warrior prone on the ground, the bystanders then went through the motions of skinning and cutting up a buffalo, pretending to butcher the warrior as they would a real buffalo. When they were done, they turned back, laughing and joyful, to the dance, while two of their number helped the warrior to his feet and escorted him away.

"How marvelous!" Eric said to himself. "How bloody well marvelous!"

It was long past midnight when Winona came over and tapped Nate on the arm. Turning, he draped an arm over her shoulders and said in her ear, "Ready to turn in?"

"Yes, husband. It has been a long day."

With one arm on Winona and another on Zach, Nate started to leave. He paused to speak to the Englishman. "We're off to sleep. Care to come?"

"No, thank you," Eric responded. "I don't want to miss a minute of this."

"Suit yourself."

Eric gave a little wave as they left, and resumed watching the dancers. Presently his attention was drawn to a nearby lodge, from which, at regular intervals, young women bundled in heavy robes would emerge with elderly warriors in tow. The pairs would then move off into the darkness. After seeing several such couples go off, and a few return, his curiosity was so aroused that he ventured over to the lodge to ascertain what custom was being enacted. At the entrance he hesitated, fearing he might break some tribal rule. But mustering his courage, he poked his head inside.

"Greetings, Nash. Come on in and sit a spell."

Glancing to his right, Eric was surprised to find Shakespeare McNair seated with his back to the wall. Entering, he sat down beside the mountain man and surveyed the interior of the lodge. Then he received his second surprise.

A circle of old warriors occupied the middle of the floor space. Some were smoking pipes, others simply sitting there as if waiting for something to happen. Among them sat Jarvis, wearing a big grin and with an air of eager anticipation.

Behind this circle sat another circle, but this one was composed exclusively of young, pretty women draped in heavy robes. Young men were also present, but they stood or moved among the aged warriors, speaking softly and gesturing at the women.

As Eric watched, one of the elderly warriors bowed forward and a younger man immediately went to one of the kneeling women, took her by the hand, and brought her around to the old man, who in turn stood and was led from the lodge by the woman. "What are they doing?" Eric whispered to McNair. "Does this have something to do with their buffalo ceremony?"

"That it does," Shakespeare replied, his eyes twinkling and the corners of his mouth twitching upward. "The Mandans don't miss a trick when they want the buffalo to draw near to their villages."

"What does all this signify? And what is Jarvis doing here?"

"He knows a good thing when he sees it."

"I beg your pardon?"

"Jarvis was invited to take part. Any white man who happens to be visiting during the buffalo dance is always asked to join in. The Mandans think it's good medicine." Shakespeare looked at Nash. "You can take a seat in the circle if you're so inclined."

"And what then?"

"Well, you sit there until one of those young warriors comes up to you and offers you his wife."

Eric's head snapped around. "What do you mean by he offers me his wife?"

"He gives his wife to you so you can take her out and do what bull buffaloes and cow buffaloes do when they want to have calves," Shakespeare explained.

"I'm not quite certain I see your point," Eric said, thinking of the mock butchery he had observed outside. "Do these women and the old men pretend to have relations?"

Shakespeare laughed and shook his head. "No wonder you English lost in 1815. No, the relations are as real as you and me."

"My word!" Eric declared, shocked by the revelation. He saw another aged warrior leaving with a comely woman, and as they passed by her buffalo robe fell open several inches permitting Eric to discover that she was completely naked. Appalled, he stared at the circle and watched two husbands beseech Jarvis to take their wives. "This is despicable!" he snapped.

"Hush," Shakespeare cautioned. "Don't let the Mandans see that you're upset or they'll be insulted."

"But what in God's name compels them to indulge in such a pagan practice?"

"The Mandans *are* pagans in the Christian sense," Shakespeare replied. "And they've practiced this custom for more years than anyone can recollect."

"Which doesn't make it right," Eric said angrily. He gestured at the nearest women. "How do they force these husbands and wives to participate?"

"They don't."

"You can't be serious."

"The husbands and wives are honored to take part because they believe they're insuring there will be plenty of buffalo for the hunt," Shakespeare detailed patiently. "They do this for the prosperity of the tribe."

The disclosure was too much for Eric, who leaned back and closed his eyes as he tried to quell the queasy sensation in the pit of his stomach. In his mind's eye he saw Morning Dew dancing among the White Buffalo Cow Women, and he blanched.

"Are you fixing to be sick?" Shakespeare inquired.

"No. I'll be all right." Eric looked at the frontiersman. "Tell me. How are the married couples picked for this affair?"

"Generally, they offer themselves for the ceremony. Since there are more of them than there are old men, the couples like to take turns."

"*All* the young couples have to participate?"

"Not if they don't want to, but anyone who doesn't is looked down on as having a faint heart and not really caring about the welfare of the tribe."

"If . . ." Eric began, and had to stop to swallow a lump in his throat. "If, say, a white man was to marry a Mandan maiden, would they also be required to take part?"

"They would if the husband is adopted into the tribe. When that happens, the white man is expected to live by the same rules as everybody else. Ask Nate. He knows all about being adopted."

"Can a white man marry a Mandan woman and want to live here in the village but refuse adoption?"

"I've never heard of that happening."

"But could he if he didn't want to be adopted?" Eric persisted, gripping McNair's wrist.

Shakespeare detected the inner turmoil mirrored in the Englishman's eyes, and he deduced the reason. "No," he said softly. "I'm sorry to say the Mandans would expect him to be adopted after a while or they'd probably kick him out. They might even make his wife stay with them."

"And here I thought . . ." Eric said, then clamped his lips shut. He had already made a fool of himself in front of Nate by extolling the supposedly pure virtues of the Mandans, and he wasn't going to commit the same mistake twice. King had tried to tell him the truth, but he hadn't listened. Now he knew better.

Eric gazed blankly at the ceiling. His perfect paradise had cracks in its foundation, and he feared the whole sterling mental image he had formed might come crashing down with the next startling insight into the habits of these inconsistent people. Most of all, he feared for Morning Dew. Specifically, for the future he had began to plan for the two of them.

Earlier his plans had been so clear-cut. He would go to St. Louis and purchase the necessary supplies, then return and live with the Mandans. His paintings and sketchings would become a permanent record of the tribe for all to behold, including generations yet unborn. And to complete the picture, he had envisioned himself courting and eventually marrying Morning Dew.

But how in the name of all that was holy, Eric asked himself, could he wed the woman knowing what lay in store for them during a subsequent buffalo ceremony? He'd be damned if he was going to share his wife with another man, whether for the good of the tribe or not!

Such an idea was ridiculous, anyway. The buffalo could no more be influenced in their actions by the dalliances of a bunch of old men and amorous women than they could be by the matings of frogs or crickets. That the Mandans believed they could only showed how backward the tribe really was.

Eric wearily rubbed his eyes. Perhaps, he reasoned, he was being unfair. He shouldn't judge the Mandans by his standards, but by their own. They had never had the benefit of his upbringing, of his education. They were lowly, superstitious primitives who combated the fickle whims of Nature the only way they knew how, with magic rituals no cultured person would ever indulge in.

What was he thinking? Eric let his chin droop to his chest, then sighed. A few hours ago he had been telling Nate that here was a new race of Adams and Eves. Now he was saying they were nothing more than ordinary ignorant savages. They couldn't be both, so which were they?

Suddenly a large pair of feet stepped into his line of vision, and Eric glanced up.

Jarvis was on his way out with one of the wives, his big face aglow with joy. "Hello, Mr. Nash. I didn't know you were here. Come to have some fun, have you?"

Eric said nothing.

"This is a bit of all right in my book," the giant declared as he stooped to go through the doorway. "Now I see why you like these people so much."

"I did," Eric said under his breath. "Now I just don't know anymore." He abruptly remembered McNair was right next to him, and he faced around to see if the mountain man had heard. But Shakespeare was staring at the circles, seemingly unaware of his comments. Relieved, Eric sank back and wished he were dead.

Chapter Nineteen

Nate King was standing with Shakespeare and Jarvis in front of the grand chief's lodge early the next morning when four warriors galloped into the village and up to where Four Bears stood nearby. Excitedly they imparted some information, and in seconds Four Bears was hurrying toward his doorway while other warriors ran to spread the news through the entire village.

"Buffalo have been sighted," Four Bears signed happily to his guests. "Every man will join in the hunt. Would you like to come?"

Since to refuse would be taken as being impolite, Nate replied that he would. So did McNair. Nate then translated for the benefit of Jarvis.

"Tell him thanks, but no, mate," the giant said. "Indian horses and I don't get along very well. Maybe I'm too heavy. But I'll stay put and keep the marquis and Diana company."

The village had been transformed into a whirl-wind of activity. Warriors were leading their prized hunting horses from their lodges while their families gathered around to wish them a safe and prosperous hunt. Bows were being strung, rifles loaded, lances sharpened.

Nate accepted the same horse Four Bears had given him the day before, and this time the animal allowed him to mount without fidgeting. He checked the Hawken and both pistols to verify they were loaded, then looked around for Shakespeare, who had promised to hurry back after fetching a horse from Stalking Wolf.

"Be careful, my husband," said a melodious voice behind him in English.

"I will, dearest," Nate told Winona, and leaned down to kiss her on the cheek as she stepped closer. How well he remembered her nervousness when he had gone on previous buffalo hunts, a fear spawned by the deaths of relatives who had died on Shoshone surrounds. Her attitude was understandable in light of the fact that next to dying in battle, buffalo hunting claimed the lives of more Indian men than any other activity. She offered a halfhearted smile, then moved aside when their son came running up, waving his long rifle.

"I just heard, Pa! Can I go along? Please?"

"Not this time," Nate said.

"Why not? You've let me hunt deer and elk. I can drop a buffalo. I know I can. So please let me go?"

"Hunting buffalo is different, son. You know that. It's very dangerous. You never know when one might turn on you and try to gore your horse, or when the whole herd might change direction and come straight at you. Shoshone boys don't go on their first buffalo hunt until they're twelve or fourteen. That's when I'll take you."

Zach had an answer ready. "But I'm only *half* Shoshone," he reminded his father.

"And that's the half that will have to stay here. Since the rest of you can't go without it, you'll remain in the village as I've told you to do."

"Awwwwww," the boy grumbled. "It's plain no fair."

Chuckling at how well he had handled the request, Nate waved to them both and rode to intercept Shakespeare, who was trotting in his direction. Suddenly he saw Eric Nash walking his way and reined up. The Englishman was misery incarnate, walking with his head held low and his shoulders slumped. Shakespeare had told Nate about the incident during the early morning hours, so Nate had an idea why Nash was so upset. "Eric!" he called out. "Care to go buffalo hunting with us?"

Nash glanced up in surprise and gazed at the bustling Indians as if noticing them for the first time. "What's that? What did you say?"

"You want to paint every aspect of Mandan life, don't you? Here's your chance to see a buffalo hunt. Not many whites get the privilege."

"I don't know the first thing about it. Is there any risk?"

"A lot. You might be killed if you're not careful."

"Really?" Eric responded, and a peculiar light came into his eyes. He hefted his rifle, glanced at Mato-tope's lodge, and nodded. "Bloody right! I'll ask Four Bears for a horse and be right with you. Wait for me, Nate."

"I'll be here," Nate said, hoping he hadn't made an error in judgment. But if there was any way to bring Nash out of the doldrums, this would do the job.

Shakespeare rode up and nodded at the retreating figure of the artist. "Don't tell me you just invited that greenhorn to come along? What are you trying to do? Get him killed?"

"He's gotten the wrong notion about Indians into his head. This might set him straight."

"Your mind is the clearer, Ajax, and your virtues the fairer. He that is proud eats up himself. Pride is his own glass, his own trumpet, his own chronicle. And whatever praises itself but in the deed, devours the deed in the praise."

"One of these days you're going to quote Shakespeare and I'll be shocked to death."

"Why so?"

"Because I'll understand what the hell you're saying."

Shakespeare exploded with mirth, which ended when he saw the sour expression on Zach. "Let me take a stab at guessing what ails your pride and joy. He wanted to go?"

Nate nodded.

"He's at a rough age," Shakespeare mentioned, then quoted again. "Not yet old enough for a man, nor young enough for a boy. As a squash is before 'tis a peascod, or a codling when 'tis almost an apple, 'tis with him in standing water, between boy and man."

"Do you have any quotes I can share with Nash?"

"Just my favorite."

"Which is?"

"To be, or not to be, that is the question," Shakespeare said. "I think Eric is wrestling with that particular dilemma himself, but in a different vein." He paused, grinning. "To love, or not to love, that is the question."

A score of warriors were bearing down on them, so they promptly moved out of the way. More soon followed, in groups or singly, all anxious to get after the buffalo before the herd moved. They were collecting just beyond the palisade, there to await the leader of their people, who presently rode past Nate and McNair, a full quiver across his back, a bow in his left hand.

"If that greenhorn doesn't hurry, we'll miss out," Shakespeare complained.

At last Nash appeared, walking from the lodge leading a brown mare. He tried to climb up but the mare pranced backwards and jerked on the rope reins, trying to pull free. Again he made the attempt with the same results.

"Do you reckon one of us should tell that greenhorn he's going about it all wrong?" Shakespeare asked.

"I will," Nate said, and rode over, doing his best to suppress a grin at the antics the Englishman was going through. Nash, apparently, didn't realize that Indians mounted on the right side of a horse, not the left as whites did. The mare had been trained in the Indian manner, and was not about to let anyone climb on her improperly. Stopping, Nate pointed this out to Nash.

"Smashing. So I've made an idiot of myself yet again," Nash replied. "Figures." Moving around the mare, he was finally able to fork her, although she did cock her head to give him a dubious look as he mounted.

Finally the three of them were off, but once outside the village they found they had been left behind. The Mandans were a quarter of a mile off, heading to the northeast.

"The blighters didn't wait," Eric commented.

"I wonder why," Shakespeare said dryly.

"Their people are depending on them for fresh meat, which is why they're in such an all-fired hurry," Nate informed the Englishman. "If you want to see how they do it, we'd best not sit here jawing." His heels touched the gelding's flanks and they were off, galloping side by side across the plain, the long grass parting under the flying hoofs of their animals, the wind whipping their hair.

Ordinarily Indians spied on a herd prior to getting down to the grisly business of killing as many as they could before the herd could flee, so Nate was confident they'd catch up before the hunt started. His gelding was the fleetest, so he had to hold it back to keep from outdistancing his friends, especially Nash on the old mare.

Nate glanced at the animal, then at the Englishman. "By the way, who gave you this horse?"

"The chief's wife. He was busy talking with some warriors so I didn't want to bother him. I ran inside and kept pointing at the horses until she got my meaning." Eric cocked his head. "Why?"

"No reason," Nate said. Truth was, if Four Bears had given the animal to Nash it would have meant the chief either didn't like the Englishman or didn't trust him. Mandan warriors owned stallions and geldings; only the women owned mares because the warriors rated them as inferior in battle and when hunting. No self-respecting Mandan brave would be caught dead on one.

The hunting party was making for a rise. They spread out as they neared the prominence, each man unlimbering his weapon. Rifles and bows were unslung, arrows notched to shafts, lances held low so the sunlight wouldn't reflect off the points and perhaps alert the herd. At the base of the rise they halted and jumped down. A number of boys who had been brought along for the purpose now held the horses while the men started up the incline.

Nate and his companions reached the bottom just as the Mandans reached the top and flattened. He dropped down, raced up the slope, and eased down beside Four Bears.

Thousands upon thousands of buffaloes covered the prairie below. To the north, the south, and the east all that could be seen was a sluggishly moving ocean of bulky brownish-black shapes. Most were grazing, others chewing their cuds, still others rolling in wallows. The air resounded to their grunts, bellows, snorts, and bawls.

Four Bears glanced at Nate and signed, "My people will eat well for many sleeps."

"My heart is glad for the Mandans," Nate responded, adding, "Your family will eat better than most. Every buffalo I shoot today is yours."

The unexpected offer touched the venerable chief, who placed his hand to Nate's chest, then signed, "If you were not an adopted Shoshone, I would adopt you into our tribe."

One of the warriors whispered urgently.

Nate looked down the rise and saw a lone bull meandering toward them as it nipped at the grass with its big teeth. Should it spy them or catch their scent, it would sound the alarm and flee, which in turn might precipitate a mass stampede. Since the Mandans would have to run to their horses before giving chase, they would not be able to slay as many of the brutes.

None of the warriors moved. They hardly appeared to breathe as the solitary bull came closer and closer. The animal shifted and began to turn, and there was an outpouring of collective relief on every face there. Then they all froze in consternation.

Eric Nash had sneezed.

Nate stiffened, his eyes on the bull. It had lifted its ponderous head and was gazing at the rim, trying to isolate the source of the strange sound it had heard. Would it keep on feeding or flee? Nate wondered. If Nash had inadvertently caused a stampede, the Mandans would be rightfully furious. He glanced at the Englishman, who was two yards below him and to his right. To his horror, he saw that Nash was unaware of what he had done. Worse, Nash's face was scrunched up and he was drawing his head back to sneeze again.

Instantly Nate launched himself into the air, letting go of the Hawken so he could wrap one arm around the Englishman's middle and clamp his other hand over Nash's nose and mouth. They both went down, rolling over and over in the soft grass, making little noise. Nate pressed his mouth to Eric's ear as they stopped and hissed, "Not another sound! Don't move!"

Eric froze, his eyes wide.

Twisting, Nate looked up the slope. He could tell the bull was still where it had been because the Mandans were as rigid as logs. Releasing Nash, he crawled back to his rifle, then inched high enough to peer over the top.

The bull was turning and heading back into the herd.

Soundlessly the Mandans slid backwards until they were low enough not to be spotted, at which point they leaped to their feet and dashed to their waiting mounts. Some gave the stupefied Englishman sour looks that implied they would rather shoot him than buffalo.

Nate ran to Nash and helped him stand. "Sorry, friend," he said, "but you about scared off the herd and I couldn't let that happen."

"It's this grass," Eric said lamely. "It makes my nose tingle sometimes."

"Make haste," Nate directed, tugging Nash along as he hustled to catch up with the Mandans. Already the warriors had split and separated, about half going north behind Stalking Wolf, the rest moving south, Four Bears leading them.

Shakespeare McNair was on his horse, a look of amusement on his face.

"You found all that funny?" Nate snapped.

"Blame Stalking Wolf. He asked me if white men can breathe with their noses chopped off and their mouths sewn shut."

In the act of taking hold of the mare's reins, Eric paused. "Was he referring to me?"

"Naw," Shakespeare answered. "He just likes to chaw about mutilating folks. Must be a mean streak in his family."

"Ignore him," Nate advised Nash as he mounted and turned the gelding to follow Four Bears. "And don't dally or we'll leave you here with the boys."

The Mandans were nearly to their respective ends of the rise. They slowed, each man hunched low over the neck of his horse. When Mato-tope halted they all did, and the chief rose so he could look over the shoulders of the men with him and see the warriors who were with Stalking Wolf. Stalking Wolf gestured. Four Bears gestured back. Then, at a screech from their leader, the entire band vented shrill whoops and swept into the open.

Nate was close on their heels and saw all that transpired. It had always amazed him how swiftly buffalo could reach top speed from a dead standstill, and these were no exception. Barely had Four Bear's voiced his cry than the whole mass was off and running to the southeast, bulls, cows, and calves churning the turf with their pounding hoofs.

The Mandans converged on their quarry, the warriors fanning right and left to give their mounts room to maneuver. Like birds of prey streaking down on game from above, the Mandans streaked toward the animals that made their existence possible. Since every shot counted, whether a shaft or a lead ball, they held their fire until they were right on the buffalo, riding abreast of the thundering beasts, in some cases inches from the shaggy, heaving sides.

Nate admired their bravery, but did not needlessly expose himself. He'd learned from hard experience not to get too close to stampeding buffalo, and armed as he was with the reliable Hawken, he didn't have to. From a range of 20 yards he sighted on a cow, struggled to hold the wavering barrel steady, and fired. At the blast the cow crashed to the ground. Those buffaloes behind her immediately skirted her on either side.

The purpose was to drop as many as humanly possible, so Nate didn't stop to claim his prize. But he did stop to reload, working feverishly while watching everything that was going on around him. Many an unwary trapper and warrior had been attacked by enraged bulls or cows while preoccupied with something else when they should have been on their guard.

Like a horde of bloodthirsty banshees, the Mandans were wreaking havoc among the herd. Flights of glittering arrows whizzed through the air, rifles cracked, spitting clouds of smoke, and lances were hurled with unerring skill. Buffaloes dropped at a staggering rate.

One stocky brave guided his galloping steed by knee pressure alone right up to a big bull. His sinew bowstring had been pulled back almost to his ear, and now, taking aim, he let the shaft fly. The arrow penetrated the bull's flesh on the right side, ripped clear through its huge body, and sailed out the other side to stick in another buffalo.

Another brave drew next to a cow, his lance held aloft. He paced her, waiting for the right moment. Then, muscles rippling, he hurled his weapon downward, burying the lance deep in the cow's body, and she smashed to the earth.

But the Mandans were not having it all their own way. Here and there more belligerent buffaloes were going after their human tormentors,

lowering their huge heads to slash and tear with
their wicked curved horns. A young brave on a
gray stallion was one of the unfortunates; a bull
rammed into his mount, upending it, and as the
frightened horse whinnied and struggled to regain
its footing, the bull charged again, rending its
stomach open with a single swipe. In acute agony,
the horse thrashed and kicked while the warrior,
who had been momentarily pinned, managed to
get to his feet. The bull saw him, and had started
to come around the horse after him when one of
his fellows, observing his plight, put two arrows
into the enraged bull one after the other.

By then Nate had his Hawken reloaded and
rejoined the chase. The buffalo were strung out
for miles and the end of the herd had not yet
passed him by. Matching the speed of a bull,
he tucked the stock to his shoulder and prepared
to fire. But then, out of the corner of his eye,
he spied Eric Nash, who had gotten ahead of
him while he reloaded. The Englishman was in
desperate straits.

Since warriors relied extensively on the reflexes
and judgment of their mounts during a buffalo hunt, only horses specifically suited to the
intensity of the chase were used. Temperamental
horses, such as those prone to frightening easily, or those that were not lightning quick, were
never ridden at such a critical time. The mare
Nash had been given, unaccustomed as it was to
hunting buffalo, had become panic-stricken and
was racing about in unbridled terror.

Eric Nash was doing his utmost to bring the
mare under control, but no matter how he lashed
the reins or slapped his legs, the animal refused

to respond. One moment she was galloping away from the roiling herd, the next she was making straight for them.

As Nate swung around he saw the mare had moved dangerously close to the edge of the surging buffalo. Nash appeared to have frozen, gaping in dread at the hairy monsters not two feet from his leg. All the Mandans were too busy to have noticed the Englishman's plight, and it was doubtful they would have gone to his aid even had they noticed. Shakespeare was nowhere to be seen. So it was entirely up to Nate to save him.

Bringing the gelding to its top speed, Nate raced to reach Nash before disaster struck. In his ears roared the drumming of a million hoofs. To his nose came the pungent odor of sweat. Dust hovered everywhere, growing thicker by the minute. He blinked to get some out of his eyes as he angled closer and closer to the Englishman.

Nate was nearly there when a bull next to the mare abruptly swerved straight at her, its right horn spearing at her side. In terror, she slanted away, and the bull pursued her, its black nose nearly touching her back hoofs. In seconds it would overtake her and bring her down.

With a smooth motion, Nate brought the Hawken up. He wasn't close enough to suit him, but he didn't dare wait. He saw the bull's horn nick the mare's leg and she broke her stride. A fraction of a second later, Nate fired.

The bull stumbled, recovered, and halted, glaring all around as blood oozed from a hole in its thick hide. It spotted Nate, whirled, and thundered toward him.

This was unforeseen. Nate had both pistols at his belt, but they lacked the stopping power of the Hawken and he had no desire to see how effective they would be in a pinch. Yet he had no other option. Drawing his right flintlock, he cut to the right, forcing the bull to move further from the herd if it wanted him, which it definitely did as evidenced by the alacrity with which it bore down on the gelding.

Nate twisted, cocked the piece, and waited for the bull to reduce the gap. He wanted to be sure because he might not get a second shot. Aiming the pistol was easier than the heavier Hawken, and he centered on a spot just above the buffalo's right eye. Twenty-five feet separated them. About 20 feet. Fifteen. Ten. And now only five.

It was then that Nate stroked the trigger and witnessed the bull's eyeball dissolve in a spray of gore. Quickly he bent to the task of gaining distance, while behind him came a loud thud. A glance showed the bull on its side, feebly striving to stand. He turned the gelding, rode in close, and dispatched the bull with his other flintlock.

Eric Nash had halted not far off and had his arms folded across his chest, his head bowed.

Nate went to him, and as he drew rein he could see the Englishman was shaking like an aspen leaf in the wind. "That was a close scare," Nate commented as he set to reloading all his guns.

"I did it again!" Nash cried, looking up. Inner pain contorted his features and drew his lips back from his teeth. "Damn my bones! I did it again!"

"Did what?" Nate asked while checking on all sides. The buffalo were still in full flight and none were showing any interest in them.

"I proved I'm a coward! I might as well lay a rod to my own back, I'm such a glutton for punishment."

"You're putting the cart before the horse."

"What?"

"A man has to learn to walk before he can run. Did you really expect to come out here after buffalo and do everything perfectly the first time? I figured you had more sense than that."

"You're missing the point," Nash said sorrowfully. "I was *scared*."

"So? The first time I hunted buffalo was with my Uncle Zeke, and I can tell you that I was so scared I nearly wet my britches."

"You were?"

Nate nodded. "Don't be so hard on yourself, Eric. You've got a damn sight more gumption than a lot of men I've known. Most wouldn't think to try to hunt buffalo the way the Indians do."

"Oh?" Eric said, and gazed at the fleeing herd. He pondered whether the trapper might have a valid point, whether he was being a bit hard on himself. There was no denying he had made great strides in his self-confidence and ability, but he would be a bloody fool to think he could match the deeds of men like King and the Mandans. Given time, though, he just might. "Thank you, Nate, for setting me straight. You're as decent a chap as I've ever met."

Nate was shoving the ramrod into his Hawken. He paused, glanced at Nash, and seized the opportunity to say, "The feeling works both ways. Once you settle down with Morning Dew, I suppose I'll have to pay you a visit every so often to see how big your brood has become."

A cloud enveloped Eric's face. "You won't have to make the effort. There won't be any brood, as you call it."

"Here I figured you were sweet on her," Nate said, and shrugged. "If you changed your mind, I don't blame you. I nearly changed mine about marrying Winona once."

"You did?"

"Yep. Her mother and father had died, and it's Shoshone custom for those who lose loved ones to cut off the tips of their fingers as a sign of their grief."

"What a revolting practice!"

"That's the way I felt too. When Winona cut off the ends of two of her fingers, I about went crazy. I figured I'd been a dunderhead to take her as my wife, and I wondered if maybe I shouldn't find myself another woman."

"Yet you stuck with her. Why?"

"The answer to that is simple. I love her." Nate was hurriedly reloading the pistols. "When a man cares for a woman, it doesn't much matter what her family is like, or the practices of her people, or the way she wears her hair, or anything else. He cares for her because she is who she is. And if she stays true to him, he'll stick with her through thick and thin."

"Your homespun philosophy never ceases to astound me," Eric confided, and would have said more had not Nate suddenly glanced to the southeast, uttered an oath, and broke into a gallop. Eric immediately did likewise, although he had no idea what they were doing until he looked in the same direction and spied a

Mandan down on the ground beside a dead horse. His eyes narrowed and he voiced a curse himself.

The warrior on the ground was Four Bears.

Chapter Twenty

The trailing ranks of the vast herd were half a mile to the south. Mato-tope lay on his stomach among dozens of fresh kills made by the warriors of his tribe. His superb stallion had been torn open from front to back and its intestines had spilled onto the grass. Beside them was a mammoth dead bull, five arrows jutting out of his body.

Nate King vaulted from the gelding before the horse came to a complete stop, and reached the grand chief in three bounds. Kneeling, he carefully rolled Four Bears over. The only wound he could find was a large welt on the chief's forehead.

"Is he alive?" Eric Nash asked as he rode up.

"Yes, and lucky for us that he is."

"In what way?"

"The Mandans would take his death as bad

medicine, and some might blame it on us."

"How daft," Eric said. "I fail to see how we could be blamed."

"They'd claim our coming brought bad medicine to the tribe. A few would want our scalps." Nate saw Mato-tope's bow lying to his right and picked it up. The ash had been splintered, the string broken, proof the chief had gone down fighting. He put the bow aside, then stood. "You stay here and keep watch. I'm going to go to the village and get another horse for him."

"What am I supposed to do while you're gone?" Eric asked.

"Shoo off any wolves that might appear," Nate said, striding to the gelding. "Sooner or later one of the other warriors will see that he's missing and they'll start a search." He swung up. "There was probably so much dust in the air that they didn't see him go down."

"Why don't I go and you stay with him?" Eric suggested, daunted by the prospect of confronting a pack of ravenous wolves. In Europe there had been many recorded instances of wolves attacking humans, and he wasn't too keen on learning if their American counterparts shared the same savage traits.

"Because the gelding is faster than the mare and you don't speak enough sign to explain what has happened," Nate responded. With that, he was off at a gallop.

"Damn," Eric muttered. Dismounting, he let the reins trail and stepped over to Mato-tope. Eric debated whether to try and rouse the chief and decided not to; someone had once told him that it was better for those unconscious from head wounds to revive in their own good time rather than be jarred to wakefulness.

Eric nervously licked his lips and made a 360-degree sweep of the vast plain. Other than the billowing dust to the south, nothing moved. He saw no sign of wolves and breathed a little easier.

Minutes passed. Flies appeared from nowhere to descend onto the bloody carcasses. From the north came a lone vulture, which in no time was joined by others. Soon ten of the ugly big birds were circling over the kills.

Eric wondered if he should shoo the vultures away too. Or the buzzards, as King and McNair called them. He raised his rifle to fire, but changed his mind. What if he should shoot and wolves appeared before he could reload? He began pacing back and forth beside Four Bears. Twice the chief groaned but didn't move.

"Hurry up, Nate," Eric said to himself. The way his luck had been going of late, he was sure wolves would arrive on the scene before the frontiersman returned. He changed his pattern and walked in a circle instead, around and around Four Bears.

More minutes went by. Eric was becoming increasingly impatient. He kept an eye on the buzzards, which seemed reluctant to land with him in the vicinity, and constantly scanned the prairie for slinking gray shapes. So it was that when something moved to the northeast, he spotted it right away.

A bull buffalo was slowly standing up 40 yards off. Blood caked its neck and side. The fletching of a single arrow protruded from under its hump. Shaking its head, the beast lumbered a few feet, stopped, and surveyed its surroundings.

Eric swallowed hard and stood still. King had told him to be on guard for wolves. Nothing had been said about wounded buffalo. What should he do? Try to shoot it or stay close to the chief and pray it departed without causing trouble? He saw the buffalo look directly at him, and hoped that Nate was right about the animals having poor eyesight. If he didn't move, it might not realize he was there.

Unfortunately, the mare picked that very moment to walk by him as it idly grazed on the lush grass.

To complicate matters, Four Bears uttered the loudest groan yet.

The bull advanced. Noisily sniffing the air, it walked to within 20 yards of the Englishman and the Mandan, then stopped.

"Please go away, you bloody brute," Eric breathed, anxiously fingering his rifle. He thought about jumping onto the mare and riding off, but he didn't care to leave Four Bears unprotected. The idea occurred to him to conceal himself behind the buffalo Four Bears had slain. Once the wounded bull could no longer see him, it might wander away.

With that purpose in mind, Eric took a step. Suddenly the bull snorted, dug its front hoofs into the ground, lowered its head, and charged. Eric's insides were transformed into mush. For several seconds he simply stood rooted to the spot, his brain and body numb.

Only when Eric's eyes focused on the bull's powerful black horns and he realized what they would do to him did the spark of life animate him to jerk up the rifle, cock the hammer, and take aim. The basic human instinct of self-preservation was taking over for the virtually paralyzed rational human mind. He held his breath as Nate had taught him and slowly pulled the trigger.

The bull was eight yards off when hit. Its front leg buckled and down it went, but not on its side. Head sagging, it slid forward across the trampled grass as if on a sheet of ice.

Eric saw the enormous dark figure growing bigger and bigger as its momentum carried it nearer and nearer, and he was tensing his muscles to leap out of the way when the bull came to a sudden stop several yards from his legs. He moved toward it, his hand falling to his pistol, then stopped when his body took to trembling. Gritting his teeth, he got a grip on himself. Warily, he approached the bull and listened for the sound of its heavy breathing. There was none.

The emotional reaction brought Eric to his knees in profound gratitude. He closed his eyes and whispered over and over again, "Thank you. Thank you. Thank you."

Suddenly a firm hand fell on his left shoulder. Eric involuntarily jumped, clawing at his flintlock in his agitation, and spun. He didn't know who had touched him; for all he knew it might be a Sioux. When he saw Four Bears behind him, smiling broadly, he slumped and released the pistol.

Mato-tope walked to the bull, said something, and gave the hump a whack. Then, laughing heartily, he walked up and clapped Eric on the shoulder.

Eric nodded dumbly. He believed the Mandan

was praising him for slaying the beast, and he gathered that Four Bears thought he had committed a courageous deed. "If you only knew," he said softly.

The sound of hoofs rose to the south. Speeding across the prairie were a score of dust-covered warriors, who shortly ringed around Eric and Four Bears, all speaking at once. Four Bears held up a hand, which silenced the braves, and proceeded to go on at some length while gesturing at the buffalo he had slain, his dead horse, the bull Eric had shot, and Eric.

Rising, the Englishman was aware of being the object of intent scrutiny. A few of the Mandans even smiled at him, showing that their annoyance over the sneezing episode had evaporated. He returned their friendly looks, then waited to see what would happen next.

A lone rider materialized to the southeast. Soon Eric recognized Shakespeare McNair. Since he expected the mountain man to inquire about what had just transpired, he sorted his thoughts to present his actions in the best possible light. The first words out of McNair's mouth, however, had nothing to do with his accomplishment.

"Where the dickens is Nate? Have you seen him? Is he hurt?"

Eric was in the process of explaining about Mato-tope's horse when the chief walked over and addressed Shakespeare in sign language. The two discoursed at some length, and when they were done McNair grinned at Eric.

"Well, now. I'll be dogged. This coon is plumb pleased to learn you have the makings of a regular mountainee man."

"I'm in their good graces, I take it?" Eric suavely responded.

"The chief here says you risked your hide to save his," Shakespeare related. "When they have their big celebration a day or two from now, you'll be his guest of honor."

"What sort of celebration?"

"To give thanks for their successful hunt," Shakespeare said. "Pretty soon the women and children will show up, and they'll get busy butchering all these buffalo. Should take 'em until late tomorrow or early the day after to cut up this many. Once all the hides have been rolled up and the meat all packed for the trip, they'll head for the village, and that night they'll have a feast fit for some of your European royalty."

"What do I do as the guest of honor?"

Shakespeare chuckled. "Nothing much except stand around and try to look noble." He stared at the bull Eric had shot. "If there's anything you'd like to ask the chief, that would be the time. I'll even translate for you if you want."

"I should think of questions to pose?"

"No. I meant anything you'd like to ask *for*, anything you want, any favor he can do you. If you want one of his horses, say so then and there and he'll be happy to oblige." The mountain man paused, then remarked, as if off-handedly, "Or could be there's something else you want. Whatever, he won't refuse."

"Anything at all?"

"Yep. Other than one of his wives. He might not like that too much."

Eric turned away, reflecting. What did he want more than anything else in the world? But was he balmy? How could he ask for her when he hardly knew her? And what sort of man took advantage of a fluke of fate to further his own ends? He scratched his chin while wrestling with his conscience.

Soon Nate King arrived leading another of Mato-tope's war horses. Upon learning of Eric's act, he walked over and congratulated the Englishman.

"To tell you the truth," Eric replied confidentially, "I don't know quite how I did it. And if I had it to do again, I'd probably botch the job."

"Don't tell Mato-tope." Nate said with a grin. "He thinks you're the bravest white man who ever lived. Nothing is too good for you."

"So McNair was saying."

While some of the warriors rode off to escort the women and children, others roamed about the prairie insuring all of the buffaloes were indeed dead.

Nate went to Shakespeare and they spent the time in idle conversation, which eventually turned to Eric Nash when the older man declared, "I'll wager ten plews our young gallant doesn't ask Mato-tope for the hand of Morning Dew."

"I'll take you up on that bet. He might surprise you. Look at what he did today."

"Tangling with a mad buffler is easy compared to finding the courage to ask a woman to be your wife."

"Hush up. Here he comes," Nate said, watching the Englishman hasten toward them wearing a disturbed expression. "Is anything wrong?" he asked.

"Do you see them?" Eric asked, aghast.

"See who?"

"Those two Mandans," Eric said, motioning at a pair of warriors who were bent over a dead cow 60 feet to the north.

"What about them?" Nate asked in feigned innocence.

"Look at what they're *doing*!"

The two in question had their butchers knives out and had sliced into the cow. One had his arms inside the animal, clean up to the elbows, and was feeling around. He now gave a glad cry and stepped back holding his bloody knife in one hand and one of the cow's dripping livers in the other. Then he raised the liver to his mouth and took a greedy bite.

"I think I'm going to be ill," Nash said, clutching his stomach. "Don't they know enough to cook their food first?"

"Cooking meat isn't important for Indians," Shakespeare revealed. "Lots of times they eat the livers and kidney raw. Sometimes they go for the intestines. And they like to crack bones so they can dig out the marrow, of course."

"But to eat it raw?"

"Don't make no never-mind to them. Me neither. Tastes just as good raw as it does cooked. Some might say it tastes better." Shakespeare grinned when Eric quivered, and went on gleefully. "Now the tongue and the hump are never eaten raw. They're special, the parts of the buffalo the Indians like the most. All Indians. They roast them real slow over a fire and savor every chunk."

"I'm surprised they don't eat the brains also," Eric said sarcastically.

"Some tribes do. Others use the brains for

curing hides, just like we did with those coyote skins. When the women show up, you'll see them crack the skulls of every buffalo that was killed."

Eric was watching the two Indians polish off the liver. "I just don't know," he commented softly. "I just don't know at all."

"About what?" Shakespeare asked.

"Nothing."

Nate had to pretend to be interested in the northern horizon so the Englishman wouldn't see the mirth that threatened to erupt into an outburst of laughter. There were times, he mused, when his mentor could be as devilish as sin. Most of the old-timers took particular delight in poking good-natured fun at greenhorns, and Shakespeare took more delight than most.

"I say! Now what are those two doing?" Nash inquired.

One of the liver-eaters had dug around inside the buffalo and removed its heart. His hands and arms covered thick with blood and gore, the warrior knelt and reverently placed the heart on the ground.

"You might say they're planting a spirit seed," Shakespeare answered.

"They're going to bury the bleeding heart?"

McNair shook his head. "They'll leave it right where it is. After all the butchering is done and the Mandans are on their way home, this whole prairie will be dotted with buffalo hearts."

"In God's name, why?"

"So there will be more buffalo next year. They believe that for every heart they leave, a new buffalo will be born in the spring. It's their way of replacing the buffalo that were killed today,"

Shakespeare elaborated. "We'd call it superstition. Or magic. The Indians call it good medicine."

Instead of registering shock, Eric knit his brow and remarked, "I must be daft. That actually makes sense to me. It's almost poetical."

"You're learning, son. Slowly but surely," Shakespeare said.

Within the hour the women and children arrived leading the packhorses that would tote the meat and hides back. Since the stallions and geldings used in warfare and hunting were far too valuable for such menial labor, they were never employed as beasts of burden. Often they were pampered to the point of being spoiled. Warriors always fed them more than the pack animals received, giving them the best grass or other feed. They were also well watered and groomed daily. Some trappers liked to joke that Indian men fussed over their horses more than they did their wives.

Butchering was a joyous time. The women sang while they worked. Older children helped while the small ones gamboled about. Everywhere the warriors held their heads up proudly and told of their prowess during the hunt.

Winona and Zach had tagged along when the mass exodus from the village occurred. Together with Nate and Shakespeare, they cut up the buffalo the two mountaineers had slain.

Nate was surprised to see Diana Templar and Jarvis ride up. They stayed long enough to see the butchering begin; then Diana addressed the giant and they both wheeled their mounts and left. Nate figured Lady Templar had been squeamish

over the gory toil the Indians were doing, until
he happened to spy Eric Nash helping Morning
Dew and her mother carve up a cow.

Night fell before the work was completed, and
the Mandans made camp right there on the plain.
Fires were lit to ward off predators and scavengers, and everyone stayed up late talking. The
next day, promptly at first light, the work was
resumed.

Once again Eric Nash spent his time in the
company of Morning Dew and her mother. From
what Nate could tell, Four Bears had no objections. In fact, the chief was very kindly disposed
toward the Englishman. Before the butchering
was done, Nash had received a fine red blanket
and a new knife as tokens of the chief's friendship. And often Four Bears would seek Nash out
to try to teach him some of the Mandan tongue.

The Indians worked swiftly out of an eagerness to reach their village; they were all looking
forward to the upcoming feast. The days after a
buffalo hunt were spent gorging themselves, and
compensated for leaner times of the year when
they sometimes had to do without meals for a
day or two.

On entering the palisade, the first order of business was to have fires started and meat racks built.
Young and old joined in. The village dogs, who
rarely ever had enough to eat, knew from past
experience what to expect and were in an excitable state. To them would be thrown the scraps,
enough to fill their bellies to the bursting point.

All was going along smoothly. Or so Nate
thought until late in the afternoon, when the
Mandans were congregating in the central plaza

for the great feast. There was a commotion ahead outside of a lodge. Men were shouting and waving their arms. A woman screamed shrilly. Nate, in the company of his wife, son, and mentor, was near the dwelling and craned his neck to see the cause of the disturbance. What he saw set his blood to racing. For locked in a life-and-death struggle on the bare earth, rolling over and over as they grappled tooth and nail, were Jarvis and two warriors.

Chapter Twenty-One

Suddenly the three men stopped rolling. One of
the Mandans had an arm looped around Jarvis's
throat from behind and was trying to throttle the
life from him, while the second Mandan was striving to pin the giant's huge arms so Jarvis would be
unable to defend himself. They were both smiling
grimly, confident of victory. But they reckoned
without the ex-soldier's enormous strength.

Jarvis wrenched his right arm free and smashed
a massive fist into the face of the warrior gripping his other arm, sending that Mandan flying. Then, twisting sharply, he reached back
over his shoulder, seized the other brave by
the hair, and swung the Mandan up and over
as effortlessly as a normal man might fling
a little girl's doll. The Mandan smacked into
the earth with a sickening thud and lay there,
dazed.

Nate saw other warriors fingering their weapons, and before any of them could move to aid their fellows he rushed forward and touched the barrel of his Hawken to the giant's temple just as Jarvis was rising.

"What the bloody hell, mate?"

"If you value your hide, don't move!" Nate cautioned, bobbing his head at the ring of warriors to accent his point.

Jarvis was in a crouch. He scanned the crowd, read their mood, and perceived the gravity of the situation. "Tell them I didn't start it," he said. "Those two blooming bastards did!"

"Why?" Nate asked.

Just then there were loud voices toward the rear of the encircling Mandans, who parted to permit Four Bears, Stalking Wolf, and Shakespeare McNair to advance. The high chief stared somberly at the two Mandans who had participated in the fight, then at Jarvis.

"What the hell went on here?" Shakespeare inquired.

"I don't know yet," Nate replied, lowering his Hawken.

The giant stood.

Mato-tope addressed the two warriors, one of whom spoke at length, often gesturing angrily at Jarvis and almost as often at an attractive woman in a trim buckskin dress standing meekly to one side. The other said only a few words. Turning to Nate, the chief signed, "I would like to hear what White Tree has to say about this."

White Tree was the name the Mandans had bestowed on Jarvis. Nate relayed the request, adding, "And don't leave out a single detail. All of us are in trouble here. If you caused this, the chief might see fit to throw us out. Or worse."

"There's not much to tell. I was minding my business near the lodge I've been staying at when this wench—" Jarvis pointed at the attractive woman "—came up to me, took me by the hand, and led me to this here lodge." He indicated the dwelling behind them. "She wasn't shy about why she'd brought me, and we were having a go when these two blighters jumped me."

"Back up a bit," Nate said. "Do you know this woman?"

"Sort of. Her name is Blue Flower, I think. She was one of those I had the other night during that fertility ceremony or whatever the hell it was."

"I remember," Shakespeare interjected. "She and you went off by yourselves twice. The first time her husband asked you to take her, but the second time he didn't look none too happy about it."

"Then you knew she was married when she came for you today," Nate said severely, thinking of the implications for all of them.

"What difference does that make? Her husband let me have her the other night."

"That was a special occasion," Nate explained. "The rest of the time the Mandans don't allow such goings-on unless the husband has given his permission."

"How was I to know? No one told me."

Nate seized on that point when detailing the giant's statements to Mato-tope. When he concluded, the chief interrogated the woman involved, Blue Flower, who hung her head in shame and answered in the barest of whispers.

Murmuring erupted among the onlookers. Mato-
tope faced the offended husband and berated
the man harshly for over a minute. Surprisingly,
the warrior offered no protest. Finally the chief
gestured. Both husband and wife went docilely
into their lodge. Tears were rolling down Blue
Flower's cheeks, and once the pair had vanished
from sight her voice could be heard as she cried
out in pleading tones.

"What the devil is happening?" Jarvis
demanded.

"We'll know in a moment," Nate said.

His expression grave, Four Bears gave a speech
using sign. "My people, it is a sad day when the
Mandans shame themselves before their white
friends who came to them in peace and who have
tried to live among us according to our ways. Blue
Flower was given to White Tree during the buffalo-
calling ceremony. She decided on her own to have
him again. She did not tell her husband. She did
not make known to White Tree that her husband
had not said she could sleep with him. So when
Beaver Tail came home and saw her in the arms
of White Tree, he became very angry. He and his
brother attacked White Tree, who had done no
wrong. Now that Beaver Tail knows this, he is
much ashamed." The chief paused, then signed
specifically at Nate. "Please tell White Tree that I
apologize on behalf of all my people, and I hope
he will not see fit to talk around white fires about
how he was deceived."

"What's he saying?" Jarvis asked, but Nate
ignored him.

"The whites are our brothers," Four Bears was
signing. "Long have we cherished the friendship

between your people and ours, and we hope this friendship will continue for more winters than anyone can count. Just as one bad berry does not spoil a berry patch, so this one misfortune should not spoil the ties that bind us."

"You need have no fear in that regard," Nate assured the chief. "This was a small misunderstanding, nothing more. We are not upset and will not be spreading stories about the Mandans, who have always treated our people with kindness and fairness."

"What's he been saying, damn it!" Jarvis broke in again. "Are they planning to skin me alive or what?"

Nate had opened his mouth to reply when from the depths of the dwelling rose a piercing shriek that caused nearby dogs to slink away in fear. The shriek wavered, faltered, and became a drawn-out wail, which in turn tapered to a protracted moan.

"God in heaven!" Jarvis blurted out, spinning around. "What is that villain doing to her?" He moved toward the lodge entrance.

"No!" Nate barked, grabbing the giant's wrist and holding fast. "Your carelessness has already caused enough harm. Don't make it worse by blundering again."

"But Blue Flower?"

"Is getting her due for shaming her husband as she did."

Jarvis halfheartedly tried to jerk loose. "But *listen* to her? What has he done?"

"We won't know for sure until she comes out in public again, which might be a while," Nate said. "It would be my guess that he either chopped off her nose or cut off one of her ears."

"*What?*" Jarvis exclaimed in utter horror, and tried to take a stride. "I'll wring his red neck!"

"Use your head!" Nate snapped. "If you go in there now, you'll start the trouble all up again. Under Indian custom, Beaver Tail has the right to do whatever he wants to her. He could kill her if he's of a mind, but I suspect he loves her too much to do that."

"God in heaven!" the giant declared, his shoulders slumping. "I had no idea! No bloody idea!"

The dispute having been resolved to the satisfaction of the Mandans, they dispersed, moving toward the plaza. Nate went on with Winona and Zach while Shakespeare lingered with Jarvis. Almost every member of the tribe was soon present. Nate saw no sign of Diana Templar, who had taken to keeping to herself or spending her time in the company of her convalescing brother.

As they stood watching the preparations, Eric Nash trotted up to them and stated, "Nate! Thank goodness I've found you. Where's Shakespeare?"

"Yonder talking to Jarvis," Nate answered, jabbing his thumb westward at the intervening lodge. "He'll be tied up a while, I expect."

"But he said he'd translate for me tonight."

"I'll do it if you'd like."

"Right!" Eric said, and anxiously motioned for them to follow him. "I'm sitting with Four Bears and his family, and I'm positive he won't mind if you join us. Please. I need you near me when the time comes."

"You seem excited," Winona mentioned.

"I tell you, I could run all the way to St. Louis right this minute and not work up a sweat," Eric replied. "I've about gone off my head over this business."

"Over what?" Nate asked, though he full well knew the answer. He hoped Shakespeare had plenty of plews to spare.

"You'll see shortly," was all Nash said.

Mato-tope's family occupied the middle of the plaza. They were seated between a pair of large crackling fires. Suspended over the flames on meat racks were choice cuts of buffalo, including several tongues and portions of hump meat. The chief's wives were watching carefully to prevent their meal from being burnt.

The grand chief had but arrived when Eric Nash hastened up with the King family. Four Bears beamed at Nate and signed, "Grizzly Killer, I have a request to make of you. Wolverine has told us that you are highly regarded by the Shoshones and considered one of their greatest warriors. After we have eaten, we would be grateful if you would entertain us by sharing the many coups you have counted and telling us about the many bears you have killed."

"I would be happy to," Nate replied to be polite, although he wasn't normally one to brag of his deeds. In many tribes the men did just that, recounting their brave acts before admiring crowds. Some, like the Sioux, held a scalp or victory dance after each successful raid, during which the warriors boasted of their daring feats. The Blackfeet practiced a curious custom whereby the warriors were required to recite the coup they had earned while repeatedly striking a special post.

Once Four Bears had taken his seat, the festivities commenced. The food was brought just as fast as it was cooked. Every morsel was greedily devoured. Roasted intestines were especially popular, as were pieces of liver or kidney flavored with drops of gall. The Mandans ate and ate until none of them could take another bite, and then they sat back, sated and content.

Shortly afterward, Four Bears pushed to his feet and made an address in Mandan and sign simultaneously in which he gave thanks to the Great Medicine Spirit for the success of their hunt, and for the presence of the white men who had brought such good medicine to the tribe. He then recounted how Eric Nash had risked his life to save Four Bears from a charging buffalo.

Nate had been translating quietly for Nash's benefit, and it was at this point that Nash held up a hand and whispered urgently, "Can you interrupt him for me?"

"We should wait until he's done."

Nash reluctantly did, his impatience transparent as he fidgeted and scratched and absently rubbed his palms up and down his legs. In due time the chief finished and sat down. "Now will you translate for me?" Nash asked urgently.

"What would you have me say?"

"I want to marry Morning Dew."

"Are you sure, Eric?"

"Are we ever sure of anything in this inconstant world in which we live?" Eric sighed. "I think I'm sure, which is the best I can do. Nate, I've worn myself out weighing the scales. Should I or shouldn't I? Am I really willing to give up any hope of returning to England for a simple but beautiful savage? Or is this a flight of fancy spawned by stupidity?" He glanced longingly at the maiden who had claimed his affection. "All I know for sure is that I want her to be mine."

"Very well." Nate shifted and raised his hands. "Four Bears has spoken well and wisely this night, and now I hope he will listen well and wisely to the request I must make on behalf of Lake Eyes."

The chief glanced at the Englishman, whose unusual eye color had made quite an impression on the dark-eyed Mandans and resulted in the name by which the tribe now knew him. "Lake Eyes saved my life. If I have it in my power to give him what his heart desires, I will do so."

"Great Chief, any man who is brave enough to stand up to a charging buffalo is a man you know you can rely on in times of danger and hardship. He would bring much good medicine to those who were his people, and to any family of which he was a member."

"This is true."

"It is also true that Lake Eyes has traveled far and wide in the white man's land and elsewhere, and in all his travels he has never met any people he respects so much as he does the Mandans. When first he entered your village, he thought he had died and gone to the great beyond."

Four Bears grinned. "His words please me."

"And I hope these next words will do the same." Nate leaned forward. "Great Chief, Lake Eyes has never known the joy of having a wife and raising a family, and this loss has long saddened him. But although he looked long and hard, he never found a woman he was willing to call his own, never met a woman who had the qualities he held dear in his heart." He stopped and gazed at Morning Dew. "Until now."

"Speak on."

"Lake Eyes is sorry he does not yet know enough of your tongue to ask you this himself. He would very much like to take your daughter, Morning Dew, for his wife."

None of Mato-tope's family displayed surprise at the news. The chief himself sat back and pursed his lips. Morning Dew had her face averted, whether from shame or joy Nate couldn't determine.

"What was all that you just said?" Eric asked. "Have you asked him yet?"

"Yes. Quiet until he answers," Nate responded.

Four Bears took his time, which was not a favorable sign. Word had been whispered among the assembled Mandans and all activity had ceased. Silence reigned. They were hanging on their leader's next words, and presently he cleared his throat and replied, using sign also as he had done before.

"Lake Eyes flatters my family by believing my daughter is special. She is. So special that I must pick her husband carefully or I would not be doing my duty as her father." Four Bears studied Nash a moment. "There are certain things every man must provide for his wife. If he does not, they cannot possibly be happy together no matter how much they are in love."

"True," Nate conceded when the chief stopped momentarily. He could foresee what was coming and felt sorry for the Englishman.

"My daughter is accustomed to living in a fine lodge and having her own horses. She is accustomed to wearing nice robes and dresses." Four Bears frowned. "I have done my best to provide for her, and her husband must also be able to do the same. Tell me, Grizzly Killer. Does Lake Eyes have a fine lodge?"

"He has no lodge."

"Does he have fine horses?"

"He has no horses."

"Can he hunt game? Has he killed many deer, many buffalo?"

"The only buffalo he has ever killed was the bull he slew protecting you."

"Does he know how to make a bow?"

"No."

"Can he cure skins?"

"No."

"What does he do, then, in the white man's world?"

"He paints pictures."

Mato-tope stared at a shield lying a few feet off, at the vivid depiction of a buffalo painted on the hide. "A wife needs more than a husband who only knows how to paint pictures. Painting does not put food in a woman's belly. Painting does not keep her warm on cold days. My heart is heavy when I say that I cannot give my daughter to Lake Eyes until he has learned how to do the things all men must know to be good husbands, good providers."

"I understand," Nate signed sadly. He was profoundly sorry he had played matchmaker and tried to convince Nash that marrying an Indian woman wasn't so terrible a fate, because now he had to deliver a devastating blow.

"Well? Well? Don't keep me in suspense all night, old chap," Eric urged. "What was his answer?"

"No."

Eric glanced at Morning Dew, whose head was bowed and hidden by her hair, then at her father, whose melancholy state was plain for all to see. "But why? What did I do to offend him? I thought he was willing to give me anything. You said as much. So did McNair."

A bitter taste formed in Nate's mouth. "We were wrong."

"Why, damn it? *Why?*"

"He doesn't think you know enough about Indian ways," Nate said, summing up the chief's objections. "He's worried you wouldn't be a good enough provider for his daughter."

"Be more specific."

Although loath to do so, Nate complied.

Eric was dumfounded. Here he had finally conquered his doubts and mustered the courage to ask for Morning Dew's hand, and he'd been refused because he didn't measure up to Indian standards of manhood? The idea was so ridiculous it was laughable, and he did laugh, coldly. Then he abruptly rose and stalked off.

In England and on the Continent Eric was accepted in the highest of circles and widely known for his artistic talent. Any upper-class woman would be delighted to receive his undivided attention. In the past, more than one had intimated she was intensely interested in him romantically. Yet always had he tactfully declined to become involved due to his love for Diana Templar. He could have had his pick of the richest, most cultured women in the world. Yet a simple heathen rated him as unworthy of marrying his daughter!

In Eric's simmering fury he was halfway through the village before he quite realized where he was going. Then, turning, he made for the palisade. He wanted to be alone with his thoughts, and once outside he could stroll under the stars and think without having to deal with any distractions.

Immersed in introspection, Eric gave little heed to his surroundings until suddenly a shadow detached itself from an dark patch between two lodges and came toward him. He glanced up, saw a skinny warrior, and kept on walking.

A moment later the back of his skull seemed to cave in.

Back in the plaza, Nate King was debating whether to go after the Englishman. It was partly his fault that Eric had been publicly humiliated, and he wanted to do something to atone. Consequently, he put his hands down to push to his feet, then hesitated on seeing Morning Dew go up to her father and whisper insistently. Her cheeks were glistening with moisture, her eyes were downcast. The chief answered, and with head held low she hastened away.

Nate relaxed, watching her. He didn't know if she was going after Eric or back to her lodge. If the former, he didn't want to intrude. So he opted to wait for a while.

The silence was broken by scores of subdued conversations, giving Nate the illusion he was seated in a hive of bees and listening to their constant buzzing. Mato-tope, Nate noticed, did not talk to anyone; he was slumped low, clearly depressed. "He looks like I feel," Nate said softly to himself.

"You are not to blame for what happened, husband," Winona commented.

"In a way I am. I gave Nash a little push in Morning Dew's direction when I should have kept hands off."

"Life is full of disappointments. Nash is a grown man. He must learn to live with them as must we all." Winona gazed in the direction the Englishman had taken. "And if he is half the man he wants to be, he will do whatever is necessary to win Morning Dew. It is not hard to learn how to hunt or how to skin game and treat the hides. He could learn if he wanted to. If he wants her badly enough."

"That's not a bad notion," Nate said. "I could teach him. Why, I bet he'd pick up on all he needs to know in no time."

"If he can show Mato-tope he has learned Indian ways, the chief will agree to the marriage."

Nate was excited by so simple a solution to their problem and he wanted to share the idea with Eric Nash right away. "Stay here, dearest. I'll be back shortly," he said. Scooping up his Hawken, he hurried to the west, threading a serpentine path through the packed Mandans.

Once Nate was among the lodges he went faster. There wasn't a living soul in sight since the whole tribe was at the feast. He passed Mato-tope's lodge, and stopped to see if Nash might be inside with Morning Dew, but neither were there.

Turning, Nate began a search, winding among the dwellings, searching in the shadows, expecting to find the pair at any moment. When a couple of minutes had gone by and he still hadn't found them, he suspected they were off by themselves in some remote corner of the village consoling one another.

After five minutes Nate was near the palisade. Since he didn't care to spend all night looking, he cupped a hand to his mouth as he rounded a lodge and tilted his head back to call the artist's name. Then he froze.

Sprawled six feet away in a dark pool of his own blood was Eric Nash.

Chapter Twenty-Two

Nate reached the Englishman in two bounds and knelt. A hasty probe revealed a vicious gash on the side of Nash's head, possibly made by a war club. The flow of blood had reduced to a trickle and was not in itself life-threatening, but Nash required immediate attention. So, slipping one arm under Nash's legs and another under his shoulders, Nate grunted, strained, and lifted.

The trek to the plaza seemed to take forever. Nate was breathing heavily when he rounded the last dwelling to be starkly illuminated by the dozens of blazing fires. Instantly Mandans were on their feet, pressing close and asking questions. Nate could only shake his head and try to get through them to where Winona sat.

A shout parted the throng as Moses had parted the Red Sea, and through the crowd came Four Bears, Winona, and Zach. Shakespeare was approaching from another direction.

"I found him like this," Nate said before anyone could pose the obvious question, and Winona
instantly translated for the chief's benefit. She
leaned over Nash, examining the gash, then
announced, "I think he will live. But we must
get him to the lodge so I can tend him."

With every last man, woman, and child trailing
behind, Nate led the way to the chief's lodge and
deposited the Englishman on a soft blanket. Nash
groaned. His eyes flickered open and shut. "Can
you hear me, Eric?" Nate asked. "Who did this to
you?"

"Indian," Nash mumbled.

Nate recalled the conflict between Jarvis and
the jealous husband earlier, and wondered if a
young brave interested in Morning Dew had tak-
en revenge on the presumptuous artist. "Did you
get a good look? Describe him."

"Indian," Nash repeated weakly. "Thin . . .
breechclout . . . red paint on face . . . bald in
front . . ."

"Bald?" Nate blurted out.

" . . . red hair in back . . . like quills," Nash continued, then collapsed, exhaling loudly.

Like a thunderbolt out of the blue the information jolted Nate to his feet and he swung toward
Mato-tope. "Sioux," he declared in sign language,
adding, "Where is Morning Dew?"

Four Bears understood immediately. Rather
than succumb to fear or fume and curse, he calmly spun and barked orders, dispatching warriors
every which way. Outside, as the news spread, others began shouting, "Sioux! Sioux! Sioux!" There
was a great pattering of rushing feet.

Nate stood aside so Winona could minister to Nash. He spied Shakespeare at the entrance and joined him. "You can keep your damn plews," he groused.

"Why? You won the wager."

"At what cost? I don't want any part of them."

The mountain man tendered an affectionate smile. "Ay, sir. To be honest, as this world goes, is to be one man picked out of ten thousand."

"If they've got her, I'm going along," Nate declared. "I want to get my hands on the bastards."

"We won't be able to leave until daylight," Shakespeare pointed out. "Can't read tracks at night, old coon."

"You're going too?"

"What? Miss the chance to add a Sioux scalp to my collection? I'd just as soon pass up the chance to shoot a white buffalo."

Out of the night materialized Diana Templar, Jarvis towering at her side. "What's happened?" she inquired. "Our host showed up a minute ago and made it clear we should come here quickly."

"The Sioux have raided the village," Nate answered. "Eric must have stumbled on them and they left him for dead."

Diana gasped and had to reach out to the giant for support. She swayed, steadied, and asked in a raspy tone, "Is he . . . ?"

"He's still breathing, missy," Shakespeare informed her. "But he won't be wrestling any panthers for a spell. Winona is inside patching him up. You might want to help her."

Lady Templar swirled past them.

Suddenly shouting broke out at the north end of the village, and was shortly echoed by shouts from the east and south. The clamor spread, becoming a general din of yells, whoops, and shrieks. Several of the warriors dispatched by Four Bears returned on the run, reported, and ran off again. With each report the chief grew more sullen, so that he was a solemn specter when he walked over to the frontiersmen and the giant.

"You are right, my friend," Mato-tope signed to Nate. "The band of Sioux struck while we were all at the feast. They killed a man and woman who had left before anyone else, they stole many horses, and they shot four dogs." He pressed a hand to his forehead. "I should have expected this. I should have insisted we put men on watch, but I forgot. I knew my daughter had grown fond of Lake Eyes, and all I could think of was them and what I would do if they wanted to share the same lodge."

A stocky, perspiring brave dashed out of the night, breathlessly relayed the grim tidings he brought, and disappeared as he had come.

Mato-tope seemed to have aged five years in five minutes. "It is worse than I thought. The number of horses missing is over thirty. My daughter is nowhere to be found, and three other women and two boys are also missing. The Sioux have taken them," he disclosed.

"That's good to hear," Shakespeare signed, and when the chief and Nate glanced at him strangely, he explained his statement. "With that many horses and captives, the Sioux can't go as fast as they normally would. If it's the same small band we saw before, there's hardly enough of them to handle so many. We should be able to catch them before the sun sets tomorrow."

"You may be right," Four Bears conceded, his tone betraying the conflict waging within him between hope and despair. "But this is not your fight. Neither of you are Mandans. You need not join us."

"We have a stake in the outcome," Nate said.

Mato-tope was not disposed to argue. "If you wish to come, do so. Two brave men such as you are always welcome." He turned to his lodge. "Now you must excuse me, my friends. I must tell my wives all I have learned and make plans." In the opening he paused and looked back. "How can a day that began so fine end with such sorrow? Our good medicine has flown on the wind." With a nod he was gone.

"I suppose I'd best turn in too," Shakespeare said. "We'll both need to be wide-eyed and bushy-tailed when we tangle with the sneaking Sioux." Turning, he headed into the darkness.

"Shakespeare?" Nate said.

The mountain man stopped and looked around. "What is it, Friar Laurence?"

"Do you figure we have the right to meddle in the affairs of others, even when we think we're doing it for their own good?"

"That's a tough question, and I doubt any man can say what's right or wrong. But this child learned long before you were born never to give advice unless it's asked for, and never, ever to stick his big nose in where it don't belong."

"So you figure I should have left well enough alone?"

"I figure we each have to do what we have to do, and damn the consequences. We can't predict how the future will turn out. Like everybody else we have to take what comes along and make the best of it." He paused. "But look at it this way and you might feel a little better." A low laugh rumbled from his chest. "If we weren't meant to speak our minds, why were we given mouths?"

"Thanks."

"Don't mention it."

The next day dawned bright and clear. Long before the sun spread its golden smile over the landscape, the Mandans were up and in pursuit of their bitter enemies. Forty warriors were selected by Mato-tope to go; the rest, who displayed much reluctance, were told to stay to safeguard the village.

There was one last-minute addition to the party. As the warriors were gathering in the plaza, Eric Nash appeared leading the mare he had ridden on the buffalo hunt. He was as pale as white linen and his head sported a tight bandage. Without saying a word, he walked over to where Nate and Shakespeare were waiting astride their mounts. Then, gripping the saddle firmly and gritting his teeth, he climbed up.

"What the dickens do you figure you're doing, son?" Shakespeare asked.

"What does it look like?" the Englishman retorted.

"You're in no condition for a long, hard ride," Nate noted. "Why don't you go back to the lodge and lay down. We'll bring her back."

"I'm going," Eric said gruffly. "And I'll shoot the first man who tries to stop me."

Four Bears and Stalking Wolf rode over. The chief raked Nash from head to toe with an inquisitive scrutiny, shifted, and addressed Nate in sign language. "Grizzly Killer, tell Lake Eyes she is my daughter. This is for me to do."

Nate dutifully translated, and was obliged to relay Nash's verbatim reply: "Not true. One day I will claim your daughter as my own, so I have as much right to go as you do."

"I made clear my wishes last night," Four Bears said.

"So you did," Nash responded through Nate. "And you were wise in refusing my request. But I will not always be as I am now. Soon, very soon, I will have learned to be a good provider. I will become so good you will have no cause to doubt me, and then you will agree to our marriage."

A kindly twinkle animated the grand chief's eyes as he smiled at the Englishman and made the sign for "Good." He added, "But be warned. If you fall behind, we cannot stop to help you. The captives and our stolen horses are more important."

"I understand," Eric assured him. "And have no fear. I will keep up even if I have to tie myself to my horse so I won't fall off."

As they rode from the village, Nate couldn't but wonder if Winona had had a hand in Nash's new attitude. She was the one, after all, who had suggested Nate teach Nash the skills the Englishman needed to learn in order to pass muster with the Mandans. And she had been the one nursing the Englishman during the night. Had Winona put the notion into Nash's head to fight for what he wanted? That would be just like her, Nate reflected, and grinned.

Finding the trail was a simple task. Since the Sioux homeland lay to the south of Mandan country, the warriors had only to swing in a loop south of the village until they found the tracks made by the fleeing band. Presently the Mandans were in full chase, racing along at a mile-eating pace.

Nate speculated on what would happen when they caught the band. The Sioux would not give up without a fierce struggle, and they might slay their captives out of sheer spite if they became aware the Mandans were after them and believed they had no hope of escaping.

They were a hardy, courageous people, the Sioux. Originally occupying land far to the east, they had migrated westward and split up. One branch had settled in the region of the Minnesota River and did more farming than they did hunting. The other branch had settled close to the wide Missouri and adopted many of the practices of the plains Indians, essentially becoming a whole new people.

They had also acquired a new name. While they referred to themselves as the Dakotas, most whites and many other tribes were calling them by a name whose origins were difficult to trace. Nate had been told that the early French-Canadians who first encountered the Dakotas had called them *Nadowessious,* which came from the Ojibwa name for the tribe, *Nadowessi.* Somehow the French name had been shortened over the years to where everyone now simply called them the *Sioux.* The name was fitting, since the Ojibwa term meant "enemy" or "small snake," and there were no sneakier or more clever horse thieves and raiders in all the broad West.

The tracks revealed the Sioux had been pushing themselves and their stolen horses to get as far from the Mandan village as they could before daylight. Further proof was provided by the fact that although their flight had taken them across the Missouri and, later on, a stream, not once had they stopped to let the animals drink.

Nate made a point of staying close to Eric Nash. The artist was holding up well so far, but his face was haggard, and now and then he would clutch at the bandage and grimace. About mid-morning Nate noticed the wound had taken to bleeding again. He moved closer to the Englishman and pointed out the blood trickling from under the bandage, but Nash simply grunted and kept on riding.

By noon they were well out on the prairie. Four Bears called a brief halt to rest their horses. He wasn't going to commit the mistake of riding their animals to the point of exhaustion. In order to catch the Sioux, they had to pace themselves so that when they did finally spot their enemies, their mounts would have a reserve reservoir of endurance to tap for the last leg of the chase.

Nate had dismounted and was stretching his legs by walking in small circles when he saw Eric Nash seated by the mare, his head cradled in his hands. Going over, Nate asked, "How are you holding up?"

"Are you daft? How you think I'm holding up?"

"You've no call to be mad at me," Nate said. "I'm your friend, remember?"

Eric glanced up, his features betraying his agony. "Sorry," he said softly. "This bloody head of mine is pounding so bad I can hardly think straight."

"Maybe you should stay here and we'll swing by on our way back."

"I'm seeing this through, Nate, and nothing Four Bears or you or anyone else says is going to stop me from pressing on." Eric winced, then continued. "Maybe I'm too stubborn by half, maybe I'm just crazy, but I refuse to quit while she's in danger. I was the one who asked for her hand in front of the whole damn tribe. This is my way of showing I was sincere."

"No one doubts your sincerity, Eric. You have nothing to prove to anyone else."

"Perhaps I have something to prove to myself."

The matter had to be dropped because a moment later Four Bears swung onto his war horse and gave the command for everyone to do likewise. In a compact group, the Mandans rode off, their best trackers in the lead.

Nate hung back, at the rear, next to Nash. The Englishman had begun to sway every so often, and occasionally he would close his eyes for yards at a time, then open them with a snap as if he had been roused from sleep. The flow of blood from under his bandage had stopped, but the bandage itself was soaked.

It was the middle of the afternoon when another small stream crossed their path. Four Bears again stopped, so they could let their animals drink. As Nash began to climb down, his arms suddenly went limp, his legs buckled, and with a groan he crashed to the ground.

Nate reached him first and gently rolled the Englishman over. Eric looked up at him, his eyes silently pleading, and gripped Nate's sleeve.

"Please. Don't let them leave me."

"Can you stand?" Nate asked.

The Englishman placed both hands down, shoved, and rose onto his elbows. His shoulders quaking, he tried to rise higher, his face turning livid from the exertion. After half a minute he gave up, groaned, and sank flat on his back. "Not at the moment," he said softly.

Four Bears and several warriors had walked over to them. The chief squatted and regarded the Englishman regretfully, then signed, "Can he ride?"

"Not for a while," Nate answered.

"I warned him. If he is not able to join us when we move on, we must leave him here to fend for himself."

"Do what you have to," Nate signed.

"I do not want to leave him, Grizzly Killer. I like him, even though in many ways he is like a small child. I hope he does one day marry my daughter."

"He will," Nate predicted.

Frowning, the chief straightened and walked off.

"What did he say?" Eric wanted to know, and when Nate had translated, he grinned and declared, "Wonderful! I knew he'd see me right, given time. Mark my words. Morning Dew is as good as mine."

"Don't count your chickens before they're hatched. First we have to rescue her from the Sioux."

"I'll be on my feet in no time. Then we'll go teach the bleeding Sioux what's what."

But although Nash tried repeatedly, he couldn't find the strength to stay on his feet. Twice he stood, and each time he would have promptly fallen on his face had Nate not been there to catch him. When Nash saw the Mandans mounting, he grew desperate and rashly lunged upright a third time. Grinning in triumph, he took a step toward the mare, faltered, moaned, and staggered dizzily.

Once again Nate had to grab hold and slowly ease the Englishman to the ground. He heard horses approach and glanced over his shoulder.

"No?" Four Bears asked.

"No," Nate signed.

"Then I have no choice. He must stay here. But we will come back this way when we return to our village and take him with us." Four Bears nodded at the gelding. "Hurry. Every moment is precious."

"You go on without me."

"You are staying too?"

"If I leave him, he might die. As you know, he does not know how to take care of himself very well." Nate sighed. "As much as I want to go with you, I gave my word I would guide Lake Eyes and his friends safely to the land of the white men, and I cannot break my promise. I must watch over them until then."

"You are a man of honor, Grizzly Killer," Four Bears said. "Stay, then." He looked at McNair. "And what about you, Wolverine? Will you come or remain?"

"I would like to go . . ." the mountain man began, then hesitated and looked at Nate.

"Go on, you old goat. I know you don't want to miss tangling with the Sioux, and Nash doesn't need two of us to nurse him. We'll be fine by ourselves."

"You're sure? I'll stay if you want me to."

"Just give the Sioux hell for me."

"I will." Shakespeare beamed and turned his horse. "Keep your eyes peeled."

"Shoot sharps the word."

For the longest while Nate knelt and watched the receding figures of the Mandans and his mentor. The drumming of hoofs faded to silence, and all that was left were lingering puffs of dust. Nate and Eric were alone in a shimmering sea of buffalo grass that rippled and waved in the mild northwesterly breeze.

The unconscious Englishman was in a bad way. His forehead was warm to Nate's touch, and he tossed and turned frequently while mumbling incoherently.

Nate used his butcher knife to cut a strip of fabric off Nash's jacket. Once the material had been dipped in the stream, he applied the drenched strip to Nash's brow and sat back. There was really nothing else he could do except let Nature take its course. He's seen the results of enough head wounds to know Nash would revive in due course and probably be none the worse for wear.

Other than the whispering of the rustling grass, all was quiet. Not even a bird chirped. Nate dipped his hands in the cool water and splashed some on his face. Rising, he made a survey of the horizon in all directions, checking for game. There was none, not even the ubiquitous antelope.

Over the next hour the only life Nate observed was a single red hawk that swooped in low to inspect them and then arced high into the air in its never-ending search for prey. Shortly thereafter the hawk dived into the tall grass to the west, and when it reappeared a struggling rabbit was clutched in its iron talons.

Nate sat down next to the Englishman, plucked a blade of grass, broke off the bottom portion of the tender stem, and stuck it between his teeth. He wondered how long it would be before Nash could move on, and whether he should scout around for something to eat right then or wait until later. The voice at his side inadvertently made him jump.

"Where are the rest?"

"They left a while ago."

"Damn them."

"If there's one thing I learned long ago, it's to never blame others for our own stupidity. You knew the risks you were taking when you came along. You're as stubborn as a mule, Eric," Nate said, grinning. "And I admire you for it. Most folks say I'm a hard-headed cuss myself."

"So what now?"

"Now we cool our heels here until they swing back this way."

"I wanted to be there when they find Morning Dew."

"Sorry, Eric. I truly am." Nate gazed up from the Englishman's dejected countenance and saw the mare straying off to the east. "Be right back," he said. Pushing to his feet, he hastened to catch her before she went too far while mentally berating himself for not hobbling both horses earlier.

Even greenhorns knew it was better to count ribs than tracks.

Nate was 15 yards from the spot where Nash lay when the sight of a hoofprint in the soft earth beside the stream gave him pause. Glancing down, he spied many more, fresh tracks of unshod horses, nine in all. The horses that made them had been moving eastward at a gallop.

Perplexed, Nate studied the ground. He absently scratched his head and mulled over the possibilities until, in a rush of insight, he realized the truth and he stiffened as if jarred by lightning. "Son of a bitch!" he exclaimed.

"What's the matter?" Eric called.

"Four Bears and the others are following the wrong trail!"

Chapter Twenty-Three

The ruse was so devilishly clever that Nate admired the Sioux for their craftiness in spite of himself. The raiders must have caught a glimpse of the Mandans far to the rear, or else a stray dust cloud or glimmer of sunlight had betrayed the avenging pursuers. In any event, the Sioux had decided they could not hope to outdistance the Mandans when they had so many stolen horses to keep under control. Consequently, rather than risk losing both the horses and their captives, they had divided their band, some of them going on with the stolen herd while the others took the captives by a different route. And because the Mandans had not thought to check the ground any distance from the main trail, they had missed seeing where the Sioux split up.

All this ran through Nate's mind as he hurried back to Nash with the mare. Quickly, he explained what he had found and his conclusions, then said, "I have to go after them, Eric. If I don't, they'll get clean away. There will be no hope for Morning Dew at all. She'll spend the rest of her life as the mate of a Sioux warrior, and his other wives will likely as not make her life unbearably miserable since she isn't one of their own kind."

Nate hoped, by painting such a bleak picture, that Nash would let him leave immediately without protest. The Englishman's reaction, though, wasn't quite what he anticipated.

Somehow Nash found the strength to stand and shuffle to the mare. "If you go, I go, my dear fellow. This is my chance to redeem myself."

"Eric—" Nate said.

"Don't waste your breath," Nash said. "I know exactly what you're going to say, and I won't listen. But I promise you this. If you try to ride off and leave me, I'll follow. If you take my horse, I'll walk. If I become too weak, I'll crawl if need be. One way or the other, though, I'm going after her."

Nate knew that Nash wouldn't last a day on his own. If Nate left, it was tantamount to killing the Englishman. Yet if he took him, Nash would slow him down. He mentioned as much.

"There's a simple solution. Tie me to this nag."

"Are you crazy? Do you have any idea what you're letting yourself in for?"

"Do it." Eric got both hands on top of the mare, heaved, and pulled himself into the saddle, where he sat rocking from side to side for a few seconds before he was able to hold himself steady. "And be quick about it. From what you told me, they can't be far ahead of us. We might catch them before sunset."

Of all the things Nash could have said, that was the one argument capable of goading Nate into complying. Since Nate believed he could overtake the Sioux swiftly, he reasoned that Eric would not have to endure too much discomfort. And so, against Nate's better judgment, he lashed Eric's legs and wrists to the mare.

Holding both the Hawken and Nash's rifle, Nate swung onto the gelding, then grasped the mare's reins. "Hang on tight," he advised. "If you feel yourself starting to slip over the side, give a yell and I'll stop."

"Don't worry. They'll hear me in Brighton."

"You'll do better if you lean forward over her neck," Nate went on. "It won't be as hard to keep your balance."

"Lead on, Hannibal. And don't spare the elephants."

"What?"

"Never mind."

"I swear. Sometimes you make as little sense as McNair."

The tracks soon made plain that the Sioux had stuck to the stream for only three miles, after which they had cut to the southeast in a wide loop that would eventually bring them into their own territory. As six of the nine horses were invariably clustered together, Nate surmised that these were the captives, which meant there were three Sioux.

By late afternoon low hills materialized in the distance, no more than blue-green mounds at first but rapidly growing larger. As the sun was sinking below the crimson western horizon, Nate reined up at the base of the northernmost one and stretched.

"Why are we stopping?" Eric asked. "Are we close?"

"I'd say an hour or two behind them."

"Then keep going. Don't stop on my account."

"We need to give the horses a breather," Nate said, a lie because the animals were hardly winded. He was more concerned about his friend, who was having so much trouble staying awake and alert that three times within the last 30 minutes Nate had been forced to stop and rouse him.

"But we're so close!"

"We rest," Nate insisted with finality. Sliding down, he untied Nash and carefully lowered him to the grass in the shade of a juniper. The Englishman's brow was still warm, although not as warm as before. Unfortunately, there was no water in their vicinity, and since they had been traveling light they didn't have any food either.

"Why don't you go on ahead?" Eric requested. "Leave my rifle with me and I'll be fine."

"When we go, we go together. Hills like these can be home to lots of bears and panthers and such, and once the sun sinks they'll be on the prowl. I don't care to leave you by yourself."

"Morning Dew matters more than I do."

"We wait," Nate said, sinking gratefully down and reclining on his back. "And don't be upset. You'll see her soon enough."

"I will?"

"Yep." Nate yawned and stretched. "Unless I miss my guess, those three Sioux will stop for the night. They didn't get any sleep last night and they must be on their last legs what with not getting a minute's rest all day." He grinned. "Come dark, I'll climb this here hill and have a look-see. They might think they've shaken the Mandans, so they'll feel safe enough to build a small fire. I should be able to spot it."

"And then?"

"We pay them a social call."

"I'm afraid I won't be much good in a pinch."

"All you'll have to do is hold the horses. I'll take care of the rest."

Eric stared at the frontiersman, trying to find the words that would eloquently express his over-whelming gratitude for all King had done for him, but in his befuddled state the best he could come up with was, "I can never thank you enough." Then he lapsed into pensive silence.

The day had been a blur for Eric. Time and again he had lapsed into unconsciousness only to revive minutes later. He had no idea how he had been able to stay on the mare, and feared if he didn't improve by the next day he wouldn't be able to ride at all. A good night's sleep might help, sleep he was unlikely to enjoy if Nate spotted the Sioux camp and they went to rescue Morning Dew and the other Mandan captives.

Morning Dew. Eric whispered her name, rolling it on the tip of his tongue, relishing every syllable. Who would have thought that he, one of the premier artists in all of England, would lose his heart to a simple Indian maiden who didn't know an easel from an English setter? Had he gone absolutely balmy?

No, Eric realized, recalling the delightful thrill he felt whenever he was in her company. He remembered working by her side when the tribe butchered buffalo, and the excitement he'd felt when their arms had not so accidentally brushed together. He recalled the perpetual happiness that enlivened her stride and put an enticing sparkle in her dark eyes.

At night, while on his buffalo robes in Manotope's lodge, Eric had lain awake thinking of Morning Dew, of the ecstasy that would be his when he could hold her in his arms and tenderly whisper the words he longed to say to her. And he knew she felt the same about him. He'd seen her devastated look when her father refused to let him take her as his wife.

Well, damn it, he would! Eric vowed. For years he had wasted his affection on a woman who had regarded him as little more than a highly amusing fop. For years he had accepted that, and fruitlessly pursued his hopeless emotional quest. No more! He'd learned his lesson too well. Only a fool let his heart be pierced time and time again by the pointed barbs of rejected love. Only an utter jackass would tolerate such unfair treatment indefinitely.

Life was meant for living, not for merely existing in a constant state of remorse or regret. And Eric dearly wanted to live, to walk hand in hand with the woman he adored, to know the unadulterated bliss of being loved body and soul by a vision every bit as lovely as a goddess.

Eric opened his eyes, then blinked in surprise. He must have dozed off for a while. Nate King was gone, and so was the sun. Twilight shrouded the landscape. Twisting, he saw the trapper working his way up the nearby hill.

Nate saw the Englishman look his way, and waved. He'd been loath to wake Nash before walking off since the man needed rest so dearly. Eric now waved back, and Nate kept on climbing. The slope wasn't steep and there was little brush, so he soon reached the crest and stopped beside a ponderosa pine. Before him were more low hills, but not many, all sparsely covered with trees.

Nate tried to think the way the Sioux did. If he were one of them, what would he do? Make camp in a hollow where the fire couldn't be seen, would be his guess. He concentrated on the lowland between the hills, but saw nothing out of the ordinary. Figuring the Sioux might not have started their campfire yet, he waited patiently while twilight gave way to murky night.

There was no moon. A multitude of stars twinkled on high, providing feeble light. Nate was disappointed when no telltale glow blossomed anywhere within range of his vision. He stayed put, hoping against hope, yet at last had to concede he had either guessed incorrectly or the Sioux were going without a fire.

Admitting defeat, Nate had turned to go when he detected a faint gleam to the west, out on the prairie, not among the hills. Swinging around, he saw only darkness, and concluded his eyes had deceived him, until the gleam reappeared for a few seconds before vanishing once again.

Nate estimated the light, whatever it was, had to be less than a quarter of a mile from the hills. He watched until the gleam flared a third time, then he turned and trotted down the slope to the juniper.

Eric Nash was sitting up, his back to the trunk. "What's your hurry?" he inquired. "Did you spot their fire?"

"I'm not rightly sure. Are you up to a short ride?"

"Definitely. And this time don't tie me."

Rather than approach the spot directly, Nate took a roundabout course, meandering along the base of the hills until he was southeast of the strange light. By then he could no longer see it, not even the intermittent gleam, which didn't bother him any. He'd been able to pinpoint its approximate location from the top of the hill, and like all competent mountain men had acquired an unerring sense of direction.

Nate rode slowly, wishing he had a robe or a blanket or buckskin he could wrap around the hoofs of the horses to muffle the dull thud of their heavy hoofs. To be safe, he stopped well short of where the gleam had originated, climbed down, and handed the gelding's reins to Nash. "I'll go on afoot. Will you be all right by yourself?"

"Don't worry about me. Just save her," Eric replied.

"I have to worry. What if you pass out again and these horses wander off? I might need to leave in a hurry, and I'd look plumb ridiculous running around in the dark like a chicken with its head chopped off trying to find you."

"I'll be here," Eric assured him.

"I sure as hell hope so," Nate said, and melted into the shadowy landscape, bent at the waist as he glided to the northeast. The prairie was level, the grass no higher than usual; there was no place at all for the Sioux to be hiding. He entertained doubts about what he had seen, and several times he halted, about to go back, but something drew him on.

Eventually Nate stopped for the last time. He'd gone much farther than he thought he should have to, yet found nothing. Sighing, he started to turn back, then froze when he detected the acrid scent of smoke. Sniffing, turning right and left, he isolated the direction the smoke was coming from, and advanced accordingly.

Nate's puzzlement grew the farther he went. Granted, the black night prevented him from seeing more than a dozen yards ahead, and that none too clearly, but all he could see now was more of the same: an unending sea of grass. Where the devil were the Sioux?

Suddenly the breeze bore to Nate's straining ears the muted sound of voices. Instantly he crouched, his Hawken at the ready, but there were no targets to shoot. He cautiously moved on, placing each sole down softly so as not to crackle the grass underfoot. A few seconds later he saw the glow.

It was at ground level, in the middle of a clear tract, and extended for 15 feet in either direction.

Nate flattened and used his elbows and knees for traction as he wriggled nearer. The voices were more distinct, those of several men speaking quietly in the Sioux tongue, a musical language he knew little of but had heard sometime back when he'd befriended an outcast Sioux warrior named Red Hawk. He went a foot further and stopped in astonishment.

A thin spiral of gray smoke was rising out of the ground itself.

Completely baffled, Nate edged closer. He heard a horse whinny, then a loud snap, like the breaking of a branch. The grass ended and the clear tract was in front of him. Only it wasn't a clear tract, after all, but simply a clear space bordering a deep gully.

Now Nate understood, and he smiled. The devious Sioux had done it again. By camping in the gully they'd practically insured they wouldn't be discovered. It had been a fluke that Nate had noticed the glow of their fire from the top of the hill.

There were additional snapping sounds, and they masked whatever slight noise Nate made as he snaked to the rim of the gully, removed his beaver hat, and peered over the side. The gully was wide enough at the bottom for two horses to stand nose to tail. Directly below was the campfire, a warrior kneeling beside it, feeding the dancing flames with branches that must have been gathered in the adjacent hills. Two other Sioux sat close at hand. To the right were the horses, all nine, tethered so they couldn't stray. To the left of the fire sat the captives, four women including Morning Dew, and two boys. All six were securely trussed at the ankles and the wrists. The women sat proudly, their postures radiating defiance, and of them all Morning Dew was the most defiant. Her chin jutted out, her eyes flashed her scorn for her captors. The boys were huddled quietly together, dejected and submissive. Both bore bruises and welts on their faces, which explained why.

Nate saw that one of the Sioux men carried a rifle, another had a bow resting near his leg, and the man feeding the fire had a lance that was lying behind him. Nate might, if he was extraordinarily lucky, drop all three before they could bring their weapons to bear. But if he missed, or if he only wounded one or two of them, the results could prove disastrous for the captives. The boys, in particular, might be killed before he could get down there to prevent the atrocity.

Nate hoped that Morning Dew would glance up and see him so he could use sign language to instruct her to cause a diversion. If the Sioux could be distracted, for just a few moments, it would be all the advantage he needed. But she continued to glare her hatred, oblivious to his presence.

Absorbed in pondering the best strategy to employ, Nate almost missed hearing the stealthy movement to his rear. When he did, his first thought was that he had miscalculated and there were four Sioux, not three.

Since any rash movements might alert the warriors in the gully and cause the man behind him to attack, Nate casually eased his right hand to his side and clutched the Hawken. Girding himself, he waited until he felt certain the person stalking him was no more than six or seven feet away. Then, in a fluid roll, he flipped onto his back and leveled the rifle.

Eric Nash was taken totally unawares. He recoiled and held up both hands. "Don't shoot!" he whispered.

Nate was flabbergasted that the Englishman had left their horses alone to follow him. But he had no time to dwell on Nash's blunder, for from out of the gully rose a sharp, questioning voice. Swiftly, he crawled to Nash, hooked a hand under the man's arm, and hauled him into the grass. Dropping flat, he held Nash down.

"I—" Eric croaked.

"Quiet, damn you!" Nate hissed, and pointed at the gully.

Emerging from the east end, up a gradual incline, were two of the three Sioux, the man with the rifle and the one with the bow. They were back to back, probing the night. At the top they separated, the rifleman going to the left, the bowman to the right.

Nate prayed the grass hid Nash and him from their view. He glanced at the spot where he had been perched on the rim and swore his heart missed a beat. Lying there at the very edge was his beaver hat!

The bowman was on the near side of the gully, but he had his back to the rim and so far was ignorant of the hat. An arrow already notched and the sinew string pulled partway back, he padded along scanning the grass until he was parallel with the hat. Then he paused.

Nate's skin prickled as if he had a rash. He held his breath, waiting to see if the bowman would turn or whether the rifleman on the other side would see his headgear. His right thumb rested on the Hawken's hammer, his forefinger on the trigger. Should they see the hat, he had to bring them both down as quickly as possible and dash to the gully to keep the last Sioux from wreaking mayhem among the captives.

The rifleman spoke a few words and the bowman responded curtly. By their attitude they were not completely sure they had heard something unusual. The warrior on the far side had also stopped to scrutinize the plain. Neither was paying any attention—yet—to the rim.

Nate was tense until both men moved slowly back toward the east end of the gully. Neither had observed any cause for alarm, and the beaver hat, shrouded in shadow as it was, had escaped detection. The warriors joked and laughed as they descended into their hideaway, apparently making light of their own nervousness.

When they were gone, Eric Nash shifted to stare at the frontiersman. "I'm bloody sorry," he whispered.

"You should be."

"I had to know if you'd found her," Eric said.

"So you risked her life and mine? If those Sioux find out we're up here, they might kill her and the rest of their captives for the hell of it."

"So what do we do?"

"*We* do nothing," Nate whispered. "*You* are going to the horses and wait there until I come back."

"I want to help."

"Forget it."

"There must be something I can do," Eric pleaded.

Nate, about to give the Englishman a piece of his mind, paused. Nash could be helpful in creating a diversion, but Nate was afraid he'd botch the task.

Eric noticed the trapper's hesitation and declared softly, "I'll do anything if it means freeing her. You tell me, and I'll follow your directions to the letter. Please, Nate. I want to have a hand in it."

Even though Nate had no other recourse, he balked. Nash was in no shape for a fight; if something went wrong, he could wind up a casualty. Nate tried to think of another way, of *any* means of saving the captives without the Englishman's assistance, and couldn't. Frustrated, he glanced around. "You give me your word you'll do exactly as I say?"

"Trust me."

"I'd rather not," Nate muttered, rising to his knees. "Lay low while I check on our friends." Head down, Hawken extended, he worked his silent way to the rim once more. The Sioux were conversing again, which was reassuring. He lowered himself onto his stomach, then inched to the edge.

The prisoners and the horses were where they had been. All three Sioux were seated at the bottom, their backs to the opposite wall.

Nate glanced westward. There the gully terminated in a sheer drop of ten or 12 feet. The Sioux wouldn't be expecting anyone to come at them from that direction, so it gave him a way of taking them by surprise provided their attention could be drawn elsewhere for the few crucial seconds he would need to leap to the bottom.

Sliding rearward, Nate put on his hat and crept back to Eric Nash. "I have a plan," he announced in a low whisper. "It won't put you in any danger if you do as I say."

"Why do you keep harping on that point?"

"Because I know you, Eric."

The Englishman smiled. "Point taken. Now let me hear my part in this scheme of yours."

Rapidly, Nate outlined the tactic he wanted to use, and when he was satisfied that Nash fully understood, he moved furtively to the west end of the gully. Once he was on his stomach above the sheer drop, he glanced toward the high grass, waiting for Eric to do his part. All Nash had to do was shout a few times, which should lure at least two of the warriors up the dirt ramp to the top of the east end of the gully, in turn enabling Nate to reach the bottom and dispatch the man who was left before they could intervene. Nate would then be between them and the captives.

That was all Nash had to do. He was supposed to wait until Nate was in position and start shouting. But a minute went by and the only sound outside the confines of the gully was the wind whipping the grass. Nate glanced impatiently at Nash's hiding place, but saw no movement whatsoever.

Simmering with anger, Nate braced his hands on the soil, and was going to ease away from the edge so he could check on the Englishman when he finally spotted Nash, not where Nash should be, but upright and within a few yards of the east end of the earthen ramp. The instant Nate laid eyes on him, Nash raised both empty hands on high and—of all things—commenced singing.

Chapter Twenty-Four

If Nate was shocked, the Sioux were astounded. They leaped to their feet and trained their weapons on the white man who had so miraculously appeared above them; then they hesitated, bewildered because he made no threatening moves and indeed appeared to be unarmed. The warrior holding the rifle was the first to break the spell transfixing them, and with a yip he bounded up the incline toward the Englishman. On his heels came both of the others.

This was not what Nate had wanted. He'd hoped to slay one of them before they knew he was there. Nash's harebrained stunt had recklessly jeopardized them both. But Nate had to stick to the original plan.

Coiling both legs under him, Nate balanced on his heels, tensed, and jumped, vaulting over the rim. He hurtled downward, the wind briefly fanning his hair. Then he landed, his legs bearing the brunt of the impact, jarring him to the bone, and his momentum swept him into a roll.

Rising into a crouch, Nate saw the three warriors had reached Nash and the Sioux with the lance had grabbed Nash's arm with one hand and touched the tip of the lance against Nash's throat with the other. Nate raised the Hawken to fire, but unexpectedly one of the Mandan women lurched awkwardly to her feet directly in his line of fire and hopped toward the crackling flames.

It was Morning Dew. Unlike the other Mandans, who had twisted at the thud of Nate's landing to see what had caused the noise, she was intent on reaching the fire, apparently so she could burn through the ropes that bound her and go to Nash's aid.

Fearing for the Englishman's life, Nate surged erect and dashed forward, past the other women and the boys. Morning Dew had reached the fire and dropped to her knees, giving him a clear shot at last. Only he couldn't shoot.

The Sioux had spotted him, and now not only was the warrior with the lance holding the weapon against Eric's throat, but the brave holding the rifle had cocked his piece and pressed the muzzle against Eric's temple. The third Sioux barked words at Nate while gesturing angrily at the artist.

Their meaning was plain. Either Nate did as they wanted, or they would slay Nash on the spot. Nate had the Hawken tucked to his shoulder, but he slowly lowered it a few inches, waiting for their next move.

The warrior with the bow motioned for the Hawken to be cast aside.

Nate wavered. If they disarmed him, he didn't stand a chance. Yet if he resisted, Nash would certainly die. The bowman motioned again, sharply, and his point was accented by the brave bearing the lance, who suddenly gouged the razor tip of his weapon into the Englishman's flesh deep enough to draw blood. Scowling in suppressed fury, Nate bent at the knees and placed the Hawken down. Then he advanced two strides and raised his hands high above his head to show them he would not give them any trouble.

There was a method to Nate's bold move. He was taking a calculated gamble, and if it paid off he might, just might, be able to turn the tables on the three braves.

By taking the two long strides, Nate had positioned himself well past the fire, near the horses and between the Sioux and Morning Dew. Should she succeed in freeing herself, the Hawken was within her reach. He could only hope she knew how to use it.

The strides had also put the front of Nate's body in shadow. From where the Sioux stood, they couldn't possibly see the pistols at his waist until they were much closer. And once they were that close, he'd bring both flintlocks to bear. But had they seen the pistols when he'd first appeared? Or had their attention been so focused on Nash and the Hawken that they had overlooked them? The answer was vital to his survival.

The bowman came partway down the dirt ramp, halted, and addressed Nate in sign language. "Move back to the fire, white dog!"

Taking another gamble, Nate stood stock still. He was hoping the Sioux would think he didn't know sign and come nearer to make him comply. Taking a breath, he said in English, "I don't savvy. Do you know how to palaver in the white man's tongue?"

The warrior with the rifle said something in Sioux and his two companions laughed. Then he unexpectedly gave Nash a brutal shove, sending the Englishman sprawling down the incline. Nash hit hard and lay in the dirt, dazed.

Nate still didn't move. He dared not make his play until the Sioux were all lower. The bowman suddenly lifted his bow, trained his shaft on Nate's chest, and came warily forward. Soon he would be near enough to distinguish the pistols. Yet the other two were still near the top of the gully.

Glancing up at them, Nate declared insolently, "What's the matter with you cowards? Are you afraid to tangle with a man who isn't half dead already?"

The Sioux had no idea what had been said, but the insulting tone was transparent. Both the brave carrying the rifle and his friend with the lance headed downward, their resentment quickening their pace.

The moment of truth was almost at hand. Nate relaxed his shoulders muscles, knowing if he was too tense he might make a mistake. The bowman was now within ten feet of where he stood, the arrow still fixed on his sternum. Nate's eyes flicked to the right, at the row of horses, at the one not a yard away. It was a Sioux war horse, as the symbols painted on its shoulders and flanks indicated. And the Sioux, like the men of nearly every other tribe on the Plains, valued their war horses above all else.

Nate let the bowman take two more steps. He let the pair on the ramp get within a foot or so of Nash. Then, in a blur of speed, he threw himself to the right, behind the war horse, as his hands flashed to the pistols and streaked them out. He was counting on the bowman not letting the arrow fly when there was a risk of hitting the war horse, and his hunch proved right.

The warrior had snapped the bow around, about to release his shaft at the very moment Nate dropped from sight. On seeing the war horse he had checked the impulse, and now was darting along the opposite wall, the bow held in front of him, seeking a target.

Nate had to kill the bowman swiftly, before the others reached the bottom. Twisting, he peered between the prancing legs of the nervous stallion and saw the bowman's midriff and leggings. Nate's right arm shot out, he cocked the flintlock, and when the Sioux was almost even with the horse, he fired. He saw the bowman double over, and then a hammer seemed to crash against his skull and he was flung backwards, landing on his back with his senses swimming.

Belatedly, Nate realized the stallion, startled by the blast and the smoke, had kicked him. He fought the black wave trying to swamp his consciousness and rose to his elbows. Through a swirling fog he could see the bowman lying in the dust in a widening pool of blood. Nate's mind shrieked at him to stand. The other two were bound to be on him any instant.

From out of the shadows flew the lance. Nate started to roll when, in a twinkling, he perceived the lance wasn't meant for him. It whizzed past and struck somewhere to his rear. A woman screamed shrilly.

Marshaling his energy, Nate got to one knee and glanced back. The lance had been thrown at Morning Dew. She had burnt the leather cords binding her wrists and ankles and had been about to grab the Hawken when the warrior had seen her and hurled his weapon. It had missed her head by inches and instead speared through the fleshy part of her upper arm, effectively pinning her to the ground. Blood was pouring out. Morning Dew, racked by acute torment, was vainly yanking at the lance, striving to pull it out.

Nate faced forward. There was nothing he could do for her until he settled accounts with the two remaining Sioux. The horses screened them from his sight, compelling him to ease onto his stomach and crawl along until he could chance a glance up the gully. What he saw alarmed him.

The two Sioux were gone. Eric Nash was lying on his back on the ramp, a red stain on his head. Evidently he had been struck again, perhaps as he was attempting to stand. For the moment, though, he was safe.

Which was more than could be said for Nate. He hugged the wall and peered up at the opposite rim. The Sioux had the advantage now; he was outnumbered and they could attack from either side or simultaneously from both. Of the two, the man with the rifle was the bigger threat, but the other one had a knife, if Nate recalled correctly, and could just as readily end Nate's life.

Nate knew he had to move, and with the thought came action. Sliding around the rump of the stallion, staying low in the deepest shadows, he hastened past the horses, then crouched against the earth wall. In front of him was the incline. On it Nash was groaning softly. By the fire Morning Dew was slumped over, grimacing. None of the other captives had moved as yet.

Where the hell were the Sioux? Nate wondered, scouring both rims for any hint of movement. Were they hoping he would go up after them so they could pick him off from the safety of the tall grass? Or were they, as usual, about to resort to some clever strategy, some trick that would take him totally unawares and end the conflict decisively?

Nate jammed the spent pistol under his belt, drew his tomahawk, and stepped gingerly toward Nash. Out of the corner of his left eye he glimpsed movement, but when he looked at the top of the gully he saw no one. Think, you dunderhead! he shouted in his mind. He had to think the way *they* would, try to foresee what they would do next before they put it into effect.

Try as Nate might, no inspiration came. He would have to rely on his instincts and his reflexes. At the incline he paused and turned his head to check on the captives and Morning Dew. As he did, a rifle roared above the west rim and a lead ball slammed into the wall a hairsbreadth from his right ear. He lifted his flintlock, but there was no one to shoot. The Sioux had vanished.

Dropping into a crouch, Nate took stock. So long as he stayed in the gully, he was at their

mercy. They could keep him pinned down indefinitely, and if they waited until daylight, he'd be
an easy target. Perhaps his wisest recourse was
to take the fight to them, to make a break for the
high grass and fight them on their own terms.

So resolved, Nate turned to scale the ramp.
Then an idea hit him. He grinned as he crawled
up to Nash and pulled the Englishman down to
the relative safety of the gully floor. Constantly
scouring the rims, he kept on going, laboriously
dragging Nash past the horses. Then rising, he
quickly worked his way along the animals, unty-
ing each and every one, speaking soothingly to
them so they wouldn't spook until he was good
and ready. When he had them all loose, he hurried back to crouch beside the stallion.

The Mandans, including Morning Dew, were all
watching him. Neither of the Sioux had shown
themselves, but that might momentarily change.
Taking a breath, Nate vented a high-pitched
screech while giving the stallion a rough swat.

In the blink of an eye the nine horses whirled
and were thundering up the incline, whinnying
in fear as they fled into the night. And right
behind them, breathing in the swirls of dust their
hoofs raised, was Nate King, racing as if his life
depended on it—which it did.

Nate hoped the ploy would see him safely to the
high grass. The Sioux would naturally be watching
their horses, which they could ill afford to lose, so
they might not spot him until it was too late. He
pounded up the incline, dug in his heels, and flew
over the crest.

Some of the horses were cutting to the right,
others to the left. From the grass to the south

came a harsh cry of rage, which was promptly answered by a shout from the west end of the gully.

Nate sprinted to the left, his arms and legs churning. He was almost to cover when above the drumming of hoofs he heard the heavy panting of strenuous breathing and the patter of flying moccasins. Too late, he spun.

The Sioux was on the frontiersman like a battering ram, leaping and plowing his powerful shoulder into Nate's stomach. Bowled over, Nate went down on his back with the Sioux on top of him. A faint glittering forewarned him a heartbeat before the warrior's knife arced at his throat, and he jerked his head aside. The blade scraped his cheek and bit into the earth underneath.

Nate bucked, attempting to throw the brave from him, realizing if he didn't prevail in the next few seconds the other Sioux would arrive and finish him off. The man clung to him tenaciously and whipped the knife into the air for another swing. Nate's right arm was pinned to his side, rendering the pistol useless, but his left was still free. He brought the tomahawk up to deflect the knife, then, with a reverse slash, sliced open the Sioux's throat.

The warrior clutched at his gushing neck and scrambled backwards.

Nate got an arm on the ground and shoved erect. His left arm flicked out, the tomahawk cleaving the brave open from shoulder to shoulder, and the Sioux tottered, lost his balance, and fell. Before Nate could close in for the kill a rifle boomed near the gully. There was a wrenching impact in Nate's forearm and his pistol went flying.

Glancing down, Nate saw a wicked gash in his buckskin sleeve. He pivoted toward the gully just as the last warrior sprang. The stock of the rifle clipped Nate on the chin, stunning him, and he reeled. A second blow on the temple felled him like a poled ox. On his knees, pain dominating his being, Nate knew he would die unless he did something and did it quickly. But his body was numb, tingling from head to toe. He was totally helpless to resist.

Nate saw the feral smirk of victory on the Sioux's face as the brave slowly drew a long knife. The warrior stepped in close, elevated the blade, and said several mocking words in the Sioux language. Then, as the loud retort of a rifle rolled across the prairie, the front of the man's forehead dissolved in an explosion of gore, brains, and blood.

Spattered by the grisly rain, Nate blinked in amazement as the Sioux's eyes fluttered. The warrior went rigid, gasped once, and toppled rearward, and beyond him materialized Eric Nash bathed in a halo of writhing gunsmoke, the smoking Hawken clutched in his hands.

"Eric?" Nate mumbled. In his benumbed state he couldn't quite grasp the reality of his deliverance.

The Englishman advanced. He stared grimly at the two dead braves, then set down the Hawken and picked up the knife of the one he had shot through the head.

"Eric?" Nate repeated, disturbed by the strange gleam in the artist's eyes.

Nash ignored him. Bending over the Sioux, he grabbed the brave's hair and held the edge of the knife close to the scalp. "Is this how it's done?" he asked hoarsely.

"Dear God. Do you know what you're doing?" Nate responded.

The Englishman looked up, toward the gully where Morning Dew stood with her wounded arm tucked tight to her bosom, her gaze locked expectantly on the man who wanted more than anything else to share his life with her. "I know what I'm gaining," he answered curtly, and bent to the task.

Two days later Four Bears, Shakespeare, and the rest of the war party arrived with the stolen horses. They had caught up with the two Sioux driving the small herd off and in a brief fight slain both men. Upon realizing the rest of the Sioux and the captives were missing, they had retraced their tracks until they reached the stream. There they had found the same trail that had led Nate and Eric eastward.

Nate had decided to stay at the gully until help came. None of the horses he had driven off returned, and he was unwilling to venture across the open plain when most of his party would have to go on foot and would be easy pickings for any wandering hostiles or roving grizzlies. He'd been confident Four Bears would come eventually, and there being plenty of game and water in the nearby hills, he'd been content to wait and allow Nash time to recover.

Under Morning Dew's loving ministrations, the Englishman did just that. In a remarkably short time, no less. For her part, she bore the pain of her wound without complaint. They were mutual balms for their hurting souls, and their unflagging smiles and good cheer were contagious. The rest of the captives had so recovered from their trials by the day after the Sioux were slain that the women were often heard humming or singing and the boys were often playing happily.

Nate had never seen the like.

When Four Bears heard of the Englishman's part in his daughter's rescue, he impetuously embraced Nash and thanked him profusely. Eric responded by doing that which would most endear him to the great warrior; he gave Four Bears the scalp he'd taken from the Sioux.

From that moment on, the chief's attitude toward the Englishman underwent a drastic transformation. Mato-tope asked Nate to inform Nash that once they were back in the Mandan village, Nash was welcome to take Morning Dew for his own if Nash still wanted her. Needless to say, the two young lovers were delirious.

So was the tribe when the war party returned without having suffered a single casualty, and with all the stolen horses recovered and the captives safe. A great victory celebration was held. For three days and nights the festivities continued, until virtually every man, woman, and child was on the verge of exhaustion. And at the end of those three days Eric Nash and Morning Dew moved into a lodge of their very own.

There was only one sour note to the whole affair. The first night of the celebration, as the

Englishman and the maiden were being joined according to Mandan custom, Nate King happened to glance back over the heads of the assembled Indians and spotted Diana Templar standing in the shadows. Her head was bent, her shoulders shaking.

Nate wasn't at all surprised when Lady Templar came up to him two days after the marriage and informed him that her brother, Jarvis, and she would be leaving the very next morning, heading down river to Independence on the boat of a Frenchman who periodically visited the Mandans to trade with them. She promised to have the money she had offered Shakespeare and him deposited in a St. Louis bank, and despite their protests she said she would pay them the full amount due and not a farthing less even though she had curtailed their services sooner than anticipated.

The parting was bittersweet.

Diana and Winona hugged, and Diana cried. Jarvis was openly sad when it came time to say good-bye to Nate and Shakespeare, but he actually had tears in his eyes when he bid farewell to Zach. Eric Nash came down to the river alone and walked up to Diana, who turned her back on him and stepped onto the boat.

William Templar, true to form, ignored them all.

Long after the trader's boat had disappeared around a bend, Nate and his family stood staring out over the water. Nate had an arm draped over Winona's shoulders. He kissed her cheek, then glanced at McNair. "Any words of wisdom to impart?" he asked sarcastically.

The mountain man was equal to the occasion. "All's well that ends well, I reckon," he said with a grin.

Three days later Nate, Winona, Zach, and Shakespeare rode out of the Mandan village on fine horses given to them by Mato-tope. In parfleches were all the provisions they would need to see them clear to the Rocky Mountains. Practically the whole village gathered to see them off, and they promised to come again just as soon as circumstances permitted.

Nate, out of concern over his wife's condition, was anxious to reach their cabin as rapidly as possible in order to insure she gave birth in the comfortable surroundings of her own home. The adventures they had along the way, though, prevented them from getting there in time.

But that is a tale for another day.

Epilogue
and Historical Note

In the summer of 1837 a devastating smallpox epidemic struck the Mandans. Out of thousands of healthy, happy people, fewer than one hundred were left when the ravaging disease ran its course. The grand chief of the Mandans, Mato-tope, lost his entire family: his wives, all his children—both the small ones and those who were married, and all his grandchildren, every last one. In his remorse he starved himself to death, and his dying words were recorded for posterity: "Four Bears never saw a white man hungry but what he gave him to eat. And how have they repaid it! I do not fear death, but to die with my face rotten, that even the wolves will shrink at seeing me, and say to themselves, 'That is Four Bears, the friend of the whites.'"

Authorities were never able to determine exactly how the Mandans were exposed to the disease.

Three months later there was a mention on the social page of a prominent London newspaper that Lady Diana Templar and Eric Nash, renowned artist, were to be married on Christmas day in St. Paul's Cathedral.